ALMAYER'S FOLLY

A Story of an Eastern River

AND

TALES OF UNREST

by

JOSEPH CONRAD

LONDON

J. M. DENT AND SONS LTD

A chronological list of Conrad's books,
with a brief biographical note and a
list of selected writings about him, will
be found at the end of this volume.

COLLECTED EDITION OF THE WORKS OF

JOSEPH CONRAD

ALMAYER'S FOLLY

and

TALES OF UNREST

ALMAYER'S FOLLY

A Story of an Eastern River

To
the memory
of
T. B.

AUTHOR'S NOTE

I AM informed that in criticizing that literature which preys on strange people and prowls in far-off countries, under the shade of palms, in the unsheltered glare of sunbeaten beaches, amongst honest cannibals and the more sophisticated pioneers of our glorious virtues, a lady—distinguished in the world of letters—summed up her disapproval of it by saying that the tales it produced were "decivilized." And in that sentence not only the tales but, I apprehend, the strange people and the far-off countries also, are finally condemned in a verdict of contemptuous dislike.

A woman's judgment: intuitive, clever, expressed with felicitous charm—infallible. A judgment that has nothing to do with justice. The critic and the judge seems to think that in those distant lands all joy is a yell and a war dance, all pathos is a howl and a ghastly grin of filed teeth, and that the solution of all problems is found in the barrel of a revolver or on the point of an assegai. And yet it is not so. But the erring magistrate may plead in excuse the misleading nature of the evidence.

The picture of life, there as here, is drawn with the same elaboration of detail, coloured with the same tints. Only in the cruel serenity of the sky, under the merciless brilliance of the sun, the dazzled eye misses the delicate detail, sees only the strong outlines, while the colours, in the steady light, seem crude and without shadow. Nevertheless it is the same picture.

And there is a bond between us and that humanity so far away. I am speaking here of men and women—not of the charming and graceful phantoms that move about in our mud and smoke and are softly luminous with the radiance of all our virtues; that are possessed of all refinements, of all sensibilities, of all wisdom— but, being only phantoms, possess no heart.

The sympathies of those are (probably) with the immortals: with the angels above or the devils below. I am content to sympathize with common mortals, no matter where they live; in houses or in tents, in the streets under a fog, or in the forests behind the dark line of dismal mangroves that fringe the vast solitude of the sea. For, their land—like ours—lies under the inscrutable eyes of the Most High. Their hearts— like ours—must endure the load of the gifts from Heaven: the curse of facts and the blessing of illusions, the bitterness of our wisdom and the deceptive consolation of our folly.

J. C.

1895

ALMAYER'S FOLLY

Qui de nous
n'a eu sa terre promise,
son jour d'extase
et sa fin en exil
AMIEL

ALMAYER'S FOLLY

CHAPTER ONE

"KASPAR! Makan!"

The well-known shrill voice startled Almayer from his dream of splendid future into the unpleasant realities of the present hour. An unpleasant voice too. He had heard it for many years, and with every year he liked it less. No matter; there would be an end to all this soon.

He shuffled uneasily, but took no further notice of the call. Leaning with both his elbows on the balustrade of the verandah, he went on looking fixedly at the great river that flowed—indifferent and hurried—before his eyes. He liked to look at it about the time of sunset; perhaps because at that time the sinking sun would spread a glowing gold tinge on the waters of the Pantai, and Almayer's thoughts were often busy with gold; gold he had failed to secure; gold the others had se-cured—dishonestly, of course—or gold he meant to secure yet, through his own honest exertions, for him-self and Nina. He absorbed himself in his dream of wealth and power away from this coast where he had dwelt for so many years, forgetting the bitterness of toil and strife in the vision of a great and splendid reward. They would live in Europe, he and his daughter. They would be rich and respected. Nobody would think of her mixed blood in the presence of her great beauty and of his immense wealth. Witnessing her triumphs

he would grow young again, he would forget the twenty-
five years of heart-breaking struggle on this coast where
he felt like a prisoner. All this was nearly within his
reach. Let only Dain return! And return soon he
must—in his own interest, for his own share. He was
now more than a week late! Perhaps he would return
to-night.

Such were Almayer's thoughts as, standing on the
verandah of his new but already decaying house—
that last failure of his life—he looked on the broad
river. There was no tinge of gold on it this evening,
for it had been swollen by the rains, and rolled an
angry and muddy flood under his inattentive eyes,
carrying small drift-wood and big dead logs, and whole
uprooted trees with branches and foliage, amongst
which the water swirled and roared angrily.

One of those drifting trees grounded on the shelving
shore, just by the house, and Almayer, neglecting his
dream, watched it with languid interest. The tree
swung slowly round, amid the hiss and foam of the
water, and soon getting free of the obstruction began
to move down stream again, rolling slowly over, raising
upwards a long, denuded branch, like a hand lifted in
mute appeal to heaven against the river's brutal and
unnecessary violence. Almayer's interest in the fate of
that tree increased rapidly. He leaned over to see if it
would clear the low point below. It did; then he drew
back, thinking that now its course was free down to the
sea, and he envied the lot of that inanimate thing now
growing small and indistinct in the deepening darkness.
As he lost sight of it altogether he began to wonder
how far out to sea it would drift. Would the current
carry it north or south? South, probably, till it drifted
in sight of Celebes, as far as Macassar, perhaps!

Macassar! Almayer's quickened fancy distanced the

tree on its imaginary voyage, but his memory lagging behind some twenty years or more in point of time saw a young and slim Almayer, clad all in white and modest-looking, landing from the Dutch mail-boat on the dusty jetty of Macassar, coming to woo fortune in the go-downs of old Hudig. It was an important epoch in his life, the beginning of a new existence for him. His father, a subordinate official employed in the Botanical Gardens of Buitenzorg, was no doubt delighted to place his son in such a firm. The young man himself too was nothing loth to leave the poisonous shores of Java, and the meagre comforts of the parental bungalow, where the father grumbled all day at the stupidity of native gardeners, and the mother from the depths of her long easy-chair bewailed the lost glories of Amsterdam, where she had been brought up, and of her position as the daughter of a cigar dealer there.

Almayer had left his home with a light heart and a lighter pocket, speaking English well, and strong in arithmetic; ready to conquer the world, never doubting that he would.

After those twenty years, standing in the close and stifling heat of a Bornean evening, he recalled with pleasurable regret the image of Hudig's lofty and cool warehouses with their long and straight avenues of gin cases and bales of Manchester goods; the big door swinging noiselessly; the dim light of the place, so delightful after the glare of the streets; the little railed-off spaces amongst piles of merchandise where the Chinese clerks, neat, cool, and sad-eyed, wrote rapidly and in silence amidst the din of the working gangs rolling casks or shifting cases to a muttered song, ending with a desper-ate yell. At the upper end, facing the great door, there was a larger space railed off, well lighted; there the noise was subdued by distance, and above it rose the soft

and continuous clink of silver guilders which other
discreet Chinamen were counting and piling up under
the supervision of Mr. Vinck, the cashier, the genius
presiding in the place—the right hand of the Master.

In that clear space Almayer worked at his table
not far from a little green painted door, by which always
stood a Malay in a red sash and turban, and whose hand,
holding a small string dangling from above, moved up
and down with the regularity of a machine. The
string worked a punkah on the other side of the green
door, where the so-called private office was, and where
old Hudig—the Master—sat enthroned, holding noisy
receptions. Sometimes the little door would fly open
disclosing to the outer world, through the bluish haze
of tobacco smoke, a long table loaded with bottles of
various shapes and tall water pitchers, rattan easy-
chairs occupied by noisy men in sprawling attitudes,
while the Master would put his head through and,
holding by the handle, would grunt confidentially to
Vinck; perhaps send an order thundering down the
warehouse, or spy a hesitating stranger and greet him
with a friendly roar, "Welgome, Gapitan! ver' you
gome vrom? Bali, eh? Got bonies? I vant bonies!
Vant all you got; ha! ha! ha! Gome in!" Then the
stranger was dragged in, in a tempest of yells, the door
was shut, and the usual noises refilled the place; the
song of the workmen, the rumble of barrels, the scratch
of rapid pens; while above all rose the musical chink
of broad silver pieces streaming ceaselessly through the
yellow fingers of the attentive Chinamen.

At that time Macassar was teeming with life and commerce. It was the point in the islands where tended
all those bold spirits who, fitting out schooners on the
Australian coast, invaded the Malay Archipelago in
search of money and adventure. Bold, reckless, keen

in business, not disinclined for a brush with the pirates
that were to be found on many a coast as yet, making
money fast, they used to have a general "rendezvous"
in the bay for purposes of trade and dissipation. The
Dutch merchants called those men English pedlars;
some of them were undoubtedly gentlemen for whom
that kind of life had a charm; most were seamen; the
acknowledged king of them all was Tom Lingard, he
whom the Malays, honest or dishonest, quiet fishermen
or desperate cut-throats, recognized as "the Rajah-
Laut"—the King of the Sea.

Almayer had heard of him before he had been three
days in Macassar, had heard the stories of his smart
business transactions, his loves, and also of his desperate
fights with the Sulu pirates, together with the romantic
tale of some child—a girl—found in a piratical prau
by the victorious Lingard, when, after a long contest,
he boarded the craft, driving the crew overboard. This
girl, it was generally known, Lingard had adopted,
was having her educated in some convent in Java, and
spoke of her as "my daughter." He had sworn a
mighty oath to marry her to a white man before he
went home and to leave her all his money. "And Captain Lingard has lots of money," would say Mr. Vinck
solemnly, with his head on one side, "lots of money;
more than Hudig!" And after a pause—just to let his
hearers recover from their astonishment at such an
incredible assertion—he would add in an explanatory
whisper, "You know, he has discovered a river."

That was it! He had discovered a river! That was
the fact placing old Lingard so much above the common
crowd of sea-going adventurers who traded with Hudig
in the daytime and drank champagne, gambled, sang
noisy songs, and made love to half-caste girls under the
broad verandah of the Sunda Hotel at night. Into that

river, whose entrances himself only knew, Lingard used
to take his assorted cargo of Manchester goods, brass
gongs, rifles and gunpowder. His brig *Flash*, which he
commanded himself, would on those occasions disappear quietly during the night from the roadstead while
his companions were sleeping off the effects of the midnight carouse, Lingard seeing them drunk under the
table before going on board, himself unaffected by any
amount of liquor. Many tried to follow him and find
that land of plenty for gutta-percha and rattans, pearl
shells and birds' nests, wax and gum-dammar, but the
little *Flash* could outsail every craft in those seas. A
few of them came to grief on hidden sandbanks and
coral reefs, losing their all and barely escaping with life
from the cruel grip of this sunny and smiling sea; others
got discouraged; and for many years the green and
peaceful-looking islands guarding the entrances to the
promised land kept their secret with all the merciless
serenity of tropical nature. And so Lingard came
and went on his secret or open expeditions, becoming a
hero in Almayer's eyes by the boldness and enormous
profits of his ventures, seeming to Almayer a very great
man indeed as he saw him marching up the warehouse,
grunting a "how are you?" to Vinck, or greeting Hudig,
the Master, with a boisterous "Hallo, old pirate! Alive
yet?" as a preliminary to transacting business behind
the little green door. Often of an evening, in the
silence of the then deserted warehouse, Almayer putting
away his papers before driving home with Mr. Vinck, in
whose household he lived, would pause listening to the
noise of a hot discussion in the private office, would hear
the deep and monotonous growl of the Master, and the
roared-out interruptions of Lingard—two mastiffs fighting over a marrowy bone. But to Almayer's ears it
sounded like a quarrel of Titans—a battle of the gods.

After a year or so Lingard, having been brought often in contact with Almayer in the course of business, took a sudden and, to the onlookers, a rather inexplicable fancy to the young man. He sang his praises, late at night, over a convivial glass to his cronies in the Sunda Hotel, and one fine morning electrified Vinck by declaring that he must have "that young fellow for a supercargo. Kind of captain's clerk. Do all my quill-driving for me." Hudig consented. Almayer, with youth's natural craving for change, was nothing loth, and packing his few belongings, started in the *Flash* on one of those long cruises when the old seaman was wont to visit almost every island in the archipelago. Months slipped by, and Lingard's friendship seemed to increase. Often pacing the deck with Almayer, when the faint night breeze, heavy with aromatic exhalations of the islands, shoved the brig gently along under the peaceful and sparkling sky, did the old seaman open his heart to his entranced listener. He spoke of his past life, of escaped dangers, of big profits in his trade, of new combinations that were in the future to bring profits bigger still. Often he had mentioned his daughter, the girl found in the pirate prau, speaking of her with a strange assumption of fatherly tenderness. "She must be a big girl now," he used to say. "It's nigh unto four years since I have seen her! Damme, Almayer, if I don't think we will run into Sourabaya this trip." And after such a declaration he always dived into his cabin muttering to himself, "Something must be done—must be done." More than once he would astonish Almayer by walking up to him rapidly, clearing his throat with a powerful "Hem!" as if he intended to say something, and then turning abruptly away to lean over the bulwarks in silence, and watch, motionless, for hours, the gleam and sparkle of the

phosphorescent sea along the ship's side. It was the
night before arriving in Sourabaya when one of those
attempts at confidential communication succeeded.
After clearing his throat he spoke. He spoke to some
purpose. He wanted Almayer to marry his adopted
daughter. ○ "And don't you kick because you're white!"
he shouted, suddenly, not giving the surprised young
man the time to say a word. "None of that with me!
Nobody will see the colour of your wife's skin. The
dollars are too thick for that, I tell you! And mind you,
they will be thicker yet before I die. There will be
millions, Kaspar! Millions I say! And all for her—
and for you, if you do what you are told."

Startled by the unexpected proposal, Almayer hesitated, and remained silent for a minute. He was gifted
with a strong and active imagination, and in that short
space of time he saw, as in a flash of dazzling light, great
piles of shining guilders, and realized all the possibilities
of an opulent existence. The consideration, the indolent ease of life—for which he felt himself so well fitted
—his ships, his warehouses, his merchandise (old Lingard would not live for ever), and, crowning all, in the
far future gleamed like a fairy palace the big mansion
in Amsterdam, that earthly paradise of his dreams,
where made king amongst men by old Lingard's money,
he would pass the evening of his days in inexpressible
splendour. As to the other side of the picture—the
companionship for life of a Malay girl, that legacy of a
boatful of pirates—there was only within him a confused
consciousness of shame that he a white man—— Still,
a convent education of four years—and then she may
mercifully die. He was always lucky, and money is
powerful! Go through it. Why not? He had a vague
idea of shutting her up somewhere, anywhere, out of his
gorgeous future. Easy enough to dispose of a Malay

woman, a slave, after all, to his Eastern mind, convent
or no convent, ceremony or no ceremony.

He lifted his head and confronted the anxious yet
irate seaman.

"I—of course—anything you wish, Captain Lingard."

"Call me father, my boy. She does," said the
mollified old adventurer. "Damme, though, if I didn't
think you were going to refuse. Mind you, Kaspar,
I always get my way, so it would have been no use.
But you are no fool."

He remembered well that time—the look, the accent,
the words, the effect they produced on him, his very
surroundings. He remembered the narrow slanting
deck of the brig, the silent sleeping coast, the smooth
black surface of the sea with a great bar of gold laid on
it by the rising moon. He remembered it all, and he
remembered his feelings of mad exultation at the
thought of that fortune thrown into his hands. He was
no fool then, and he was no fool now. Circumstances
had been against him; the fortune was gone, but hope
remained.

He shivered in the night air, and suddenly became
aware of the intense darkness which, on the sun's
departure, had closed in upon the river, blotting out the
outlines of the opposite shore. Only the fire of dry
branches lit outside the stockade of the Rajah's compound called fitfully into view the ragged trunks of the
surrounding trees, putting a stain of glowing red half-
way across the river where the drifting logs were hurrying toward the sea through the impenetrable gloom.
He had a hazy recollection of having been called some
time during the evening by his wife. To his dinner
probably. But a man busy contemplating the wreckage of his past in the dawn of new hopes cannot be

hungry whenever his rice is ready. Time he went
home, though; it was getting late.

He stepped cautiously on the loose planks towards
the ladder. A lizard, disturbed by the noise, emitted a
plaintive note and scurried through the long grass
growing on the bank. Almayer descended the ladder
carefully, now thoroughly recalled to the realities of
life by the care necessary to prevent a fall on the uneven
ground where the stones, decaying planks, and half-
sawn beams were piled up in inextricable confusion.
As he turned towards the house where he lived—"my
old house" he called it—his ear detected the splash of
paddles away in the darkness of the river. He stood
still in the path, attentive and surprised at anybody
being on the river at this late hour during such a heavy
freshet. Now he could hear the paddles distinctly,
and even a rapidly exchanged word in low tones, the
heavy breathing of men fighting with the current, and
hugging the bank on which he stood. Quite close,
too, but it was too dark to distinguish anything under
the overhanging bushes.

"Arabs, no doubt," muttered Almayer to himself,
peering into the solid blackness. "What are they up
to now? Some of Abdulla's business; curse him!"

The boat was very close now.

"Oh, ya! Man!" hailed Almayer.

The sound of voices ceased, but the paddles worked
as furiously as before. Then the bush in front of Almayer shook, and the sharp sound of the paddles falling into the canoe rang in the quiet night. They were
holding on to the bush now; but Almayer could hardly
make out an indistinct dark shape of a man's head and
shoulders above the bank.

"You Abdulla?" said Almayer, doubtfully.

A grave voice answered—

"Tuan Almayer is speaking to a friend. There is no Arab here."

Almayer's heart gave a great leap.

"Dain!" he exclaimed. "At last! at last! I have been waiting for you every day and every night. I had nearly given you up."

"Nothing could have stopped me from coming back here," said the other, almost violently. "Not even death," he whispered to himself.

"This is a friend's talk, and is very good," said Almayer, heartily. "Drop down to the jetty and let your men cook their rice in my campong while we talk in the house."

There was no answer to that invitation.

"What is it?" asked Almayer, uneasily. "There is nothing wrong with the brig, I hope?"

"The brig is where no Orang Blanda can lay his hands on her," said Dain, with a gloomy tone in his voice, which Almayer, in his elation, failed to notice.

"Right," he said. "But where are all your men? There are only two with you."

"Listen, Tuan Almayer," said Dain. "To-morrow's sun shall see me in your house, and then we will talk. Now I must go to the Rajah."

"To the Rajah! Why? What do you want with Lakamba?"

"Tuan, to-morrow we talk like friends. I must see Lakamba to-night."

"Dain, you are not going to abandon me now, when all is ready?" asked Almayer, in a pleading voice.

"Have I not returned? But I must see Lakamba first for your good and mine."

The shadowy head disappeared abruptly. The bush, released from the grasp of the bowman, sprung back with a swish, scattering a shower of muddy water over Almayer, as he bent forward, trying to see.

In a little while the canoe shot into the streak of light that streamed on the river from the big fire on the opposite shore, disclosing the outline of two men bending to their work, and a third figure in the stern flourishing the steering paddle, his head covered with an enormous round hat, like a fantastically exaggerated mushroom.

Almayer watched the canoe till it passed out of the line of light. Shortly after the murmur of many voices reached him across the water. He could see the torches being snatched out of the burning pile, and rendering visible for a moment the gate in the stockade round which they crowded. Then they went in; the torches disappeared, and the scattered fire sent out only a dim and fitful glare.

Almayer stepped homewards with long strides and mind uneasy. Surely Dain was not thinking of playing him false. It was absurd. Dain and Lakamba were both too much interested in the success of his scheme. Trusting to Malays was poor work; but then even Malays have some sense and understand their own interest. All would be well—must be well. At this point in his meditation he found himself at the foot of the steps leading to the verandah of his home. From the low point of land where he stood he could see both branches of the river. The main stream of the Pantai was lost in complete darkness, for the fire at the Rajah's had gone out altogether; but up the Sambir reach his eye could follow the long line of Malay houses crowding the bank, with here and there a dim light twinkling through bamboo walls, or a smoky torch burning on the platforms built out over the river. Further away, where the island ended in a low cliff, rose a dark mass of buildings towering above the Malay structures. Founded solidly on a firm ground with plenty of space, starred by many lights burning strong and white, with a suggestion of paraffin and lamp-glasses, stood the house and the godowns of Abdulla bin Selim, the great trader of Sambir. To Almayer the sight was very distasteful, and he shook his fist towards the buildings that in their evident prosperity looked to him cold and insolent, and contemptuous of his own fallen fortunes.

He mounted the steps of his house slowly.

In the middle of the verandah there was a round table. On it a paraffin lamp without a globe shed a hard glare on the three inner sides. The fourth side was open, and faced the river. Between the rough supports of the high-pitched roof hung torn rattan screens. There was no ceiling, and the harsh brilliance of the lamp was toned above into a soft half-light that lost itself in the obscurity amongst the rafters. The front wall was cut in two by the doorway of a central passage closed by a red curtain. The women's room opened into that passage, which led to the back court-yard and to the cooking shed. In one of the side walls there was a doorway. Half obliterated words—"Office: Lingard and Co."—were still legible on the dusty door, which looked as if it had not been opened for a very long time. Close to the other side wall stood a bent-wood rocking chair, and by the table and about the verandah four wooden armchairs straggled forlornly, as if ashamed of their shabby surroundings. A heap of common mats lay in one corner, with an old hammock slung diagonally above. In the other corner, his head wrapped in a piece of red calico, huddled into a shapeless heap, slept a Malay, one of Almayer's domestic slaves—"my own people," he used to call them. A numerous and representative assembly of moths were holding high revels round the lamp to the spirited music of swarming mosquitoes. Under the palm-leaf thatch lizards raced on the beams calling softly. A monkey, chained to one of the verandah supports—retired for the night under the eaves—peered and grinned at Almayer, as it swung to one of the bamboo roof sticks and caused a shower of dust and bits of dried leaves to settle on the shabby table. The floor was uneven, with many withered plants and dried earth scattered about. A general air of squalid neglect pervaded the place. The light breeze from the river swayed gently the tattered blinds, sending from the woods opposite a faint and sickly perfume as of decaying flowers.

Under Almayer's heavy tread the boards of the verandah creaked loudly. The sleeper in the corner moved uneasily, muttering indistinct words. There was a slight rustle behind the curtained doorway, and a soft voice asked in Malay, "Is it you, father?"

"Yes, Nina. I am hungry. Is everybody asleep in this house?"

Almayer spoke jovially and dropped with a contented sigh into the armchair nearest to the table. Nina Almayer came through the curtained doorway followed by an old Malay woman, who busied herself in setting upon the table a plateful of rice and fish, a jar of water and a bottle half full of genever. After carefully placing before her master a cracked glass tumbler and a tin spoon she went away noiselessly. Nina stood by the table, one hand lightly resting on its edge, the other hanging listlessly by her side. Her face turned towards the outer darkness, through which her dreamy eyes seemed to see some entrancing picture, wore a look of impatient expectancy. She was tall for a half-caste, with the correct profile of the father, modified and

strengthened by the squareness of the lower part of the
face inherited from her maternal ancestors—the Sulu
pirates.   Her firm mouth, with the lips slightly parted
and disclosing a gleam of white teeth, put a vague suggestion of ferocity into the impatient expression of her
features.   And yet her dark and perfect eyes had all
the tender softness common to Malay women, but with
a gleam of superior intelligence; they looked out gravely,
wide open and steady, as if facing something invisible
to all other eyes.   She stood there all in white, straight,
flexible, graceful, unconscious of herself, her low but
broad forehead crowned with a shining mass of long
black hair that fell in heavy tresses over her shoulders,
and made her pale olive complexion look paler still by
the contrast of its coal-black hue.

Almayer attacked his rice greedily, but after a few
mouthfuls he paused, spoon in hand, and looked at his
daughter curiously.

"Did you hear a boat pass about half an hour ago,
Nina?" he asked.

The girl gave him a quick glance, and moving
away from the light stood with her back to the
table.

"I heard nothing," she said, slowly.

"There was a boat.   At last!   Dain himself; and he
went on to Lakamba.   I know it, for he told me so.   I
spoke to him, but he would not come here to-night.
Promised to come to-morrow."

He swallowed another spoonful, then said—

"I am almost happy to-night, Nina.   I can see the
end of a long road, and it leads us away from this
miserable swamp.   We shall soon get away from here,
I and you, my dear little girl, and then——"

He rose from the table and stood looking fixedly
before him as if contemplating some enchanting vision.

"And then," he went on, "we shall be happy, you and I. Live rich and respected far from here, and forget this life, and all this struggle, and all this misery."

He approached his daughter and passed his hand caressingly over her hair.

"It is bad to have to trust a Malay," he said, "but I must own that this Dain is a perfect gentleman—a perfect gentleman," he repeated.

"Did you ask him to come here, father?" inquired Nina, not looking at him.

"Well, of course. We shall start on the day after to-morrow," said Almayer, joyously. "We must not lose any time. Are you glad, little girl?"

She was as tall as himself, but he liked to recall the time when she was little and they were all in all to each other.

"I am glad," she said, very low.

"Of course," said Almayer, vivaciously, "you cannot imagine what is before you. I myself have not been to Europe, but I have heard my mother talk so often that I seem to know all about it. We shall live a—a glorious life. You shall see."

Again he stood silent by his daughter's side looking at that enchanting vision. After a while he shook his fist towards the sleeping settlement.

"Ah! my friend Abdulla," he cried, "we shall see who will have the best of it after all these years!"

He looked up the river and remarked calmly:

"Another thunderstorm. Well! No thunder will keep me awake to-night, I know! Good-night, little girl," he whispered tenderly, kissing her cheek. "You do not seem to be very happy to-night, but to-morrow you will show a brighter face. Eh?"

Nina had listened to her father, unmoved, with her

half-closed eyes still gazing into the night now made
more intense by a heavy thunder-cloud that had crept
down from the hills blotting out the stars, merging sky,
forest, and river into one mass of almost palpable blackness. The faint breeze had died out, but the distant
rumble of thunder and pale flashes of lightning gave
warning of the approaching storm. With a sigh the
girl turned towards the table.

Almayer was in his hammock now, already half
asleep.

"Take the lamp, Nina," he muttered, drowsily.
"This place is full of mosquitoes. Go to sleep, daughter."

But Nina put the lamp out and turned back again
towards the balustrade of the verandah. She stood with
her arm round the wooden support looking eagerly
towards the Pantai reach. And motionless there in the
oppressive calm of the tropical night she could see at
each flash of lightning the forest lining both banks up the
river, bending before the furious blast of wind the upper reach of the river whipped into white foam, and
the black clouds torn into fantastic shapes trailing low
over the swaying trees. Round her all was as yet
stillness and peace, but she could hear afar off the
driving roar, and hiss of heavy rain, the wash of the
waves on the tormented river. It came nearer and
nearer, with loud thunder-claps and long flashes of vivid
lightning, followed by short periods of appalling blackness. When the storm reached the low point dividing
the river, the whole house shook while the rain pattered
loudly on the palm-leaf roof. The thunder spoke in one
prolonged roll, and the incessant lightning disclosed a
turmoil of leaping waters, driving logs, and the big trees
bending before a brutal and merciless force.

Undisturbed by the nightly event of the rainy monsoon, the father slept quietly, oblivious alike of his hopes, his misfortunes, his friends, and his enemies; and the daughter stood motionless, at each flash of lightning eagerly scanning the broad river with a steady and anxious gaze.

CHAPTER TWO

WHEN, in compliance with Lingard's abrupt demand, Almayer consented to wed the Malay girl, no one knew that on the day when the interesting young convert had lost all her natural relations and found a white father, she had been fighting desperately like the rest of them on board the prau, and was only prevented from leaping overboard, like the few other survivors, by a severe wound in the leg. There, on the fore-deck of the prau, old Lingard found her under a heap of dead and dying pirates, and had her carried on the poop of the *Flash* before the Malay craft was set on fire and sent adrift. She was conscious, and in the great peace and stillness of the tropical evening succeeding the turmoil of the battle, she watched all she held dear on earth after her own savage manner, drift away into the gloom in a great roar of flame and smoke. She lay there unheeding the careful hands attending to her wound, silent and absorbed in gazing at the funeral pile of those brave men she had so much admired and so well helped in their contest with the redoubtable "Rajah-Laut."

The light night breeze fanned the brig gently to the southwards, and the great blaze of light got smaller and smaller till it twinkled only on the horizon like a setting star. It set: the heavy canopy of smoke reflected the glare of hidden flames for a short time and then disappeared also.

She realized that with this vanishing gleam her old life departed too. Thenceforth there was slavery in the far countries, amongst strangers, in unknown and perhaps terrible surroundings. There was in her the dread of the unknown; but otherwise she accepted her position calmly, after the manner of her people, and even considered it quite natural; for was she not a daughter of warriors, conquered in battle, and did she not belong rightfully to the victorious Rajah? Even the evident kindness of the terrible old man must spring, she thought, from admiration for his captive, and the flattered vanity eased for her the pangs of sorrow after such an awful calamity. Perhaps had she known of the high walls, the quiet gardens, and the silent nuns of the Samarang convent, where her destiny was leading her, she would have sought death in her dread and hate of such a restraint. But in imagination she pictured to herself the usual life of a Malay girl—the usual succession of heavy work and fierce love, of intrigues, gold ornaments, of domestic drudgery, and of that great but occult influence which is one of the few rights of half-savage womankind. But her destiny in the rough hands of the old sea-dog, acting under unreasoning impulses of the heart, took a strange and to her a terrible shape. She bore it all—the restraint and the teaching and the new faith—with calm submission, concealing her hate and contempt for all that new life. She learned the language very easily, yet understood but little of the new faith the good sisters taught her, assimilating quickly only the superstitious elements of the religion. She called Lingard father, gently and caressingly, at each of his short and noisy visits, under the clear impression that he was a great and dangerous power it was good to propitiate. Was he not now her master? And during those long four years she nourished a hope of finding favour in his eyes and ultimately becoming his wife, counsellor, and guide.

Those dreams of the future were dispelled by the Rajah Laut's "fiat," which made Almayer's fortune, as that young man fondly hoped. And dressed in the hateful finery of Europe, the young convert stood before the altar with an unknown and sulky-looking white man. For Almayer was uneasy, a little disgusted, and greatly inclined to run away. A judicious fear of the adopted father-in-law and a just regard for his own material welfare prevented him from making a scandal; yet, while swearing fidelity, he was concocting plans for getting rid of the pretty Malay girl in a more or less distant future. She, however, had retained enough of conventual teaching to understand well that according to white men's law she was going to be Almayer's companion and not his slave, and promised to herself to act accordingly.

So when the *Flash* freighted with materials for building a new house left the harbour of Batavia, taking away the young couple into the unknown Borneo, she did not carry on her deck so much love and happiness as old Lingard was wont to boast of before his casual friends in the verandahs of various hotels. The old seaman himself was perfectly happy. Now he had done his duty by the girl. "You know I made her an orphan," he often concluded solemnly, when talking about his own affairs to a scratch audience of shore loafers—as it was his habit to do. And the approbative shouts of his half-intoxicated auditors filled his simple soul with delight and pride. "I carry everything right through," was another of his sayings, and in pursuance of that principle he pushed the building of house and godowns on the Pantai River with feverish haste. The house for the young couple; the godowns for the big trade Almayer was going to develop while he (Lingard) would be able to give himself up to some

mysterious work which was only spoken of in hints,
but was understood to relate to gold and diamonds in the
interior of the island. Almayer was impatient too.
Had he known what was before him he might not have
been so eager and full of hope as he stood watching the
last canoe of the Lingard expedition disappear in the
bend up the river. When, turning round, he beheld the
pretty little house, the godowns built neatly by an
army of Chinese carpenters, the new jetty round which
were clustered the trading canoes, he felt a sudden elation in the thought that the world was his.

But the world had to be conquered first, and its
conquest was not so easy as he thought. He was very
soon made to understand that he was not wanted in that
corner of it where old Lingard and his own weak will
placed him, in the midst of unscrupulous intrigues and
of a fierce trade competition. The Arabs had found out
the river, had established a trading post in Sambir, and
where they traded they would be masters and suffer no
rival. Lingard returned unsuccessful from his first
expedition, and departed again spending all the profits
of the legitimate trade on his mysterious journeys.
Almayer struggled with the difficulties of his position,
friendless and unaided, save for the protection given to
him for Lingard's sake by the old Rajah, the predecessor
of Lakamba. Lakamba himself, then living as a private
individual on a rice clearing, seven miles down the river,
exercised all his influence towards the help of the white
man's enemies, plotting against the old Rajah and Almayer with a certainty of combination, pointing clearly
to a profound knowledge of their most secret affairs.
Outwardly friendly, his portly form was often to be seen
on Almayer's verandah; his green turban and gold-
embroidered jacket shone in the front rank of the decorous throng of Malays coming to greet Lingard on his

returns from the interior; his salaams were of the lowest, and his hand-shakings of the heartiest, when welcoming the old trader. But his small eyes took in the signs of the times, and he departed from those interviews with a satisfied and furtive smile to hold long consultations with his friend and ally, Syed Abdulla, the chief of the Arab trading post, a man of great wealth and of great influence in the islands.

It was currently believed at that time in the settlement that Lakamba's visits to Almayer's house were not limited to those official interviews. Often on moonlight nights the belated fishermen of Sambir saw a small canoe shooting out from the narrow creek at the back of the white man's house, and the solitary occupant paddle cautiously down the river in the deep shadows of the bank; and those events, duly reported, were discussed round the evening fires far into the night with the cynicism of expression common to Malays. Almayer went on struggling desperately, but with a feebleness of purpose depriving him of all chance of success against men so unscrupulous and resolute as his rivals the Arabs. The trade fell away from the large godowns, and the godowns themselves rotted piecemeal. The old man's banker, Hudig of Macassar, failed, and with this went the whole available capital. The profits of past years had been swallowed up in Lingard's exploring craze. Lingard was in the interior—perhaps dead—at all events giving no sign of life. Almayer stood alone in the midst of those adverse circumstances, deriving only a little comfort from the companionship of his little daughter, born two years after the marriage, and at the time some six years old. His wife had soon commenced to treat him with a savage contempt expressed by sulky silence, only occasionally varied by outbursts of savage invective. He felt she hated him, and saw her jealous eyes watching himself and the child with almost an expression of hate. She was jealous of the little girl's evident preference for the father, and Almayer felt he was not safe with that woman in the house. While she was burning the furniture, and tearing down the pretty curtains in her unreasoning hate of those signs of civilization, Almayer, cowed by these outbursts of savage nature, meditated in silence on the best way of getting rid of her. He thought of everything; even planned murder in an undecided and feeble sort of way, but dared do nothing—expecting every day the return of Lingard with news of some immense good fortune.　Lingard returned indeed, but aged, ill, a ghost of his former self, with the fire of fever burning in his sunken eyes, almost the only survivor of the numerous expedition. But he was successful at last! Untold riches were in his grasp; he wanted more money—only a little more to realize a dream of fabulous fortune. And Hudig had failed! Almayer scraped all he could together, but the old man wanted more. If Almayer could not get it he would go to Singapore—to Europe even, but before all to Singapore; and he would take the little Nina with him. The child must be brought up decently. He had good friends in Singapore who would take care of her and have her taught properly. All would be well, and that girl, upon whom the old seaman seemed to have transferred all his former affection for the mother, would be the richest woman in the East —in the world even. So old Lingard shouted, pacing the verandah with his heavy quarter-deck step, gesticulating with a smouldering cheroot; ragged, dishevelled, enthusiastic; and Almayer, sitting huddled up on a pile of mats, thought with dread of the separation with the only human being he loved—with greater dread still, perhaps, of the scene with his wife, the savage tigress deprived of her young. She will poison me, thought the poor wretch, well aware of that easy and final manner of solving the social, political, or family problems in Malay life.

To his great surprise she took the news very quietly, giving only him and Lingard a furtive glance, and saying not a word. This, however, did not prevent her the next day from jumping into the river and swimming after the boat in which Lingard was carrying away the nurse with the screaming child. Almayer had to give chase with his whale-boat and drag her in by the hair in the midst of cries and curses enough to make heaven fall. Yet after two days spent in wailing, she returned to her former mode of life, chewing betel-nut, and sitting all day amongst her women in stupefied idleness. She aged very rapidly after that, and only roused herself from her apathy to acknowledge by a scathing remark or an insulting exclamation the accidental presence of her husband. He had built for her a riverside hut in the compound where she dwelt in perfect seclusion. Lakamba's visits had ceased when, by a convenient decree of Providence the old ruler of Sambir departed this life. Lakamba reigned in his stead now, having been well served by his Arab friends with the Dutch authorities. Syed Abdulla was the great man and trader of the Pantai. Almayer lay ruined and helpless under the close-meshed net of their intrigues, owing his life only to his supposed knowledge of Lingard's valuable secret. Lingard had disappeared. He wrote once from Singapore saying the child was well, and under the care of a Mrs. Vinck, and that he himself was going to Europe to raise money for the great enterprise. He was coming back soon. There would be no difficulties, he wrote. People would rush in with their money. Evidently they did not, for there was only

one letter more from him saying he was ill, had found
no relation living, but little else besides. Then came a
complete silence. Europe had swallowed up the Rajah
Laut apparently, and Almayer looked vainly westward
for a ray of light out of the gloom of his shattered hopes.
Years passed, and the rare letters from Mrs. Vinck,
later from the girl herself, were the only thing to be
looked to to make life bearable amongst the triumphant
savagery of the river. Almayer lived now alone, having
even ceased to visit his debtors who would not pay, sure
of Lakamba's protection. The faithful Sumatrese Ali
cooked his rice and made his coffee, for he dared not
trust any one else, and least of all his wife. He killed
time wandering sadly in the overgrown paths round the
house, visiting the ruined godowns where a few brass
guns covered with verdigris and only a few broken cases
of mouldering Manchester goods reminded him of the
good early times when all this was full of life and merchandise, and he overlooked a busy scene on the river
bank, his little daughter by his side. Now the up-
country canoes glided past the little rotten wharf of
Lingard and Co., to paddle up the Pantai branch, and
cluster round the new jetty belonging to Abdulla.
Not that they loved Abdulla, but they dared not trade
with the man whose star had set. Had they done so
they knew there was no mercy to be expected from Arab
or Rajah; no rice to be got on credit in times of scarcity
from either; and Almayer could not help them, having
at times hardly enough for himself. Almayer, in his
isolation and despair, often envied his near neighbour
the Chinaman, Jim-Eng, whom he could see stretched
on a pile of cool mats, a wooden pillow under his head,
an opium pipe in his nerveless fingers. He did not
seek, however, consolation in opium—perhaps it was
too expensive—perhaps his white man's pride saved him

from that degradation; but most likely it was the thought of his little daughter in the far-off Straits Settlements. He heard from her oftener since Abdulla bought a steamer, which ran now between Singapore and the Pantai settlement every three months or so. Almayer felt himself nearer his daughter. He longed to see her, and planned a voyage to Singapore, but put off his departure from year to year, always expecting some favourable turn of fortune. He did not want to meet her with empty hands and with no words of hope on his lips. He could not take her back into that savage life to which he was condemned himself. He was also a little afraid of her. What would she think of him? He reckoned the years. A grown woman. A civilized woman, young and hopeful; while he felt old and hopeless, and very much like those savages round him. He asked himself what was going to be her future. He could not answer that question yet, and he dared not face her. And yet he longed after her. He hesitated for years.

His hesitation was put an end to by Nina's unexpected appearance in Sambir. She arrived in the steamer under the captain's care. Almayer beheld her with surprise not unmixed with wonder. During those ten years the child had changed into a woman, black-haired, olive-skinned, tall, and beautiful, with great sad eyes, where the startled expression common to Malay womankind was modified by a thoughtful tinge inherited from her European ancestry. Almayer thought with dismay of the meeting of his wife and daughter, of what this grave girl in European clothes would think of her betel-nut chewing mother, squatting in a dark hut, disorderly, half naked, and sulky. He also feared an outbreak of temper on the part of that pest of a woman he had hitherto managed to keep

tolerably quiet, thereby saving the remnants of his
dilapidated furniture. And he stood there before the
closed door of the hut in the blazing sunshine listening
to the murmur of voices, wondering what went on inside, wherefrom all the servant-maids had been expelled
at the beginning of the interview, and now stood clustered by the palings with half-covered faces in a chatter
of curious speculation. He forgot himself there trying
to catch a stray word through the bamboo walls, till
the captain of the steamer (who had walked up with the
girl) fearing a sunstroke, took him under the arm and
led him into the shade of his own verandah where Nina's
trunk stood already, having been landed by the steamer's men. As soon as Captain Ford had his glass before
him and his cheroot lighted, Almayer asked for the
explanation of his daughter's unexpected arrival.
Ford said little beyond generalizing in vague but violent
terms upon the foolishness of women in general, and of
Mrs. Vinck in particular.

"You know, Kaspar," said he, in conclusion, to the
excited Almayer, "it is deucedly awkward to have a
half-caste girl in the house. There's such a lot of fools
about. There was that young fellow from the bank who
used to ride to the Vinck bungalow early and late.
That old woman thought it was for that Emma of hers.
When she found out what he wanted exactly, there was
a row, I can tell you. She would not have Nina—not
an hour longer—in the house. Fact is, I heard of this
affair and took the girl to my wife. My wife is a pretty
good woman—as women go—and upon my word we
would have kept the girl for you, only she would not
stay. Now, then! Don't flare up, Kaspar. Sit still.
What can you do? It is better so. Let her stay with
you. She was never happy over there. Those two
Vinck girls are no better than dressed-up monkeys.

They slighted her. You can't make her white. It's no use you swearing at me. You can't. She is a good girl for all that, but she would not tell my wife anything. If you want to know, ask her yourself; but if I was you I would leave her alone. You are welcome to her passage money, old fellow, if you are short now." And the skipper, throwing away his cigar, walked off to "wake them up on board," as he expressed it.

Almayer vainly expected to hear of the cause of his daughter's return from his daughter's lips. Not that day, not on any other day did she ever allude to her Singapore life. He did not care to ask, awed by the calm impassiveness of her face, by those solemn eyes looking past him on the great, still forests sleeping in majestic repose to the murmur of the broad river. He accepted the situation, happy in the gentle and protecting affection the girl showed him, fitfully enough, for she had (as he called it) her bad days when she used to visit her mother and remain long hours in the riverside hut, coming out as inscrutable as ever, but with a contemptuous look and a short word ready to answer any of his speeches. He got used even to that, and on those days kept quiet, although greatly alarmed by his wife's influence upon the girl. Otherwise Nina adapted herself wonderfully to the circumstances of a half-savage and miserable life. She accepted without question or apparent disgust the neglect, the decay, the poverty of the household, the absence of furniture, and the preponderance of rice diet on the family table. She lived with Almayer in the little house (now sadly decaying) built originally by Lingard for the young couple. The Malays discussed eagerly her arrival. There were at the beginning crowded levées of Malay women with their children, seeking eagerly after "Ubat" for all the ills of the flesh from the young Mem Putih. In the cool of the evening grave Arabs in long white shirts and yellow sleeveless jackets walked slowly on the dusty path by the riverside towards Almayer's gate, and made solemn calls upon that Unbeliever under shallow pretences of business, only to get a glimpse of the young girl in a highly decorous manner. Even Lakamba came out of his stockade in a great pomp of war canoes and red umbrellas, and landed on the rotten little jetty of Lingard and Co. He came, he said, to buy a couple of brass guns as a present to his friend the chief of Sambir Dyaks; and while Almayer, suspicious but polite, busied himself in unearthing the old popguns in the godowns, the Rajah sat on an armchair in the verandah, surrounded by his respectful retinue waiting in vain for Nina's appearance. She was in one of her bad days, and remained in her mother's hut watching with her the ceremonious proceedings on the verandah. The Rajah departed, baffled but courteous, and soon Almayer began to reap the benefit of improved relations with the ruler in the shape of the recovery of some debts, paid to him with many apologies and many a low salaam by debtors till then considered hopelessly insolvent. Under these improving circumstances Almayer brightened up a little. All was not lost perhaps. Those Arabs and Malays saw at last that he was a man of some ability, he thought. And he began, after his manner, to plan great things, to dream of great fortunes for himself and Nina. Especially for Nina! Under these vivifying impulses he asked Captain Ford to write to his friends in England making inquiries after Lingard. Was he alive or dead? If dead, had he left any papers, documents; any indications or hints as to his great enterprise? Meantime he had found amongst the rubbish in one of the empty rooms a notebook belonging to the old adventurer. He studied the crabbed handwriting of its pages and often grew meditative over it. Other things also woke him up from his apathy. The stir made in the whole of the island by the establishment of the British Borneo Company affected even the sluggish flow of the Pantai life. Great changes were expected; annexation was talked of; the Arabs grew civil. Almayer began building his new house for the use of the future engineers, agents, or settlers of the new Company. He spent every available guilder on it with a confiding heart. One thing only disturbed his happiness; his wife came out of her seclusion, importing her green jacket, scant sarongs, shrill voice, and witch-like appearance, into his quiet life in the small bungalow. And his daughter seemed to accept that savage intrusion into their daily existence with wonderful equanimity. He did not like it, but dared say nothing.

CHAPTER THREE

THE deliberations conducted in London have a far-reaching importance, and so the decision issued from the fog-veiled offices of the Borneo Company darkened for Almayer the brilliant sunshine of the Tropics, and added another drop of bitterness to the cup of his disenchantments. The claim to that part of the East Coast was abandoned, leaving the Pantai river under the nominal power of Holland. In Sambir there was joy and excitement. The slaves were hurried out of sight into the forest and jungle, and the flags were run up to tall poles in the Rajah's compound in expectation of a visit from Dutch man-of-war boats.

The frigate remained anchored outside the mouth of the river, and the boats came up in tow of the steam launch, threading their way cautiously amongst a crowd of canoes filled with gaily dressed Malays. The officer in command listened gravely to the loyal speeches of Lakamba, returned the salaams of Abdulla, and assured those gentlemen in choice Malay of the great Rajah's—down in Batavia—friendship and good-will towards the ruler and inhabitants of this model state of Sambir.

Almayer from his verandah watched across the river the festive proceedings, heard the report of brass guns saluting the new flag presented to Lakamba, and the deep murmur of the crowd of spectators surging round the stockade. The smoke of the firing rose in white clouds on the green background of the forests, and he could not help comparing his own fleeting hopes to the rapidly disappearing vapour. He was by no means patriotically elated by the event, yet he had to force himself into a gracious behaviour when, the official reception being over, the naval officers of the Commission crossed the river to pay a visit to the solitary white man of whom they had heard, no doubt wishing also to catch a glimpse of his daughter. In that they were disappointed, Nina refusing to show herself; but they seemed easily consoled by the gin and cheroots set before them by the hospitable Almayer; and sprawling comfortably on the lame armchairs under the shade of the verandah, while the blazing sunshine outside seemed to set the great river simmering in the heat, they filled the little bungalow with the unusual sounds of European languages, with noise and laughter produced by naval witticisms at the expense of the fat Lakamba whom they had been complimenting so much that very morning. The younger men in an access of good fellowship made their host talk, and Almayer, excited by the sight of European faces, by the sound of European voices, opened his heart before the sympathizing strangers, unaware of the amusement the recital of his many misfortunes caused to those future admirals. They drank his health, wished him many big diamonds and a mountain of gold, expressed even an envy of the high destinies awaiting him yet. Encouraged by so much friendliness, the grey-headed and foolish dreamer invited his guests to visit his new house. They went there through the long grass in a straggling procession while their boats were got ready for the return down the river in the cool of the evening. And in the great empty rooms where the tepid wind entering through the sashless windows whirled gently the dried leaves and the dust of many days of neglect, Almayer in his white jacket and flowered sarong, surrounded by a circle of

glittering uniforms, stamped his foot to show the so-
lidity of the neatly-fitting floors and expatiated upon the
beauties and convenience of the building. They listened and assented, amazed by the wonderful simplicity
and the foolish hopefulness of the man, till Almayer,
carried away by his excitement, disclosed his regret at
the non-arrival of the English, "who knew how to develop a rich country," as he expressed it. There was
a general laugh amongst the Dutch officers at that un-
sophisticated statement, and a move was made towards
the boats; but when Almayer, stepping cautiously on
the rotten boards of the Lingard jetty, tried to approach the chief of the Commission with some timid
hints anent the protection required by the Dutch subject against the wily Arabs, that salt water diplomat
told him significantly that the Arabs were better subjects than Hollanders who dealt illegally in gunpowder
with the Malays. The innocent Almayer recognized
there at once the oily tongue of Abdulla and the solemn
persuasiveness of Lakamba, but ere he had time to
frame an indignant protest the steam launch and the
string of boats moved rapidly down the river leaving
him on the jetty, standing open-mouthed in his surprise
and anger. There are thirty miles of river from Sambir
to the gem-like islands of the estuary where the frigate
was awaiting the return of the boats. The moon rose
long before the boats had traversed half that distance,
and the black forest sleeping peacefully under her cold
rays woke up that night to the ringing laughter in the
small flotilla provoked by some reminiscence of Almayer's lamentable narrative. Salt-water jests at the
poor man's expense were passed from boat to boat,
the non-appearance of his daughter was commented
upon with severe displeasure, and the half-finished house
built for the reception of Englishmen received on that

joyous night the name of "Almayer's Folly" by the unanimous vote of the lighthearted seamen.

For many weeks after this visit life in Sambir resumed its even and uneventful flow. Each day's sun shooting its morning rays above the tree-tops lit up the usual scene of daily activity. Nina walking on the path that formed the only street in the settlement saw the accustomed sight of men lolling on the shady side of the houses, on the high platforms; of women busily engaged in husking the daily rice; of naked brown children racing along the shady and narrow paths leading to the clearings. Jim-Eng, strolling before his house, greeted her with a friendly nod before climbing up indoors to seek his beloved opium pipe. The elder children clustered round her, daring from long acquaintance, pulling the skirts of her white robe with their dark fingers, and showing their brilliant teeth in expectation of a shower of glass beads. She greeted them with a quiet smile, but always had a few friendly words for a Siamese girl, a slave owned by Bulangi, whose numerous wives were said to be of a violent temper. Well-founded rumour said also that the domestic squabbles of that industrious cultivator ended generally in a combined assault of all his wives upon the Siamese slave. The girl herself never complained—perhaps from dictates of prudence, but more likely through the strange, resigned apathy of half-savage womankind. From early morning she was to be seen on the paths amongst the houses—by the riverside or on the jetties, the tray of pastry, it was her mission to sell, skilfully balanced on her head. During the great heat of the day she usually sought refuge in Almayer's campong, often finding shelter in a shady corner of the verandah, where she squatted with her tray before her, when invited by Nina. For "Mem Putih" she had always a smile, but the presence of

Mrs. Almayer, the very sound of her shrill voice, was the signal for a hurried departure.

To this girl Nina often spoke; the other inhabitants of Sambir seldom or never heard the sound of her voice. They got used to the silent figure moving in their midst calm and white-robed, a being from another world and incomprehensible to them. Yet Nina's life for all her outward composure, for all the seeming detachment from the things and people surrounding her, was far from quiet, in consequence of Mrs. Almayer being much too active for the happiness and even safety of the household. She had resumed some intercourse with Lakamba, not personally, it is true (for the dignity of that potentate kept him inside his stockade), but through the agency of that potentate's prime minister, harbour master, financial adviser, and general factotum. That gentleman—of Sulu origin—was certainly endowed with statesmanlike qualities, although he was totally devoid of personal charms. In truth he was perfectly repulsive, possessing only one eye and a pock-marked face, with nose and lips horribly disfigured by the smallpox. This unengaging individual often strolled into Almayer's garden in unofficial costume, composed of a piece of pink calico round his waist. There at the back of the house, squatting on his heels on scattered embers, in close proximity to the great iron boiler, where the family daily rice was being cooked by the women under Mrs. Almayer's superintendence, did that astute negotiator carry on long conversations in Sulu language with Almayer's wife. What the subject of their discourses was might have been guessed from the subsequent domestic scenes by Almayer's hearthstone.

Of late Almayer had taken to excursions up the river. In a small canoe with two paddlers and the faithful Ali for a steersman he would disappear for a few days at a time. All his movements were no doubt closely watched by Lakamba and Abdulla, for the man once in the confidence of Rajah Laut was supposed to be in possession of valuable secrets. The coast population of Borneo believes implicitly in diamonds of fabulous value, in gold mines of enormous richness in the interior. And all those imaginings are heightened by the difficulty of penetrating far inland, especially on the northeast coast, where the Malays and the river tribes of Dyaks or Head-hunters are eternally quarrelling. It is true enough that some gold reaches the coast in the hands of those Dyaks when, during short periods of truce in the desultory warfare, they visit the coast settlements of Malays. And so the wildest exaggerations are built up and added to on the slight basis of that fact.

Almayer in his quality of white man—as Lingard before him—had somewhat better relations with the up-river tribes. Yet even his excursions were not without danger, and his returns were eagerly looked for by the impatient Lakamba. But every time the Rajah was disappointed. Vain were the conferences by the rice-pot of his factotum Babalatchi with the white man's wife. The white man himself was impenetrable—impenetrable to persuasion, coaxing, abuse; to soft words and shrill revilings; to desperate beseechings or murderous threats; for Mrs. Almayer, in her extreme desire to persuade her husband into an alliance with Lakamba, played upon the whole gamut of passion. With her soiled robe wound tightly under the armpits across her lean bosom, her scant greyish hair tumbled in disorder over her projecting cheek-bones, in suppliant attitude, she depicted with shrill volubility the advantages of close union with a man so good and so fair dealing.

"Why don't you go to the Rajah?" she screamed.

"Why do you go back to those Dyaks in the great forest? They should be killed. You cannot kill them, you cannot; but our Rajah's men are brave! You tell the Rajah where the old white man's treasure is. Our Rajah is good! He is our very grandfather. He will kill those wretched Dyaks, and you shall have half the treasure. Oh, Kaspar, tell where the treasure is! Tell me! Tell me out of the old man's surat where you read so often at night."

On those occasions Almayer sat with rounded shoulders bending to the blast of this domestic tempest, accentuating only each pause in the torrent of his wife's eloquence by an angry growl, "There is no treasure! Go away, woman!" Exasperated by the sight of his patiently bent back, she would at last walk round so as to face him across the table, and clasping her robe with one hand she stretched the other lean arm and claw-like hand to emphasize, in a passion of anger and contempt, the rapid rush of scathing remarks and bitter cursings heaped on the head of the man unworthy to associate with brave Malay chiefs. It ended generally by Almayer rising slowly, his long pipe in hand, his face set into a look of inward pain, and walking away in silence. He descended the steps and plunged into the long grass on his way to the solitude of his new house, dragging his feet in a state of physical collapse from disgust and fear before that fury. She followed to the head of the steps, and sent the shafts of indiscriminate abuse after the retreating form. And each of those scenes was concluded by a piercing shriek, reaching him far away. "You know, Kaspar, I am your wife! your own Christian wife after your own Blanda law!" For she knew that this was the bitterest thing of all; the greatest regret of that man's life.

All these scenes Nina witnessed unmoved. She

might have been deaf, dumb, without any feeling as far as any expression of opinion went. Yet oft when her father had sought the refuge of the great dusty rooms of "Almayer's Folly," and her mother, exhausted by rhetorical efforts, squatted wearily on her heels with her back against the leg of the table, Nina would approach her curiously, guarding her skirts from betel juice besprinkling the floor, and gaze down upon her as one might look into the quiescent crater of a volcano after a destructive eruption. Mrs. Almayer's thoughts after these scenes were usually turned into a channel of childhood reminiscences, and she gave them utterance in a kind of monotonous recitative—slightly disconnected, but generally describing the glories of the Sultan of Sulu, his great splendour, his power, his great prowess, the fear which benumbed the hearts of white men at the sight of his swift piratical praus. And these muttered statements of her grandfather's might were mixed up with bits of later recollections, where the great fight with the "White Devil's" brig and the convent life in Samarang occupied the principal place. At that point she usually dropped the thread of her narrative, and pulling out the little brass cross, always suspended round her neck, she contemplated it with superstitious awe. That superstitious feeling connected with some vague talismanic properties of the little bit of metal and the still more hazy but terrible notion of some bad Djinns and horrible torments invented, as she thought, for her especial punishment by the good Mother Superior in case of the loss of the above charm, were Mrs. Almayer's only theological outfit for the stormy road of life. Mrs. Almayer had at least something tangible to cling to, but Nina, brought up under the Protestant wing of the proper Mrs. Vinck, had not even a little piece of brass to remind her of past teaching.

And listening to the recital of those savage glories, those barbarous fights and savage feasting, to the story of deeds valorous, albeit somewhat bloodthirsty, where men of her mother's race shone far above the Orang Blanda, she felt herself irresistibly fascinated, and saw with vague surprise the narrow mantle of civilized morality, in which good-meaning people had wrapped her young soul, fall away and leave her shivering and helpless as if on the edge of some deep and unknown abyss. Strangest of all, this abyss did not frighten her when she was under the influence of the witch-like being she called her mother. She seemed to have forgotten in civilized surroundings her life before the time when Lingard had, so to speak, kidnapped her from Brow. Since then she had had Christian teaching, social education, and a good glimpse of civilized life. Unfortunately her teachers did not understand her nature, and the education ended in a scene of humiliation, in an outburst of contempt from white people for her mixed blood. And now she had lived on the river for three years with a savage mother and a father walking about amongst pitfalls, with his head in the clouds, weak, irresolute, and unhappy. She had lived a life devoid of all the decencies of civilization, in miserable domestic conditions; she had breathed the atmosphere of sordid plottings for gain, of the no less disgusting intrigues and crimes for lust or money; and those things, together with the domestic quarrels, were the only events of her three years' existence. She did not die from despair and disgust the first month, as she expected and almost hoped for. On the contrary, at the end of half a year it had seemed to her that she had known no other life. Her young mind having been unskilfully permitted to glance at better things, and then thrown back again into the hopeless quagmire of barbarism, full of strong and uncontrolled passions, had lost the power to discriminate. It seemed to Nina that there was no change and no difference Whether they traded in brick godowns or on the muddy river bank; whether they reached after much or little; whether they made love under the shadows of the great trees or in the shadow of the cathedral on the Singapore promenade; whether they plotted for their own ends under the protection of laws and according to the rules of Christian conduct, or whether they sought the gratification of their desires with the savage cunning and the unrestrained fierceness of natures as innocent of culture as their own immense and gloomy forests, Nina saw only the same manifestations of love and hate and of sordid greed chasing the uncertain dollar in all its multifarious and vanishing shapes. To her resolute nature, however, after all these years, the savage and uncompromising sincerity of purpose shown by her Malay kinsmen seemed at last preferable to the sleek hypocrisy, to the polite disguises, to the virtuous pretences of such white people as she had had the misfortune to come in contact with. After all it was her life; it was going to be her life, and so thinking she fell more and more under the influence of her mother. Seeking, in her ignorance, a better side to that life, she listened with avidity to the old woman's tales of the departed glories of the Rajahs, from whose race she had sprung, and she became gradually more indifferent, more contemptuous of the white side of her descent represented by a feeble and traditionless father.

Almayer's difficulties were by no means diminished by the girl's presence in Sambir. The stir caused by her arrival had died out, it is true, and Lakamba had not renewed his visits; but about a year after the departure of the man-of-war boats the nephew of Abdulla, Syed

Reshid, returned from his pilgrimage to **Mecca**, rejoicing in a green jacket and the proud title of Hadji. There was a great letting off of rockets on board the steamer which brought him in, and a great beating of drums all night in Abdulla's compound, while the feast of welcome was prolonged far into the small hours of the morning. Reshid was the favourite nephew and heir of Abdulla, and that loving uncle, meeting Almayer one day by the riverside, stopped politely to exchange civilities and to ask solemnly for an interview. Almayer suspected some attempt at a swindle, or at any rate something unpleasant, but of course consented with a great show of rejoicing. Accordingly the next evening, after sunset, Abdulla came, accompanied by several other grey-beards and by his nephew. That young man—of a very rakish and dissipated appearance—affected the greatest indifference as to the whole of the proceedings. When the torch-bearers had grouped themselves below the steps, the visitors had seated themselves on various lame chairs, Reshid stood apart in the shadow, examining his aristocratically small hands with great attention. Almayer, surprised by the great solemnity of his visitors, perched himself on the corner of the table with a characteristic want of dignity quickly noted by the Arabs with grave disapproval. But Abdulla spoke now, looking straight past Almayer at the red curtain hanging in the doorway, where a slight tremor disclosed the presence of women on the other side. He began by neatly complimenting Almayer upon the long years they had dwelt together in cordial neighbourhood, and called upon Allah to give him many more years to gladden the eyes of his friends by his welcome presence. He made a polite allusion to the great consideration shown him (Almayer) by the Dutch "Commissie," and drew thence the flattering inference of Almayer's great importance amongst his own people. He—Abdulla—was also important amongst all the Arabs, and his nephew Reshid would be heir of that social position and of great riches. Now Reshid was a Hadji. He was possessor of several Malay women, went on Abdulla, but it was time he had a favourite wife, the first of the four allowed by the Prophet. And, speaking with well-bred politeness, he explained further to the dumbfounded Almayer that, if he would consent to the alliance of his offspring with that true believer and virtuous man Reshid, she would be mistress of all the splendours of Reshid's house, the first wife of the first Arab in the Islands, when he—Abdulla—had been called to the joys of Paradise by Allah the All-merciful. "You know, Tuan," he said, in conclusion, "the other women would be her slaves, and Reshid's house is great. From Bombay he has brought great divans, and costly carpets, and European furniture. There is also a great looking-glass in a frame shining like gold. What could a girl want more?" And while Almayer looked upon him in silent dismay Abdulla spoke in a more confidential tone, waving his attendants away, and finished his speech by pointing out the material advantages of such an alliance, and offering to settle upon Almayer three thousand dollars as a sign of his sincere friendship and the price of the girl.

Poor Almayer was nearly having a fit. Burning with the desire of taking Abdulla by the throat, he had but to think of his helpless position in the midst of lawless men to comprehend the necessity of diplomatic conciliation. He mastered his impulses, and spoke politely and coldly, saying the girl was young and was the apple of his eye. Tuan Reshid, a Faithful and a Hadji, would not want an infidel woman in his harem;

and, seeing Abdulla smile sceptically at that last objection, he remained silent, not trusting himself to speak more, not daring to refuse point-blank, nor yet to say anything compromising. Abdulla understood the meaning of that silence, and rose to take leave with a grave salaam. He wished his friend Almayer "a thousand years," and moved down the steps, helped dutifully by Reshid. The torch-bearers shook their torches, scattering a shower of sparks into the river, and the cortege moved off, leaving Almayer agitated but greatly relieved by their departure. He dropped into a chair and watched the glimmer of the lights amongst the tree trunks till they disappeared and complete silence succeeded the tramp of feet and the murmur of voices. He did not move till the curtain rustled and Nina came out on the verandah and sat in the rocking-chair, where she used to spend many hours every day. She gave a slight rocking motion to her seat, leaning back with half-closed eyes, her long hair shading her face from the smoky light of the lamp on the table. Almayer looked at her furtively, but the face was as impassible as ever. She turned her head slightly towards her father, and, speaking, to his great surprise, in English, asked—

"Was that Abdulla here?"

"Yes," said Almayer—"just gone."

"And what did he want, father?"

"He wanted to buy you for Reshid," answered Almayer, brutally, his anger getting the better of him, and looking at the girl as if in expectation of some outbreak of feeling. But Nina remained apparently unmoved, gazing dreamily into the black night outside.

"Be careful, Nina," said Almayer, after a short silence and rising from his chair, "when you go paddling alone into the creeks in your canoe. That Reshid is a violent

scoundrel, and there is no saying what he may do.   Do
you hear me?"

She was standing now, ready to go in, one hand grasping the curtain in the doorway.   She turned round,
throwing her heavy tresses back by a sudden gesture.

"Do you think he would dare?" she asked, quickly,
and then turned again to go in, adding in a lower tone,
"He would not dare.   Arabs are all cowards."

Almayer looked after her, astonished.   He did not
seek the repose of his hammock.   He walked the floor
absently, sometimes stopping by the balustrade to
think.   The lamp went out.   The first streak of dawn
broke over the forest; Almayer shivered in the damp air.
"I give it up," he muttered to himself, lying down
wearily.   "Damn those women!   Well!   If the girl
did not look as if she wanted to be kidnapped!"

And he felt a nameless fear creep into his heart,
making him shiver again.

CHAPTER FOUR

THAT year, towards the breaking up of the southwest monsoon, disquieting rumours reached Sambir. Captain Ford, coming up to Almayer's house for an evening's chat, brought late numbers of the *Straits Times* giving the news of Acheen war and of the unsuccessful Dutch expedition. The Nakhodas of the rare trading praus ascending the river paid visits to Lakamba, discussing with that potentate the unsettled state of affairs, and wagged their heads gravely over the recital of Orang Blanda exaction, severity, and general tyranny, as exemplified in the total stoppage of gunpowder trade and the rigorous visiting of all suspicious craft trading in the straits of Macassar. Even the loyal soul of Lakamba was stirred into a state of inward discontent by the withdrawal of his license for powder and by the abrupt confiscation of one hundred and fifty barrels of that commodity by the gunboat *Princess Amelia*, when, after a hazardous voyage, it had almost reached the mouth of the river. The unpleasant news was given him by Reshid, who, after the unsuccessful issue of his matrimonial projects, had made a long voyage amongst the islands for trading purposes; had bought the powder for his friend, and was overhauled and deprived of it on his return when actually congratulating himself on his acuteness in avoiding detection. Reshid's wrath was principally directed against Almayer, whom he suspected of having notified the Dutch authorities of the desultory warfare carried on by the Arabs and the Rajah with the up-river Dyak tribes.

To Reshid's great surprise the Rajah received his complaints very coldly, and showed no signs of vengeful disposition towards the white man. In truth, Lakamba knew very well that Almayer was perfectly innocent of any meddling in state affairs; and besides, his attitude towards that much persecuted individual was wholly changed in consequence of a reconciliation effected between him and his old enemy by Almayer's newly-found friend, Dain Maroola.

Almayer had now a friend. Shortly after Reshid's departure on his commercial journey, Nina, drifting slowly with the tide in the canoe on her return home after one of her solitary excursions, heard in one of the small creeks a splashing of heavy ropes dropping in the water and the prolonged song of Malay seamen when some heavy pulling is to be done. Through the thick fringe of bushes hiding the mouth of the creek she saw the tall spars of some European-rigged sailing vessel overtopping the summits of the Nipa palms. A brig was being hauled out of the small creek into the main stream. The sun had set, and during the short moments of twilight Nina saw the brig, aided by the evening breeze and the flowing tide, head towards Sambir under her set foresail The girl turned her canoe out of the main river into one of the many narrow channels amongst the wooded islets, and paddled vigorously over the black and sleepy backwaters towards Sambir. Her canoe brushed the water-palms, skirted the short spaces of muddy bank where sedate alligators looked at her with lazy unconcern, and, just as darkness was setting in, shot out into the broad junction of the two main branches of the river, where the brig was already at anchor with sails furled, yards squared, and decks seemingly untenanted by any human being. Nina had to cross the river and pass pretty close to the brig in order to reach home on the low promontory between the two branches of the Pantai. Up both branches, in the houses built on the banks and over the water, the lights twinkled already, reflected in the still waters below. The hum of voices, the occasional cry of a child, the rapid and abruptly interrupted roll of a wooden drum, together with some distant hailing in the darkness by the returning fishermen, reached her over the broad expanse of the river. She hesitated a little before crossing, the sight of such an unusual object as an European-rigged vessel causing her some uneasiness, but the river in its wide expansion was dark enough to render a small canoe invisible. She urged her small craft with swift strokes of her paddle, kneeling in the bottom and bending forward to catch any suspicious sound while she steered towards the little jetty of Lingard and Co., to which the strong light of the paraffin lamp shining on the whitewashed verandah of Almayer's bungalow served as a convenient guide. The jetty itself, under the shadow of the bank overgrown by drooping bushes, was hidden in darkness. Before even she could see it she heard the hollow bumping of a large boat against its rotten posts, and heard also the murmur of whispered conversation in that boat whose white paint and great dimensions, faintly visible on nearer approach, made her rightly guess that it belonged to the brig just anchored. Stopping her course by a rapid motion of her paddle, with another swift stroke she sent it whirling away from the wharf and steered for a little rivulet which gave access to the back courtyard of the house. She landed at the muddy head of the creek and made her way towards the house over the trodden grass of the courtyard. To the left, from the cooking shed, shone a red glare through the banana plantation she skirted, and the noise of feminine laughter reached her from there in the silent evening. She rightly judged her mother was not near, laughter and Mrs. Almayer not being close neighbours. She must be in the house, thought Nina, as she ran lightly up the inclined plane of shaky planks leading to the back door of the narrow passage dividing the house in two. Outside the doorway, in the black shadow, stood the faithful Ali.

"Who is there?" asked Nina.

"A great Malay man has come," answered Ali, in a tone of suppressed excitement. "He is a rich man. There are six men with lances. Real Soldat, you understand. And his dress is very brave. I have seen his dress. It shines! What jewels! Don't go there, Mem Nina. Tuan said not; but the old Mem is gone. Tuan will be angry. Merciful Allah! what jewels that man has got!"

Nina slipped past the outstretched hand of the slave into the dark passage where, in the crimson glow of the hanging curtain, close by its other end, she could see a small dark form crouching near the wall. Her mother was feasting her eyes and ears with what was taking place on the front verandah, and Nina approached to take her share in the rare pleasure of some novelty. She was met by her mother's extended arm and by a low murmured warning not to make a noise.

"Have you seen them, mother?" asked Nina, in a breathless whisper.

Mrs. Almayer turned her face towards the girl, and her sunken eyes shone strangely in the red half-light of the passage.

"I saw him," she said, in an almost inaudible tone, pressing her daughter's hand with her bony fingers. "A great Rajah has come to Sambir—a Son of Heaven," muttered the old woman to herself. "Go away, girl!"

The two women stood close to the curtain, Nina wishing to approach the rent in the stuff, and her mother defending the position with angry obstinacy. On the other side there was a lull in the conversation, but the occasional light tinkling of some ornaments, the clink of metal scabbards, or of brass siri-vessels passed from hand to hand, was audible during the short pause. The women struggled silently, when there was a shuffling noise and the shadow of Almayer's burly form fell on the curtain.

The women ceased struggling and remained motionless. Almayer had stood up to answer his guest, turning his back to the doorway, unaware of what was going on on the other side. He spoke in a tone of regretful irritation.

"You have come to the wrong house, Tuan Maroola, if you want to trade as you say. I was a trader once, not now, whatever you may have heard about me in Macassar. And if you want anything, you will not find it here; I have nothing to give, and want nothing myself. You should go to the Rajah here; you can see in the daytime his houses across the river, there, where those fires are burning on the shore. He will help you and trade with you. Or, better still, go to the Arabs over there," he went on bitterly, pointing with his hand towards the houses of Sambir. "Abdulla is the man you want. There is nothing he would not buy, and there is nothing he would not sell; believe me, I know him well."

He waited for an answer a short time, then added—

"All that I have said is true, and there is nothing more."

Nina, held back by her mother, heard a soft voice reply with a calm evenness of intonation peculiar to the better class Malays—

"Who would doubt a white Tuan's words? A man seeks his friends where his heart tells him. Is this not true also? I have come, although so late, for I have something to say which you may be glad to hear. To-morrow I shall go to the Sultan; a trader wants the friendship of great men. Then I shall return here to speak serious words, if Tuan permits. I shall not go to the Arabs; their lies are very great! What are they? Chelakka!"

Almayer's voice sounded a little more pleasantly in reply.

"Well, as you like. I can hear you to-morrow at any time if you have anything to say. Bah! After you have seen the Sultan Lakamba you will not want to return here, Inchi Dain. You will see. Only mind, I will have nothing to do with Lakamba. You may tell him so. What is your business with me, after all?"

"To-morrow we talk, Tuan, now I know you," answered the Malay. "I speak English a little, so we can talk and nobody will understand, and then——"

He interrupted himself suddenly, asking surprised, "What's that noise, Tuan?"

Almayer had also heard the increasing noise of the scuffle recommenced on the women's side of the curtain. Evidently Nina's strong curiosity was on the point of overcoming Mrs. Almayer's exalted sense of social proprieties. Hard breathing was distinctly audible, and the curtain shook during the contest, which was mainly physical, although Mrs. Almayer's voice was heard in angry remonstrance with its usual want of strictly logical reasoning, but with the well-known richness of invective.

"You shameless woman! Are you a slave?" shouted shrilly the irate matron. "Veil your face, abandoned wretch! You white snake, I will not let you!"

Almayer's face expressed annoyance and also doubt as to the advisability of interfering between mother and daughter. He glanced at his Malay visitor, who was waiting silently for the end of the uproar in an attitude of amused expectation, and waving his hand contemptuously he murmured—

"It is nothing. Some women."

The Malay nodded his head gravely, and his face assumed an expression of serene indifference, as etiquette demanded after such an explanation. The contest was ended behind the curtain, and evidently the younger will had its way, for the rapid shuffle and click of Mrs. Almayer's high-heeled sandals died away in the distance. The tranquillized master of the house was going to resume the conversation when, struck by an unexpected change in the expression of his guest's countenance, he turned his head and saw Nina standing in the doorway.

After Mrs. Almayer's retreat from the field of battle, Nina, with a contemptuous exclamation, "It's only a trader," had lifted the conquered curtain and now stood in full light, framed in the dark background of the passage, her lips slightly parted, her hair in disorder after the exertion, the angry gleam not yet faded out of her glorious and sparkling eyes. She took in at a glance the group of white-clad lancemen standing motionless in the shadow of the far-off end of the verandah, and her gaze rested curiously on the chief of that imposing cortege. He stood, almost facing her, a little on one side, and struck by the beauty of the unexpected apparition had bent low, elevating his joint hands above his head in a sign of respect accorded by Malays only to the great of this earth. The crude light of the lamp shone on the gold embroidery of his black silk jacket, broke in a thousand sparkling rays on the jewelled hilt of his kriss protruding from under the many folds of the red sarong gathered into a sash round his waist, and played on the precious stones of the many rings on his dark fingers. He straightened himself up quickly after the low bow, putting his hand with a graceful ease on the hilt of his heavy short sword ornamented with brilliantly dyed fringes of horsehair. Nina, hesitating on the threshold, saw an erect lithe figure of medium height with a breadth of shoulder suggesting great power. Under the folds of a blue turban, whose fringed ends hung gracefully over the left shoulder, was a face full of determination and expressing a reckless good-humour, not devoid, however, of some dignity. The squareness of lower jaw, the full red lips, the mobile nostrils, and the proud carriage of the head gave the impression of a being half-savage, untamed, perhaps cruel, and corrected the liquid softness of the almost feminine eye, that general characteristic of the race. Now, the first surprise over, Nina saw those eyes fixed upon her with such an uncontrolled expression of admiration and desire that she felt a hitherto unknown feeling of shyness, mixed with alarm and some delight, enter and penetrate her whole being. Confused by those unusual sensations she stopped in the doorway and instinctively drew the lower part of the curtain across her face, leaving only half a rounded cheek, a stray tress, and one eye exposed, wherewith to contemplate the gorgeous and bold being so unlike in appearance to the rare specimens of traders she had seen before on that same verandah.

Dain Maroola, dazzled by the unexpected vision, forgot the confused Almayer, forgot his brig, his escort staring in open-mouthed admiration, the object of his visit and all things else, in his overpowering desire to prolong the contemplation of so much loveliness met so suddenly in such an unlikely place—as he thought.

"It is my daughter," said Almayer, in an embarrassed manner. "It is of no consequence. White women have their customs, as you know Tuan, having travelled much, as you say. However, it is late; we will finish our talk to-morrow."

Dain bent low trying to convey in a last glance towards the girl the bold expression of his overwhelming admiration. The next minute he was shaking Almayer's hand with grave courtesy, his face wearing a look of stolid unconcern as to any feminine presence. His men filed off, and he followed them quickly, closely attended by a thick-set, savage-looking Sumatrese he had introduced before as the commander of his brig. Nina walked to the balustrade of the verandah and saw the sheen of moonlight on the steel spear-heads and heard the rhythmic jingle of brass anklets as the men moved in single file towards the jetty. The boat shoved off after a little while, looming large in the full light of the moon, a black shapeless mass in the slight haze hanging over the water. Nina fancied she could distinguish the graceful figure of the trader standing erect in the stern sheets, but in a little while all the outlines got blurred, confused, and soon disappeared in the folds of white vapour shrouding the middle of the river.

Almayer had approached his daughter, and leaning with both arms over the rail, was looking moodily down on the heap of rubbish at the foot of the verandah.

"What was all that noise just now?" he growled peevishly, without looking up. "Confound you and your mother! What did she want? What did you come out for?"

"She did not want to let me come out," said Nina. "She is angry. She says the man just gone is some Rajah. I think she is right now."

"I believe all you women are crazy," snarled Almayer. "What's that to you, to her, to anybody? The man wants to collect trepang and birds' nests on the islands. He told me so, that Rajah of yours. He will come to-morrow. I want you both to keep away from the house, and let me attend to my business in peace."

Dain Maroola came the next day and had a long conversation with Almayer. This was the beginning of a close and friendly intercourse which, at first, was much remarked in Sambir, till the population got used to the frequent sight of many fires burning in Almayer's campong, where Maroola's men were warming themselves during the cold nights of the northeast monsoon, while their master had long conferences with the Tuan Putih—as they styled Almayer amongst themselves. Great was the curiosity in Sambir on the subject of the new trader. Had he seen the Sultan? What did the Sultan say? Had he given any presents? What would he sell? What would he buy? Those were the questions broached eagerly by the inhabitants of bamboo houses built over the river. Even in more substantial buildings, in Abdulla's house, in the residences of principal traders, Arab, Chinese, and Bugis, the excitement ran high, and lasted many days. With inborn suspicion they would not believe the simple account of himself the young trader was always ready to give. Yet it had all the appearance of truth. He said he was a trader, and sold rice. He did not want to buy gutta-percha or beeswax, because he intended to employ his numerous crew in collecting trepang on the coral reefs outside the river, and also in seeking for birds' nests on the mainland. Those two articles he professed himself ready to buy if there were any to be obtained in that way. He said he was from Bali, and a Brahmin, which

c

last statement he made good by refusing all food during his often repeated visits to Lakamba's and Almayer's houses. To Lakamba he went generally at night and had long audiences. Babalatchi, who was always a third party at those meetings of potentate and trader, knew how to resist all attempts on the part of the curious to ascertain the subject of so many long talks. When questioned with languid courtesy by the grave Abdulla he sought refuge in a vacant stare of his one eye, and in the affectation of extreme simplicity.

"I am only my master's slave," murmured Babalatchi, in a hesitating manner. Then as if making up his mind suddenly for a reckless confidence he would inform Abdulla of some transaction in rice, repeating the words, "A hundred big bags the Sultan bought; a hundred, Tuan!" in a tone of mysterious solemnity. Abdulla, firmly persuaded of the existence of some more important dealings, received, however, the information with all the signs of respectful astonishment. And the two would separate, the Arab cursing inwardly the wily dog, while Babalatchi went on his way walking on the dusty path, his body swaying, his chin with its few grey hairs pushed forward, resembling an inquisitive goat bent on some unlawful expedition. Attentive eyes watched his movements. Jim-Eng, descrying Babalatchi far away, would shake off the stupor of an habitual opium smoker and, tottering on to the middle of the road, would await the approach of that important person, ready with hospitable invitation. But Babalatchi's discretion was proof even against the combined assaults of good fellowship and of strong gin generously administered by the open-hearted Chinaman. Jim-Eng, owning himself beaten, was left uninformed with the empty bottle, and gazed sadly after the departing form of the statesman of

Sambir pursuing his devious and unsteady way, which, as usual, led him to Almayer's compound. Ever since a reconciliation had been effected by Dain Maroola between his white friend and the Rajah, the one-eyed diplomatist had again become a frequent guest in the Dutchman's house. To Almayer's great disgust he was to be seen there at all times, strolling about in an abstracted kind of way on the verandah, skulking in the passages, or else popping round unexpected corners, always willing to engage Mrs. Almayer in confidential conversation. He was very shy of the master himself, as if suspicious that the pent-up feelings of the white man towards his person might find vent in a sudden kick. But the cooking shed was his favourite place, and he became an habitual guest there, squatting for hours amongst the busy women, with his chin resting on his knees, his lean arms clasped round his legs, and his one eye roving uneasily—the very picture of watchful ugliness. Almayer wanted more than once to complain to Lakamba of his Prime Minister's intrusion, but Dain dissuaded him. "We cannot say a word here that he does not hear," growled Almayer.

"Then come and talk on board the brig," retorted Dain, with a quiet smile. "It is good to let the man come here. Lakamba thinks he knows much. Perhaps the Sultan thinks I want to run away. Better let the one-eyed crocodile sun himself in your campong, Tuan."

And Almayer assented unwillingly muttering vague threats of personal violence, while he eyed malevolently the aged statesman sitting with quiet obstinacy by his domestic rice-pot.

CHAPTER FIVE

AT LAST the excitement had died out in Sambir. The inhabitants got used to the sight of comings and goings between Almayer's house and the vessel, now moored to the opposite bank, and speculation as to the feverish activity displayed by Almayer's boatmen in repairing old canoes ceased to interfere with the due discharge of domestic duties by the women of the Settlement. Even the baffled Jim-Eng left off troubling his muddled brain with secrets of trade, and relapsed by the aid of his opium pipe into a state of stupefied bliss, letting Babalatchi pursue his way past his house uninvited and seemingly unnoticed.

So on that warm afternoon, when the deserted river sparkled under the vertical sun, the statesman of Sambir could, without any hindrance from friendly inquirers, shove off his little canoe from under the bushes, where it was usually hidden during his visits to Almayer's compound. Slowly and languidly Babalatchi paddled, crouching low in the boat, making himself small under his enormous sun hat to escape the scorching heat reflected from the water. He was not in a hurry; his master, Lakamba, was surely reposing at this time of the day. He would have ample time to cross over and greet him on his waking with important news. Will he be displeased? Will he strike his ebony wood staff angrily on the floor, frightening him by the incoherent violence of his exclamations; or will he squat down with a good-humoured smile, and, rubbing his hands gently over his stomach with a familiar gesture, expectorate copiously into the brass siri-vessel, giving vent to a low, approbative murmur? Such were Babalatchi's thoughts as he skilfully handled his paddle, crossing the river on his way to the Rajah's campong, whose stockades showed from behind the dense foliage of the bank just opposite to Almayer's bungalow.

Indeed, he had a report to make. Something certain at last to confirm the daily tale of suspicions, the daily hints of familiarity, of stolen glances he had seen, of short and burning words he had overheard exchanged between Dain Maroola and Almayer's daughter. Lakamba had, till then, listened to it all, calmly and with evident distrust; now he was going to be convinced, for Babalatchi had the proof; had it this very morning, when fishing at break of day in the creek over which stood Bulangi's house. There from his skiff he saw Nina's long canoe drift past, the girl sitting in the stern bending over Dain, who was stretched in the bottom with his head resting on the girl's knees. He saw it. He followed them, but in a short time they took to the paddles and got away from under his observant eye. A few minutes afterwards he saw Bulangi's slave-girl paddling in a small dug-out to the town with her cakes for sale. She also had seen them in the grey dawn. And Babalatchi grinned confidentially to himself at the recollection of the slave-girl's discomposed face, of the hard look in her eyes, of the tremble in her voice, when answering his questions. That little Taminah evidently admired Dain Maroola. That was good! And Babalatchi laughed aloud at the notion; then becoming suddenly serious, he began by some strange association of ideas to speculate upon the price for which Bulangi would, possibly, sell the girl. He shook his head sadly at the thought that Bulangi was a hard man, and had refused one hundred dollars for that

same Taminah only a few weeks ago; then he became
suddenly aware that the canoe had drifted too far down
during his meditation. He shook off the despondency
caused by the certitude of Bulangi's mercenary disposition, and, taking up his paddle, in a few strokes
sheered alongside the water-gate of the Rajah's house.

That afternoon Almayer, as was his wont lately,
moved about on the water-side, overlooking the repairs
to his boats. He had decided at last. Guided by
the scraps of information contained in old Lingard's
pocket-book, he was going to seek for the rich gold-
mine, for that place where he had only to stoop to
gather up an immense fortune and realize the dream of
his young days. To obtain the necessary help he had
shared his knowledge with Dain Maroola, he had consented to be reconciled with Lakamba, who gave his
support to the enterprise on condition of sharing the
profits; he had sacrificed his pride, his honour, and his
loyalty in the face of the enormous risk of his undertaking, dazzled by the greatness of the results to be
achieved by this alliance so distasteful yet so necessary.
The dangers were great, but Maroola was brave; his
men seemed as reckless as their chief, and with Lakamba's aid success seemed assured.

For the last fortnight Almayer was absorbed in the
preparations, walking amongst his workmen and slaves
in a kind of waking trance, where practical details
as to the fitting out of the boats were mixed up with
vivid dreams of untold wealth, where the present misery
of burning sun, of the muddy and malodorous river
bank disappeared in a gorgeous vision of a splendid
future existence for himself and Nina. He hardly saw
Nina during these last days, although the beloved
daughter was ever present in his thoughts. He hardly
took notice of Dain, whose constant presence in his

house had become a matter of course to him now they were connected by a community of interests. When meeting the young chief he gave him an absent greeting and passed on, seemingly wishing to avoid him, bent upon forgetting the hated reality of the present by absorbing himself in his work, or else by letting his imagination soar far above the tree-tops into the great white clouds away to the westward, where the paradise of Europe was awaiting the future Eastern millionaire. And Maroola, now the bargain was struck and there was no more business to be talked over, evidently did not care for the white man's company. Yet Dain was always about the house, but he seldom stayed long by the riverside. On his daily visits to the white man the Malay chief preferred to make his way quietly through the central passage of the house, and would come out into the garden at the back, where the fire was burning in the cooking shed, with the rice kettle swinging over it, under the watchful supervision of Mrs. Almayer. Avoiding that shed, with its black smoke and the warbling of soft, feminine voices, Dain would turn to the left. There, on the edge of a banana plantation, a clump of palms and mango trees formed a shady spot, a few scattered bushes giving it a certain seclusion into which only the serving women's chatter or an occasional burst of laughter could penetrate. Once in, he was invisible; and hidden there, leaning against the smooth trunk of a tall palm, he waited with gleaming eyes and an assured smile to hear the faint rustle of dried grass under the light footsteps of Nina.

From the very first moment when his eyes beheld this—to him—perfection of loveliness he felt in his inmost heart the conviction that she would be his; he felt the subtle breath of mutual understanding passing between their two savage natures, and he did not want

Mrs. Almayer's encouraging smiles to take every opportunity of approaching the girl; and every time he spoke to her, every time he looked into her eyes, Nina, although averting her face, felt as if this bold-looking being who spoke burning words into her willing ear was the embodiment of her fate, the creature of her dreams—reckless, ferocious, ready with flashing kriss for his enemies, and with passionate embrace for his beloved—the ideal Malay chief of her mother's tradition.

She recognized with a thrill of delicious fear the mysterious consciousness of her identity with that being. Listening to his words, it seemed to her she was born only then to a knowledge of a new existence, that her life was complete only when near him, and she abandoned herself to a feeling of dreamy happiness, while with half-veiled face and in silence—as became a Malay girl—she listened to Dain's words giving up to her the whole treasure of love and passion his nature was capable of with all the unrestrained enthusiasm of a man totally untrammelled by any influence of civilized self-discipline.

And they used to pass many a delicious and fast fleeting hour under the mango trees behind the friendly curtain of bushes till Mrs. Almayer's shrill voice gave the signal of unwilling separation. Mrs. Almayer had undertaken the easy task of watching her husband lest he should interrupt the smooth course of her daughter's love affair, in which she took a great and benignant interest. She was happy and proud to see Dain's infatuation, believing him to be a great and powerful chief, and she found also a gratification of her mercenary instincts in Dain's open-handed generosity.

On the eve of the day when Babalatchi's suspicions were confirmed by ocular demonstration, Dain and Nina had remained longer than usual in their shady retreat. Only Almayer's heavy step on the verandah and his querulous clamour for food decided Mrs. Almayer to lift a warning cry. Maroola leaped lightly over the low bamboo fence, and made his way through the banana plantation down to the muddy shore of the back creek, while Nina walked slowly towards the house to minister to her father's wants, as was her wont every evening. Almayer felt happy enough that evening; the preparations were nearly completed; to-morrow he would launch his boats. In his mind's eye he saw the rich prize in his grasp; and, with tin spoon in his hand, he was forgetting the plateful of rice before him in the fanciful arrangement of some splendid banquet to take place on his arrival in Amsterdam. Nina, reclining in the long chair, listened absently to the few disconnected words escaping from her father's lips. Expedition! Gold! What did she care for all that? But at the name of Maroola mentioned by her father she was all attention. Dain was going down the river with his brig to-morrow to remain away for a few days, said Almayer. It was very annoying, this delay. As soon as Dain returned they would have to start without loss of time, for the river was rising. He would not be surprised if a great flood was coming. And he pushed away his plate with an impatient gesture on rising from the table. But now Nina heard him not. Dain going away! That's why he had ordered her, with that quiet masterfulness it was her delight to obey, to meet him at break of day in Bulangi's creek. Was there a paddle in her canoe? she thought. Was it ready? She would have to start early—at four in the morning, in a very few hours.

She rose from her chair, thinking she would require rest before the long pull in the early morning. The lamp was burning dimly, and her father, tired with

*c

the day's labour, was already in his hammock. Nina put the lamp out and passed into a large room she shared with her mother on the left of the central passage. Entering, she saw that Mrs. Almayer had deserted the pile of mats serving her as bed in one corner of the room, and was now bending over the opened lid of her large wooden chest. Half a shell of cocoanut filled with oil, where a cotton rag floated for a wick, stood on the floor, surrounding her with a ruddy halo of light shining through the black and odorous smoke. Mrs. Almayer's back was bent, and her head and shoulders hidden in the deep box. Her hands rummaged in the interior, where a soft clink as of silver money could be heard. She did not notice at first her daughter's approach, and Nina, standing silently by her, looked down on many little canvas bags ranged in the bottom of the chest, wherefrom her mother extracted handfuls of shining guilders and Mexican dollars, letting them stream slowly back again through her claw-like fingers. The music of tinkling silver seemed to delight her, and her eyes sparkled with the reflected gleam of freshly-minted coins. She was muttering to herself: "And this, and this, and yet this! Soon he will give more—as much more as I ask. He is a great Rajah—a Son of Heaven! And she will be a Ranee— he gave all this for her! Who ever gave anything for me? I am a slave! Am I? I am the mother of a great Ranee!" She became aware suddenly of her daughter's presence, and ceased her droning, shutting the lid down violently; then, without rising from her crouching position, she looked up at the girl standing by with a vague smile on her dreamy face.

"You have seen. Have you?" she shouted, shrilly. "That is all mine, and for you. It is not enough! He will have to give more before he takes you away to the southern island where his father is king. You hear me? You are worth more, granddaughter of Rajahs! More! More!"

The sleepy voice of Almayer was heard on the verandah recommending silence. Mrs. Almayer extinguished the light and crept into her corner of the room. Nina laid down on her back on a pile of soft mats, her hands entwined under her head, gazing through the shutterless hole, serving as a window at the stars twinkling on the black sky; she was awaiting the time of start for her appointed meeting-place. With quiet happiness she thought of that meeting in the great forest, far from all human eyes and sounds. Her soul, lapsing again into the savage mood, which the genius of civilization working by the hand of Mrs. Vinck could never destroy, experienced a feeling of pride and of some slight trouble at the high value her worldly-wise mother had put upon her person; but she remembered the expressive glances and words of Dain, and, tranquillized, she closed her eyes in a shiver of pleasant anticipation.

There are some situations where the barbarian and the, so-called, civilized man meet upon the same ground. It may be supposed that Dain Maroola was not exceptionally delighted with his prospective mother-in-law, nor that he actually approved of that worthy woman's appetite for shining dollars. Yet on that foggy morning when Babalatchi, laying aside the cares of state, went to visit his fish-baskets in the Bulangi creek, Maroola had no misgivings, experienced no feelings but those of impatience and longing, when paddling to the east side of the island forming the backwater in question. He hid his canoe in the bushes and strode rapidly across the islet, pushing with impatience through the twigs of heavy undergrowth intercrossed over his path. From motives of prudence he would not take his canoe to the meeting-place, as Nina had done. He had left it in the main stream till his return from the other side of the island. The heavy warm fog was closing rapidly round him, but he managed to catch a fleeting glimpse of a light away to the left, proceeding from Bulangi's house. Then he could see nothing in the thickening vapour, and kept to the path only by a sort of instinct, which also led him to the very point on the opposite shore he wished to reach. A great log had stranded there, at right angles to the bank, forming a kind of jetty against which the swiftly flowing stream broke with a loud ripple. He stepped on it with a quick but steady motion, and in two strides found himself at the outer end, with the rush and swirl of the foaming water at his feet.

Standing there alone, as if separated from the world; the heavens, earth; the very water roaring under him swallowed up in the thick veil of the morning fog, he breathed out the name of Nina before him into the apparently limitless space, sure of being heard, instinctively sure of the nearness of the delightful creature; certain of her being aware of his near presence as he was aware of hers.

The bow of Nina's canoe loomed up close to the log, canted high out of the water by the weight of the sitter in the stern. Maroola laid his hand on the stem and leaped lightly in, giving it a vigorous shove off. The light craft, obeying the new impulse, cleared the log by a hair's breadth, and the river, with obedient complicity, swung it broadside to the current, and bore it off silently and rapidly between the invisible banks. And once more Dain, at the feet of Nina, forgot the world, felt himself carried away helpless by a great wave of supreme emotion, by a rush of joy, pride, and desire; understood once more with overpowering certitude that there was no life possible without that being he held clasped in his arms with passionate strength in a prolonged embrace.

Nina disengaged herself gently with a low laugh.

"You will overturn the boat, Dain," she whispered.

He looked into her eyes eagerly for a minute and let her go with a sigh, then lying down in the canoe he put his head on her knees, gazing upwards and stretching his arms backwards till his hands met round the girl's waist. She bent over him, and, shaking her head, framed both their faces in the falling locks of her long black hair.

And so they drifted on, he speaking with all the rude eloquence of a savage nature giving itself up without restraint to an overmastering passion, she bending low to catch the murmur of words sweeter to her than life itself. To those two nothing existed then outside the gunwales of the narrow and fragile craft. It was their world, filled with their intense and all-absorbing love. They took no heed of thickening mist, or of the breeze dying away before sunrise; they forgot the existence of the great forests surrounding them, of all the tropical nature awaiting the advent of the sun in a solemn and impressive silence.

Over the low river-mist hiding the boat with its freight of young passionate life and all-forgetful happiness, the stars paled, and a silvery-grey tint crept over the sky from the eastward. There was not a breath of wind, not a rustle of stirring leaf, not a splash of leaping fish to disturb the serene repose of all living things on the banks of the great river. Earth, river, and sky were wrapped up in a deep sleep from which it seemed there would be no waking. All the seething life and movement of tropical nature seemed concentrated in the ardent eyes, in the tumultuously beating hearts of the two beings drifting in the canoe, under the white canopy of mist, over the smooth surface of the river.

Suddenly a great sheaf of yellow rays shot upwards from behind the black curtain of trees lining the banks of the Pantai. The stars went out; the little black clouds at the zenith glowed for a moment with crimson tints, and the thick mist, stirred by the gentle breeze, the sigh of waking nature, whirled round and broke into fantastically torn pieces, disclosing the wrinkled surface of the river sparkling in the broad light of day. Great flocks of white birds wheeled screaming above the swaying tree-tops. The sun had risen on the east coast.

Dain was the first to return to the cares of everyday life. He rose and glanced rapidly up and down the river. His eye detected Babalatchi's boat astern, and another small black speck on the glittering water, which was Taminah's canoe. He moved cautiously forward, and, kneeling, took up a paddle; Nina at the stern took hers. They bent their bodies to the work, throwing up the water at every stroke, and the small craft went swiftly ahead, leaving a narrow wake fringed with a lacelike border of white and gleaming foam. Without turning his head, Dain spoke.

"Somebody behind us, Nina. We must not let him gain. I think he is too far to recognize us."

"Somebody before us also," panted out Nina, without ceasing to paddle.

"I think I know," rejoined Dain. "The sun shines over there, but I fancy it is the girl Taminah. She comes down every morning to my brig to sell cakes—stays often all day. It does not matter; steer more into the bank; we must get under the bushes. My canoe is hidden not far from here."

As he spoke his eyes watched the broad-leaved nipas

which they were brushing in their swift and silent course.

"Look out, Nina," he said at last; "there, where the water palms end and the twigs hang down under the leaning tree. Steer for the big green branch."

He stood up attentive, and the boat drifted slowly in shore, Nina guiding it by a gentle and skilful movement of her paddle. When near enough Dain laid hold of the big branch, and leaning back shot the canoe under a low green archway of thickly matted creepers giving access to a miniature bay formed by the caving in of the bank during the last great flood. His own boat was there anchored by a stone, and he stepped into it, keeping his hand on the gunwale of Nina's canoe. In a moment the two little nutshells with their occupants floated quietly side by side, reflected by the black water in the dim light struggling through a high canopy of dense foliage; while above, away up in the broad day, flamed immense red blossoms sending down on their heads a shower of great dew-sparkling petals that descended rotating slowly in a continuous and perfumed stream; and over them, under them, in the sleeping water; all around them in a ring of luxuriant vegetation bathed in the warm air charged with strong and harsh perfumes, the intense work of tropical nature went on: plants shooting upward, entwined, interlaced in inextricable confusion, climbing madly and brutally over each other in the terrible silence of a desperate struggle towards the life-giving sunshine above—as if struck with sudden horror at the seething mass of corruption below, at the death and decay from which they sprang.

"We must part now," said Dain, after a long silence. "You must return at once, Nina. I will wait till the brig drifts down here, and shall get on board then."

"And will you be long away, Dain?" asked Nina, in a low voice.

"Long!" exclaimed Dain. "Would a man willingly remain long in a dark place? When I am not near you, Nina, I am like a man that is blind. What is life to me without light?"

Nina leaned over, and with a proud and happy smile took Dain's face between her hands, looking into his eyes with a fond yet questioning gaze. Apparently she found there the confirmation of the words just said, for a feeling of grateful security lightened for her the weight of sorrow at the hour of parting. She believed that he, the descendant of many great Rajahs, the son of a great chief, the master of life and death, knew the sunshine of life only in her presence. An immense wave of gratitude and love welled forth out of her heart towards him. How could she make an outward and visible sign of all she felt for the man who had filled her heart with so much joy and so much pride? And in the great tumult of passion, like a flash of lightning came to her the reminiscence of that despised and almost forgotten civilization she had only glanced at in her days of restraint, of sorrow, and of anger. In the cold ashes of that hateful and miserable past she would find the sign of love, the fitting expression of the boundless felicity of the present, the pledge of a bright and splendid future. She threw her arms around Dain's neck and pressed her lips to his in a long and burning kiss. He closed his eyes, surprised and frightened at the storm raised in his breast by the strange and to him hitherto unknown contact, and long after Nina had pushed her canoe into the river he remained motionless, without daring to open his eyes, afraid to lose the sensation of intoxicating delight he had tasted for the first time.

Now he wanted but immortality, he thought, to be the

equal of gods, and the creature that could open so the
gates of paradise must be his—soon would be his for ever!

He opened his eyes in time to see through the archway
of creepers the bows of his brig come slowly into view,
as the vessel drifted past on its way down the river. He
must go on board now, he thought; yet he was loth to
leave the place where he had learned to know what
happiness meant. "Time yet. Let them go," he
muttered to himself; and he closed his eyes again under
the red shower of scented petals, trying to recall the
scene with all its delight and all its fear.

He must have been able to join his brig in time, after
all, and found much occupation outside, for it was in
vain that Almayer looked for his friend's speedy return.
The lower reach of the river where he so often and so
impatiently directed his eyes remained deserted, save
for the rapid flitting of some fishing canoe; but down the
upper reaches came black clouds and heavy showers
heralding the final setting in of the rainy season with its
thunderstorms and great floods making the river almost
impossible of ascent for native canoes.

Almayer, strolling along the muddy beach between
his houses, watched uneasily the river rising inch by
inch, creeping slowly nearer to the boats, now ready
and hauled up in a row under the cover of dripping
Kajang-mats. Fortune seemed to elude his grasp,
and in his weary tramp backwards and forwards under
the steady rain falling from the lowering sky, a sort
of despairing indifference took possession of him. What
did it matter? It was just his luck! Those two infernal savages, Lakamba and Dain, induced him, with
their promises of help, to spend his last dollar in the
fitting out of boats, and now one of them was gone
somewhere, and the other shut up in his stockade would
give no sign of life. No, not even the scoundrelly

Babalatchi, thought Almayer, would show his face near him, now they had sold him all the rice, brass gongs, and cloth necessary for his expedition. They had his very last coin, and did not care whether he went or stayed. And with a gesture of abandoned discouragement Almayer would climb up slowly to the verandah of his new house to get out of the rain, and leaning on the front rail with his head sunk between his shoulders he would abandon himself to the current of bitter thoughts, oblivious of the flight of time and the pangs of hunger, deaf to the shrill cries of his wife calling him to the evening meal. When, roused from his sad meditations by the first roll of the evening thunderstorm, he stumbled slowly towards the glimmering light of his old house, his half-dead hope made his ears preternaturally acute to any sound on the river. Several nights in succession he had heard the splash of paddles and had seen the indistinct form of a boat, but when hailing the shadowy apparition, his heart bounding with sudden hope of hearing Dain's voice, he was disappointed each time by the sulky answer conveying to him the intelligence that the Arabs were on the river, bound on a visit to the home-staying Lakamba. This caused him many sleepless nights, spent in speculating upon the kind of villainy those estimable personages were hatching now. At last, when all hope seemed dead, he was overjoyed on hearing Dain's voice; but Dain also appeared very anxious to see Lakamba, and Almayer felt uneasy owing to a deep and ineradicable distrust as to that ruler's disposition towards himself. Still, Dain had returned at last. Evidently he meant to keep to his bargain. Hope revived, and that night Almayer slept soundly, while Nina watched the angry river under the lash of the thunderstorm sweeping onward towards the sea.

CHAPTER SIX

Dain was not long in crossing the river after leaving
Almayer. He landed at the water-gate of the stockade
enclosing the group of houses which composed the
residence of the Rajah of Sambir. Evidently somebody
was expected there, for the gate was open, and men with
torches were ready to precede the visitor up the inclined
plane of planks leading to the largest house where
Lakamba actually resided, and where all the business
of state was invariably transacted. The other buildings
within the enclosure served only to accommodate the
numerous household and the wives of the ruler.

Lakamba's own house was a strong structure of
solid planks, raised on high piles, with a verandah of
split bamboos surrounding it on all sides; the whole was
covered in by an immensely high-pitched roof of palm-
leaves, resting on beams blackened by the smoke of
many torches.

The building stood parallel to the river, one of its
long sides facing the water-gate of the stockade. There
was a door in the short side looking up the river, and
the inclined plank-way led straight from the gate to
that door. By the uncertain light of smoky torches,
Dain noticed the vague outlines of a group of armed
men in the dark shadows to his right. From that group
Babalatchi stepped forward to open the door, and Dain
entered the audience chamber of the Rajah's residence.
About one-third of the house was curtained off, by
heavy stuff of European manufacture, for that purpose;
close to the curtain there was a big arm-chair of some

black wood, much carved, and before it a rough deal table. Otherwise the room was only furnished with mats in great profusion. To the left of the entrance stood a rude arm-rack, with three rifles with fixed bayonets in it. By the wall, in the shadow, the body-guard of Lakamba—all friends or relations—slept in a confused heap of brown arms, legs, and multi-coloured garments, from whence issued an occasional snore or a subdued groan of some uneasy sleeper. An European lamp with a green shade standing on the table made all this indistinctly visible to Dain.

"You are welcome to your rest here," said Baba-latchi, looking at Dain interrogatively.

"I must speak to the Rajah at once," answered Dain.

Babalatchi made a gesture of assent, and, turning to the brass gong suspended under the arm-rack, struck two sharp blows.

The ear-splitting din woke up the guard. The snores ceased; outstretched legs were drawn in; the whole heap moved, and slowly resolved itself into in-dividual forms with much yawning and rubbing of sleepy eyes; behind the curtains there was a burst of feminine chatter; then the bass voice of Lakamba was heard.

"Is that the Arab trader?"

"No, Tuan," answered Babalatchi; "Dain has re-turned at last. He is here for an important talk, bitcharra—if you mercifully consent."

Evidently Lakamba's mercy went so far—for in a short while he came out from behind the curtain—but it did not go to the length of inducing him to make an extensive toilet. A short red sarong tightened hastily round his hips was his only garment. The merciful ruler of Sambir looked sleepy and rather sulky. He sat in the arm-chair, his knees well apart, his elbows on the arm-rests, his chin on his breast, breathing heavily and waiting malevolently for Dain to open the important talk.

But Dain did not seem anxious to begin. He directed his gaze towards Babalatchi, squatting comfortably at the feet of his master, and remained silent with a slightly bent head as if in attentive expectation of coming words of wisdom.

Babalatchi coughed discreetly, and, leaning forward, pushed over a few mats for Dain to sit upon, then lifting up his squeaky voice he assured him with eager volubility of everybody's delight at this long-looked-for return. His heart had hungered for the sight of Dain's face, and his ears were withering for the want of the refreshing sound of his voice. Everybody's hearts and ears were in the same sad predicament, according to Babalatchi, as he indicated with a sweeping gesture the other bank of the river where the settlement slumbered peacefully, unconscious of the great joy awaiting it on the morrow when Dain's presence amongst them would be disclosed. "For"—went on Babalatchi— "what is the joy of a poor man if not the open hand of a generous trader or of a great——"

Here he checked himself abruptly with a calculated embarrassment of manner, and his roving eye sought the floor, while an apologetic smile dwelt for a moment on his misshapen lips. Once or twice during this opening speech an amused expression flitted across Dain's face, soon to give way, however, to an appearance of grave concern. On Lakamba's brow a heavy frown had settled, and his lips moved angrily as he listened to his Prime Minister's oratory. In the silence that fell upon the room when Babalatchi ceased speaking arose a chorus of varied snores from the corner where the body-guard had resumed their interrupted slumbers, but the distant rumble of thunder filling then Nina's heart with apprehension for the safety of her lover passed unheeded by those three men intent each on their own purposes, for life or death.

After a short silence, Babalatchi, discarding now the flowers of polite eloquence, spoke again, but in short and hurried sentences and in a low voice. They had been very uneasy. Why did Dain remain so long absent? The men dwelling on the lower reaches of the river heard the reports of big guns and saw a fire-ship of the Dutch amongst the islands of the estuary. So they were anxious. Rumours of a disaster had reached Abdulla a few days ago, and since then they had been waiting for Dain's return under the apprehension of some misfortune. For days they had closed their eyes in fear, and woke up alarmed, and walked abroad trembling, like men before an enemy. And all on account of Dain. Would he not allay their fears for his safety, not for themselves? They were quiet and faithful, and devoted to the great Rajah in Batavia— may his fate lead him ever to victory for the joy and profit of his servants! "And here," went on Babalatchi, "Lakamba my master was getting thin in his anxiety for the trader he had taken under his protection; and so was Abdulla, for what would wicked men not say if perchance——"

"Be silent, fool!" growled Lakamba, angrily.

Babalatchi subsided into silence with a satisfied smile, while Dain, who had been watching him as if fascinated, turned with a sigh of relief towards the ruler of Sambir. Lakamba did not move, and, without raising his head, looked at Dain from under his eyebrows, breathing audibly, with pouted lips, in an air of general discontent.

"Speak! O Dain!" he said at last. "We have heard many rumours. Many nights in succession has my friend Reshid come here with bad tidings. News travels fast along the coast. But they may be untrue; there are more lies in men's mouths in these days than when I was young, but I am not easier to deceive now."

"All my words are true," said Dain, carelessly. "If you want to know what befell my brig, then learn that it is in the hands of the Dutch. Believe me, Rajah," he went on, with sudden energy, "the Orang Blanda have good friends in Sambir, or else how did they know I was coming thence?"

Lakamba gave Dain a short and hostile glance. Babalatchi rose quietly, and, going to the arm-rack, struck the gong violently.

Outside the door there was a shuffle of bare feet; inside, the guard woke up and sat staring in sleepy surprise.

"Yes, you faithful friend of the white Rajah," went on Dain, scornfully, turning to Babalatchi, who had returned to his place, "I have escaped, and I am here to gladden your heart. When I saw the Dutch ship I ran the brig inside the reefs and put her ashore. They did not dare to follow with the ship, so they sent the boats. We took to ours and tried to get away, but the ship dropped fireballs at us, and killed many of my men. But I am left, O Babalatchi! The Dutch are coming here. They are seeking for me. They're coming to ask their faithful friend Lakamba and his slave Babalatchi. Rejoice!"

But neither of his hearers appeared to be in a joyful mood. Lakamba had put one leg over his knee. and went on gently scratching it with a meditative air, while Babalatchi, sitting cross-legged, seemed suddenly to become smaller and very limp, staring straight before him vacantly. The guard evinced some interest in the proceedings, stretching themselves full length on the

mats to be nearer the speaker. One of them got up
and now stood leaning against the arm-rack, playing
absently with the fringes of his sword-hilt.

Dain waited till the crash of thunder had died away
in distant mutterings before he spoke again.

"Are you dumb, O ruler of Sambir, or is the son of a
great Rajah unworthy of your notice? I am come here
to seek refuge and to warn you, and want to know what
you intend doing."

"You came here because of the white man's daughter," retorted Lakamba, quickly. "Your refuge was
with your father, the Rajah of Bali, the Son of Heaven,
the 'Anak Agong' himself. What am I to protect great
princes? Only yesterday I planted rice in a burnt
clearing; to-day you say I hold your life in my hand."

Babalatchi glanced at his master. "No man can
escape his fate," he murmured piously. "When love
enters a man's heart he is like a child—without any
understanding. Be merciful, Lakamba," he added,
twitching the corner of the Rajah's sarong warningly.

Lakamba snatched away the skirt of the sarong
angrily. Under the dawning comprehension of intolerable embarrassments caused by Dain's return to Sambir
he began to lose such composure as he had been, till
then, able to maintain; and now he raised his voice
loudly above the whistling of the wind and the patter of
rain on the roof in the hard squall passing over the
house.

"You came here first as a trader with sweet words
and great promises, asking me to look the other way
while you worked your will on the white man there.
And I did. What do you want now? When I was
young I fought. Now I am old, and want peace. It
is easier for me to have you killed than to fight the
Dutch. It is better for me."

The squall had now passed, and, in the short stillness of the lull in the storm, Lakamba repeated softly, as if to himself, "Much easier. Much better."

Dain did not seem greatly discomposed by the Rajah's threatening words. While Lakamba was speaking he had glanced once rapidly over his shoulder, just to make sure that there was nobody behind him, and, tranquillized in that respect, he had extracted a siri-box out of the folds of his waist-cloth, and was wrapping carefully the little bit of betel-nut and a small pinch of lime in the green leaf tendered him politely by the watchful Babalatchi. He accepted this as a peace-offering from the silent statesman—a kind of mute protest against his master's undiplomatic violence, and as an omen of a possible understanding to be arrived at yet. Otherwise Dain was not uneasy. Although recognizing the justice of Lakamba's surmise that he had come back to Sambir only for the sake of the white man's daughter, yet he was not conscious of any childish lack of understanding, as suggested by Babalatchi. In fact, Dain knew very well that Lakamba was too deeply implicated in the gunpowder smuggling to care for an investigation by the Dutch authorities into that matter. When sent off by his father, the independent Rajah of Bali, at the time when the hostilities between Dutch and Malays threatened to spread from Sumatra over the whole archipelago, Dain had found all the big traders deaf to his guarded proposals, and above the temptation of the great prices he was ready to give for gunpowder. He went to Sambir as a last and almost hopeless resort, having heard in Macassar of the white man there, and of the regular steamer trading from Singapore—allured also by the fact that there was no Dutch resident on the river, which would make things easier, no doubt. His hopes

got nearly wrecked against the stubborn loyalty of
Lakamba arising from well-understood self-interest;
but at last the young man's generosity, his persuasive
enthusiasm, the prestige of his father's great name,
overpowered the prudent hesitation of the ruler of Sambir. Lakamba would have nothing to do himself with
any illegal traffic. He also objected to the Arabs being
made use of in that matter; but he suggested Almayer,
saying that he was a weak man easily persuaded, and
that his friend, the English captain of the steamer,
could be made very useful—very likely even would join
in the business, smuggling the powder in the steamer
without Abdulla's knowledge. There again Dain met
in Almayer an unexpected resistance; Lakamba had
to send Babalatchi over with the solemn promise that
his eyes would be shut in friendship for the white man,
Dain paying for the promise and the friendship in good
silver guilders of the hated Orang Blanda. Almayer,
at last consenting, said the powder would be obtained,
but Dain must trust him with dollars to send to Singapore in payment for it. He would induce Ford to buy
and smuggle it in the steamer on board the brig. He
did not want any money for himself out of the transaction, but Dain must help him in his great enterprise
after sending off the brig. Almayer had explained to
Dain that he could not trust Lakamba alone in that
matter; he would be afraid of losing his treasure and his
life through the cupidity of the Rajah; yet the Rajah
had to be told, and insisted on taking a share in that
operation, or else his eyes would remain shut no longer.
To this Almayer had to submit. Had Dain not seen
Nina he would have probably refused to engage himself
and his men in the projected expedition to Gunong
Mas—the mountain of gold. As it was he intended
to return with half of his men as soon as the brig was

clear of the reefs, but the persistent chase given him by the Dutch frigate had forced him to run south and ultimately to wreck and destroy his vessel in order to preserve his liberty or perhaps even his life. Yes, he had come back to Sambir for Nina, although aware that the Dutch would look for him there, but he had also calculated his chances of safety in Lakamba's hands. For all his ferocious talk, the merciful ruler would not kill him, for he had long ago been impressed with the notion that Dain possessed the secret of the white man's treasure; neither would he give him up to the Dutch, for fear of some fatal disclosure of complicity in the treasonable trade. So Dain felt tolerably secure as he sat meditating quietly his answer to the Rajah's bloodthirsty speech. Yes, he would point out to him the aspect of his position should he—Dain—fall into the hands of the Dutch and should he speak the truth. He would have nothing more to lose then, and he would speak the truth. And if he did return to Sambir, disturbing thereby Lakamba's peace of mind, what then? He came to look after his property. Did he not pour a stream of silver into Mrs. Almayer's greedy lap? He had paid, for the girl, a price worthy of a great prince, although unworthy of that delightfully maddening creature for whom his untamed soul longed in an intensity of desire far more tormenting than the sharpest pain. He wanted his happiness. He had the right to be in Sambir.

He rose, and, approaching the table, leaned both his elbows on it; Lakamba responsively edged his seat a little closer, while Babalatchi scrambled to his feet and thrust his inquisitive head between his master's and Dain's. They interchanged their ideas rapidly, speaking in whispers into each other's faces, very close now, Dain suggesting, Lakamba contradicting, Baba-

latchi conciliating and anxious in his vivid apprehension
of coming difficulties. He spoke most, whispering
earnestly, turning his head slowly from side to side so
as to bring his solitary eye to bear upon each of his
interlocutors in turn. Why should there be strife? said
he. Let Tuan Dain, whom he loved only less than his
master, go trustfully into hiding. There were many
places for that. Bulangi's house away in the clearing
was best. Bulangi was a safe man. In the network
of crooked channels no white man could find his way.
White men were strong, but very foolish. It was un-
desirable to fight them, but deception was easy. They
were like silly women—they did not know the use of
reason, and he was a match for any of them—went on
Babalatchi, with all the confidence of deficient experience. Probably the Dutch would seek Almayer.
Maybe they would take away their countryman if
they were suspicious of him. That would be good.
After the Dutch went away Lakamba and Dain would
get the treasure without any trouble, and there would
be one person less to share it. Did he not speak wisdom? Will Tuan Dain go to Bulangi's house till the
danger is over, go at once?

Dain accepted this suggestion of going into hiding
with a certain sense of conferring a favour upon Lakamba and the anxious statesman, but he met the proposal
of going at once with a decided no, looking Babalatchi
meaningly in the eye. The statesman sighed as a
man accepting the inevitable would do, and pointed
silently towards the other bank of the river. Dain
bent his head slowly.

"Yes, I am going there," he said.

"Before the day comes?" asked Babalatchi.

"I am going there now," answered Dain, decisively.
"The Orang Blanda will not be here before to-morrow

night, perhaps, and I must tell Almayer of our arrangements."

"No, Tuan. No; say nothing," protested Babalatchi. "I will go over myself at sunrise and let him know."

"I will see," said Dain, preparing to go.

The thunderstorm was recommencing outside, the heavy clouds hanging low overhead now. There was a constant rumble of distant thunder punctuated by the nearer sharp crashes, and in the continuous play of blue lightning the woods and the river showed fitfully, with all the elusive distinctness of detail characteristic of such a scene. Outside the door of the Rajah's house Dain and Babalatchi stood on the shaking verandah as if dazed and stunned by the violence of the storm. They stood there amongst the cowering forms of the Rajah's slaves and retainers seeking shelter from the rain, and Dain called aloud to his boatmen, who responded with an unanimous "Ada! Tuan!" while they looked uneasily at the river.

"This is a great flood!" shouted Babalatchi into Dain's ear. "The river is very angry. Look! Look at the drifting logs! Can you go?"

Dain glanced doubtfully on the livid expanse of seething water bounded far away on the other side by the narrow black line of the forests. Suddenly, in a vivid white flash, the low point of land with the bending trees on it and Almayer's house, leaped into view, flickered and disappeared. Dain pushed Babalatchi aside and ran down to the water-gate followed by his shivering boatmen.

Babalatchi backed slowly in and closed the door, then turned round and looked silently upon Lakamba. The Rajah sat still, glaring stonily upon the table, and Babalatchi gazed curiously at the perplexed mood of

the man he had served so many years through good and
evil fortune. No doubt the one-eyed statesman felt
within his savage and much sophisticated breast the
unwonted feelings of sympathy with, and perhaps even
pity for, the man he called his master. From the safe
position of a confidential adviser, he could, in the dim
vista of past years, see himself—a casual cut-throat—
finding shelter under that man's roof in the modest
rice-clearing of early beginnings. Then came a long
period of unbroken success, of wise counsels, and deep
plottings resolutely carried out by the fearless Lakamba,
till the whole east coast from Poulo Laut to Tanjong
Batu listened to Babalatchi's wisdom speaking through
the mouth of the ruler of Sambir. In those long years
how many dangers escaped, how many enemies bravely
faced, how many white men successfully circumvented!
And now he looked upon the result of so many years of
patient toil: the fearless Lakamba cowed by the shadow
of an impending trouble. The ruler was growing old,
and Babalatchi, aware of an uneasy feeling at the pit
of his stomach, put both his hands there with a suddenly
vivid and sad perception of the fact that he himself was
growing old too; that the time of reckless daring was
past for both of them, and that they had to seek refuge
in prudent cunning. They wanted peace; they were
disposed to reform; they were ready even to retrench
so as to have the wherewithal to bribe the evil days
away, if bribed away they could be. Babalatchi
sighed for the second time that night as he squatted
again at his master's feet and tendered him his betel-nut
box in mute sympathy. And they sat there in close yet
silent communion of betel-nut chewers, moving their jaws
slowly, expectorating decorously into the wide-mouthed
brass vessel they passed to one another, and listening
to the awful din of the battling elements outside.

"There is a very great flood," remarked Babalatchi, sadly.

"Yes," said Lakamba. "Did Dain go?"

"He went, Tuan. He ran down to the river like a man possessed of the Sheitan himself."

There was another long pause.

"He may get drowned," suggested Lakamba at last, with some show of interest.

"The floating logs are many," answered Babalatchi, "but he is a good swimmer," he added languidly.

"He ought to live," said Lakamba; "he knows where the treasure is."

Babalatchi assented with an ill-humoured grunt. His want of success in penetrating the white man's secret as to the locality where the gold was to be found was a sore point with the statesman of Sambir, as the only conspicuous failure in an otherwise brilliant career.

A great peace had now succeeded the turmoil of the storm. Only the little belated clouds, which hurried past overhead to catch up the main body flashing silently in the distance, sent down short showers that pattered softly with a soothing hiss over the palm-leaf roof.

Lakamba roused himself from his apathy with an appearance of having grasped the situation at last.

"Babalatchi," he called briskly, giving him a slight kick.

"Ada Tuan! I am listening."

"If the Orang Blanda come here, Babalatchi, and take Almayer to Batavia to punish him for smuggling gunpowder, what will he do, you think?"

"I do not know, Tuan."

"You are a fool," commented Lakamba, exultingly. "He will tell them where the treasure is, so as to find mercy. He will."

Babalatchi looked up at his master and nodded his head with by no means a joyful surprise. He had not thought of this; there was a new complication.

"Almayer must die," said Lakamba, decisively, "to make our secret safe. He must die quietly, Babalatchi. You must do it."

Babalatchi assented, and rose wearily to his feet. "To-morrow?" he asked.

"Yes; before the Dutch come. He drinks much coffee," answered Lakamba, with seeming irrelevancy.

Babalatchi stretched himself yawning, but Lakamba, in the flattering consciousness of a knotty problem solved by his own unaided intellectual efforts, grew suddenly very wakeful.

"Babalatchi," he said to the exhausted statesman, "fetch the box of music the white captain gave me. I cannot sleep."

At this order a deep shade of melancholy settled upon Babalatchi's features. He went reluctantly behind the curtain and soon reappeared carrying in his arms a small hand-organ, which he put down on the table with an air of deep dejection. Lakamba settled himself comfortably in his arm-chair.

"Turn, Babalatchi, turn," he murmured, with closed eyes.

Babalatchi's hand grasped the handle with the energy of despair, and as he turned, the deep gloom on his countenance changed into an expression of hopeless resignation. Through the open shutter the notes of Verdi's music floated out on the great silence over the river and forest. Lakamba listened with closed eyes and a delighted smile; Babalatchi turned, at times dozing off and swaying over, then catching himself up in a great fright with a few quick turns of the handle. Nature slept in an exhausted repose after the fierce turmoil, while under the unsteady hand of the statesman of Sambir the Trovatore fitfully wept, wailed, and bade good-bye to his Leonore again and again in a mournful round of tearful and endless iteration.

CHAPTER SEVEN

THE bright sunshine of the clear mistless morning, after the stormy night, flooded the main path of the settlement leading from the low shore of the Pantai branch of the river to the gate of Abdulla's compound. The path was deserted this morning; it stretched its dark yellow surface, hard beaten by the tramp of many bare feet, between the clusters of palm trees, whose tall trunks barred it with strong black lines at irregular intervals, while the newly risen sun threw the shadows of their leafy heads far away over the roofs of the buildings lining the river, even over the river itself as it flowed swiftly and silently past the deserted houses. For the houses were deserted too. On the narrow strip of trodden grass intervening between their open doors and the road, the morning fires smouldered untended, sending thin fluted columns of smoke into the cool air, and spreading the thinnest veil of mysterious blue haze over the sunlit solitude of the settlement. Almayer, just out of his hammock, gazed sleepily at the unwonted appearance of Sambir, wondering vaguely at the absence of life. His own house was very quiet; he could not hear his wife's voice, nor the sound of Nina's footsteps in the big room, opening on the verandah, which he called his sitting-room, whenever, in the company of white men, he wished to assert his claims to the commonplace decencies of civilization. Nobody ever sat there; there was nothing there to sit upon, for Mrs. Almayer in her savage moods, when excited by the reminiscences of the piratical period of her life, had

torn off the curtains to make sarongs for the slave-girls,
and had burnt the showy furniture piecemeal to cook
the family rice. But Almayer was not thinking of his
furniture now. He was thinking of Dain's return, of
Dain's nocturnal interview with Lakamba, of its possible
influence on his long-matured plans, now nearing the
period of their execution. He was also uneasy at the
non-appearance of Dain who had promised him an
early visit. "The fellow had plenty of time to cross
the river," he mused, "and there was so much to be
done to-day. The settling of details for the early
start on the morrow; the launching of the boats; the
thousand and one finishing touches. For the expedition must start complete, nothing should be forgotten,
nothing should——"

The sense of the unwonted solitude grew upon him
suddenly, and in the unusual silence he caught himself
longing even for the usually unwelcome sound of his
wife's voice to break the oppressive stillness which
seemed, to his frightened fancy, to portend the advent
of some new misfortune. "What has happened?" he
muttered half aloud, as he shuffled in his imperfectly
adjusted slippers towards the balustrade of the verandah.
"Is everybody asleep or dead?"

The settlement was alive and very much awake.
It was awake ever since the early break of day, when
Mahmat Banjer, in a fit of unheard-of energy, arose
and, taking up his hatchet, stepped over the sleeping
forms of his two wives and walked shivering to the
water's edge to make sure that the new house he was
building had not floated away during the night.

The house was being built by the enterprising Mahmat on a large raft, and he had securely moored it
just inside the muddy point of land at the junction of
the two branches of the Pantai so as to be out of the

way of drifting logs that would no doubt strand on the point during the freshet. Mahmat walked through the wet grass saying bourrouh, and cursing softly to himself the hard necessities of active life that drove him from his warm couch into the cold of the morning. A glance showed him that his house was still there, and he congratulated himself on his foresight in hauling it out of harm's way, for the increasing light showed him a confused wrack of drift-logs, half-stranded on the muddy flat, interlocked into a shapeless raft by their branches, tossing to and fro and grinding together in the eddy caused by the meeting currents of the two branches of the river. Mahmat walked down to the water's edge to examine the rattan moorings of his house just as the sun cleared the trees of the forest on the opposite shore. As he bent over the fastenings he glanced again carelessly at the unquiet jumble of logs and saw there something that caused him to drop his hatchet and stand up, shading his eyes with his hand from the rays of the rising sun. It was something red, and the logs rolled over it, at times closing round it, sometimes hiding it. It looked to him at first like a strip of red cloth. The next moment Mahmat had made it out and raised a great shout.

"Ah ya! There!" yelled Mahmat. "There's a man amongst the logs." He put the palms of his hand to his lips and shouted, enunciating distinctly, his face turned towards the settlement: "There's a body of a man in the river! Come and see! A dead—stranger!"

The women of the nearest house were already outside kindling the fires and husking the morning rice. They took up the cry shrilly, and it travelled so from house to house, dying away in the distance. The men rushed out excited but silent, and ran towards the muddy point

where the unconscious logs tossed and ground and
bumped and rolled over the dead stranger with the
stupid persistency of inanimate things. The women
followed, neglecting their domestic duties and disre-
garding the possibilities of domestic discontent, while
groups of children brought up the rear, warbling joyously, in the delight of unexpected excitement.

Almayer called aloud for his wife and daughter,
but receiving no response, stood listening intently.
The murmur of the crowd reached him faintly, bringing
with it the assurance of some unusual event. He
glanced at the river just as he was going to leave the
verandah and checked himself at the sight of a small
canoe crossing over from the Rajah's landing-place.
The solitary occupant (in whom Almayer soon recognized Babalatchi) effected the crossing a little below
the house and paddled up to the Lingard jetty in the
dead water under the bank. Babalatchi clambered
out slowly and went on fastening his canoe with fastidi-
ous care, as if not in a hurry to meet Almayer, whom he
saw looking at him from the verandah. This delay
gave Almayer time to notice and greatly wonder at
Babalatchi's official get-up. The statesman of Sambir
was clad in a costume befitting his high rank. A loudly
checkered sarong encircled his waist and from its many
folds peeped out the silver hilt of the kriss that saw the
light only on great festivals or during official receptions.
Over the left shoulder and across the otherwise unclad
breast of the aged diplomatist glistened a patent
leather belt bearing a brass plate with the arms of
Netherlands under the inscription, "Sultan of Sambir."
Babalatchi's head was covered by a red turban, whose
fringed ends falling over the left cheek and shoulder
gave to his aged face a ludicrous expression of joyous
recklessness. When the canoe was at last fastened to

his satisfaction he straightened himself up, shaking
down the folds of his sarong, and moved with long
strides towards Almayer's house, swinging regularly his
long ebony staff, whose gold head ornamented with
precious stones flashed in the morning sun. Almayer
waved his hand to the right towards the point of land,
to him invisible, but in full view from the jetty.

"Oh, Babalatchi! oh!" he called out; "what is the
matter there? can you see?"

Babalatchi stopped and gazed intently at the crowd
on the river bank, and after a little while the astonished
Almayer saw him leave the path, gather up his sarong
in one hand, and break into a trot through the grass
towards the muddy point. Almayer, now greatly interested, ran down the steps of the verandah. The
murmur of men's voices and the shrill cries of women
reached him quite distinctly now, and as soon as he
turned the corner of his house he could see the crowd on
the low promontory swaying and pushing round some
object of interest. He could indistinctly hear Babalatchi's voice, then the crowd opened before the aged
statesman and closed after him with an excited hum,
ending in a loud shout.

As Almayer approached the throng a man ran out
and rushed past him towards the settlement, unheeding
his call to stop and explain the cause of this excitement.
On the very outskirts of the crowd Almayer found himself arrested by an unyielding mass of humanity, regardless of his entreaties for a passage, insensible to his
gentle pushes as he tried to work his way through it
towards the riverside.

In the midst of his gentle and slow progress he fancied
suddenly he had heard his wife's voice in the thickest
of the throng. He could not mistake very well Mrs.
Almayer's high-pitched tones, yet the words were too

indistinct for him to understand their purport. He paused in his endeavours to make a passage for himself, intending to get some intelligence from those around him, when a long and piercing shriek rent the air, silencing the murmurs of the crowd and the voices of his informants. For a moment Almayer remained as if turned into stone with astonishment and horror, for he was certain now that he had heard his wife wailing for the dead. He remembered Nina's unusual absence, and maddened by his apprehensions as to her safety, he pushed blindly and violently forward, the crowd falling back with cries of surprise and pain before his frantic advance.

On the point of land in a little clear space lay the body of the stranger just hauled out from amongst the logs. On one side stood Babalatchi, his chin resting on the head of his staff and his one eye gazing steadily at the shapeless mass of broken limbs, torn flesh, and bloodstained rags. As Almayer burst through the ring of horrified spectators, Mrs. Almayer threw her own head-veil over the upturned face of the drowned man, and, squatting by it, with another mournful howl, sent a shiver through the now silent crowd. Mahmat, dripping wet, turned to Almayer, eager to tell his tale.

In the first moment of reaction from the anguish of his fear the sunshine seemed to waver before Almayer's eyes, and he listened to words spoken around him without comprehending their meaning. When, by a strong effort of will, he regained the possession of his senses, Mahmat was saying—

"That is the way, Tuan. His sarong was caught in the broken branch, and he hung with his head under water. When I saw what it was I did not want it here. I wanted it to get clear and drift away. Why should we bury a stranger in the midst of our houses for his

ghost to frighten our women and children? Have we
not enough ghosts about this place?"

A murmur of approval interrupted him here. Mahmat looked reproachfully at Babalatchi.

"But the Tuan Babalatchi ordered me to drag the
body ashore"—he went on looking round at his audience, but addressing himself only to Almayer—"and
I dragged him by the feet; in through the mud I have
dragged him, although my heart longed to see him
float down the river to strand perchance on Bulangi's
clearing—may his father's grave be defiled!"

There was subdued laughter at this, for the enmity
of Mahmat and Bulangi was a matter of common no-
toriety and of undying interest to the inhabitants of
Sambir. In the midst of that mirth Mrs. Almayer
wailed suddenly again.

"Allah! What ails the woman!" exclaimed Mahmat, angrily. "Here, I have touched this carcass
which came from nobody knows where, and have most
likely defiled myself before eating rice. By orders of
Tuan Babalatchi I did this thing to please the white
man. Are you pleased, O Tuan Almayer? And what
will be my recompense? Tuan Babalatchi said a recompense there will be, and from you. Now consider.
I have been defiled and if not defiled I may be under
the spell. Look at his anklets! Who ever heard of a
corpse appearing during the night amongst the logs
with gold anklets on its legs? There is witchcraft there.
However," added Mahmat, after a reflective pause,
"I will have the anklet if there is permission, for I have
a charm against the ghosts and am not afraid. God is
great!"

A fresh outburst of noisy grief from Mrs. Almayer
checked the flow of Mahmat's eloquence. Almayer,
bewildered, looked in turn at his wife, at Mahmat, at

Babalatchi, and at last arrested his fascinated gaze on the body lying on the mud with covered face in a grotesquely unnatural contortion of mangled and broken limbs, one twisted and lacerated arm, with white bones protruding in many places through the torn flesh, stretched out; the hand with outspread fingers nearly touching his foot.

"Do you know who this is?" he asked of Babalatchi, in a low voice.

Babalatchi, staring straight before him, hardly moved his lips, while Mrs. Almayer's persistent lamentations drowned the whisper of his murmured reply intended only for Almayer's ear.

"It was fate. Look at your feet, white man. I can see a ring on those torn fingers which I know well."

Saying this, Babalatchi stepped carelessly forward, putting his foot as if accidentally on the hand of the corpse and pressing it into the soft mud. He swung his staff menacingly towards the crowd, which fell back a little.

"Go away," he said sternly, "and send your women to their cooking fires, which they ought not to have left to run after a dead stranger. This is men's work here. I take him now in the name of the Rajah. Let no man remain here but Tuan Almayer's slaves. Now go!"

The crowd reluctantly began to disperse. The women went first, dragging away the children that hung back with all their weight on the maternal hand. The men strolled slowly after them in ever forming and changing groups that gradually dissolved as they neared the settlement and every man regained his own house with steps quickened by the hungry anticipation of the morning rice. Only on the slight elevation where the land sloped down towards the muddy point a few men, either friends or enemies of Mahmat, remained gazing

*D

curiously for some time longer at the small group standing around the body on the river bank.

"I do not understand what you mean, Babalatchi," said Almayer. "What is the ring you are talking about? Whoever he is, you have trodden the poor fellow's hand right into the mud. Uncover his face," he went on, addressing Mrs. Almayer, who, squatting by the head of the corpse, rocked herself to and fro, shaking from time to time her dishevelled grey locks, and muttering mournfully.

"Hai!" exclaimed Mahmat, who had lingered close by. "Look, Tuan; the logs came together so," and here he pressed the palms of his hands together, "and his head must have been between them, and now there is no face for you to look at. There are his flesh and his bones, the nose, and the lips, and maybe his eyes, but nobody could tell the one from the other. It was written the day he was born that no man could look at him in death and be able to say, 'This is my friend's face.'"

"Silence, Mahmat; enough!" said Babalatchi, "and take thy eyes off his anklet, thou eater of pigs flesh. Tuan Almayer," he went on, lowering his voice, "have you seen Dain this morning?"

Almayer opened his eyes wide and looked alarmed. "No," he said quickly; "haven't you seen him? Is he not with the Rajah? I am waiting; why does he not come?"

Babalatchi nodded his head sadly.

"He is come, Tuan. He left last night when the storm was great and the river spoke angrily. The night was very black, but he had within him a light that showed the way to your house as smooth as a narrow backwater, and the many logs no bigger than wisps of dried grass. Therefore he went; and now he lies here." And Babalatchi nodded his head towards the body.

"How can you tell?" said Almayer, excitedly, pushing his wife aside. He snatched the cover off and looked at the formless mass of flesh, hair, and drying mud, where the face of the drowned man should have been. "Nobody can tell," he added, turning away with a shudder.

Babalatchi was on his knees wiping the mud from the stiffened fingers of the outstretched hand. He rose to his feet and flashed before Almayer's eyes a gold ring set with a large green stone.

"You know this well," he said. "This never left Dain's hand. I had to tear the flesh now to get it off. Do you believe now?"

Almayer raised his hands to his head and let them fall listlessly by his side in the utter abandonment of despair. Babalatchi, looking at him curiously, was astonished to see him smile. A strange fancy had take possession of Almayer's brain, distracted by this new misfortune. It seemed to him that for many years he had been falling into a deep precipice. Day after day, month after month, year after year, he had been falling, falling, falling; it was a smooth, round, black thing, and the black walls had been rushing upwards with wearisome rapidity. A great rush, the noise of which he fancied he could hear yet; and now, with an awful shock, he had reached the bottom, and behold! he was alive and whole, and Dain was dead with all his bones broken. It struck him as funny. A dead Malay; he had seen many dead Malays without any emotion; and now he felt inclined to weep, but it was over the fate of a white man he knew; a man that fell over a deep precipice and did not die. He seemed somehow to himself to be standing on one side, a little way off, looking at a certain Almayer who was in great trouble. Poor, poor fellow! Why doesn't he cut his throat? He wished to encourage him; he was very anxious to see him lying dead over that other corpse. Why does he not die and end this suffering? He groaned aloud unconsciously and started with affright at the sound of his own voice. Was he going mad? Terrified by the thought he turned away and ran towards his house repeating to himself, "I am not going mad; of course not, no, no, no!" He tried to keep a firm hold of the idea. Not mad, not mad. He stumbled as he ran blindly up the steps repeating fast and ever faster those words wherein seemed to lie his salvation. He saw Nina standing there, and wished to say something to her, but could not remember what, in his extreme anxiety not to forget that he was not going mad, which he still kept repeating mentally as he ran round the table, till he stumbled against one of the arm-chairs and dropped into it exhausted. He sat staring wildly at Nina, still assuring himself mentally of his own sanity and wondering why the girl shrank from him in open-eyed alarm. What was the matter with her? This was foolish. He struck the table violently with his clenched fist and shouted hoarsely, "Give me some gin! Run!" Then, while Nina ran off, he remained in the chair, very still and quiet, astonished at the noise he had made.

Nina returned with a tumbler half filled with gin, and found her father staring absently before him. Almayer felt very tired now, as if he had come from a long journey. He felt as if he had walked miles and miles that morning and now wanted to rest very much. He took the tumbler with a shaking hand, and as he drank his teeth chattered against the glass which he drained and set down heavily on the table. He turned his eyes slowly towards Nina standing beside him, and said steadily—

"Now all is over, Nina. He is dead, and I may as well burn all my boats."

He felt very proud of being able to speak so calmly. Decidedly he was not going mad. This certitude was very comforting, and he went on talking about the finding of the body, listening to his own voice complacently. Nina stood quietly, her hand resting lightly on her father's shoulder, her face unmoved, but every line of her features, the attitude of her whole body expressing the most keen and anxious attention.

"And so Dain is dead," she said coldly, when her father ceased speaking.

Almayer's elaborately calm demeanour gave way in a moment to an outburst of violent indignation.

"You stand there as if you were only half alive, and talk to me," he exclaimed angrily, "as if it was a matter of no importance. Yes, he is dead! Do you understand? Dead! What do you care? You never cared; you saw me struggle, and work, and strive, unmoved; and my suffering you could never see. No, never. You have no heart, and you have no mind, or you would have understood that it was for you, for your happiness I was working. I wanted to be rich; I wanted to get away from here. I wanted to see white men bowing low before the power of your beauty and your wealth. Old as I am I wished to seek a strange land, a civilization to which I am a stranger, so as to find a new life in the contemplation of your high fortunes, of your triumphs, of your happiness. For that I bore patiently the burden of work, of disappointment, of humiliation amongst these savages here, and I had it all nearly in my grasp."

He looked at his daughter's attentive face and jumped to his feet upsetting the chair.

"Do you hear? I had it all there; so; within reach of my hand."

He paused, trying to keep down his rising anger, and failed.

"Have you no feeling?" he went on. "Have you lived without hope?" Nina's silence exasperated him; his voice rose, although he tried to master his feelings.

"Are you content to live in this misery and die in this wretched hole? Say something, Nina; have you no sympathy? Have you no word of comfort for me? I that loved you so."

He waited for a while for an answer, and receiving none shook his fist in his daughter's face.

"I believe you are an idiot!" he yelled.

He looked round for the chair, picked it up and sat down stiffly. His anger was dead within him, and he felt ashamed of his outburst, yet relieved to think that now he had laid clear before his daughter the inner meaning of his life. He thought so in perfect good faith, deceived by the emotional estimate of his motives, unable to see the crookedness of his ways, the unreality of his aims, the futility of his regrets. And now his heart was filled only with a great tenderness and love for his daughter. He wanted to see her miserable, and to share with her his despair; but he wanted it only as all weak natures long for a companionship in misfortune with beings innocent of its cause. If she suffered herself she would understand and pity him; but now she would not, or could not, find one word of comfort or love for him in his dire extremity. The sense of his absolute loneliness came home to his heart with a force that made him shudder. He swayed and fell forward with his face on the table, his arms stretched straight out, extended and rigid. Nina made a quick movement towards her father and stood looking at the

grey head, on the broad shoulders shaken convulsively
by the violence of feelings that found relief at last in
sobs and tears.

Nina sighed deeply and moved away from the table.
Her features lost the appearance of stony indifference
that had exasperated her father into his outburst of
anger and sorrow. The expression of her face, now
unseen by her father, underwent a rapid change. She
had listened to Almayer's appeal for sympathy, for
one word of comfort, apparently indifferent, yet with
her breast torn by conflicting impulses raised unexpectedly by events she had not foreseen, or at least did
not expect to happen so soon. With her heart deeply
moved by the sight of Almayer's misery, knowing it in
her power to end it with a word, longing to bring peace
to that troubled heart, she heard with terror the voice
of her overpowering love commanding her to be silent.
And she submitted after a short and fierce struggle of
her old self against the new principle of her life. She
wrapped herself up in absolute silence, the only safe-
guard against some fatal admission. She could not
trust herself to make a sign, to murmur a word for fear
of saying too much; and the very violence of the feelings
that stirred the innermost recesses of her soul seemed to
turn her person into a stone. The dilated nostrils and
the flashing eyes were the only signs of the storm raging within, and those signs of his daughter's emotion
Almayer did not see, for his sight was dimmed by self-
pity, by anger, and by despair.

Had Almayer looked at his daughter as she leant over
the front rail of the verandah he could have seen the
expression of indifference give way to a look of pain
and that again pass away, leaving the glorious beauty
of her face marred by deep-drawn lines of watchful
anxiety. The long grass in the neglected courtyard

stood very straight before her eyes in the noonday heat.
From the river-bank there were voices and a shuffle
of bare feet approaching the house; Babalatchi could be
heard giving directions to Almayer's men, and Mrs.
Almayer's subdued wailing became audible as the small
procession bearing the body of the drowned man and
headed by that sorrowful matron turned the corner of
the house. Babalatchi had taken the broken anklet
off the man's leg, and now held it in his hand as he
moved by the side of the bearers, while Mahmat lingered behind timidly, in the hopes of the promised
reward.

"Lay him there," said Babalatchi to Almayer's men,
pointing to a pile of drying planks in front of the verandah. "Lay him there. He was a Kaffir and the son
of a dog, and he was the white man's friend. He drank
the white man's strong water," he added, with affected
horror. "That I have seen myself."

The men stretched out the broken limbs on two
planks they had laid level, while Mrs. Almayer covered
the body with a piece of white cotton cloth, and after
whispering for some time with Babalatchi departed to
her domestic duties. Almayer's men, after laying down
their burden, dispersed themselves in quest of shady
spots wherein to idle the day away. Babalatchi was
left alone by the corpse that laid rigid under the white
cloth in the bright sunshine.

Nina came down the steps and joined Babalatchi,
who put his hand to his forehead, and squatted down
with great deference.

"You have a bangle there," said Nina, looking down
on Babalatchi's upturned face and into his solitary eye.

"I have, Mem Putih," returned the polite statesman.
Then turning towards Mahmat he beckoned him closer,
calling out, "Come here!"

Mahmat approached with some hesitation. He avoided looking at Nina, but fixed his eyes on Babalatchi.

"Now, listen," said Babalatchi, sharply. "The ring and the anklet you have seen, and you know they belonged to Dain the trader, and to no other. Dain returned last night in a canoe. He spoke with the Rajah, and in the middle of the night left to cross over to the white man's house. There was a great flood, and this morning you found him in the river."

"By his feet I dragged him out," muttered Mahmat under his breath. "Tuan Babalatchi, there will be a recompense!" he exclaimed aloud.

Babalatchi held up the gold bangle before Mahmat's eyes. "What I have told you, Mahmat, is for all ears. What I give you now is for your eyes only. Take."

Mahmat took the bangle eagerly and hid it in the folds of his waist-cloth. "Am I a fool to show this thing in a house with three women in it?" he growled. "But I shall tell them about Dain the trader, and there will be talk enough."

He turned and went away, increasing his pace as soon as he was outside Almayer's compound.

Babalatchi looked after him till he disappeared behind the bushes. "Have I done well, Mem Putih?" he asked, humbly addressing Nina.

"You have," answered Nina. "The ring you may keep yourself."

Babalatchi touched his lips and forehead, and scrambled to his feet. He looked at Nina, as if expecting her to say something more, but Nina turned towards the house and went up the steps, motioning him away with her hand.

Babalatchi picked up his staff and prepared to go. It was very warm, and he did not care for the long pull to the Rajah's house. Yet he must go and tell the Rajah—tell of the event; of the change in his plans; of all his suspicions. He walked to the jetty and began casting off the rattan painter of his canoe.

The broad expanse of the lower reach, with its shimmering surface dotted by the black specks of the fishing canoes, lay before his eyes. The fishermen seemed to be racing. Babalatchi paused in his work, and looked on with sudden interest. The man in the foremost canoe, now within hail of the first houses of Sambir, laid in his paddle and stood up shouting—

"The boats! the boats! The man-of-war's boats are coming! They are here!"

In a moment the settlement was again alive with people rushing to the riverside. The men began to unfasten their boats, the women stood in groups looking towards the bend down the river. Above the trees lining the reach a slight puff of smoke appeared like a black stain on the brilliant blue of the cloudless sky.

Babalatchi stood perplexed, the painter in his hand. He looked down the reach, then up towards Almayer's house, and back again at the river as if undecided what to do. At last he made the canoe fast again hastily, and ran towards the house and up the steps of the verandah.

"Tuan! Tuan!" he called, eagerly. "The boats are coming. The man-of-war's boats. You had better get ready. The officers will come here, I know."

Almayer lifted his head slowly from the table, and looked at him stupidly.

"Mem Putih!" exclaimed Babalatchi to Nina, "look at him. He does not hear. You must take care," he added meaningly.

Nina nodded to him with an uncertain smile, and was going to speak, when a sharp report from the gun

mounted in the bow of the steam launch that was just
then coming into view arrested the words on her parted
lips. The smile died out, and was replaced by the old
look of anxious attention. From the hills far away the
echo came back like a long-drawn and mournful sigh,
as if the land had sent it in answer to the voice of its
masters.

CHAPTER EIGHT

THE news as to the identity of the body lying now in Almayer's compound spread rapidly over the settlement. During the forenoon most of the inhabitants remained in the long street discussing the mysterious return and the unexpected death of the man who had become known to them as the trader. His arrival during the northeast monsoon, his long sojourn in their midst, his sudden departure with his brig, and, above all, the mysterious appearance of the body, said to be his, amongst the logs, were subjects to wonder at and to talk over and over again with undiminished interest. Mahmat moved from house to house and from group to group, always ready to repeat his tale: how he saw the body caught by the sarong in a forked log; how Mrs. Almayer coming, one of the first, at his cries, recognized it, even before he had it hauled on shore; how Babalatchi ordered him to bring it out of the water. "By the feet I dragged him in, and there was no head," exclaimed Mahmat, "and how could the white man's wife know who it was? She was a witch, it was well known. And did you see how the white man himself ran away at the sight of the body? Like a deer he ran!" And here Mahmat imitated Almayer's long strides, to the great joy of the beholders. And for all his trouble he had nothing. The ring with the green stone Tuan Babalatchi kept. "Nothing! Nothing!" He spat down at his feet in sign of disgust, and left that group to seek further on a fresh audience.

The news spreading to the furthermost parts of the

settlement found out Abdulla in the cool recess of his godown, where he sat overlooking his Arab clerks and the men loading and unloading the up-country canoes. Reshid, who was busy on the jetty, was summoned into his uncle's presence and found him, as usual, very calm and even cheerful, but very much surprised. The rumour of the capture or destruction of Dain's brig had reached the Arab's ears three days before from the sea-fishermen and through the dwellers on the lower reaches of the river. It had been passed upstream from neighbour to neighbour till Bulangi, whose clearing was nearest to the settlement, had brought that news himself to Abdulla whose favour he courted. But rumour also spoke of a fight and of Dain's death on board his own vessel. And now all the settlement talked of Dain's visit to the Rajah and of his death when crossing the river in the dark to see Almayer. They could not understand this. Reshid thought that it was very strange. He felt uneasy and doubtful. But Abdulla, after the first shock of surprise, with the old age's dislike for solving riddles, showed a becoming resignation. He remarked that the man was dead now at all events, and consequently no more dangerous. Where was the use to wonder at the decrees of Fate, especially if they were propitious to the True Believers? And with a pious ejaculation to Allah the Merciful, the Compassionate, Abdulla seemed to regard the incident as closed for the present.

Not so Reshid. He lingered by his uncle, pulling thoughtfully his neatly trimmed beard.

"There are many lies," he murmured. "He has been dead once before, and came to life to die again now. The Dutch will be here before many days and clamour for the man. Shall I not believe my eyes sooner than the tongues of women and idle men?"

"They say that the body is being taken to Almayer's compound," said Abdulla. "If you want to go there you must go before the Dutch arrive here. Go late. It should not be said that we have been seen inside that man's enclosure lately."

Reshid assented to the truth of this last remark and left his uncle's side. He leaned against the lintel of the big doorway and looked idly across the courtyard through the open gate on to the main road of the settlement. It lay empty, straight, and yellow under the flood of light. In the hot noontide the smooth trunks of palm trees, the outlines of the houses, and away there at the other end of the road the roof of Almayer's house visible over the bushes on the dark background of forest, seemed to quiver in the heat radiating from the steaming earth. Swarms of yellow butterflies rose, and settled to rise again in short flights before Reshid's half-closed eyes. From under his feet arose the dull hum of insects in the long grass of the courtyard. He looked on sleepily.

From one of the side paths amongst the houses a woman stepped out on the road, a slight girlish figure walking under the shade of a large tray balanced on its head. The consciousness of something moving stirred Reshid's half-sleeping senses into a comparative wakefulness. He recognized Taminah, Bulangi's slave-girl, with her tray of cakes for sale—an apparition of daily recurrence and of no importance whatever. She was going towards Almayer's house. She could be made useful. He roused himself up and ran towards the gate calling out, "Taminah O!" The girl stopped, hesitated, and came back slowly. Reshid waited, signing to her impatiently to come nearer.

When near Reshid Taminah stood with downcast eyes. Reshid looked at her a while before he asked—

"Are you going to Almayer's house? They say in the settlement that Dain the trader, he that was found drowned this morning, is lying in the white man's campong."

"I have heard this talk," whispered Taminah; "and this morning by the riverside I saw the body. Where it is now I do not know."

"So you have seen it?" asked Reshid, eagerly. "Is it Dain? You have seen him many times. You would know him."

The girl's lips quivered and she remained silent for a while breathing quickly.

"I have seen him, not a long time ago," she said at last. "The talk is true; he is dead. What do you want from me, Tuan? I must go."

Just then the report of the gun fired on board the steam launch was heard, interrupting Reshid's reply. Leaving the girl he ran to the house, and met in the courtyard Abdulla coming towards the gate.

"The Orang Blanda are come," said Reshid, "and now we shall have our reward."

Abdulla shook his head doubtfully. "The white men's rewards are long in coming," he said. "White men are quick in anger and slow in gratitude. We shall see."

He stood at the gate stroking his grey beard and listening to the distant cries of greeting at the other end of the settlement. As Taminah was turning to go he called her back.

"Listen, girl," he said: "there will be many white men in Almayer's house. You shall be there selling your cakes to the men of the sea. What you see and what you hear you may tell me. Come here before the sun sets and I will give you a blue handkerchief with red spots. Now go, and forget not to return."

He gave her a push with the end of his long staff as she was going away and made her stumble.

"This slave is very slow," he remarked to his nephew, looking after the girl with great disfavour.

Taminah walked on, her tray on the head, her eyes fixed on the ground. From the open doors of the houses were heard, as she passed, friendly calls inviting her within for business purposes, but she never heeded them, neglecting her sales in the preoccupation of intense thinking. Since the very early morning she had heard much, she had also seen much that filled her heart with a joy mingled with great suffering and fear. Before the dawn, before she left Bulangi's house to paddle up to Sambir she had heard voices outside the house when all in it, but herself were asleep. And now, with her knowledge of the words spoken in the darkness, she held in her hand a life and carried in her breast a great sorrow. Yet from her springy step, erect figure, and face veiled over by the every-day look of apathetic indifference, nobody could have guessed of the double load she carried under the visible burden of the tray piled up high with cakes manufactured by the thrifty hands of Bulangi's wives. In that supple figure straight as an arrow, so graceful and free in its walk, behind those soft eyes that spoke of nothing but of unconscious resignation, there slept all feelings and all passions, all hopes and all fears, the curse of life and the consolation of death. And she knew nothing of it all. She lived like the tall palms amongst whom she was passing now, seeking the light, desiring the sunshine, fearing the storm, unconscious of either. The slave had no hope, and knew of no change. She knew of no other sky, no other water, no other forest, no other world, no other life. She had no wish, no hope, no love, no fear except of a blow, and no vivid feeling but that of occasional

hunger, which was seldom, for Bulangi was rich and
rice was plentiful in the solitary house in his clearing.
The absence of pain and hunger was her happiness, and
when she felt unhappy she was simply tired, more than
usual, after the day's labour. Then in the hot nights
of the southwest monsoon she slept dreamlessly under
the bright stars on the platform built outside the house
and over the river. Inside they slept too: Bulangi by
the door; his wives further in; the children with their
mothers. She could hear their breathing; Bulangi's
sleepy voice; the sharp cry of a child soon hushed with
tender words. And she closed her eyes to the murmur
of the water below her, to the whisper of the warm wind
above, ignorant of the never-ceasing life of that tropical
nature that spoke to her in vain with the thousand faint
voices of the near forest, with the breath of tepid wind;
in the heavy scents that lingered around her head; in
the white wraiths of morning mist that hung over her in
the solemn hush of all creation before the dawn.

Such had been her existence before the coming of the
brig with the strangers. She remembered well that
time; the uproar in the settlement, the never-ending
wonder, the days and nights of talk and excitement.
She remembered her own timidity with the strange men,
till the brig moored to the bank became in a manner part
of the settlement, and the fear wore off in the familiarity
of constant intercourse. The call on board then became part of her daily round. She walked hesitatingly
up the slanting planks of the gangway amidst the encouraging shouts and more or less decent jokes of the
men idling over the bulwarks. There she sold her
wares to those men that spoke so loud and carried
themselves so free. There was a throng, a constant
coming and going; calls interchanged, orders given and
executed with shouts; the rattle of blocks, the flinging

about of coils of rope. She sat out of the way under the
shade of the awning, with her tray before her, the veil
drawn well over her face, feeling shy amongst so many
men. She smiled at all buyers, but spoke to none, letting their jests pass with stolid unconcern. She heard
many tales told around her of far-off countries, of
strange customs, of events stranger still. Those men
were brave; but the most fearless of them spoke of their
chief with fear. Often the man they called their master
passed before her, walking erect and indifferent, in the
pride of youth, in the flash of rich dress, with a tinkle of
gold ornaments, while everybody stood aside watching
anxiously for a movement of his lips, ready to do his
bidding. Then all her life seemed to rush into her
eyes, and from under her veil she gazed at him, charmed
yet fearful to attract attention. One day he noticed
her and asked, "Who is that girl?" "A slave, Tuan!
A girl that sells cakes," a dozen voices replied together.
She rose in terror to run on shore, when he called her
back; and as she stood trembling with head hung down
before him, he spoke kind words, lifting her chin with
his hand and looking into her eyes with a smile. "Do
not be afraid," he said. He never spoke to her any
more. Somebody called out from the river-bank; he
turned away and forgot her existence. Taminah saw
Almayer standing on the shore with Nina on his arm.
She heard Nina's voice calling out gaily, and saw Dain's
face brighten with joy as he leaped on shore. She hated
the sound of that voice ever since.

After that day she left off visiting Almayer's compound, and passed the noon hours under the shade of
the brig awning. She watched for his coming with
heart beating quicker and quicker, as he approached,
into a wild tumult of newly-aroused feelings of joy and
hope and fear that died away with Dain's retreating

figure, leaving her tired out, as if after a struggle, sitting still for a long time in dreamy languor. Then she paddled home slowly in the afternoon, often letting her canoe float with the lazy stream in the quiet backwater of the river. The paddle hung idle in the water as she sat in the stern, one hand supporting her chin, her eyes wide open, listening intently to the whispering of her heart that seemed to swell at last into a song of extreme sweetness. Listening to that song she husked the rice at home; it dulled her ears to the shrill bickerings of Bulangi's wives, to the sound of angry reproaches addressed to herself. And when the sun was near its setting she walked to the bathing-place and heard it as she stood on the tender grass of the low bank, her robe at her feet, and looked at the reflection of her figure on the glass-like surface of the creek. Listening to it she walked slowly back, her wet hair hanging over her shoulders; laying down to rest under the bright stars, she closed her eyes to the murmur of the water below, of the warm wind above; to the voice of nature speaking through the faint noises of the great forest, and to the song of her own heart.

She heard, but did not understand, and drank in the dreamy joy of her new existence without troubling about its meaning or its end, till the full consciousness of life came to her through pain and anger. And she suffered horribly the first time she saw Nina's long canoe drift silently past the sleeping house of Bulangi, bearing the two lovers into the white mist of the great river. Her jealousy and rage culminated into a paroxysm of physical pain that left her lying panting on the riverbank, in the dumb agony of a wounded animal. But she went on moving patiently in the enchanted circle of slavery, going through her task day after day with all the pathos of the grief she could not express, even to her-

self, locked within her breast. She shrank from Nina
as she would have shrunk from the sharp blade of a
knife cutting into her flesh, but she kept on visiting the
brig to feed her dumb, ignorant soul on her own despair.
She saw Dain many times. He never spoke, he never
looked. Could his eyes see only one woman's image?
Could his ears hear only one woman's voice? He never
noticed her; not once.

And then he went away. She saw him and Nina for
the last time on that morning when Babalatchi, while
visiting his fish baskets, had his suspicions of the white
man's daughter's love affair with Dain confirmed beyond
the shadow of doubt. Dain disappeared, and Taminah's heart, where lay useless and barren the seeds of all
love and of all hate, the possibilities of all passions and
of all sacrifices, forgot its joys and its sufferings when
deprived of the help of the senses. Her half-formed,
savage mind, the slave of her body—as her body was
the slave of another's will—forgot the faint and vague
image of the ideal that had found its beginning in the
physical promptings of her savage nature. She dropped back into the torpor of her former life and found
consolation—even a certain kind of happiness—in the
thought that now Nina and Dain were separated,
probably for ever. He would forget. This thought
soothed the last pangs of dying jealousy that had nothing now to feed upon, and Taminah found peace. It
was like the dreary tranquillity of a desert, where there
is peace only because there is no life.

And now he had returned. She had recognized his
voice calling aloud in the night for Bulangi. She had
crept out after her master to listen closer to the intoxicating sound. Dain was there, in a boat, talking to
Bulangi. Taminah, listening with arrested breath,
heard another voice. The maddening joy, that only a

second before she thought herself incapable of containing
within her fast-beating heart, died out, and left her
shivering in the old anguish of physical pain that she
had suffered once before at the sight of Dain and Nina.
Nina spoke now, ordering and entreating in turns, and
Bulangi was refusing, expostulating, at last consenting.
He went in to take a paddle from the heap lying behind
the door. Outside the murmur of two voices went on,
and she caught a word here and there. She understood
that he was fleeing from white men, that he was seeking
a hiding-place, that he was in some danger. But she
heard also words which woke the rage of jealousy that
had been asleep for so many days in her bosom. Crouching low on the mud in the black darkness amongst the
piles, she heard the whisper in the boat that made light
of toil, of privation, of danger, of life itself, if in exchange there could be but a short moment of close embrace, a look from the eyes, the feel of light breath, the
touch of soft lips. So spoke Dain as he sat in the canoe
holding Nina's hands while waiting for Bulangi's return; and Taminah, supporting herself by the slimy
pile, felt as if a heavy weight was crushing her down,
down into the black oily water at her feet. She wanted
to cry out; to rush at them and tear their vague shadows
apart; to throw Nina into the smooth water, cling to her
close, hold her to the bottom where that man could not
find her. She could not cry, she could not move. Then
footsteps were heard on the bamboo platform above her
head; she saw Bulangi get into his smallest canoe and
take the lead, the other boat following, paddled by Dain
and Nina. With a slight splash of the paddles dipped
stealthily into the water, their indistinct forms passed
before her aching eyes and vanished in the darkness of
the creek.

She remained there in the cold and wet, powerless to

move, breathing painfully under the crushing weight
that the mysterious hand of Fate had laid so suddenly
upon her slender shoulders, and shivering, she felt
within a burning fire, that seemed to feed upon her very
life. When the breaking day had spread a pale golden
ribbon over the black outline of the forests, she took
up her tray and departed towards the settlement, going
about her task purely from the force of habit. As she
approached Sambir she could see the excitement and
she heard with momentary surprise of the finding of
Dain's body. It was not true, of course. She knew it
well. She regretted that he was not dead. She should
have liked Dain to be dead, so as to be parted from that
woman—from all women. She felt a strong desire to
see Nina, but without any clear object. She hated her,
and feared her, and she felt an irresistible impulse
pushing her towards Almayer's house to see the white
woman's face, to look close at those eyes, to hear again
that voice, for the sound of which Dain was ready to
risk his liberty, his life even. She had seen her many
times; she had heard her voice daily for many months
past. What was there in her? What was there in that
being to make a man speak as Dain had spoken, to make
him blind to all other faces, deaf to all other voices?

She left the crowd by the riverside, and wandered
aimlessly among the empty houses, resisting the impulse
that pushed her towards Almayer's campong to seek
there in Nina's eyes the secret of her own misery. The
sun mounting higher, shortened the shadows and poured
down upon her a flood of light and of stifling heat as
she passed on from shadow to light, from light to shadow
amongst the houses, the bushes, the tall trees, in her
unconscious flight from the pain in her own heart. In
the extremity of her distress she could find no words
to pray for relief, she knew of no heaven to send her

prayer to, and she wandered on with tired feet in the dumb surprise and terror at the injustice of the suffering inflicted upon her without cause and without redress.

The short talk with Reshid, the proposal of Abdulla steadied her a little and turned her thoughts into another channel. Dain was in some danger. He was hiding from white men. So much she had overheard last night. They all thought him dead. She knew he was alive, and she knew of his hiding-place. What did the Arabs want to know about the white men? The white men want with Dain? Did they wish to kill him? She could tell them all—no, she would say nothing, and in the night she would go to him and sell him his life for a word, for a smile, for a gesture even, and be his slave in far-off countries, away from Nina. But there were dangers. The one-eyed Babalatchi who knew everything; the white man's wife!—she was a witch. Perhaps they would tell. And then there was Nina. She must hurry on and see.

In her impatience she left the path and ran towards Almayer's dwelling through the undergrowth between the palm trees. She came out at the back of the house, where a narrow ditch, full of stagnant water that overflowed from the river, separated Almayer's campong from the rest of the settlement. The thick bushes growing on the bank were hiding from her sight the large courtyard with its cooking shed. Above them rose several thin columns of smoke, and from behind the sound of strange voices informed Taminah that the Men of the Sea belonging to the warship had already landed and were camped between the ditch and the house. To the left one of Almayer's slave-girls came down to the ditch and bent over the shiny water, washing a kettle. To the right the tops of the banana

plantation, visible above the bushes, swayed and shook
under the touch of invisible hands gathering the fruit.
On the calm water several canoes moored to a heavy
stake were crowded together, nearly bridging the ditch
just at the place where Taminah stood. The voices
in the courtyard rose at times into an outburst of calls,
replies, and laughter, and then died away into a silence
that soon was broken again by a fresh clamour. Now
and again the thin blue smoke rushed out thicker and
blacker, and drove in odorous masses over the creek,
wrapping her for a moment in a suffocating veil; then,
as the fresh wood caught well alight, the smoke vanished
in the bright sunlight, and only the scent of aromatic
wood drifted afar, to leeward of the crackling fires.

Taminah rested her tray on a stump of a tree, and
remained standing with her eyes turned towards Almayer's house, whose roof and part of a whitewashed
wall were visible over the bushes. The slave-girl
finished her work, and after looking for a while curiously
at Taminah, pushed her way through the dense thicket
back to the courtyard. Round Taminah there was now
a complete solitude. She threw herself down on the
ground, and hid her face in her hands. Now when so
close she had no courage to see Nina. At every burst of
louder voices from the courtyard she shivered in the
fear of hearing Nina's voice. She came to the resolution
of waiting where she was till dark, and then going
straight to Dain's hiding-place. From where she was
she could watch the movements of white men, of Nina,
of all Dain's friends, and of all his enemies. Both were
hateful alike to her, for both would take him away beyond her reach. She hid herself in the long grass to
wait anxiously for the sunset that seemed so slow to
come.

On the other side of the ditch, behind the bush, by

the clear fires, the seamen of the frigate had encamped on the hospitable invitation of Almayer. Almayer, roused out of his apathy by the prayers and importunity of Nina, had managed to get down in time to the jetty so as to receive the officers at their landing. The lieutenant in command accepted his invitation to his house with the remark that in any case their business was with Almayer—and perhaps not very pleasant, he added. Almayer hardly heard him. He shook hands with them absently and led the way towards the house. He was scarcely conscious of the polite words of welcome he greeted the strangers with, and afterwards repeated several times over again in his efforts to appear at ease. The agitation of their host did not escape the officer's eyes, and the chief confided to his subordinate, in a low voice, his doubts as to Almayer's sobriety. The young sub-lieutenant laughed and expressed in a whisper the hope that the white man was not intoxicated enough to neglect the offer of some refreshments. "He does not seem very dangerous," he added, as they followed Almayer up the steps of the verandah.

"No, he seems more of a fool than a knave; I have heard of him," returned the senior.

They sat around the table. Almayer with shaking hands made gin cocktails, offered them all round, and drank himself, with every gulp feeling stronger, steadier, and better able to face all the difficulties of his position. Ignorant of the fate of the brig he did not suspect the real object of the officer's visit. He had a general notion that something must have leaked out about the gunpowder trade, but apprehended nothing beyond some temporary inconvenience. After emptying his glass he began to chat easily, lying back in his chair with one of his legs thrown negligently over the arm. The lieutenant astride on his chair, a glowing cheroot

E

in the corner of his mouth, listened with a sly smile from
behind the thick volumes of smoke that escaped from
his compressed lips. The young sub-lieutenant, leaning with both elbows on the table, his head between his
hands, looked on sleepily in the torpor induced by fatigue and the gin. Almayer talked on—

"It is a great pleasure to see white faces here. I
have lived here many years in great solitude. The
Malays, you understand, are not company for a white
man; moreover they are not friendly; they do not understand our ways. Great rascals they are. I believe I
am the only white man on the east coast that is a settled resident. We get visitors from Macassar or Singapore sometimes—traders, agents, or explorers, but they
are rare. There was a scientific explorer here a year or
more ago. He lived in my house: drank from morning
to night. He lived joyously for a few months, and
when the liquor he brought with him was gone he returned to Batavia with a report on the mineral wealth
of the interior. Ha, ha, ha! Good, is it not?"

He ceased abruptly and looked at his guests with a
meaningless stare. While they laughed he was reciting
to himself the old story: "Dain dead, all my plans destroyed. This is the end of all hope and of all things."
His heart sank within him. He felt a kind of deadly
sickness.

"Very good. Capital!" exclaimed both officers.

Almayer came out of his despondency with another
burst of talk.

"Eh! what about the dinner? You have got a cook
with you. That's all right. There is a cooking shed
in the other courtyard. I can give you a goose. Look
at my geese—the only geese on the east coast—perhaps on the whole island. Is that your cook? Very
good. Here, Ali, show this Chinaman the cooking place

and tell Mem Almayer to let him have room there.   My wife, gentlemen, does not come out; my daughter may. Meantime have some more drink.   It is a hot day."

The lieutenant took the cigar out of his mouth, looked at the ash critically, shook it off and turned towards Almayer.

"We have a rather unpleasant business with you," he said.

"I am sorry," returned Almayer.   "It can be nothing very serious, surely."

"If you think an attempt to blow up forty men at least, not a serious matter you will not find many people of your opinion," retorted the officer sharply.

"Blow up! What? I know nothing about it," exclaimed Almayer. "Who did that, or tried to do it?"

"A man with whom you had some dealings," answered the lieutenant. "He passed here under the name of Dain Maroola. You sold him the gunpowder he had in that brig we captured."

"How did you hear about the brig?" asked Almayer. "I know nothing about the powder he may have had."

"An Arab trader of this place has sent the information about your goings on here to Batavia, a couple of months ago," said the officer. "We were waiting for the brig outside, but he slipped past us at the mouth of the river, and we had to chase the fellow to the southward. When he sighted us he ran inside the reefs and put the brig ashore. The crew escaped in boats before we could take possession. As our boats neared the craft it blew up with a tremendous explosion; one of the boats being too near got swamped. Two men drowned —that is the result of your speculation, Mr. Almayer. Now we want this Dain. We have good grounds to suppose he is hiding in Sambir. Do you know where he is? You had better put yourself right with the authorities as much as possible by being perfectly frank with me. Where is this Dain?"

Almayer got up and walked towards the balustrade of the verandah. He seemed not to be thinking of the officer's question. He looked at the body laying straight and rigid under its white cover on which the sun, declining amongst the clouds to the westward, threw a pale tinge of red. The lieutenant waited for the answer, taking quick pulls at his half-extinguished cigar. Behind them Ali moved noiselessly laying the table, ranging solemnly the ill-assorted and shabby crockery, the tin spoons, the forks with broken prongs, and the knives with saw-like blades and loose handles. He had almost forgotten how to prepare the table for white men. He felt aggrieved; Mem Nina would not help him. He stepped back to look at his work admiringly, feeling very proud. This must be right; and if the master afterwards is angry and swears, then so much the worse for Mem Nina. Why did she not help? He left the verandah to fetch the dinner.

"Well, Mr. Almayer, will you answer my question as frankly as it is put to you?" asked the lieutenant, after a long silence.

Almayer turned round and looked at his interlocutor steadily. "If you catch this Dain what will you do with him?" he asked.

The officer's face flushed. "This is not an answer," he said, annoyed.

"And what will you do with me?" went on Almayer, not heeding the interruption.

"Are you inclined to bargain?" growled the other. "It would be bad policy, I assure you. At present I have no orders about your person, but we expected your assistance in catching this Malay."

"Ah!" interrupted Almayer, "just so: you can do

nothing without me, and I, knowing the man well, am to help you in finding him."

"This is exactly what we expect," assented the officer. "You have broken the law, Mr. Almayer, and you ought to make amends."

"And save myself?"

"Well, in a sense yes. Your head is not in any danger," said the lieutenant, with a short laugh.

"Very well," said Almayer, with decision, "I shall deliver the man up to you."

Both officers rose to their feet quickly, and looked for their side-arms which they had unbuckled. Almayer laughed harshly.

"Steady, gentlemen!" he exclaimed. "In my own time and in my own way. After dinner, gentlemen, you shall have him."

"This is preposterous," urged the lieutenant. "Mr. Almayer, this is no joking matter. The man is a criminal. He deserves to hang. While we dine he may escape; the rumour of our arrival——"

Almayer walked towards the table. "I give you my word of honour, gentlemen, that he shall not escape; I have him safe enough."

"The arrest should be effected before dark," remarked the young sub.

"I shall hold you responsible for any failure. We are ready, but can do nothing just now without you," added the senior, with evident annoyance.

Almayer made a gesture of assent. "On my word of honour," he repeated vaguely. "And now let us dine," he added briskly.

Nina came through the doorway and stood for a moment holding the curtain aside for Ali and the old Malay woman bearing the dishes; then she moved towards the three men by the table.

"Allow me," said Almayer, pompously. "This is my daughter. Nina, these gentlemen, officers of the frigate outside, have done me the honour to accept my hospitality."

Nina answered the low bows of the two officers by a slow inclination of the head and took her place at the table opposite her father. All sat down. The coxswain of the steam launch came up carrying some bottles of wine.

"You will allow me to have this put upon the table?" said the lieutenant to Almayer.

"What! Wine! You are very kind. Certainly. I have none myself. Times are very hard."

The last words of his reply were spoken by Almayer in a faltering voice. The thought that Dain was dead recurred to him vividly again, and he felt as if an invisible hand was gripping his throat. He reached for the gin bottle while they were uncorking the wine and swallowed a big gulp. The lieutenant, who was speaking to Nina, gave him a quick glance. The young sub began to recover from the astonishment and confusion caused by Nina's unexpected appearance and great beauty. "She was very beautiful and imposing," he reflected, "but after all a half-caste girl." This thought caused him to pluck up heart and look at Nina sideways. Nina, with composed face, was answering in a low, even voice the elder officer's polite questions as to the country and her mode of life. Almayer pushed his plate away and drank his guest's wine in gloomy silence.

CHAPTER NINE

"CAN I believe what you tell me? It is like a tale for men that listen only half awake by the camp fire, and it seems to have run off a woman's tongue."

"Who is there here for me to deceive, O Rajah?" answered Babalatchi. "Without you I am nothing. All I have told you I believe to be true. I have been safe for many years in the hollow of your hand. This is no time to harbour suspicions. The danger is very great. We should advise and act at once, before the sun sets."

"Right. Right," muttered Lakamba, pensively.

They had been sitting for the last hour together in the audience chamber of the Rajah's house, for Babalatchi, as soon as he had witnessed the landing of the Dutch officers, had crossed the river to report to his master the events of the morning, and to confer with him upon the line of conduct to pursue in the face of altered circumstances. They were both puzzled and frightened by the unexpected turn the events had taken. The Rajah, sitting crosslegged on his chair, looked fixedly at the floor; Babalatchi was squatting close by in an attitude of deep dejection.

"And where did you say he is hiding now?" asked Lakamba, breaking at last the silence full of gloomy forebodings in which they both had been lost for a long while.

"In Bulangi's clearing—the furthest one, away from the house. They went there that very night. The white man's daughter took him there. She told me so

herself, speaking to me openly, for she is half white and
has no decency.   She said she was waiting for him while
he was here; then, after a long time, he came out of the
darkness and fell at her feet exhausted.   He lay like
one dead, but she brought him back to life in her arms,
and made him breathe again with her own breath.
That is what she said, speaking to my face, as I am
speaking now to you, Rajah.   She is like a white
woman and knows no shame."

He paused, deeply shocked.   Lakamba nodded his
head.   "Well, and then?" he asked.

"They called the old woman," went on Babalatchi,
"and he told them all—about the brig, and how he tried
to kill many men.   He knew the Orang Blanda were
very near, although he had said nothing to us about
that; he knew his great danger.   He thought he had
killed many, but there were only two dead, as I have
heard from the men of the sea that came in the warship's
boats."

"And the other man, he that was found in the river?"
interrupted Lakamba.

"That was one of his boatmen.   When his canoe
was overturned by the logs those two swam together,
but the other man must have been hurt.   Dain swam,
holding him up.   He left him in the bushes when he
went up to the house.   When they all came down his
heart had ceased to beat; then the old woman spoke;
Dain thought it was good.   He took off his anklet and
broke it, twisting it round the man's foot.   His ring he
put on that slave's hand.   He took off his sarong and
clothed that thing that wanted no clothes, the two
women holding it up meanwhile, their intent being to
deceive all eyes and to mislead the minds in the settlement, so that they could swear to the thing that was
not, and that there could be no treachery when the

white men came. Then Dain and the white woman departed to call up Bulangi and find a hiding-place. The old woman remained by the body."

"Hai!" exclaimed Lakamba. "She has wisdom."

"Yes, she has a Devil of her own to whisper counsel in her ear," assented Babalatchi. "She dragged the body with great toil to the point where many logs were stranded. All these things were done in the darkness after the storm had passed away. Then she waited. At the first sign of daylight she battered the face of the dead with a heavy stone, and she pushed him amongst the logs. She remained near, watching. At sunrise Mahmat Banjer came and found him. They all believed; I myself was deceived, but not for long. The white man believed, and, grieving, fled to his house. When we were alone, I, having doubts, spoke to the woman, and she, fearing my anger and your might, told me all, asking for help in saving Dain."

"He must not fall into the hands of the Orang Blanda," said Lakamba; "but let him die, if the thing can be done quietly."

"It cannot, Tuan! Remember there is that woman who, being half white, is ungovernable, and would raise a great outcry. Also the officers are here. They are angry enough already. Dain must escape; he must go. We must help him now for our own safety."

"Are the officers very angry?" inquired Lakamba, with interest.

"They are. The principal chief used strong words when speaking to me—to me when I salaamed in your name. I do not think," added Babalatchi, after a short pause and looking very worried—"I do not think I saw a white chief so angry before. He said we were careless or even worse. He told me he would speak to the Rajah, and that I was of no account."

*E

"Speak to the Rajah!" repeated Lakamba, thoughtfully. "Listen, Babalatchi: I am sick, and shall withdraw; you cross over and tell the white men."

"Yes," said Babalatchi, "I am going over at once; and as to Dain?"

"You get him away as you can best. This is a great trouble in my heart," sighed Lakamba.

Babalatchi got up, and, going close to his master, spoke earnestly.

"There is one of our praus at the southern mouth of the river. The Dutch warship is to the northward watching the main entrance. I shall send Dain off to-night in a canoe, by the hidden channels, on board the prau. His father is a great prince, and shall hear of our generosity. Let the prau take him to Ampanam. Your glory shall be great, and your reward in powerful friendship. Almayer will no doubt deliver the dead body as Dain's to the officers, and the foolish white men shall say, 'This is very good; let there be peace.' And the trouble shall be removed from your heart, Rajah."

"True! true!" said Lakamba.

"And, this being accomplished by me who am your slave, you shall reward with a generous hand. That I know! The white man is grieving for the lost treasure, in the manner of white men who thirst after dollars. Now, when all other things are in order, we shall perhaps obtain the treasure from the white man. Dain must escape, and Almayer must live."

"Now go, Babalatchi, go!" said Lakamba, getting off his chair. "I am very sick, and want medicine. Tell the white chief so."

But Babalatchi was not to be got rid of in this summary manner. He knew that his master, after the manner of the great, liked to shift the burden of toil and danger on to his servants' shoulders, but in the

difficult straits in which they were now the Rajah must
play his part. He may be very sick for the white men,
for all the world if he liked, as long as he would take
upon himself the execution of part at least of Babalatchi's carefully thought-of plan. Babalatchi wanted a
big canoe manned by twelve men to be sent out after
dark towards Bulangi's clearing. Dain may have to be
overpowered. A man in love cannot be expected to
see clearly the path of safety if it leads him away from
the object of his affections, argued Babalatchi, and in
that case they would have to use force in order to make
him go. Would the Rajah see that trusty men manned
the canoe? The thing must be done secretly. Perhaps
the Rajah would come himself, so as to bring all the
weight of his authority to bear upon Dain if he should
prove obstinate and refuse to leave his hiding-place.
The Rajah would not commit himself to a definite
promise, and anxiously pressed Babalatchi to go, being
afraid of the white men paying him an unexpected visit.
The aged statesman reluctantly took his leave and went
into the courtyard.

Before going down to his boat Babalatchi stopped for
a while in the big open space where the thick-leaved
trees put black patches of shadow which seemed to
float on a flood of smooth, intense light that rolled up
to the houses and down to the stockade and over the
river, where it broke and sparkled in thousands of glittering wavelets, like a band woven of azure and gold
edged with the brilliant green of the forests guarding
both banks of the Pantai. In the perfect calm before
the coming of the afternoon breeze the irregularly
jagged line of tree-tops stood unchanging, as if traced
by an unsteady hand on the clear blue of the hot sky.
In the space sheltered by the high palisades there lingered the smell of decaying blossoms from the surround-

ing forest, a taint of drying fish; with now and then a whiff of acrid smoke from the cooking fires when it eddied down from under the leafy boughs and clung lazily about the burnt-up grass.

As Babalatchi looked up at the flagstaff overtopping a group of low trees in the middle of the courtyard the tricolour flag of the Netherlands stirred slightly for the first time since it had been hoisted that morning on the arrival of the man-of-war boats. With a faint rustle of trees the breeze came down in light puffs, playing capriciously for a time with this emblem of Lakamba's power, that was also the mark of his servitude; then the breeze freshened in a sharp gust of wind, and the flag flew out straight and steady above the trees. A dark shadow ran along the river, rolling over and covering up the sparkle of declining sunlight. A big white cloud sailed slowly across the darkening sky, and hung to the westward as if waiting for the sun to join it there. Men and things shook off the torpor of the hot afternoon and stirred into life under the first breath of the sea breeze.

Babalatchi hurried down to the water-gate; yet before he passed through it he paused to look round the courtyard, with its light and shade, with its cheery fires, with the groups of Lakamba's soldiers and retainers scattered about. His own house stood amongst the other buildings in that enclosure, and the statesman of Sambir asked himself with a sinking heart when and how would it be given him to return to that house. He had to deal with a man more dangerous than any wild beast of his experience: a proud man, a man wilful after the manner of princes, a man in love. And he was going forth to speak to that man words of cold and worldly wisdom. Could anything be more appalling? What if that man should take umbrage at some fancied

slight to his honour or disregard of his affections and
suddenly "amok"? The wise adviser would be the
first victim, no doubt, and death would be his reward.
And underlying the horror of this situation there was
the danger of those meddlesome fools, the white men.
A vision of comfortless exile in far-off Madura rose up
before Babalatchi. Wouldn't that be worse than death
itself? And there was that half-white woman with
threatening eyes. How could he tell what an incomprehensible creature of that sort would or would not do?
She knew so much that she made the killing of Dain an
impossibility. That much was certain. And yet the
sharp, rough-edged kriss is a good and discreet friend,
thought Babalatchi, as he examined his own lovingly,
and put it back in the sheath, with a sigh of regret,
before unfastening his canoe. As he cast off the painter,
pushed out into the stream, and took up his paddle, he
realized vividly how unsatisfactory it was to have
women mixed up in state affairs. Young women, of
course. For Mrs. Almayer's mature wisdom, and for
the easy aptitude in intrigue that comes with years to
the feminine mind, he felt the most sincere respect.

He paddled leisurely, letting the canoe drift down as
he crossed towards the point. The sun was high yet,
and nothing pressed. His work would commence only
with the coming of darkness. Avoiding the Lingard
jetty, he rounded the point, and paddled up the creek
at the back of Almayer's house. There were many
canoes lying there, their noses all drawn together,
fastened all to the same stake. Babalatchi pushed his
little craft in amongst them and stepped on shore. On
the other side of the ditch something moved in the
grass.

"Who's that hiding?" hailed Babalatchi. "Come
out and speak to me."

Nobody answered. Babalatchi crossed over, passing from boat to boat, and poked his staff viciously in the suspicious place. Taminah jumped up with a cry.

"What are you doing here?" he asked, surprised. "I have nearly stepped on your tray. Am I a Dyak that you should hide at my sight?"

"I was weary, and—I slept," whispered Taminah, confusedly.

"You slept! You have not sold anything to-day, and you will be beaten when you return home," said Babalatchi.

Taminah stood before him abashed and silent. Babalatchi looked her over carefully with great satisfaction. Decidedly he would offer fifty dollars more to that thief Bulangi. The girl pleased him.

"Now you go home. It is late," he said sharply. "Tell Bulangi that I shall be near his house before the night is half over, and that I want him to make all things ready for a long journey. You understand? A long journey to the southward. Tell him that before sunset, and do not forget my words."

Taminah made a gesture of assent, and watched Babalatchi recross the ditch and disappear through the bushes bordering Almayer's compound. She moved a little further off the creek and sank in the grass again, lying down on her face, shivering in dry-eyed misery.

Babalatchi walked straight towards the cooking-shed looking for Mrs. Almayer. - The courtyard was in a great uproar. A strange Chinaman had possession of the kitchen fire and was noisily demanding another saucepan. He hurled objurgations, in the Canton dialect and bad Malay, against the group of slave-girls standing a little way off, half frightened, half amused, at his violence. From the camping fires round which the seamen of the frigate were sitting came words of encouragement, mingled with laughter and jeering. In the midst of this noise and confusion Babalatchi met Ali, an empty dish in his hand.

"Where are the white men?" asked Babalatchi.

"They are eating in the front verandah," answered Ali. "Do not stop me, Tuan. I am giving the white men their food and am busy."

"Where's Mem Almayer?"

"Inside the passage. She is listening to the talk."

Ali grinned and passed on; Babalatchi ascended the plankway to the rear verandah, and beckoning out Mrs. Almayer, engaged her in earnest conversation. Through the long passage, closed at the further end by the red curtain, they could hear from time to time Almayer's voice mingling in conversation with an abrupt loudness that made Mrs. Almayer look significantly at Babalatchi.

"Listen," she said. "He has drunk much."

"He has," whispered Babalatchi. "He will sleep heavily to-night."

Mrs. Almayer looked doubtful.

"Sometimes the devil of strong gin makes him keep awake, and he walks up and down the verandah all night, cursing; then we stand afar off," explained Mrs. Almayer, with the fuller knowledge born of twenty odd years of married life.

"But then he does not hear, nor understand, and his hand, of course, has no strength. We do not want him to hear to-night."

"No," assented Mrs. Almayer, energetically, but in a cautiously subdued voice. "If he hears he will kill."

Babalatchi looked incredulous.

"Hai Tuan, you may believe me. Have I not lived many years with that man? Have I not seen death in that man's eyes more than once when I was younger and he guessed at many things. Had he been a man of my own people I would not have seen such a look twice; but he——"

With a contemptuous gesture she seemed to fling unutterable scorn on Almayer's weak-minded aversion to sudden bloodshed.

"If he has the wish but not the strength, then what do we fear?" asked Babalatchi, after a short silence during which they both listened to Almayer's loud talk till it subsided into the murmur of general conversation. "What do we fear?" repeated Babalatchi again.

"To keep the daughter whom he loves he would strike into your heart and mine without hesitation," said Mrs. Almayer. "When the girl is gone he will be like the devil unchained. Then you and I had better beware."

"I am an old man and fear not death," answered Babalatchi, with a mendacious assumption of indifference. "But what will you do?"

"I am an old woman, and wish to live," retorted Mrs. Almayer. "She is my daughter also. I shall seek safety at the feet of our Rajah, speaking in the name of the past when we both were young, and he——"

Babalatchi raised his hand.

"Enough. You shall be protected," he said soothingly.

Again the sound of Almayer's voice was heard, and again interrupting their talk, they listened to the confused but loud utterance coming in bursts of unequal strength, with unexpected pauses and noisy repetitions that made some words and sentences fall clear and distinct on their ears out of the meaningless jumble of excited shoutings emphasized by the thumping of Almayer's fist upon the table. On the short intervals of silence, the high complaining note of tumblers, standing close together and vibrating to the shock, lingered, growing fainter, till it leapt up again into tumultuous ringing, when a new idea started a new rush of words and brought down the heavy hand again. At last the quarrelsome shouting ceased, and the thin plaint of disturbed glass died away into reluctant quietude.

Babalatchi and Mrs. Almayer had listened curiously, their bodies bent and their ears turned towards the passage. At every louder shout they nodded at each other with a ridiculous affectation of scandalized propriety, and they remained in the same attitude for some time after the noise had ceased.

"This is the devil of gin," whispered Mrs. Almayer. "Yes; he talks like that sometimes when there is nobody to hear him."

"What does he say?" inquired Babalatchi, eagerly. "You ought to understand."

"I have forgotten their talk. A little I understood. He spoke without any respect of the white ruler in Batavia, and of protection, and said he had been wronged; he said that several times. More I did not understand. Listen! Again he speaks!"

"Tse! tse! tse!" clicked Babalatchi, trying to appear shocked, but with a joyous twinkle of his solitary eye. "There will be great trouble between those white men. I will go round now and see. You tell your daughter that there is a sudden and a long journey before her, with much glory and splendour at the end. And tell her that Dain must go, or he must die, and that he will not go alone."

"No, he will not go alone," slowly repeated Mrs. Almayer, with a thoughtful air, as she crept into the passage after seeing Babalatchi disappear round the corner of the house.

The statesman of Sambir, under the impulse of vivid curiosity, made his way quickly to the front of the house, but once there he moved slowly and cautiously as he crept step by step up the stairs of the verandah. On the highest step he sat down quietly, his feet on the steps below, ready for flight should his presence prove unwelcome. He felt pretty safe so. The table stood nearly endways to him, and he saw Almayer's back; at Nina he looked full face, and had a side view of both officers; but of the four persons sitting at the table only Nina and the younger officer noticed his noiseless arrival. The momentary dropping of Nina's eyelids acknowledged Babalatchi's presence; she then spoke at once to the young sub, who turned towards her with attentive alacrity, but her gaze was fastened steadily on her father's face while Almayer was speaking uproariously.

". . . disloyalty and unscrupulousness! What have you ever done to make me loyal? You have no grip on this country. I had to take care of myself, and when I asked for protection I was met with threats and contempt, and had Arab slander thrown in my face. I! a white man!"

"Don't be violent, Almayer," remonstrated the lieutenant; "I have heard all this already."

"Then why do you talk to me about scruples? I wanted money, and I gave powder in exchange. How could I know that some of your wretched men were going to be blown up? Scruples! Pah!"

He groped unsteadily amongst the bottles, trying one after another, grumbling to himself the while. "No more wine," he muttered discontentedly.

"You have had enough, Almayer," said the lieutenant, as he lighted a cigar. "Is it not time to deliver to us your prisoner? I take it you have that Dain Maroola stowed away safely somewhere. Still we had better

get that business over, and then we shall have more
drink. Come! don't look at me like this."

. Almayer was staring with stony eyes, his trembling
fingers fumbling about his throat.

"Gold," he said with difficulty. "Hem! A hand
on the windpipe, you know. Sure you will excuse.
I wanted to say—a little gold for a little powder.
What's that?"

"I know, I know," said the lieutenant soothingly.

"No! You don't know. Not one of you knows!"
shouted Almayer. "The government is a fool, I tell
you. Heaps of gold. I am the man that knows; I and
another one. But he won't speak. He is——"

He checked himself with a feeble smile, and, making
an unsuccessful attempt to pat the officer on the
shoulder, knocked over a couple of empty bottles.

"Personally you are a fine fellow," he said very distinctly, in a patronizing manner. His head nodded
drowsily as he sat muttering to himself.

The two officers looked at each other helplessly.

"This won't do," said the lieutenant, addressing his
junior. "Have the men mustered in the compound
here. I must get some sense out of him. Hi! Almayer! Wake up, man. Redeem your word. You
gave your word. You gave your word of honour, you
know."

Almayer shook off the officer's hand with impatience,
but his ill-humour vanished at once, and he looked up,
putting his forefinger to the side of his nose.

"You are very young; there is time for all things,"
he said, with an air of great sagacity.

The lieutenant turned towards Nina, who, leaning
back in her chair, watched her father steadily.

"Really I am very much distressed by all this for
your sake," he exclaimed. "I do not know," he went

on, speaking with some embarrassment, "whether I
have any right to ask you anything, unless, perhaps,
to withdraw from this painful scene, but I feel that I
must—for your father's good—suggest that you should
—I mean if you have any influence over him you ought
to exert it now to make him keep the promise he gave me
before he—before he got into this state."

He observed with discouragement that she seemed not
to take any notice of what he said, sitting still with half-
closed eyes.

"I trust——" he began again.

"What is the promise you speak of?" abruptly asked
Nina, leaving her seat and moving towards her father.

"Nothing that is not just and proper. He promised
to deliver to us a man who in time of profound peace
took the lives of innocent men to escape the punishment
he deserved for breaking the law. He planned his
mischief on a large scale. It is not his fault if it failed,
partially. Of course you have heard of Dain Maroola.
Your father secured him, I understand. We know he
escaped up this river. Perhaps you——"

"And he killed white men!" interrupted Nina.

"I regret to say they were white. Yes, two white
men lost their lives through that scoundrel's freak."

"Two only!" exclaimed Nina.

The officer looked at her in amazement.

"Why! why! You——" he stammered, confused.

"There might have been more," interrupted Nina.
"And when you get this—this scoundrel, will you go?"

The lieutenant, still speechless, bowed his assent.

"Then I would get him for you if I had to seek him
in a burning fire," she burst out with intense energy.
"I hate the sight of your white faces. I hate the sound
of your gentle voices. That is the way you speak to
women, dropping sweet words before any pretty face.

I have heard your voices before. I hoped to live here without seeing any other white face but this," she added in a gentler tone, touching lightly her father's cheek.

Almayer ceased his mumbling and opened his eyes. He caught hold of his daughter's hand and pressed it to his face, while Nina with the other hand smoothed his rumpled grey hair, looking defiantly over her father's head at the officer, who had now regained his composure and returned her look with a cool, steady stare. Below, in front of the verandah, they could hear the tramp of seamen mustering there according to orders. The sub-lieutenant came up the steps, while Babalatchi stood up uneasily and, with finger on lip, tried to catch Nina's eye.

"You are a good girl," whispered Almayer, absently, dropping his daughter's hand.

"Father! father!" she cried, bending over him with passionate entreaty. "See those two men looking at us. Send them away. I cannot bear it any more. Send them away. Do what they want and let them go."

She caught sight of Babalatchi and ceased speaking suddenly, but her foot tapped the floor with rapid beats in a paroxysm of nervous restlessness. The two officers stood close together looking on curiously.

"What has happened? What is the matter?" whispered the younger man.

"Don't know," answered the other, under his breath. "One is furious, and the other is drunk. Not so drunk, either. Queer this. Look!"

Almayer had risen, holding on to his daughter's arm. He hesitated a moment, then he let go his hold and lurched half-way across the verandah. There he pulled himself together, and stood very straight, breathing hard and glaring round angrily.

"Are the men ready?" asked the lieutenant.

"All ready, sir."

"Now, Mr. Almayer, lead the way," said the lieutenant.

Almayer rested his eyes on him as if he saw him for the first time.

"Two men," he said thickly. The effort of speaking seemed to interfere with his equilibrium. He took a quick step to save himself from a fall, and remained swaying backwards and forwards. "Two men," he began again, speaking with difficulty. "Two white men —men in uniform—honourable men. I want to say— men of honour. Are you?"

"Come! None of that," said the officer impatiently. "Let us have that friend of yours."

"What do you think I am?" asked Almayer, fiercely.

"You are drunk, but not so drunk as not to know what you are doing. Enough of this tomfoolery," said the officer sternly, "or I will have you put under arrest in your own house."

"Arrest!" laughed Almayer, discordantly. "Ha! ha! ha! Arrest! Why, I have been trying to get out of this infernal place for twenty years, and I can't. You hear, man! I can't, and never shall! Never!"

He ended his words with a sob, and walked unsteadily down the stairs. When in the courtyard the lieutenant approached him, and took him by the arm. The sub-lieutenant and Babalatchi followed close.

"That's better, Almayer," said the officer encouragingly. "Where are you going to? There are only planks there. Here," he went on, shaking him slightly, "do we want the boats?"

"No," answered Almayer, viciously. "You want a grave."

"What? Wild again! Try to talk sense."

"Grave!" roared Almayer, struggling to get himself

free. "A hole in the ground. Don't you understand? You must be drunk. Let me go! Let go, I tell you!"

He tore away from the officer's grasp, and reeled towards the planks where the body lay under its white cover; then he turned round quickly, and faced the semicircle of interested faces. The sun was sinking rapidly, throwing long shadows of house and trees over the courtyard, but the light lingered yet on the river, where the logs went drifting past in midstream, looking very distinct and black in the pale red glow. The trunks of the trees in the forest on the east bank were lost in gloom while their highest branches swayed gently in the departing sunlight. The air felt heavy and cold in the breeze, expiring in slight puffs that came over the water.

Almayer shivered as he made an effort to speak, and again with an uncertain gesture he seemed to free his throat from the grip of an invisible hand. His blood-shot eyes wandered aimlessly from face to face.

"There!" he said at last. "Are you all there? He is a dangerous man."

He dragged at the cover with hasty violence, and the body rolled stiffly off the planks and fell at his feet in rigid helplessness.

"Cold, perfectly cold," said Almayer, looking round with a mirthless smile. "Sorry can do no better. And you can't hang him, either. As you observe, gentlemen," he added gravely, "there is no head, and hardly any neck."

The last ray of light was snatched away from the tree-tops, the river grew suddenly dark, and in the great stillness the murmur of the flowing water seemed to fill the vast expanse of grey shadow that descended upon the land.

"This is Dain," went on Almayer to the silent group

that surrounded him. "And I have kept my word.
First one hope, then another, and this is my last.
Nothing is left now. You think there is one dead man
here? Mistake, I 'sure you. I am much more dead.
Why don't you hang me?" he suggested suddenly, in a
friendly tone, addressing the lieutenant. "I assure,
assure you it would be a mat—matter of form altog—
altogether."

These last words he muttered to himself, and walked
zigzagging towards his house. "Get out!" he thundered at Ali, who was approaching timidly with offers
of assistance. From afar, scared groups of men and
women watched his devious progress. He dragged
himself up the stairs by the banister, and managed to
reach a chair into which he fell heavily. He sat for
awhile panting with exertion and anger, and looking
round vaguely for Nina; then making a threatening
gesture towards the compound, where he had heard
Babalatchi's voice, he overturned the table with his
foot in a great crash of smashed crockery. He muttered yet menacingly to himself, then his head fell on his
breast, his eyes closed, and with a deep sigh he fell
asleep.

That night—for the first time in its history—the
peaceful and flourishing settlement of Sambir saw the
lights shining about "Almayer's Folly." These were
the lanterns of the boats hung up by the seamen under
the verandah where the two officers were holding a court
of inquiry into the truth of the story related to them by
Babalatchi. Babalatchi had regained all his importance. He was eloquent and persuasive, calling Heaven
and Earth to witness the truth of his statements. There
were also other witnesses. Mahmat Banjer and a good
many others underwent a close examination that dragged its weary length far into the evening. A messenger

was sent for Abdulla, who excused himself from coming
on the score of his venerable age, but sent Reshid.
Mahmat had to produce the bangle, and saw with rage
and mortification the lieutenant put it in his pocket
as one of the proofs of Dain's death, to be sent in with
the official report of the mission. Babalatchi's ring
was also impounded for the same purpose, but the experienced statesman was resigned to that loss from the
very beginning. He did not mind as long as he was sure
that the white men believed. He put that question to
himself earnestly as he left, one of the last, when the
proceedings came to a close. He was not certain.
Still, if they believed only for a night, he would put
Dain beyond their reach and feel safe himself. He
walked away fast, looking from time to time over his
shoulder in the fear of being followed, but he saw and
heard nothing.

"Ten o'clock," said the lieutenant, looking at his
watch and yawning. "I shall hear some of the captain's complimentary remarks when we get back.
Miserable business, this."

"Do you think all this is true?" asked the younger
man.

"True! It is just possible. But if it isn't true what
can we do? If we had a dozen boats we could patrol
the creeks; and that wouldn't be much good. That
drunken madman was right; we haven't enough hold on
this coast. They do what they like. Are our ham-
mocks slung?"

"Yes, I told the coxswain. Strange couple over
there," said the sub, with a wave of his hand towards
Almayer's house.

"Hem! Queer, certainly. What have you been
telling her? I was attending to the father most of the
time."

"I assure you I have been perfectly civil," protested the other warmly.

"All right. Don't get excited. She objects to civility, then, from what I understand. I thought you might have been tender. You know we are on service."

"Well, of course. Never forget that. Coldly civil. That's all."

They both laughed a little, and not feeling sleepy began to pace the verandah side by side. The moon rose stealthily above the trees, and suddenly changed the river into a stream of scintillating silver. The forest came out of the black void and stood sombre and pensive over the sparkling water. The breeze died away into a breathless calm.

Seamanlike, the two officers tramped measuredly up and down without exchanging a word. The loose planks rattled rhythmically under their steps with obtrusive dry sound in the perfect silence of the night. As they were wheeling round again the younger man stood attentive.

"Did you hear that?" he asked.

"No!" said the other. "Hear what?"

"I thought I heard a cry. Ever so faint. Seemed a woman's voice. In that other house. Ah! Again! Hear it?"

"No," said the lieutenant, after listening awhile. "You young fellows always hear women's voices. If you are going to dream you had better get into your hammock. Good-night."

The moon mounted higher, and the warm shadows grew smaller and crept away as if hiding before the cold and cruel light.

CHAPTER TEN

"It has set at last," said Nina to her mother pointing towards the hills behind which the sun had sunk. "Listen, mother, I am going now to Bulangi's creek, and if I should never return——"

She interrupted herself, and something like doubt dimmed for a moment the fire of suppressed exaltation that had glowed in her eyes and had illuminated the serene impassiveness of her features with a ray of eager life during all that long day of excitement—the day of joy and anxiety, of hope and terror, of vague grief and indistinct delight. While the sun shone with that dazzling light in which her love was born and grew till it possessed her whole being, she was kept firm in her unwavering resolve by the mysterious whisperings of desire which filled her heart with impatient longing for the darkness that would mean the end of danger and strife, the beginning of happiness, the fulfilling of love, the completeness of life. It had set at last! The short tropical twilight went out before she could draw the long breath of relief; and now the sudden darkness seemed to be full of menacing voices calling upon her to rush headlong into the unknown; to be true to her own impulses to give herself up to the passion she had evoked and shared. He was waiting! In the solitude of the secluded clearing, in the vast silence of the forest he was waiting alone, a fugitive in fear of his life. Indifferent to his danger he was waiting for her. It was for her only that he had come; and now as the time approached when he should have his reward, she asked her-

self with dismay what meant that chilling doubt of her
own will and of her own desire? With an effort she
shook off the fear of the passing weakness. He should
have his reward. Her woman's love and her woman's
honour overcame the faltering distrust of that unknown future waiting for her in the darkness of the
river.

"No, you will not return," muttered Mrs. Almayer,
prophetically. "Without you he will not go, and if he
remains here——" She waved her hand towards the
lights of "Almayer's Folly," and the unfinished sentence
died out in a threatening murmur.

The two women had met behind the house, and now
were walking slowly together towards the creek where
all the canoes were moored. Arrived at the fringe of
bushes they stopped by a common impulse, and Mrs.
Almayer, laying her hand on her daughter's arm, tried
in vain to look close into the girl's averted face. When
she attempted to speak her first words were lost in a
stifled sob that sounded strangely coming from that
woman who, of all human passions, seemed to know only
those of anger and hate.

"You are going away to be a great Ranee," she said
at last, in a voice that was steady enough now, "and
if you be wise you shall have much power that will endure many days, and even last into your old age. What
have I been? A slave all my life, and I have cooked
rice for a man who had no courage and no wisdom.
Hai! I! even I, was given in gift by a chief and a warrior to a man that was neither. Hai! Hai!"

She wailed to herself softly, lamenting the lost possibilities of murder and mischief that could have fallen
to her lot had she been mated with a congenial spirit.
Nina bent down over Mrs. Almayer's slight form and
scanned attentively, under the stars that had rushed out

on the black sky and now hung breathless over that
strange parting, her mother's shrivelled features, and
looked close into the sunken eyes that could see into
her own dark future by the light of a long and a painful
experience. Again she felt herself fascinated, as of old,
by her mother's exalted mood and by the oracular certainty of expression which, together with her fits of
violence, had contributed not a little to the reputation
for witchcraft she enjoyed in the settlement.

"I was a slave, and you shall be a queen," went on
Mrs. Almayer, looking straight before her; "but remember men's strength and their weakness. Tremble
before his anger, so that he may see your fear in the
light of day; but in your heart you may laugh, for after
sunset he is your slave."

"A slave! He! The master of life! You do not
know him, mother."

Mrs. Almayer condescended to laugh contemptuously.

"You speak like a fool of a white woman," she exclaimed. "What do you know of men's anger and of
men's love? Have you watched the sleep of men weary
of dealing death? Have you felt about you the strong
arm that could drive a kriss keep into a beating heart?
Yah! you are a white woman, and ought to pray to a
woman god!"

"Why do you say this? I have listened to your
words so long that I have forgotten my old life. If I
was white would I stand here, ready to go? Mother,
I shall return to the house and look once more at my
father's face."

"No!" said Mrs. Almayer, violently. "No, he
sleeps now the sleep of gin; and if you went back he
might awake and see you. No, he shall never see you.

When the terrible old man took you away from me when you were little, you remember——"

"It was such a long time ago," murmured Nina.

"I remember," went on Mrs. Almayer, fiercely. "I wanted to look at your face again. He said no! I heard you cry and jumped into the river. You were his daughter then; you are my daughter now. Never shall you go back to that house; you shall never cross this courtyard again. No! no!"

Her voice rose almost to a shout. On the other side of the creek there was a rustle in the long grass. The two women heard it, and listened for a while in startled silence.

"I shall go," said Nina, in a cautious but intense whisper. "What is your hate or your revenge to me?"

She moved towards the house, Mrs. Almayer clinging to her and trying to pull her back.

"Stop, you shall not go!" she gasped.

Nina pushed away her mother impatiently and gathered up her skirts for a quick run, but Mrs. Almayer ran forward and turned round, facing her daughter with outstretched arms.

"If you move another step," she exclaimed, breathing quickly, "I shall cry out. Do you see those lights in the big house? There sit two white men, angry because they cannot have the blood of the man you love. And in those dark houses," she continued, more calmly as she pointed towards the settlement, "my voice could wake up men that would lead the Orang Blanda soldiers to him who is waiting—for you."

She could not see her daughter's face, but the white figure before her stood silent and irresolute in the darkness. Mrs. Almayer pursued her advantage.

"Give up your old life! Forget!" she said in entreating tones. "Forget that you ever looked at a white face; forget their words; forget their thoughts. They speak lies.   And they think lies because they despise us that are better than they are, but not so strong. Forget their friendship and their contempt; forget their many gods.   Girl, why do you want to remember the past when there is a warrior and a chief ready to give many lives—his own life—for one of your smiles?"

While she spoke she pushed gently her daughter towards the canoes, hiding her own fear, anxiety, and doubt under the flood of passionate words that left Nina no time to think and no opportunity to protest, even if she had wished it.   But she did not wish it now. At the bottom of that passing desire to look again at her father's face there was no strong affection.   She felt no scruples and no remorse at leaving suddenly that man whose sentiment towards herself she could not understand, she could not even see.   There was only an instinctive clinging to old life, to old habits, to old faces; that fear of finality which lurks in every human breast and prevents so many heroisms and so many crimes.   For years she had stood between her mother and her father, the one so strong in her weakness, the other so weak where he could have been strong.   Between those two beings so dissimilar, so antagonistic, she stood with mute heart wondering and angry at the fact of her own existence.   It seemed so unreasonable, so humiliating to be flung there in that settlement and to see the days rush by into the past, without a hope, a desire, or an aim that would justify the life she had to endure in ever-growing weariness.   `She had little belief and no sympathy for her father's dreams; but the savage ravings of her mother chanced to strike a responsive chord, deep down somewhere in her despairing heart; and she dreamed dreams of her own with the persistent absorption of a captive thinking of liberty within the walls of his prison cell. With the coming of Dain she found the road to freedom by obeying the voice of the new-born impulses, and with surprised joy she thought she could read in his eyes the answer to all the questionings of her heart. She understood now the reason and the aim of life; and in the triumphant unveiling of that mystery she threw away disdainfully her past with its sad thoughts, its bitter feelings and its faint affections, now withered and dead in contact with her fierce passion.

Mrs. Almayer unmoored Nina's own canoe and, straightening herself painfully, stood, painter in hand, looking at her daughter.

"Quick," she said; "get away before the moon rises, while the river is dark. I am afraid of Abdulla's slaves. The wretches prowl in the night often, and might see and follow you. There are two paddles in the canoe."

Nina approached her mother and touched lightly with her lips the wrinkled forehead. Mrs. Almayer snorted contemptuously in protest against that tenderness which she, nevertheless, feared could be contagious.

"Shall I ever see you again, mother?"- murmured Nina.

"No," said Mrs. Almayer, after a short silence. "Why should you return here where it is my fate to die? You will live far away in splendour and might. When I hear of white men driven from the islands, then I shall know that you are alive, and that you remember my words."

"I shall always remember," returned Nina, earnestly; "but where is my power, and what can I do?"

"Do not let him look too long in your eyes, nor lay his head on your knees without reminding him that men should fight before they rest. And if he lingers, give him his kriss yourself and bid him go, as the wife of a

mighty prince should do when the enemies are near.
Let him slay the white men that come to us to trade,
with prayers on their lips and loaded guns in their
hands. Ah"—she ended with a sigh—"they are on
every sea, and on every shore; and they are very
many!"

She swung the bow of the canoe towards the river, but
did not let go the gunwale, keeping her hand on it in
irresolute thoughtfulness. Nina put the point of the
paddle against the bank, ready to shove off into the
stream.

"What is it, mother?" she asked, in a low voice.
"Do you hear anything?"

"No," said Mrs. Almayer, absently. "Listen, Nina,"
she continued, abruptly, after a slight pause, "in after
years there will be other women——"

A stifled cry in the boat interrupted her, and the
paddle rattled in the canoe as it slipped from Nina's
hands, which she put out in a protesting gesture. Mrs.
Almayer fell on her knees on the bank and leaned over
the gunwale so as to bring her own face close to her
daughter's.

"There will be other women," she repeated firmly;
"I tell you that, because you are half white, and may
forget that he is a great chief, and that such things
must be. Hide your anger, and do not let him see
on your face the pain that will eat your heart. Meet
him with joy in your eyes and wisdom on your lips, for
to you he will turn in sadness or in doubt. As long as
he looks upon many women your power will last, but
should there be one, one only with whom he seems to
forget you, then——"

"I could not live," exclaimed Nina, covering her
face with both her hands. "Do not speak so, mother;
it could not be."

F

"Then," went on Mrs. Almayer, steadily, "to that woman, Nina, show no mercy."

She moved the canoe down towards the stream by the gunwale, and gripped it with both her hands, the bow pointing into the river.

"Are you crying?" she asked sternly of her daughter, who sat still with covered face. "Arise, and take your paddle, for he has waited long enough. And remember, Nina, no mercy; and if you must strike, strike with a steady hand."

She put out all her strength, and swinging her body over the water, shot the light craft far into the stream. When she recovered herself from the effort she tried vainly to catch a glimpse of the canoe that seemed to have dissolved suddenly into the white mist trailing over the heated waters of the Pantai. After listening for a while intently on her knees, Mrs. Almayer rose with a deep sigh, while two tears wandered slowly down her withered cheeks. She wiped them off quickly with a wisp of her grey hair as if ashamed of herself, but could not stifle another loud sigh, for her heart was heavy and she suffered much, being unused to tender emotions. This time she fancied she had heard a faint noise, like the echo of her own sigh, and she stopped, straining her ears to catch the slightest sound, and peering apprehensively towards the bushes near her.

"Who is there?" she asked, in an unsteady voice, while her imagination peopled the solitude of the riverside with ghost-like forms. "Who is there?" she repeated faintly.

There was no answer: only the voice of the river murmuring in sad monotone behind the white veil seemed to swell louder for a moment, to die away again in a soft whisper of eddies washing against the bank.

Mrs. Almayer shook her head as if in answer to her

own thoughts, and walked quickly away from the bushes, looking to the right and left watchfully. She went straight towards the cooking-shed, observing that the embers of the fire there glowed more brightly than usual, as if somebody had been adding fresh fuel to the fires during the evening. As she approached, Babalatchi, who had been squatting in the warm glow, rose and met her in the shadow outside.

"Is she gone?" asked the anxious statesman, hastily.

"Yes," answered Mrs. Almayer. "What are the white men doing? When did you leave them?"

"They are sleeping now, I think. May they never wake!" exclaimed Babalatchi, fervently. "Oh! but they are devils, and made much talk and trouble over that carcase. The chief threatened me twice with his hand, and said he would have me tied up to a tree. Tie me up to a tree! Me!" he repeated, striking his breast violently.

Mrs. Almayer laughed tauntingly.

"And you salaamed and asked for mercy. Men with arms by their side acted otherwise when I was young."

"And where are they, the men of your youth? You mad woman!" retorted Babalatchi, angrily. "Killed by the Dutch. Aha! But I shall live to deceive them. A man knows when to fight and when to tell peaceful lies. You would know that if you were not a woman."

But Mrs. Almayer did not seem to hear him. With bent body and outstretched arm she appeared to be listening to some noise behind the shed.

"There are strange sounds," she whispered, with evident alarm. "I have heard in the air the sounds of grief, as of a sigh and weeping. That was by the riverside. And now again I heard——"

"Where?" asked Babalatchi, in an altered voice. "What did you hear?"

"Close here. It was like a breath long drawn. I wish I had burnt the paper over the body before it was buried."

"Yes," assented Babalatchi. "But the white men had him thrown into a hole at once. You know he found his death on the river," he added cheerfully, "and his ghost may hail the canoes, but would leave the land alone."

Mrs. Almayer, who had been craning her neck to look round the corner of the shed, drew back her head.

"There is nobody there," she said, reassured. "Is it not time for the Rajah war-canoe to go to the clearing?"

"I have been waiting for it here, for I myself must go," explained Babalatchi. "I think I will go over and see what makes them late. When will you come? The Rajah gives you refuge."

"I shall paddle over before the break of day. I cannot leave my dollars behind," muttered Mrs. Almayer.

They separated. Babalatchi crossed the courtyard towards the creek to get his canoe, and Mrs. Almayer walked slowly to the house, ascended the plankway, and passing through the back verandah entered the passage leading to the front of the house; but before going in she turned in the doorway and looked back at the empty and silent courtyard, now lit up by the rays of the rising moon. No sooner she had disappeared, however, than a vague shape flitted out from amongst the stalks of the banana plantation, darted over the moonlit space, and fell in the darkness at the foot of the verandah. It might have been the shadow of a driving cloud, so noiseless and rapid was its passage, but for the trail of disturbed grass, whose feathery heads trembled and swayed for a long time in the moonlight before they rested motionless and gleaming, like a design of silver sprays embroidered on a sombre background.

Mrs. Almayer lighted the cocoanut lamp, and lifting cautiously the red curtain, gazed upon her husband, shading the light with her hand. Almayer, huddled up in the chair, one of his arms hanging down, the other thrown across the lower part of his face as if to ward off an invisible enemy, his legs stretched straight out, slept heavily, unconscious of the unfriendly eyes that looked upon him in disparaging criticism. At his feet lay the overturned table, amongst a wreck of crockery and broken bottles. The appearance as of traces left by a desperate struggle was accentuated by the chairs, which seemed to have been scattered violently all over the place, and now lay about the verandah with a lamentable aspect of inebriety in their helpless attitudes. Only Nina's big rocking-chair, standing black and motionless on its high runners, towered above the chaos of demoralized furniture, unflinchingly dignified and patient, waiting for its burden.

With a last scornful look towards the sleeper, Mrs. Almayer passed behind the curtain into her own room. A couple of bats, encouraged by the darkness and the peaceful state of affairs, resumed their silent and oblique gambols above Almayer's head, and for a long time the profound quiet of the house was unbroken, save for the deep breathing of the sleeping man and the faint tinkle of silver in the hands of the woman preparing for flight. In the increasing light of the moon that had risen now above the night mist, the objects on the verandah came out strongly outlined in black splashes of shadow with all the uncompromising ugliness of their disorder, and a caricature of the sleeping Almayer appeared on the dirty whitewash of the wall behind him in a grotesquely exaggerated detail of attitude and feature enlarged to a heroic size. The discontented bats departed in quest of darker places, and a lizard came out in short, nervous rushes, and, pleased with the white table-cloth, stopped on it in breathless immobility that would have suggested sudden death had it not been for the melodious call he exchanged with a less adventurous friend hiding amongst the lumber in the courtyard. Then the boards in the passage creaked, the lizard vanished, and Almayer stirred uneasily with a sigh: slowly, out of the senseless annihilation of drunken sleep, he was returning, through the land of dreams, to waking consciousness. Almayer's head rolled from shoulder to shoulder in the oppression of his dream; the heavens had descended upon him like a heavy mantle, and trailed in starred folds far under him. Stars above, stars all round him; and from the stars under his feet rose a whisper full of entreaties and tears, and sorrowful faces flitted amongst the clusters of light filling the infinite space below. How escape from the importunity of lamentable cries and from the look of staring, sad eyes in the faces which pressed round him till he gasped for breath under the crushing weight of worlds that hung over his aching shoulders? Get away! But how? If he attempted to move he would step off into nothing, and perish in the crashing fall of that universe of which he was the only support. And what were the voices saying? Urging him to move! Why? Move to destruction! Not likely! The absurdity of the thing filled him with indignation. He got a firmer foothold and stiffened his muscles in heroic resolve to carry his burden to all eternity. And ages passed in the superhuman labour, amidst the rush of circling worlds; in the plaintive murmur of sorrowful voices urging him to desist before it was too late—till the mysterious power that had laid upon him the giant task seemed at last to seek his destruction. With terror he felt an irresistible hand shaking him by the shoulder, while the chorus of voices swelled louder into an agonized prayer to go, go before it is too late. He felt himself slipping, losing his balance, as something dragged at his legs, and he fell. With a faint cry he glided out of the anguish of perishing creation into an imperfect waking that seemed to be still under the spell of his dream.

"What? What?" he murmured sleepily, without moving or opening his eyes. His head still felt heavy, and he had not the courage to raise his eyelids. In his ears there still lingered the sound of entreating whisper. —"Am I awake?—Why do I hear the voices?" he argued to himself, hazily.—"I cannot get rid of the horrible nightmare yet.—I have been very drunk.—What is that shaking me? I am dreaming yet.—I must open my eyes and be done with it. I am only half awake, it is evident."

He made an effort to shake off his stupor and saw a face close to his, glaring at him with staring eyeballs. He closed his eyes again in amazed horror and sat up straight in the chair, trembling in every limb. What was this apparition?—His own fancy, no doubt.— His nerves had been much tried the day before—and then the drink! He would not see it again if he had the courage to look.—He would look directly.—Get a little steadier first.—So.—Now.

He looked. The figure of a woman standing in the steely light, her hands stretched forth in a suppliant gesture, confronted him from the far-off end of the verandah; and in the space between him and the obstinate phantom floated the murmur of words that fell

on his ears in a jumble of torturing sentences, the
meaning of which escaped the utmost efforts of his
brain. Who spoke the Malay words? Who ran away?
Why too late—and too late for what? What meant
those words of hate and love mixed so strangely together, the ever-recurring names falling on his ears
again and again—Nina, Dain; Dain, Nina? Dain was
dead, and Nina was sleeping, unaware of the terrible
experience through which he was now passing. Was
he going to be tormented for ever, sleeping or waking,
and have no peace either night or day? What was the
meaning of this?

He shouted the last words aloud. The shadowy
woman seemed to shrink and recede a little from him
towards the doorway, and there was a shriek. Exasperated by the incomprehensible nature of his torment,
Almayer made a rush upon the apparition, which eluded
his grasp, and he brought up heavily against the wall.
Quick as lightning he turned round and pursued fiercely
the mysterious figure fleeing from him with piercing
shrieks that were like fuel to the flames of his anger.
Over the furniture, round the overturned table, and now
he had it cornered behind Nina's chair. To the left,
to the right they dodged, the chair rocking madly
between them, she sending out shriek after shriek at
every feint, and he growling meaningless curses through
his hard set teeth. "Oh! the fiendish noise that split
his head and seemed to choke his breath.—It would
kill him.—It must be stopped!" An insane desire to
crush that yelling thing induced him to cast himself
recklessly over the chair with a desperate grab, and
they came down together in a cloud of dust amongst
the splintered wood. The last shriek died out under
him in a faint gurgle, and he had secured the relief
of absolute silence.

He looked at the woman's face under him. A real woman. He knew her. By all that is wonderful! Taminah! He jumped up ashamed of his fury and stood perplexed, wiping his forehead. The girl struggled to a kneeling posture and embraced his legs in a frenzied prayer for mercy.

"Don't be afraid," he said, raising her. "I shall not hurt you. Why do you come to my house in the night? And if you had to come, why not go behind the curtain where the women sleep?"

"The place behind the curtain is empty," gasped Taminah, catching her breath between the words. "There are no women in your house any more, Tuan. I saw the old Mem go away before I tried to wake you. I did not want your women, I wanted you."

"Old Mem!" repeated Almayer. "Do you mean my wife?"

She nodded her head.

"But of my daughter you are not afraid?" said Almayer.

"Have you not heard me?" she exclaimed. "Have I not spoken for a long time when you lay there with eyes half open? She is gone too."

"I was asleep. Can you not tell when a man is sleeping and when awake?"

"Sometimes," answered Taminah in a low voice; "sometimes the spirit lingers close to a sleeping body and may hear. I spoke a long time before I touched you, and I spoke softly for fear it would depart at a sudden noise and leave you sleeping for ever. I took you by the shoulder only when you began to mutter words I could not understand. Have you not heard, then, and do you know nothing?"

"Nothing of what you said. What is it? Tell again if you want me to know."

*F

He took her by the shoulder and led her unresisting
to the front of the verandah into a stronger light. She
wrung her hands with such an appearance of grief that
he began to be alarmed.

"Speak," he said. "You made noise enough to
wake even dead men. And yet nobody living came,"
he added to himself in an uneasy whisper. "Are you
mute? Speak!" he repeated.

In a rush of words which broke out after a short
struggle from her trembling lips she told him the tale
of Nina's love and her own jealousy. Several times he
looked angrily into her face and told her to be silent;
but he could not stop the sounds that seemed to him
to run out in a hot stream, swirl about his feet, and rise
in scalding waves about him, higher, higher, drowning
his heart, touching his lips with a feel of molten lead,
blotting out his sight in scorching vapour, closing over
his head, merciless and deadly. When she spoke of
the deception as to Dain's death of which he had been
the victim only that day, he glanced again at her with
terrible eyes, and made her falter for a second, but he
turned away directly, and his face suddenly lost all
expression in a stony stare far away over the river.
Ah! the river! His old friend and his old enemy,
speaking always with the same voice as he runs from
year to year bringing fortune or disappointment, happiness or pain, upon the same varying but unchanged
surface of glancing currents and swirling eddies. For
many years he had listened to the passionless and
soothing murmur that sometimes was the song of
hope, at times the song of triumph, of encouragement;
more often the whisper of consolation that spoke of
better days to come. For so many years! So many
years! And now to the accompaniment of that murmur he listened to the slow and painful beating of his

heart. He listened attentively, wondering at the regularity of its beats. He began to count mechanically. One, two. Why count? At the next beat it must stop. No heart could suffer so and beat so steadily for long. Those regular strokes as of a muffled hammer that rang in his ears must stop soon. Still beating unceasing and cruel. No man can bear this: and is this the last, or will the next one be the last?— How much longer? O God! how much longer? His hand weighed heavier unconsciously on the girl's shoulder, and she spoke the last words of her story crouching at his feet with tears of pain and shame and anger. Was her revenge to fail her? This white man was like a senseless stone. Too late! Too late!

"And you saw her go?" Almayer's voice sounded harshly above her head.

"Did I not tell you?" she sobbed, trying to wriggle gently out from under his grip. "Did I not tell you that I saw the witchwoman push the canoe? I lay hidden in the grass and heard all the words. She that we used to call the white Mem wanted to return to look at your face, but the witchwoman forbade her, and——"

She sank lower yet on her elbow, turning half round under the downward push of the heavy hand, her face lifted up to him with spiteful eyes.

"And she obeyed," she shouted out in a half-laugh, half-cry of pain. "Let me go, Tuan. Why are you angry with me? Hasten, or you will be too late to show your anger to the deceitful woman."

Almayer dragged her up to her feet and looked close into her face while she struggled, turning her head away from his wild stare.

"Who sent you here to torment me?" he asked, violently. "I do not believe you. You lie."

He straightened his arm suddenly and flung her across the verandah towards the doorway, where she lay immobile and silent, as if she had left her life in his grasp, a dark heap, without a sound or a stir.

"Oh! Nina!" whispered Almayer, in a voice in which reproach and love spoke together in pained tenderness. "Oh! Nina! I do not believe."

A light draught from the river ran over the courtyard in a wave of bowing grass and, entering the verandah, touched Almayer's forehead with its cool breath, in a caress of infinite pity. The curtain in the women's doorway blew out and instantly collapsed with startling helplessness. He stared at the fluttering stuff.

"Nina!" cried Almayer. "Where are you, Nina?" The wind passed out of the empty house in a tremulous sigh, and all was still.

Almayer hid his face in his hands as if to shut out a loathsome sight. When, hearing a slight rustle, he uncovered his eyes, the dark heap by the door was gone.

CHAPTER ELEVEN

IN THE middle of a shadowless square of moonlight, shining on a smooth and level expanse of young rice-shoots, a little shelter-hut perched on high posts, the pile of brushwood near by and the glowing embers of a fire with a man stretched before it, seemed very small and as if lost in the pale green iridescence reflected from the ground. On three sides of the clearing, appearing very far away in the deceptive light, the big trees of the forest, lashed together with manifold bonds by a mass of tangled creepers, looked down at the growing young life at their feet with the sombre resignation of giants that had lost faith in their strength. And in the midst of them the merciless creepers clung to the big trunks in cable-like coils, leaped from tree to tree, hung in thorny festoons from the lower boughs, and, sending slender tendrils on high to seek out the smallest branches, carried death to their victims in an exulting riot of silent destruction.

On the fourth side, following the curve of the bank of that branch of the Pantai that formed the only access to the clearing, ran a black line of young trees, bushes, and thick second growth, unbroken save for a small gap chopped out in one place. At that gap began the narrow footpath leading from the water's edge to the grass-built shelter used by the night watchers when the ripening crop had to be protected from the wild pigs. The pathway ended at the foot of the piles on which the hut was built, in a circular space covered with ashes and bits of burnt wood. In the middle of that space, by the dim fire, lay Dain.

He turned over on his side with an impatient sigh, and, pillowing his head on his bent arm, lay quietly with his face to the dying fire. The glowing embers shone redly in a small circle, throwing a gleam into his wide-open eyes. His body was weary with the exertion of the past few days, his mind more weary still with the strain of solitary waiting for his fate. Never before had he felt so helpless. He had heard the report of the gun fired on board the launch, and he knew that his life was in untrustworthy hands, and that his enemies were very near.

During the slow hours of the afternoon he had roamed about on the edge of the forest, or, hiding in the bushes, watched the creek with unquiet eyes for some sign of danger. He feared not death, yet he desired ardently to live, for life to him was Nina. She had promised to come, to follow him, to share his danger and his splendour. But with her by his side he cared not for danger, and without her there could be no splendour and no joy in existence. Crouching in his shady hiding-place, he closed his eyes, trying to evoke the gracious and charming image of the white figure that for him was the beginning and the end of life. With eyes shut tight, his teeth hard set, he tried in a great effort of passionate will to keep his hold on that vision of supreme delight. In vain! His heart grew heavy as the figure of Nina faded away to be replaced by another vision this time—a vision of armed men, of angry faces, of glittering arms—and he seemed to hear the hum of excited and triumphant voices as they discovered him in his hiding-place. Startled by the vividness of his fancy, he would open his eyes, and, leaping out into the sunlight, resume his aimless wanderings around the clearing. As he skirted in his weary march the edge of the forest he glanced now and then into its dark

shade, so enticing in its deceptive appearance of cool-
ness, so repellent with its unrelieved gloom, where lay,
entombed and rotting, countless generations of trees,
and where their successors stood as if mourning, in
dark green foliage, immense and helpless, awaiting their
turn. Only the parasites seemed to live there in a
sinuous rush upwards into the air and sunshine, feeding
on the dead and the dying alike, and crowning their
victims with pink and blue flowers that gleamed
amongst the boughs, incongruous and cruel, like a
strident and mocking note in the solemn harmony of
the doomed trees.

A man could hide there, thought Dain, as he approached a place where the creepers had been torn and
hacked into an archway that might have been the beginning of a path. As he bent down to look through
he heard angry grunting, and a sounder of wild pig
crashed away in the undergrowth. An acrid smell of
damp earth and of decaying leaves took him by the
throat, and he drew back with a scared face, as if he
had been touched by the breath of Death itself. The
very air seemed dead in there—heavy and stagnating,
poisoned with the corruption of countless ages. He
went on, staggering on his way, urged by the nervous
restlessness that made him feel tired yet caused him
to loathe the very idea of immobility and repose.
Was he a wild man to hide in the woods and perhaps be
killed there—in the darkness—where there was no
room to breathe? He would wait for his enemies in
the sunlight, where he could see the sky and feel the
breeze. He knew how a Malay chief should die.
The sombre and desperate fury, that peculiar inherit-
ance of his race, took possession of him, and he glared
savagely across the clearing towards the gap in the
bushes by the riverside. They would come from there.

In imagination he saw them now. He saw the bearded faces and the white jackets of the officers, the light on the levelled barrels of the rifles. What is the bravery of the greatest warrior before the firearms in the hand of a slave? He would walk towards them with a smiling face, with his hands held out in a sign of submission till he was very near them. He would speak friendly words—come nearer yet—yet nearer—so near that they could touch him with their hands and stretch them out to make him a captive. That would be the time; with a shout and a leap he would be in the midst of them, kriss in hand, killing, killing, killing, and would die with the shouts of his enemies in his ears, their warm blood spurting before his eyes.

Carried away by his excitement, he snatched the kriss hidden in his sarong, and, drawing a long breath, rushed forward, struck at the empty air, and fell on his face. He lay as if stunned in the sudden reaction from his exaltation, thinking that, even if he died thus gloriously, it would have to be before he saw Nina. Better so. If he saw her again he felt that death would be too terrible. With horror he, the descendant of Rajahs and of conquerors, had to face the doubt of his own bravery. His desire of life tormented him in a paroxysm of agonizing remorse. He had not the courage to stir a limb. He had lost faith in himself, and there was nothing else in him of what makes a man. The suffering remained, for it is ordered that it should abide in the human body even to the last breath, and fear remained. Dimly he could look into the depths of his passionate love, see its strength and its weakness, and felt afraid.

The sun went down slowly. The shadow of the western forest marched over the clearing, covered the man's scorched shoulders with its cool mantle, and went

on hurriedly to mingle with the shadows of other forests
on the eastern side. The sun lingered for a while
amongst the light tracery of the higher branches, as
if in friendly reluctance to abandon the body stretched
in the green paddy-field. Then Dain, revived by the
cool of the evening breeze, sat up and stared round him.
As he did so the sun dipped sharply, as if ashamed
of being detected in a sympathizing attitude, and the
clearing, which during the day was all light, became
suddenly all darkness, where the fire gleamed like an
eye. Dain walked slowly towards the creek, and,
divesting himself of his torn sarong, his only garment,
entered the water cautiously. He had had nothing
to eat that day, and had not dared show himself in
daylight by the water-side to drink. Now, as he swam
silently, he swallowed a few mouthfuls of water that
lapped about his lips. This did him good, and he
walked with greater confidence in himself and others as
he returned towards the fire. Had he been betrayed
by Lakamba all would have been over by this. He
made up a big blaze, and while it lasted dried himself,
and then lay down by the embers. He could not sleep,
but he felt a great numbness in all his limbs. His
restlessness was gone, and he was content to lie still,
measuring the time by watching the stars that rose in
endless succession above the forests, while the slight
puffs of wind under the cloudless sky seemed to fan
their twinkle into a greater brightness. Dreamily he
assured himself over and over again that she would
come, till the certitude crept into his heart and filled
him with a great peace. Yes, when the next day
broke, they would be together on the great blue sea that
was like life—away from the forests that were like
death. He murmured the name of Nina into the silent
space with a tender smile: this seemed to break the

spell of stillness, and far away by the creek a frog croaked loudly as if in answer. A chorus of loud roars and plaintive calls rose from the mud along the line of bushes. He laughed heartily; doubtless it was their love-song. He felt affectionate towards the frogs and listened, pleased with the noisy life near him.

When the moon peeped above the trees he felt the old impatience and the old restlessness steal over him. Why was she so late? True, it was a long way to come with a single paddle. With what skill and what endurance could those small hands manage a heavy paddle! It was very wonderful—such small hands, such soft little palms that knew how to touch his cheek with a feel lighter than the fanning of a butterfly's wing. Wonderful! He lost himself lovingly in the contemplation of this tremendous mystery, and when he looked at the moon again it had risen a hand's breadth above the trees. Would she come? He forced himself to lie still, overcoming the impulse to rise and rush round the clearing again. He turned this way and that; at last, quivering with the effort, he lay on his back, and saw her face among the stars looking down on him.

The croaking of frogs suddenly ceased. With the watchfulness of a hunted man Dain sat up, listening anxiously, and heard several splashes in the water as the frogs took rapid headers into the creek. He knew that they had been alarmed by something, and stood up suspicious and attentive. A slight grating noise, then the dry sound as of two pieces of wood struck against each other. Somebody was about to land! He took up an armful of brushwood, and, without taking his eyes from the path, held it over the embers of his fire. He waited, undecided, and saw something gleam amongst the bushes; then a white figure came out of the shadows and seemed to float towards him in the pale light. His heart gave a great leap and stood still, then went on shaking his frame in furious beats. He dropped the brushwood upon the glowing coals, and had an impression of shouting her name—of rushing to meet her; yet he emitted no sound, he stirred not an inch, but he stood silent and motionless like chiselled bronze under the moonlight that streamed over his naked shoulders. As he stood still, fighting with his breath, as if bereft of his senses by the intensity of his delight, she walked up to him with quick, resolute steps, and, with the appearance of one about to leap from a dangerous height, threw both her arms round his neck with a sudden gesture. A small blue gleam crept amongst the dry branches, and the crackling of reviving fire was the only sound as they faced each other in the speechless emotion of that meeting; then the dry fuel caught at once, and a bright hot flame shot upwards in a blaze as high as their heads, and in its light they saw each other's eyes.

Neither of them spoke. He was regaining his senses in a slight tremor that ran upwards along his rigid body and hung about his trembling lips. She drew back her head and fastened her eyes on his in one of those long looks that are a woman's most terrible weapon; a look that is more stirring than the closest touch, and more dangerous than the thrust of a dagger, because it also whips the soul out of the body, but leaves the body alive and helpless, to be swayed here and there by the capricious tempests of passion and desire; a look that enwraps the whole body, and that penetrates into the innermost recesses of the being, bringing terrible defeat in the delirious uplifting of accomplished conquest. It has the same meaning for the man of the forests and the sea as for the man threading the paths of the more dangerous wilderness of houses and streets.

Men that had felt in their breasts the awful exultation such a look awakens become mere things of to-day—which is paradise; forget yesterday—which was suffering; care not for to-morrow—which may be perdition. They wish to live under that look for ever. It is the look of woman's surrender.

He understood, and, as if suddenly released from his invisible bonds, fell at her feet with a shout of joy, and, embracing her knees, hid his head in the folds of her dress, murmuring disjointed words of gratitude and love. Never before had he felt so proud as now, when at the feet of that woman that half belonged to his enemies. Her fingers played with his hair in an absent-minded caress as she stood absorbed in thought. The thing was done. Her mother was right. The man was her slave. As she glanced down at his kneeling form she felt a great pitying tenderness for that man she was used to call—even in her thoughts—the master of life. She lifted her eyes and looked sadly at the southern heavens under which lay the path of their lives—her own, and that man's at her feet. Did he not say himself that she was the light of his life? She would be his light and his wisdom; she would be his greatness and his strength; yet hidden from the eyes of all men she would be, above all, his only and lasting weakness. A very woman! In the sublime vanity of her kind she was thinking already of moulding a god from the clay at her feet. A god for others to worship. She was content to see him as he was now, and to feel him quiver at the slightest touch of her light fingers. And while her eyes looked sadly at the southern stars a faint smile seemed to be playing about her firm lips. Who can tell in the fitful light of a camp fire? It might have been a smile of triumph, or of conscious power, or of tender pity, or, perhaps, of love.

She spoke softly to him, and he rose to his feet, putting his arm round her in quiet consciousness of his ownership; she laid her head on his shoulder with a sense of defiance to all the world in the encircling protection of that arm. He was hers with all his qualities and his faults. His strength and his courage, his recklessness and his daring, his simple wisdom and his savage cunning—all were hers. As they passed together out of the red light of the fire into the silver shower of rays that fell upon the clearing he bent his head over her face, and she saw in his eyes the dreamy intoxication of boundless felicity from the close touch of her slight figure clasped to his side. With a rhythmical swing of their bodies they walked through the light towards the outlying shadows of the forests that seemed to guard their happiness in solemn immobility. Their forms melted in the play of light and shadow at the foot of the big trees, but the murmur of tender words lingered over the empty clearing, grew faint, and died out. A sigh as of immense sorrow passed over the land in the last effort of the dying breeze, and in the deep silence which succeeded, the earth and the heavens were suddenly hushed up in the mournful contemplation of human love and human blindness.

They walked slowly back to the fire. He made for her a seat out of the dry branches, and, throwing himself down at her feet, lay his head in her lap and gave himself up to the dreamy delight of the passing hour. Their voices rose and fell, tender or animated as they spoke of their love and of their future. She, with a few skilful words spoken from time to time, guided his thoughts, and he let his happiness flow in a stream of talk passionate and tender, grave or menacing, according to the mood which she evoked. He spoke to her of his own island, where the gloomy forests and the muddy rivers were unknown. He spoke of its terraced fields, of the murmuring clear rills of sparkling water that flowed down the sides of great mountains, bringing life to the land and joy to its tillers. And he spoke also of the mountain peak that rising lonely above the belt of trees knew the secrets of the passing clouds, and was the dwelling-place of the mysterious spirit of his race, of the guardian genius of his house. He spoke of vast horizons swept by fierce winds that whistled high above the summits of burning mountains. He spoke of his forefathers that conquered ages ago the island of which he was to be the future ruler. And then as, in her interest, she brought her face nearer to his, he, touching lightly the thick tresses of her long hair, felt a sudden impulse to speak to her of the sea he loved so well; and he told her of its never-ceasing voice, to which he had listened as a child, wondering at its hidden meaning that no living man has penetrated yet; of its enchanting glitter; of its senseless and capricious fury; how its surface was for ever changing, and yet always enticing, while its depths were for ever the same, cold and cruel, and full of the wisdom of destroyed life. He told her how it held men slaves of its charm for a lifetime, and then, regardless of their devotion, swallowed them up, angry at their fear of its mystery, which it would never disclose, not even to those that loved it most. While he talked, Nina's head had been gradually sinking lower, and her face almost touched his now. Her hair was over his eyes, her breath was on his forehead, her arms were about his body. No two beings could be closer to each other, yet she guessed rather than understood the meaning of his last words that came out after a slight hesitation in a faint murmur, dying out imperceptibly into a profound and significant silence: "The sea, O Nina, is like a woman's heart."

She closed his lips with a sudden kiss, and answered in a steady voice—

"But to the men that have no fear, O master of my life, the sea is ever true."

Over their heads a film of dark, thread-like clouds, looking like immense cobwebs drifting under the stars, darkened the sky with the presage of the coming thunderstorm. From the invisible hills the first distant rumble of thunder came in a prolonged roll which, after tossing about from hill to hill, lost itself in the forests of the Pantai. Dain and Nina stood up, and the former looked at the sky uneasily.

"It is time for Babalatchi to be here," he said. "The night is more than half gone. Our road is long, and a bullet travels quicker than the best canoe."

"He will be here before the moon is hidden behind the clouds," said Nina. "I heard a splash in the water," she added. "Did you hear it too?"

"Alligator," answered Dain shortly, with a careless glance towards the creek. "The darker the night," he continued, "the shorter will be our road, for then we could keep in the current of the main stream, but if it is light—even no more than now—we must follow the small channels of sleeping water, with nothing to help our paddles."

"Dain," interposed Nina, earnestly, "it was no alligator. I heard the bushes rustling near the landing-place."

"Yes," said Dain, after listening awhile. "It cannot be Babalatchi, who would come in a big war canoe, and openly. Those that are coming, whoever they are, do not wish to make much noise. But you have heard, and now I can see," he went on quickly. "It is but one man. Stand behind me, Nina. If he is a friend he is welcome; if he is an enemy you shall see him die."

He laid his hand on his kriss, and waited the approach of his unexpected visitor. The fire was burning very low, and small clouds—precursors of the storm—crossed the face of the moon in rapid succession, and their flying shadows darkened the clearing. He could not make out who the man might be, but he felt uneasy at the steady advance of the tall figure walking on the path with a heavy tread, and hailed it with a command to stop. The man stopped at some little distance, and Dain expected him to speak, but all he could hear was his deep breathing. Through a break in the flying clouds a sudden and fleeting brightness descended upon the clearing. Before the darkness closed in again Dain saw a hand holding some glittering object extended towards him, heard Nina's cry of "Father!" and in an instant the girl was between him and Almayer's revolver. Nina's loud cry woke up the echoes of the sleeping woods, and the three stood still as if waiting for the return of silence before they would give expression to their various feelings. At the appearance of Nina, Almayer's arm fell by his side, and he made a step forward. Dain pushed the girl gently aside.

"Am I a wild beast that you should try to kill me suddenly and in the dark, Tuan Almayer?" said Dain, breaking the strained silence. "Throw some brushwood on the fire," he went on, speaking to Nina, "while I watch my white friend, lest harm should come to you or to me, O delight of my heart!"

Almayer ground his teeth and raised his arm again. With a quick bound Dain was at his side: there was a short scuffle, during which one chamber of the revolver went off harmlessly, then the weapon, wrenched out of Almayer's hand, whirled through the air and fell in the bushes. The two men stood close together, breathing hard. The replenished fire threw out an unsteady circle of light and shone on the terrified face of Nina, who looked at them with outstretched hands.

"Dain!" she cried out warningly, "Dain!"

He waved his hand towards her in a reassuring gesture, and, turning to Almayer, said with great courtesy—

"Now we may talk, Tuan. It is easy to send out death, but can your wisdom recall the life? She might have been harmed," he continued, indicating Nina. "Your hand shook much; for myself I was not afraid."

"Nina!" exclaimed Almayer, "come to me at once. What is this sudden madness? What bewitched you? Come to your father, and together we shall try to forget this horrible nightmare!"

He opened his arms with the certitude of clasping her to his breast in another second. She did not move. As it dawned upon him that she did not mean to obey he felt a deadly cold creep into his heart, and pressing the palms of his hands to his temples, he looked down on the ground in mute despair. Dain took Nina by the arm and led her towards her father.

"Speak to him in the language of his people," he said. "He is grieving—as who would not grieve at losing thee, my pearl! Speak to him the last words he shall hear spoken by that voice, which must be very sweet to him, but is all my life to me."

He released her, and, stepping back a few paces out of the circle of light, stood in the darkness looking at them with calm interest. The reflection of a distant flash of lightning lit up the clouds over their heads, and was followed after a short interval by the faint rumble of thunder, which mingled with Almayer's voice as he began to speak.

"Do you know what you are doing? Do you know what is waiting for you if you follow that man? Have you no pity for yourself? Do you know that you shall be at first his plaything and then a scorned slave, a drudge, and a servant of some new fancy of that man?"

She raised her hand to stop him, and turning her head slightly, asked—

"You hear this Dain! Is it true?"

"By all the gods!" came the impassioned answer from the darkness—"by heaven and earth, by my head and thine I swear: this is a white man's lie. I have delivered my soul into your hands for ever; I breathe with your breath, I see with your eyes, I think with your mind, and I take you into my heart for ever."

"You thief!" shouted the exasperated Almayer.

A deep silence succeeded this outburst, then the voice of Dain was heard again.

"Nay, Tuan," he said in a gentle tone, "that is not true also. The girl came of her own will. I have done no more but to show her my love like a man; she heard the cry of my heart, and she came, and the dowry I have given to the woman you call your wife."

Almayer groaned in his extremity of rage and shame. Nina laid her hand lightly on his shoulder, and the contact, light as the touch of a falling leaf, seemed to calm him. He spoke quickly, and in English this time.

" Tell me," he said—" tell me, what have they done to you, your mother and that man? What made you give yourself up to that savage? For he is a savage. Between him and you there is a barrier that nothing can remove. I can see in your eyes the look of those who commit suicide when they are mad. You are mad. Don't smile. It breaks my heart. If I were to see you drowning before my eyes, and I without the power to help you, I could not suffer a greater torment. Have you forgotten the teaching of so many years?"

"No," she interrupted, "I remember it well. I remember how it ended also. Scorn for scorn, contempt for contempt, hate for hate. I am not of your race. Between your people and me there is also a barrier that nothing can remove. You ask why I want to go, and I ask you why I should stay."

He staggered as if struck in the face, but with a quick, unhesitating grasp she caught him by the arm and steadied him.

"Why you should stay!" he repeated slowly, in a dazed manner, and stopped short, astounded at the completeness of his misfortune.

"You told me yesterday," she went on again, "that I could not understand or see your love for me: it is so. How can I? No two human beings understand each other. They can understand but their own voices. You wanted me to dream your dreams, to see your own visions—the visions of life amongst the white faces of those who cast me out from their midst in angry contempt. But while you spoke I listened to the voice of my own self; then this man came, and all was still; there was only the murmur of his love. You call him a savage! What do you call my mother, your wife?"

"Nina!" cried Almayer, "take your eyes off my face."

She looked down directly, but continued speaking only a little above a whisper.

"In time," she went on, "both our voices, that man's and mine, spoke together in a sweetness that was intelligible to our ears only. You were speaking of gold then, but our ears were filled with the song of our love, and we did not hear you. Then I found that we could see through each other's eyes: that he saw things that nobody but myself and he could see. We entered a land where no one could follow us, and least of all you. Then I began to live."

She paused. Almayer sighed deeply. With her eyes still fixed on the ground she began speaking again.

"And I mean to live. I mean to follow him. I have been rejected with scorn by the white people, and now I am a Malay! He took me in his arms, he laid his life at my feet. He is brave; he will be powerful, and I hold his bravery and his strength in my hand, and I shall make him great. His name shall be remembered long after both our bodies are laid in the dust. I love you no less than I did before, but I shall never leave him, for without him I cannot live."

"If he understood what you have said," answered Almayer, scornfully, "he must be highly flattered. You want him as a tool for some incomprehensib'e ambition of yours. Enough, Nina. If you do not go down at once to the creek, where Ali is waiting with my canoe, I shall tell him to return to the settlement and bring the Dutch officers here. You cannot escape from this clearing, for I have cast adrift your canoe. If the Dutch catch this hero of yours they will hang him as sure as I stand here. Now go."

He made a step towards his daughter and laid hold of her by the shoulder, his other hand pointing down the path to the landing-place.

"Beware!" exclaimed Dain; "this woman belongs to me!"

Nina wrenched herself free and looked straight at Almayer's angry face.

"No, I will not go," she said with desperate energy. "If he dies I shall die too!"

"You die?" said Almayer, contemptuously. "Oh, no! You shall live a life cf lies and deception till some other vagabond comes along to sing; how did you say that? The song of love to you! Make up your mind quickly."

He waited for a while, and then added meaningly—
"Shall I call out to Ali?"

"Call out," she answered in Malay, "you that cannot
be true to your own countrymen. Only a few days
ago you were selling the powder of their destruction;
now you want to give up to them the man that yesterday you called your friend. Oh, Dain," she said, turning towards the motionless but attentive figure in the
darkness, "instead of bringing you life I bring you
death, for he will betray unless I leave you for ever!"

Dain came into the circle of light, and, throwing his
arm around Nina's neck, whispered in her ear—

"I can kill him where he stands, before a sound can
pass his lips. For you it is to say yes or no. Babalatchi
cannot be far now."

He straightened himself up, taking his arm off her
shoulder, and confronted Almayer, who looked at them
both with an expression of concentrated fury.

"No!" she cried, clinging to Dain in wild alarm. "No!
Kill me! Then perhaps he will let you go. You do not
know the mind of a white man. He would rather see
me dead than standing where I am. Forgive me, your
slave, but you must not." She fell at his feet sobbing
violently and repeating, "Kill me! Kill me!"

"I want you alive" said Almayer, speaking also in
Malay, with sombre calmness. "You go, or he hangs.
Will you obey?"

Dain shook Nina off, and, making a sudden lunge,
struck Almayer full in the chest with the handle of his
kriss, keeping the point towards himself.

"Hai, look! It was easy for me to turn the point
the other way," he said in his even voice. "Go, Tuan
Putih," he added with dignity. "I give you your life,
my life, and her life. I am the slave of this woman's
desire, and she wills it so."

There was not a glimmer of light in the sky now, and the tops of the trees were as invisible as their trunks, being lost in the mass of clouds that hung low over the woods, the clearing, and the river. Every outline had disappeared in the intense blackness that seemed to have destroyed everything but space. Only the fire glimmered like a star forgotten in this annihilation of all visible things, and nothing was heard after Dain ceased speaking but the sobs of Nina, whom he held in his arms, kneeling beside the fire. Almayer stood looking down at them in gloomy thoughtfulness. As he was opening his lips to speak they were startled by a cry of warning by the riverside, followed by the splash of many paddles and the sound of voices.

"Babalatchi!" shouted Dain, lifting up Nina as he got upon his feet quickly.

"Ada! Ada!" came the answer from the panting statesman who ran up the path and stood amongst them. "Run to my canoe," he said to Dain excitedly, without taking any notice of Almayer. "Run! we must go. That woman has told them all!"

"What woman?" asked Dain, looking at Nina. Just then there was only one woman in the whole world for him.

"The she-dog with white teeth; the seven times accursed slave of Bulangi. She yelled at Abdulla's gate till she woke up all Sambir. Now the white officers are coming guided by her and Reshid. If you want to live, do not look at me, but go!"

"How do you know this?" asked Almayer.

"Oh, Tuan! what matters how I know! I have only one eye, but I saw lights in Abdulla's house and in his campong as we were paddling past. I have ears, and while we lay under the bank I have heard the messengers sent out to the white men's house."

"Will you depart without that woman who is my daughter?" said Almayer, addressing Dain, while Babalatchi stamped with impatience, muttering, "Run! Run at once!"

"No," answered Dain, steadily, "I will not go; to no man will I abandon this woman."

"Then kill me and escape yourself," sobbed out Nina. He clasped her close, looking at her tenderly, and whispered, "We will never part, O Nina!"

"I shall not stay here any longer," broke in Babalatchi, angrily. "This is great foolishness. No woman is worth a man's life. I am an old man, and I know."

He picked up his staff, and, turning to go, looked at Dain as if offering him his last chance of escape. But Dain's face was hidden amongst Nina's black tresses, and he did not see this last appealing glance.

Babalatchi vanished in the darkness. Shortly after his disappearance they heard the war canoe leave the landing-place in the swish of the numerous paddles dipped in the water together. Almost at the same time Ali came up from the riverside, two paddles on his shoulder.

"Our canoe is hidden up the creek, Tuan Almayer," he said, "in the dense bush where the forest comes down to the water. I took it there because I heard from Babalatchi's paddlers that the white men are coming here."

"Wait for me there," said Almayer, "but keep the canoe hidden."

He remained silent, listening to Ali's footsteps, then turned to Nina.

"Nina," he said sadly "will you have no pity for me?"

There was no answer. She did not even turn her head, which was pressed close to Dain's breast.

He made a movement as if to leave them and stopped. By the dim glow of the burning-out fire he saw their two motionless figures. The woman's back turned to him with the long black hair streaming down over the white dress, and Dain's calm face looking at him above her head.

"I cannot," he muttered to himself. After a long pause he spoke again a little lower, but in an unsteady voice, "It would be too great a disgrace. I am a white man." He broke down completely there, and went on tearfully, "I am a white man, and of good family. Very good family," he repeated, weeping bitterly. "It would be a disgrace . . . all over the island, . . . the only white man on the east coast. No, it cannot be . . . white men finding my daughter with this Malay. My daughter!" he cried aloud, with a ring of despair in his voice.

He recovered his composure after a while and said distinctly—

"I will never forgive you, Nina—never! If you were to come back to me now, the memory of this night would poison all my life. I shall try to forget. I have no daughter. There used to be a half-caste woman in my house, but she is going even now. You, Dain, or whatever your name may be, I shall take you and that woman to the island at the mouth of the river myself. Come with me."

He led the way, following the bank as far as the forest. Ali answered to his call, and, pushing their way through the dense bush, they stepped into the canoe hidden under the overhanging branches. Dain laid Nina in the bottom, and sat holding her head on his knees. Almayer and Ali each took up a paddle. As they were going to push out Ali hissed warningly. All listened.

In the great stillness before the bursting out of the

thunderstorm they could hear the sound of oars working regularly in their row-locks. The sound approached steadily, and Dain, looking through the branches, could see the faint shape of a big white boat. A woman's voice said in a cautious tone—

"There is the place where you may land white men; a little higher—there!"

The boat was passing them so close in the narrow creek that the blades of the long oars nearly touched the canoe.

"Way enough! Stand by to jump on shore! He is alone and unarmed," was the quiet order in a man's voice, and in Dutch.

Somebody else whispered: "I think I can see a glimmer of a fire through the bush." And then the boat floated past them, disappearing instantly in the darkness.

"Now," whispered Ali, eagerly, "let us push out and paddle away."

The little canoe swung into the stream, and as it sprung forward in response to the vigorous dig of the paddles they could hear an angry shout.

"He is not by the fire. Spread out, men, and search for him!"

Blue lights blazed out in different parts of the clearing, and the shrill voice of a woman cried in accents of rage and pain—

"Too late! O senseless white men! He has escaped!"

CHAPTER TWELVE

"THAT is the place," said Dain, indicating with the blade of his paddle a small islet about a mile ahead of the canoe—"that is the place where Babalatchi promised that a boat from the prau would come for me when the sun is overhead. We will wait for that boat there."

Almayer, who was steering, nodded without speaking, and by a slight sweep of his paddle laid the head of the canoe in the required direction.

They were just leaving the southern outlet of the Pantai, which lay behind them in a straight and long vista of water shining between two walls of thick verdure that ran downwards and towards each other, till at last they joined and sank together in the far-away distance. The sun, rising above the calm waters of the Straits, marked its own path by a streak of light that glided upon the sea and darted up the wide reach of the river, a hurried messenger of light and life to the gloomy forests of the coast; and in this radiance of the sun's pathway floated the black canoe heading for the islet which lay bathed in sunshine, the yellow sands of its encircling beach shining like an inlaid golden disc on the polished steel of the unwrinkled sea. To the north and south of it rose other islets, joyous in their brilliant colouring of green and yellow, and on the main coast the sombre line of mangrove bushes ended to the southward in the reddish cliffs of Tanjong Mirrah, advancing into the sea, steep and shadowless under the clear light of the early morning.

The bottom of the canoe grated upon the sand as the little craft ran upon the beach. Ali leaped on shore and held on while Dain stepped out carrying Nina in his arms, exhausted by the events and the long travelling during the night. Almayer was the last to leave the boat, and together with Ali ran it higher up on the beach. Then Ali, tired out by the long paddling, laid down in the shade of the canoe, and incontinently fell asleep. Almayer sat sideways on the gunwale, and with his arms crossed on his breast, looked to the southward upon the sea.

After carefully laying Nina down in the shade of the bushes growing in the middle of the islet, Dain threw himself beside her and watched in silent concern the tears that ran down from under her closed eyelids, and lost themselves in that fine sand upon which they both were lying face to face. These tears and this sorrow were for him a profound and disquieting mystery. Now, when the danger was past, why should she grieve? He doubted her love no more than he would have doubted the fact of his own existence, but as he lay looking ardently in her face, watching her tears, her parted lips, her very breath, he was uneasily conscious of something in her he could not understand. Doubtless she had the wisdom of perfect beings. He sighed. He felt something invisible that stood between them, something that would let him approach her so far, but no farther. No desire, no longing, no effort of will or length of life could destroy this vague feeling of their difference. With awe but also with great pride he concluded that it was her own incomparable perfection. She was his, and yet she was like a woman from another world. His! His! He exulted in the glorious thought; nevertheless her tears pained him.

With a wisp of her own hair which he took in his hand

with timid reverence he tried in an access of clumsy
tenderness to dry the tears that trembled on her eyelashes. He had his reward in a fleeting smile that
brightened her face for the short fraction of a second,
but soon the tears fell faster than ever, and he could
bear it no more. He rose and walked towards Almayer,
who still sat absorbed in his contemplation of the sea.
It was a very, very long time since he had seen the sea—
that sea that leads everywhere, brings everything, and
takes away so much. He had almost forgotten why he
was there, and dreamily he could see all his past life on
the smooth and boundless surface that glittered before
his eyes.

Dain's hand laid on Almayer's shoulder recalled
him with a start from some country very far away
indeed. He turned round, but his eyes seemed to look
rather at the place where Dain stood than at the man
himself. Dain felt uneasy under the unconscious gaze.

"What do you want?" asked Almayer.

"She is crying," murmured Dain, softly.

"She is crying! Why?" asked Almayer, indifferently.

"I came to ask you. My Ranee smiles when looking
at the man she loves. It is the white woman that is
crying now. You would know."

Almayer shrugged his shoulders and turned away
again towards the sea.

"Go, Tuan Putih," urged Dain. "Go to her; her
tears are more terrible to me than the anger of gods."

"Are they? You will see them more than once.
She told me she could not live without you," answered
Almayer, speaking without the faintest spark of expression in his face, "so it behoves you to go to her
quick, for fear you may find her dead."

He burst into a loud and unpleasant laugh which

made Dain stare at him with some apprehension, but got off the gunwale of the boat and moved slowly towards Nina, glancing up at the sun as he walked.

"And you go when the sun is overhead?" he said.

"Yes, Tuan. Then we go," answered Dain.

"I have not long to wait," muttered Almayer. "It is most important for me to see you go. Both of you. Most important," he repeated, stopping short and looking at Dain fixedly.

He went on again towards Nina, and Dain remained behind. Almayer approached his daughter and stood for a time looking down on her. She did not open her eyes, but hearing footsteps near her, murmured in a low sob, "Dain."

Almayer hesitated for a minute and then sank on the sand by her side. She, not hearing a responsive word, not feeling a touch, opened her eyes—saw her father, and sat up suddenly with a movement of terror.

"Oh, father!" she murmured faintly, and in that word there was expressed regret and fear and dawning hope.

"I shall never forgive you, Nina," said Almayer, in a dispassionate voice. "You have torn my heart from me while I dreamt of your happiness. You have deceived me. Your eyes that for me were like truth itself lied to me in every glance—for how long? You know that best. When you were caressing my cheek you were counting the minutes to the sunset that was the signal for your meeting with that man—there!"

He ceased, and they both sat silent side by side, not looking at each other, but gazing at the vast expanse of the sea. Almayer's words had dried Nina's tears, and her look grew hard as she stared before her into the limitless sheet of blue that shone limpid, unwaving, and steady like heaven itself. He looked at

it also, but his features had lost all expression, and life
in his eyes seemed to have gone out. The face was a
blank, without a sign of emotion, feeling, reason, or
even knowledge of itself. All passion, regret, grief,
hope, or anger—all were gone, erased by the hand of
fate, as if after this last stroke everything was over
and there was no need for any record. Those few who
saw Almayer during the short period of his remaining
days were always impressed by the sight of that face
that seemed to know nothing of what went on within:
like the blank wall of a prison enclosing sin, regrets,
and pain, and wasted life, in the cold indifference of
mortar and stones.

"What is there to forgive?" asked Nina, not addressing Almayer directly, but more as if arguing with herself. "Can I not live my own life as you have lived
yours? The path you would have wished me to follow
has been closed to me by no fault of mine."

"You never told me," muttered Almayer.

"You never asked me," she answered, "and I
thought you were like the others and did not care.
I bore the memory of my humiliation alone, and why
should I tell you that it came to me because I am your
daughter? I knew you could not avenge me."

"And yet I was thinking of that only," interrupted
Almayer, "and I wanted to give you years of happiness
for the short day of your suffering. I only knew of
one way."

"Ah! but it was not my way!" she replied. "Could
you give me happiness without life? Life!" she repeated with sudden energy that sent the word ringing
over the sea. "Life that means power and love," she
added in a low voice.

"That!" said Almayer, pointing his finger at Dain
standing close by and looking at them in curious wonder.

"Yes, that!" she replied, looking her father full in the face and noticing for the first time with a slight gasp of fear the unnatural rigidity of his features.

"I would have rather strangled you with my own hands," said Almayer, in an expressionless voice which was such a contrast to the desperate bitterness of his feelings that it surprised even himself. He asked himself who spoke, and, after looking slowly round as if expecting to see somebody, turned again his eyes towards the sea.

"You say that because you do not understand the meaning of my words," she said sadly. "Between you and my mother there never was any love. When I returned to Sambir I found the place which I thought would be a peaceful refuge for my heart, filled with weariness and hatred—and mutual contempt. I have listened to your voice and to her voice. Then I saw that you could not understand me; for was I not part of that woman? Of her who was the regret and shame of your life? I had to choose—I hesitated. Why were you so blind? Did you not see me struggling before your eyes? But, when he came, all doubt disappeared, and I saw only the light of the blue and cloudless heaven——"

"I will tell you the rest," interrupted Almayer: "when that man came I also saw the blue and the sunshine of the sky. A thunderbolt has fallen from that sky, and suddenly all is still and dark around me for ever. I will never forgive you, Nina; and to-morrow I shall forget you! I shall never forgive you," he repeated with mechanical obstinacy while she sat, her head bowed down as if afraid to look at her father.

To him it seemed of the utmost importance that he should assure her of his intention of never forgiving. He was convinced that his faith in her had been the foundation of his hopes, the motive of his courage, of his determination to live and struggle, and to be victorious for her sake. And now his faith was gone, destroyed by her own hands; destroyed cruelly, treacherously, in the dark; in the very moment of success. In the utter wreck of his affections and of all his feelings, in the chaotic disorder of his thoughts, above the confused sensation of physical pain that wrapped him up in a sting as of a whiplash curling round him from his shoulders down to his feet, only one idea remained clear and definite—not to forgive her; only one vivid desire —to forget her. And this must be made clear to her— and to himself—by frequent repetition. That was his idea of his duty to himself—to his race—to his respectable connections; to the whole universe unsettled and shaken by this frightful catastrophe of his life. He saw it clearly and believed he was a strong man. He had always prided himself upon his unflinching firmness. And yet he was afraid. She had been all in all to him. What if he should let the memory of his love for her weaken the sense of his dignity? She was a remarkable woman; he could see that; all the latent greatness of his nature—in which he honestly believed—had been transfused into that slight, girlish figure. Great things could be done! What if he should suddenly take her to his heart, forget his shame, and pain, and anger, and —follow her! What if he changed his heart if not his skin and made her life easier between the two loves that would guard her from any mischance! His heart yearned for her. What if he should say that his love for her was greater than . . .

"I will never forgive you, Nina!" he shouted, leaping up madly in the sudden fear of his dream,

This was the last time in his life that he was heard to raise his voice. Henceforth he spoke always in a monotonous whisper like an instrument of which all the strings but one are broken in a last ringing clamour under a heavy blow.

She rose to her feet and looked at him. The very violence of his cry soothed her in an intuitive conviction of his love, and she hugged to her breast the lamentable remnants of that affection with the unscrupulous greediness of women who cling desperately to the very scraps and rags of love, any kind of love, as a thing that of right belongs to them and is the very breath of their life. She put both her hands on Almayer's shoulders, and looking at him half tenderly, half playfully, she said—

"You speak so because you love me."

Almayer shook his head.

"Yes, you do," she insisted softly; then after a short pause she added, "and you will never forget me."

Almayer shivered slightly. She could not have said a more cruel thing.

"Here is the boat coming now," said Dain, his arm outstretched towards a black speck on the water between the coast and the islet.

They all looked at it and remained standing in silence till the little canoe came gently on the beach and a man landed and walked towards them. He stopped some distance off and hesitated.

"What news?" asked Dain.

"We have had orders secretly and in the night to take off from this islet a man and a woman. I see the woman. Which of you is the man?"

"Come, delight of my eyes," said Dain to Nina. "Now we go, and your voice shall be for my ears only. You have spoken your last words to the Tuan Putih, your father. Come."

She hesitated for a while, looking at Almayer, who

*G

kept his eyes steadily on the sea, then she touched his forehead in a lingering kiss, and a tear—one of her tears—fell on his cheek and ran down his immovable face.

"Good-bye," she whispered, and remained irresolute till he pushed her suddenly into Dain's arms.

"If you have any pity for me," murmured Almayer, as if repeating some sentence learned by heart, "take that woman away."

He stood very straight, his shoulders thrown back, his head held high, and looked at them as they went down the beach to the canoe, walking enlaced in each other's arms. He looked at the line of their footsteps marked in the sand. He followed their figures moving in the crude blaze of the vertical sun, in that light violent and vibrating, like a triumphal flourish of brazen trumpets. He looked at the man's brown shoulders, at the red sarong round his waist; at the tall, slender, dazzling white figure he supported. He looked at the white dress, at the falling masses of the long black hair. He looked at them embarking, and at the canoe growing smaller in the distance, with rage, despair, and regret in his heart, and on his face a peace as that of a carved image of oblivion. Inwardly he felt himself torn to pieces, but Ali who—now aroused—stood close to his master, saw on his features the blank expression of those who live in that hopeless calm which sightless eyes only can give.

The canoe disappeared, and Almayer stood motionless with his eyes fixed on its wake. Ali from under the shade of his hand examined the coast curiously. As the sun declined, the sea-breeze sprang up from the northward and shivered with its breath the glassy surface of the water.

"Dapat!" exclaimed Ali, joyously. "Got him,

'master! Got prau! Not there! Look more Tanah
Mirrah side. Aha! That way! Master, see? Now
plain. See?"

Almayer followed Ali's forefinger with his eyes for a
long time in vain. At last he sighted a triangular
patch of yellow light on the red background of the cliffs
of Tanjong Mirrah. It was the sail of the prau that
had caught the sunlight and stood out, distinct with
its gay tint, on the dark red of the cape. The yellow
triangle crept slowly from cliff to cliff, till it cleared the
last point of land and shone brilliantly for a fleeting
minute on the blue of the open sea. Then the prau
bore up to the southward: the light went out of the sail,
and all at once the vessel itself disappeared, vanishing
in the shadow of the steep headland that looked on,
patient and lonely, watching over the empty sea.

Almayer never moved. Round the little islet the
air was full of the talk of the rippling water. The
crested wavelets ran up the beach audaciously, joyously, with the lightness of young life, and died quickly,
unresistingly, and graciously, in the wide curves of
transparent foam on the yellow sand. Above the
white clouds sailed rapidly southwards as if intent upon
overtaking something. Ali seemed anxious.

"Master," he said timidly, "time to get house now.
Long way off to pull. All ready, sir."

"Wait," whispered Almayer.

Now she was gone his business was to forget, and he
had a strange notion that it should be done systemati-
cally and in order. To Ali's great dismay he fell on his
hands and knees, and, creeping along the sand, erased
carefully with his hand all traces of Nina's footsteps.
He piled up small heaps of sand, leaving behind him
a line of miniature graves right down to the water.
After burying the last slight imprint of Nina's slipper

he stood up, and, turning his face towards the headland
where he had last seen the prau, he made an effort
to shout out loud again his firm resolve to never forgive.
Ali watching him uneasily saw only his lips move, but
heard no sound. He brought his foot down with a
stamp. He was a firm man—firm as a rock. Let her
go. He never had a daughter. He would forget. He
was forgetting already.

Ali approached him again, insisting on immediate
departure, and this time he consented, and they went
together towards their canoe, Almayer leading. For all
his firmness he looked very dejected and feeble as he
dragged his feet slowly through the sand on the beach;
and by his side—invisible to Ali—stalked that particular fiend whose mission it is to jog the memories of men,
lest they should forget the meaning of life. He whispered into Almayer's ear a childish prattle of many years
ago. Almayer, his head bent on one side, seemed
to listen to his invisible companion, but his face was
like the face of a man that has died struck from behind
—a face from which all feelings and all expression are
suddenly wiped off by the hand of unexpected death.

They slept on the river that night, mooring their
canoe under the bushes and lying down in the bottom
side by side, in the absolute exhaustion that kills hunger, thirst, all feeling and all thought in the overpowering desire for that deep sleep which is like the temporary
annihilation of the tired body. Next day they started
again and fought doggedly with the current all the
morning, till about midday they reached the settlement and made fast their little craft to the jetty of
Lingard and Co. Almayer walked straight to the
house, and Ali followed, paddles on shoulder, thinking
that he would like to eat something. As they crossed

the front courtyard they noticed the abandoned look of the place. Ali looked in at the different servants' houses: all were empty. In the back courtyard there was the same absence of sound and life. In the cooking-shed the fire was out and the black embers were cold. A tall, lean man came stealthily out of the banana plantation, and went away rapidly across the open space looking at them with big, frightened eyes over his shoulder. Some vagabond without a master; there were many such in the settlement, and they looked upon Almayer as their patron. They prowled about his premises and picked their living there, sure that nothing worse could befall them than a shower of curses when they got in the way of the white man, whom they trusted and liked, and called a fool amongst themselves. In the house, which Almayer entered through the back verandah, the only living thing that met his eyes was his small monkey, which hungry and unnoticed for the last two days, began to cry and complain in monkey language as soon as it caught sight of the familiar face. Almayer soothed it with a few words and ordered Ali to bring in some bananas, then while Ali was gone to get them he stood in the doorway of the front verandah looking at the chaos of overturned furniture. `Finally he picked up the table and sat on it while the monkey let itself down from the roof-stick by its chain and perched on his shoulder. When the bananas came they had their breakfast together; both hungry, both eating greedily and showering the skins round them recklessly, in the trusting silence of perfect friendship. Ali went away, grumbling, to cook some rice himself, for all the women about the house had disappeared; he did not know where. Almayer did not seem to care, and, after he finished eating, he sat on the table swinging his legs and staring at the river as if lost in thought.

After some time he got up and went to the door of a room on the right of the verandah. That was the office. The office of Lingard and Co. He very seldom went in there. There was no business now, and he did not want an office. The door was locked, and he stood biting his lower lip, trying to think of the place where the key could be. Suddenly he remembered: in the women's room hung upon a nail. He went over to the doorway where the red curtain hung down in motionless folds, and hesitated for a moment before pushing it aside with his shoulder as if breaking down some solid obstacle. A great square of sunshine entering through the window lay on the floor. On the left he saw Mrs. Almayer's big wooden chest, the lid thrown back, empty; near it the brass nails of Nina's European trunk shone in the large initials N. A. on the cover. A few of Nina's dresses hung on wooden pegs, stiffened in a look of offended dignity at their abandonment. He remembered making the pegs himself and noticed that they were very good pegs. Where was the key? He looked round and saw it near the door where he stood. It was red with rust. He felt very much annoyed at that, and directly afterwards wondered at his own feeling. What did it matter? There soon would be no key—no door—nothing! He paused, key in hand, and asked himself whether he knew well what he was about. He went out again on the verandah and stood by the table thinking. The monkey jumped down, and, snatching a banana skin, absorbed itself in picking it to shreds industriously.

"Forget!" muttered Almayer, and that word started before him a sequence of events, a detailed programme of things to do. He knew perfectly well what was to be done now. First this, then that, and then forget-fulness would come easy. Very easy. He had a fixed idea that if he should not forget before he died he would have to remember to all eternity. Certain things had to be taken out of his life, stamped out of sight, destroyed, forgotten. For a long time he stood in deep thought, lost in the alarming possibilities of unconquerable memory, with the fear of death and eternity before him. "Eternity!" he said aloud, and the sound of that word recalled him out of his reverie. The monkey started, dropped the skin, and grinned up at him amicably.

He went towards the office door and with some difficulty managed to open it. He entered in a cloud of dust that rose under his feet. Books open with torn pages bestrewed the floor; other books lay about grimy and black, looking as if they had never been opened. Account books. In those books he had intended to keep day by day a record of his rising fortunes. Long time ago. A very long time. For many years there had been no record to keep on the blue and red ruled pages! In the middle of the room the big office desk, with one of its legs broken, careened over like the hull of a stranded ship; most of the drawers had fallen out, disclosing heaps of paper yellow with age and dirt. The revolving office chair stood in its place, but he found the pivot set fast when he tried to turn it. No matter. He desisted, and his eyes wandered slowly from object to object. All those things had cost a lot of money at the time. The desk, the paper, the torn books, and the broken shelves, all under a thick coat of dust. The very dust and bones of a dead and gone business. He looked at all these things, all that was left after so many years of work, of strife, of weariness, of discouragement, conquered so many times. And all for what? He stood thinking mournfully of his past life till he heard distinctly the clear voice of a child speaking amongst all this wreck, ruin, and waste. He started with a great fear in his heart, and feverishly began to rake in the papers scattered on the floor, broke the chair into bits, splintered the drawers by banging them against the desk, and made a big heap of all that rubbish in one corner of the room.

He came out quickly, slammed the door after him, turned the key, and, taking it out, ran to the front rail of the verandah, and, with a great swing of his arm, sent the key whizzing into the river. This done he went back slowly to the table, called the monkey down, unhooked its chain, and induced it to remain quiet in the breast of his jacket. Then he sat again on the table and looked fixedly at the door of the room he had just left. He listened also intently. He heard a dry sound of rustling sharp cracks as of dry wood snapping; a whirr like that of a bird's wings when it rises suddenly, and then he saw a thin stream of smoke come through the keyhole. The monkey struggled under his coat. Ali appeared with his eyes starting out of his head.

"Master! House burn!" he shouted.

Almayer stood up holding by the table. He could hear the yells of alarm and surprise in the settlement. Ali wrung his hands, lamenting aloud.

"Stop this noise, fool!" said Almayer, quietly. "Pick up my hammock and blankets and take them to the other house. Quick, now!"

The smoke burst through the crevices of the door, and Ali, with the hammock in his arms, cleared in one bound the steps of the verandah.

"It has caught well," muttered Almayer to himself. "Be quiet, Jack," he added, as the monkey made a frantic effort to escape from its confinement.

The door split from top to bottom, and a rush of flame and smoke drove Almayer away from the table

to the front rail of the verandah. He held on there till
a great roar overhead assured him that the roof was
ablaze. Then he ran down the steps of the verandah,
coughing, half choked with the smoke that pursued
him in bluish wreaths curling about his head.

On the other side of the ditch, separating Almayer's
courtyard from the settlement, a crowd of the inhabitants of Sambir looked at the burning house of the
white man. In the calm air the flames rushed up on
high, coloured pale brick-red, with violet gleams in the
strong sunshine. The thin column of smoke ascended
straight and unwavering till it lost itself in the clear blue
of the sky, and in the great empty space between the
two houses the interested spectators could see the tall
figure of the Tuan Putih, with bowed head and dragging
feet, walking slowly away from the fire towards the
shelter of "Almayer's Folly."

In that manner did Almayer move into his new house.
He took possession of the new ruin, and in the undying
folly of his heart set himself to wait in anxiety and pain
for that forgetfulness which was so slow to come. He
had done all he could. Every vestige of Nina's existence had been destroyed; and now with every sunrise
he asked himself whether the longed-for oblivion would
come before sunset, whether it would come before he
died? He wanted to live only long enough to be able to
forget, and the tenacity of his memory filled him with
dread and horror of death; for should it come before
he could accomplish the purpose of his life he would
have to remember for ever! He also longed for loneliness. He wanted to be alone. But he was not. In
the dim light of the rooms with their closed shutters,
in the bright sunshine of the verandah, wherever he
went, whichever way he turned, he saw the small figure
of a little maiden with pretty olive face, with long black

hair, her little pink robe slipping off her shoulders, her big eyes looking up at him in the tender trustfulness of a petted child. Ali did not see anything, but he also was aware of the presence of a child in the house. In his long talks by the evening fires of the settlement he used to tell his intimate friends of Almayer's strange doings. His master had turned sorcerer in his old age. Ali said that often when Tuan Putih had retired for the night he could hear him talking to something in his room. Ali thought that it was a spirit in the shape of a child. He knew his master spoke to a child from certain expressions and words his master used. His master spoke in Malay a little, but mostly in English, which he, Ali, could understand. Master spoke to the child at times tenderly, then he would weep over it, laugh at it, scold it, beg of it to go away; curse it. It was a bad and stubborn spirit. Ali thought his master had imprudently called it up, and now could not get rid of it. His master was very brave; he was not afraid to curse this spirit in the very Presence; and once he fought with it. Ali had heard a great noise as of running about inside the room and groans. His master groaned. Spirits do not groan. His master was brave, but foolish. You cannot hurt a spirit. Ali expected to find his master dead next morning, but he came out very early, looking much older than the day before, and had no food all day.

So far Ali to the settlement. To Captain Ford he was much more communicative, for the good reason that Captain Ford had the purse and gave orders. On each of Ford's monthly visits to Sambir Ali had to go on board with a report about the inhabitant of "Almayer's Folly." On his first visit to Sambir, after Nina's departure, Ford had taken charge of Almayer's affairs. They were not cumbersome. The shed for the storage of goods was empty, the boats had disappeared, appropriated—generally in night-time—by various citizens of Sambir in need of means of transport. During a great flood the jetty of Lingard and Co. left the bank and floated down the river, probably in search of more cheerful surroundings; even the flock of geese—"the only geese on the east coast"—departed somewhere, preferring the unknown dangers of the bush to the desolation of their old home. As time went on the grass grew over the black patch of ground where the old house used to stand, and nothing remained to mark the place of the dwelling that had sheltered Almayer's young hopes, his foolish dream of splendid future, his awakening, and his despair.

Ford did not often visit Almayer, for visiting Almayer was not a pleasant task. At first he used to respond listlessly to the old seaman's boisterous inquiries about his health; he even made efforts to talk, asking for news in a voice that made it perfectly clear that no news from this world had any interest for him. Then gradually he became more silent—not sulkily—but as if he was forgetting how to speak. He used also to hide in the darkest rooms of the house where Ford had to seek him out guided by the patter of the monkey galloping before him. The monkey was always there to receive and introduce Ford. The little animal seemed to have taken complete charge of its master, and whenever it wished for his presence on the verandah it would tug perseveringly at his jacket, till Almayer obediently came out into the sunshine, which he seemed to dislike so much.

One morning Ford found him sitting on the floor of the verandah, his back against the wall, his legs stretched stiffly out, his arms hanging by his side. His expressionless face, his eyes open wide with immobile pupils, and the rigidity of his pose, made him look like an immense man-doll broken and flung there out of the way. As Ford came up the steps he turned his head slowly.

"Ford," he murmured from the floor, "I cannot forget."

"Can't you?" said Ford, innocently, with an attempt at joviality: "I wish I was like you. I am losing my memory—age, I suppose; only the other day my mate——"

He stopped, for Almayer had got up, stumbled, and steadied himself on his friend's arm.

"Hallo! You are better to-day. Soon be all right," said Ford, cheerfully, but feeling rather scared.

Almayer let go his arm and stood very straight with his head up and shoulders thrown back, looking stonily at the multitude of suns shining in ripples of the river. His jacket and his loose trousers flapped in the breeze on his thin limbs.

"Let her go!" he whispered in a grating voice. "Let her go. To-morrow I shall forget. I am a firm man, . . . firm as a . . . rock, . . . firm. . . ."

Ford looked at his face—and fled. The skipper was a tolerably firm man himself—as those who had sailed with him could testify—but Almayer's firmness was altogether too much for his fortitude.

Next time the steamer called in Sambir Ali came on board early with a grievance. He complained to Ford that Jim-Eng the Chinaman had invaded Almayer's house, and actually had lived there for the last month.

"And they both smoke," added Ali.

"Phew! Opium, you mean?"

Ali nodded, and Ford remained thoughtful; then he muttered to himself, "Poor devil! The sooner the better now." In the afternoon he walked up to the house.

"What are you doing here?" he asked of Jim-Eng, whom he found strolling about on the verandah.

Jim-Eng explained in bad Malay, and speaking in that monotonous, uninterested voice of an opium smoker pretty far gone, that his house was old, the roof leaked, and the floor was rotten. So, being an old friend for many, many years, he took his money, his opium, and two pipes, and came to live in this big house.

"There is plenty of room. He smokes, and I live here. He will not smoke long," he concluded.

"Where is he now?" asked Ford.

"Inside. He sleeps," answered Jim-Eng, wearily.

Ford glanced in through the doorway. In the dim light of the room he could see Almayer lying on his back on the floor, his head on a wooden pillow, the long white beard scattered over his breast, the yellow skin of the face, the half-closed eyelids showing the whites of the eye only. . . .

He shuddered and turned away. As he was leaving he noticed a long strip of faded red silk, with some Chinese letters on it, which Jim-Eng had just fastened to one of the pillars.

"What's that?" he asked.

"That," said Jim-Eng, in his colourless voice, "that is the name of the house. All the same like my house. Very good name."

Ford looked at him for awhile and went away. He did not know what the crazy-looking maze of the Chinese inscription on the red silk meant. Had he asked Jim-Eng, that patient Chinaman would have informed him with proper pride that its meaning was: "House of heavenly delight."

In the evening of the same day Babalatchi called on

Captain Ford. The captain's cabin opened on deck, and Babalatchi sat astride on the high step, while Ford smoked his pipe on the settee inside. The steamer was leaving next morning, and the old statesman came as usual for a last chat.

"We had news from Bali last moon," remarked Babalatchi. "A grandson is born to the old Rajah, and there is great rejoicing."

Ford sat up interested.

"Yes," went on Babalatchi, in answer to Ford's look. "I told him. That was before he began to smoke."

"Well, and what?" asked Ford.

"I escaped with my life," said Babalatchi, with perfect gravity, "because the white man is very weak and fell as he rushed upon me." Then, after a pause, he added, "She is mad with joy."

"Mrs. Almayer, you mean?"

"Yes, she lives in our Rajah's house. She will not die soon. Such women live a long time," said Babalatchi, with a slight tinge of regret in his voice. "She has dollars, and she has buried them, but we know where. We had much trouble with those people. We had to pay a fine and listen to threats from the white men, and now we have to be careful." He sighed and remained silent for a long while. Then with energy:

"There will be fighting. There is a breath of war on the islands. Shall I live long enough to see? . . . Ah, Tuan!" he went on, more quietly, "the old times were best. Even I have sailed with Lanun men, and boarded in the night silent ships with white sails. That was before an English Rajah ruled in Kuching. Then we fought amongst ourselves and were happy. Now when we fight with you we can only die!"

He rose to go. "Tuan," he said, "you remember the

girl that man Bulangi had? Her that caused all the
trouble?"

"Yes," said Ford. "What of her?"

"She grew thin and could not work. Then Bulangi,
who is a thief and a pig-eater, gave her to me for fifty
dollars. I sent her amongst my women to grow fat.
I wanted to hear the sound of her laughter, but she
must have been bewitched, and   .   .   .   she died two
days ago. Nay, Tuan. Why do you speak bad words?
I am old—that is true—but why should I not like the
sight of a young face and the sound of a young voice in
my house?" He paused, and then added with a little
mournful laugh, "I am like a white man talking too
much of what is not men's talk when they speak to one
another."

And he went off looking very sad.

*   *   *   *   *

The crowd massed in a semicircle before the steps
of "Almayer's Folly," swayed silently backwards and
forwards, and opened out before the group of white-
robed and turbaned men advancing through the grass
towards the house. Abdulla walked first, supported by
Reshid and followed by all the Arabs in Sambir. As
they entered the lane made by the respectful throng
there was a subdued murmur of voices, where the word
"Mati" was the only one distinctly audible. Abdulla
stopped and looked round slowly.

"Is he dead?" he asked.

"May you live!" answered the crowd in one shout,
and then there succeeded a breathless silence.

Abdulla made a few paces forward and found himself
for the last time face to face with his old enemy. Whatever he might have been once he was not dangerous

now, lying stiff and lifeless in the tender light of the early day. The only white man on the east coast was dead, and his soul, delivered from the trammels of his earthly folly, stood now in the presence of Infinite Wisdom. On the upturned face there was that serene look which follows the sudden relief from anguish and pain, and it testified silently before the cloudless heaven that the man lying there under the gaze of indifferent eyes had been permitted to forget before he died.

Abdulla looked down sadly at this Infidel he had fought so long and had bested so many times. Such was the reward of the Faithful! Yet in the Arab's old heart there was a feeling of regret for that thing gone out of his life. He was leaving fast behind him friendships, and enmities, successes, and disappointments—all that makes up a life; and before him was only the end. Prayer would fill up the remainder of the days allotted to the True Believer! He took in his hand the beads that hung at his waist.

"I found him here, like this, in the morning," said Ali, in a low and awed voice.

Abdulla glanced coldly once more at the serene face. "Let us go," he said, addressing Reshid.

And as they passed through the crowd that fell back before them, the beads in Abdulla's hand clicked, while in a solemn whisper he breathed out piously the name of Allah! The Merciful! The Compassionate!

THE END

TALES OF UNREST

AUTHOR'S NOTE

OF THE five stories in this volume The Lagoon, the last in order, is the earliest in date. It is the first short story I ever wrote and marks, in a manner of speaking, the end of my first phase, the Malayan phase with its special subject and its verbal suggestions. Conceived in the same mood which produced "Almayer's Folly" and "An Outcast of the Islands," it is told in the same breath (with what was left of it, that is, after the end of An Outcast), seen with the same vision, rendered in the same method—if such a thing as method did exist then in my conscious relation to this new adventure of writing for print. I doubt it very much. One does one's work first and theorizes about it afterwards. It is a very amusing and egotistical occupation of no use whatever to any one and just as likely as not to lead to false conclusions.

Anybody can see that between the last paragraph of An Outcast and the first of The Lagoon there has been no change of pen, figuratively speaking. It happens also to be literally true. It was the same pen: a common steel pen. Having been charged with a certain lack of emotional faculty I am glad to be able to say that on one occasion at least I did give way to a sentimental impulse. I thought the pen had been a good pen and that it had done enough for me, and so, with the idea of keeping it for a sort of memento on which I could look later with tender eyes, I put it into my waistcoat pocket. Afterwards it used to turn up in all sorts of places, at the bottom of small drawers, among my studs in cardboard boxes, till at last it found permanent rest in a large wooden bowl containing some loose keys, bits of sealing wax, bits of string, small broken chains, a few buttons, and similar minute wreckage that washes out of a man's life into such receptacles. I would catch sight of it from time to time with a distinct feeling of satisfaction till, one day, I perceived with horror that there were two old pens in there. How the other pen found its way into the bowl instead of the fireplace or wastepaper basket I can't imagine, but there the two were, lying side by side, both encrusted with ink and completely undistinguishable from each other. It was very distressing, but being determined not to share my sentiment between two pens or run the risk of sentimentalizing over a mere stranger, I threw them both out of the window into a flower bed—which strikes me now as a poetical grave for the remnants of one's past.

But the tale remained. It was first fixed in print in the *Cornhill Magazine*, being my first appearance in a serial of any kind; and I have lived long enough to see it most agreeably guyed by Mr. Max Beerbohm in a volume of parodies entitled "A Christmas Garland," where I found myself in very good company. I was immensely gratified. I began to believe in my public existence. I have much to thank The Lagoon for.

My next effort in short story writing was a departure —I mean a departure from the Malay Archipelago. Without premeditation, without sorrow, without rejoicing and almost without noticing it, I stepped into the very different atmosphere of An Outpost of Progress. I found there a different moral attitude. I seemed able to capture new reactions, new suggestions, and even new rhythms for my paragraphs. For a moment I fancied myself a new man—a most exciting illusion. It clung to me for some time, monstrous, half conviction and half hope as to its body, with an iridescent tail of dreams and with a changeable head like a plastic mask. It was only later that I perceived that in common with the rest of men nothing could deliver me from my fatal consistency. We cannot escape from ourselves.

An Outpost of Progress is the lightest part of the loot I carried off from Central Africa, the main portion being of course "The Heart of Darkness." Other men have found a lot of quite different things there and I have the comfortable conviction that what I took would not have been of much use to anybody else. And it must be said that it was but a very small amount of plunder. All of it could go into one's breast pocket when folded neatly. As for the story itself it is true enough in its essentials. The sustained invention of a really telling lie demands a talent which I do not possess.

The Idiots is such an obviously derivative piece of work that it is impossible for me to say anything about it here. The suggestion of it was not mental but visual: the actual idiots. It was after an interval of long groping amongst vague impulses and hesitations which ended in the production of the Nigger that I turned to my third short story in the order of time, the first in this volume: Karain: A Memory.

Reading it after many years Karain produced on me the effect of something seen through a pair of glasses from a rather advantageous position. In that story I had not gone back to the Archipelago, I had only turned for another look at it. I admit that I was absorbed by the distant view, so absorbed that I didn't notice then that the *motif* of the story is almost identical with the *motif* of The Lagoon. However, the idea at the back is very different; but the story is mainly made memorable to me by the fact that it was my first contribution to *Blackwoods' Magazine* and that it led to my personal acquaintance with Mr. William Blackwood whose guarded appreciation I felt nevertheless to be genuine, and prized accordingly. Karain was begun on a sudden impulse only three days after I wrote the last line of the Nigger, and the recollection of its difficulties is mixed up with the worries of the unfinished Return, the last pages of which I took up again at the time; the only instance in my life when I made an attempt to write with both hands at once as it were.

Indeed my innermost feeling, now, is that The Return is a left-handed production. Looking through that story lately I had the material impression of sitting under a large and expensive umbrella in the loud drumming of a furious rain-shower. It was very distracting. In the general uproar one could hear every individual drop strike on the stout and distended silk. Mentally, the reading rendered me dumb for the remainder of the day, not exactly with astonishment but with a sort of dismal wonder. I don't want to talk disrespectfully of any pages of mine. Psychologically there were no doubt good reasons for my attempt; and it was worth while, if only to see of what excesses I was capable in that sort of virtuosity. In this connection I should like to confess my surprise on finding that notwithstanding all its apparatus of analysis the story consists for the most part of physical impressions; impressions of sound and sight, railway station, streets, a trotting horse, reflections in mirrors and so on, rendered as if for their own sake and combined with a sublimated description of a desirable middle class town-residence which somehow manages to produce a sinister effect. For the rest any kind word about The Return (and there have been such words said at different times) awakens in me the liveliest gratitude, for I know how much the writing of that fantasy has cost me in sheer toil, in temper and in disillusion.

J. C.

CONTENTS

CONTENTS

TALES OF UNREST

'Be it thy course to busy giddy minds
With foreign quarrels'

SHAKESPEARE

TALES OF UNREST

KARAIN: A MEMORY

I

WE KNEW him in those unprotected days when we were content to hold in our hands our lives and our property. None of us, I believe, has any property now, and I hear that many, negligently, have lost their lives; but I am sure that the few who survive are not yet so dim-eyed as to miss in the befogged respectability of their newspapers the intelligence of various native risings in the Eastern Archipelago. Sunshine gleams between the lines of those short paragraphs—sunshine and the glitter of the sea. A strange name wakes up memories; the printed words scent the smoky atmosphere of to-day faintly, with the subtle and penetrating perfume as of land breezes breathing through the starlight of bygone nights; a signal fire gleams like a jewel on the high brow of a sombre cliff; great trees, the advanced sentries of immense forests, stand watchful and still over sleeping stretches of open water; a line of white surf thunders on an empty beach, the shallow water foams on the reefs; and green islets scattered through the calm of noonday lie upon the level of a polished sea, like a handful of emeralds on a buckler of steel.

There are faces too—faces dark, truculent, and smiling; the frank audacious faces of men barefooted, well

armed and noiseless. They thronged the narrow length
of our schooner's decks with their ornamented and barbarous crowd, with the variegated colours of checkered
sarongs, red turbans, white jackets, embroideries; with
the gleam of scabbards, gold rings, charms, armlets,
lance blades, and jewelled handles of their weapons.
They had an independent bearing, resolute eyes, a restrained manner; and we seem yet to hear their soft
voices speaking of battles, travels, and escapes; boast-
ing with composure, joking quietly; sometimes in well-
bred murmurs extolling their own valour, our generosity; or celebrating with loyal enthusiasm the virtues
of their ruler. We remember the faces, the eyes, the
voices, we see again the gleam of silk and metal; the
murmuring stir of that crowd, brilliant, festive, and
martial; and we seem to feel the touch of friendly
brown hands that, after one short grasp, return to rest
on a chased hilt. They were Karain's people—a
devoted following. Their movements hung on his
lips; they read their thoughts in his eyes; he murmured
to them nonchalantly of life and death, and they accepted his words humbly, like gifts of fate. They were
all free men, and when speaking to him said, "Your
slave." On his passage voices died out as though he
had walked guarded by silence; awed whispers followed
him. They called him their war-chief. He was the
ruler of three villages on a narrow plain; the master
of an insignificant foothold on the earth—of a conquered
foothold that, shaped like a young moon, lay ignored
between the hills and the sea.

From the deck of our schooner, anchored in the
middle of the bay, he indicated by a theatrical sweep
of his arm along the jagged outline of the hills the
whole of his domain; and the ample movement seemed
to drive back its limits, augmenting it suddenly into

something so immense and vague that for a moment it appeared to be bounded only by the sky. And really, looking at that place, landlocked from the sea and shut off from the land by the precipitous slopes of mountains, it was difficult to believe in the existence of any neighbourhood. It was still, complete, unknown, and full of a life that went on stealthily with a troubling effect of solitude; of a life that seemed unaccountably empty of anything that would stir the thought, touch the heart, give a hint of the ominous sequence of days. It appeared to us a land without memories, regrets, and hopes; a land where nothing could survive the coming of the night, and where each sunrise, like a dazzling act of special creation, was disconnected from the eve and the morrow.

Karain swept his hand over it. "All mine!" He struck the deck with his long staff; the gold head flashed like a falling star; very close behind him a silent old fellow in a richly embroidered black jacket alone of all the Malays around did not follow the masterful gesture with a look. He did not even lift his eyelids. He bowed his head behind his master, and without stirring held hilt up over his right shoulder a long blade in a silver scabbard. He was there on duty, but without curiosity, and seemed weary, not with age, but with the possession of a burdensome secret of existence. Karain, heavy and proud, had a lofty pose and breathed calmly. It was our first visit, and we looked about curiously.

The bay was like a bottomless pit of intense light. The circular sheet of water reflected a luminous sky, and the shores enclosing it made an opaque ring of earth floating in an emptiness of transparent blue. The hills, purple and arid, stood out heavily on the sky: their summits seemed to fade into a coloured tremble

*H

as of ascending vapour; their steep sides were streaked with the green of narrow ravines; at their foot lay rice-fields, plantain-patches, yellow sands. A torrent wound about like a dropped thread. Clumps of fruit-trees marked the villages; slim palms put their nodding heads together above the low houses; dried palm-leaf roofs shone afar, like roofs of gold, behind the dark colonnades of tree-trunks; figures passed vivid and vanishing; the smoke of fires stood upright above the masses of flowering bushes; bamboo fences glittered, running away in broken lines between the fields. A sudden cry on the shore sounded plaintive in the distance, and ceased abruptly, as if stifled in the downpour of sunshine. A puff of breeze made a flash of darkness on the smooth water, touched our faces, and became forgotten. Nothing moved. The sun blazed down into a shadowless hollow of colours and stillness.

It was the stage where, dressed splendidly for his part, he strutted, incomparably dignified, made important by the power he had to awaken an absurd expectation of something heroic going to take place— a burst of action or song—upon the vibrating tone of a wonderful sunshine. He was ornate and disturbing, for one could not imagine what depth of horrible void such an elaborate front could be worthy to hide. He was not masked—there was too much life in him, and a mask is only a lifeless thing; but he presented himself essentially as an actor, as a human being aggressively disguised. His smallest acts were prepared and unexpected, his speeches grave, his sentences ominous like hints and complicated like arabesques. He was treated with a solemn respect accorded in the irreverent West only to the monarchs of the stage, and he accepted the profound homage with a sustained dignity seen nowhere else but behind the footlights and in the condensed falseness of some grossly tragic situation. It was almost impossible to remember who he was— only a petty chief of a conveniently isolated corner of Mindanao, where we could in comparative safety break the law against the traffic in firearms and ammunition with the natives. What would happen should one of the moribund Spanish gun-boats be suddenly galvanized into a flicker of active life did not trouble us, once we were inside the bay—so completely did it appear out of the reach of a meddling world; and besides, in those days we were imaginative enough to look with a kind of joyous equanimity on any chance there was of being quietly hanged somewhere out of the way of diplomatic remonstrance. As to Karain, nothing could happen to him unless what happens to all—failure and death; but his quality was to appear clothed in the illusion of unavoidable success. He seemed too effective, too necessary there, too much of an essential condition for the existence of his land and his people, to be destroyed by anything short of an earthquake. He summed up his race, his country, the elemental force of ardent life, of tropical nature. He had its luxuriant strength, its fascination; and, like it, he carried the seed of peril within.

In many successive visits we came to know his stage well—the purple semicircle of hills, the slim trees leaning over houses, the yellow sands, the streaming green of ravines. All that had the crude and blended colouring, the appropriateness almost excessive, the suspicious immobility of a painted scene; and it enclosed so perfectly the accomplished acting of his amazing pretences that the rest of the world seemed shut out forever from the gorgeous spectacle. There could be nothing outside. It was as if the earth had gone on spinning, and had left that crumb of its surface alone

in space. He appeared utterly cut off from everything
but the sunshine, and that even seemed to be made
for him alone. Once when asked what was on the other
side of the hills, he said, with a meaning smile, "Friends
and enemies—many enemies; else why should I buy
your rifles and powder?" He was always like this—
word-perfect in his part, playing up faithfully to the
mysteries and certitudes of his surroundings. "Friends
and enemies"—nothing else. It was impalpable and
vast. The earth had indeed rolled away from under
his land, and he, with his handful of people, stood
surrounded by a silent tumult as of contending shades.
Certainly no sound came from outside. "Friends
and enemies!" He might have added, "and memories," at least as far as he himself was concerned;
but he neglected to make that point then. It made
itself later on, though; but it was after the daily perfor-
mance—in the wings, so to speak, and with the lights
out. Meantime he filled the stage with barbarous
dignity. Some ten years ago he had led his people
—a scratch lot of wandering Bugis—to the conquest
of the bay, and now in his august care they had forgotten all the past, and had lost all concern for the
future. He gave them wisdom, advice, reward, punishment, life or death, with the same serenity of attitude and voice. He understood irrigation and the art
of war—the qualities of weapons and the craft of boat-
building. He could conceal his heart; had more endurance; he could swim longer, and steer a canoe better
than any of his people; he could shoot straighter, and
negotiate more tortuously than any man of his race I
knew. He was an adventurer of the sea, an outcast,
a ruler—and my very good friend. I wish him a quick
death in a stand-up fight, a death in sunshine; for he had
known remorse and power, and no man can demand

more from life. Day after day he appeared before us incomparably faithful to the illusions of the stage, and at sunset the night descended upon him quickly, like a falling curtain. The seamed hills became black shadows towering high upon a clear sky; above them the glittering confusion of stars resembled a mad turmoil stilled by a gesture; sounds ceased, men slept, forms vanished—and the reality of the universe alone remained—a marvellous thing of darkness and glimmers.

II

BUT it was at night that he talked openly, forgetting the exactions of his stage. In the daytime there were affairs to be discussed in state. There were at first between him and me his own splendour, my shabby suspicions, and the scenic landscape that intruded upon the reality of our lives by its motionless fantasy of outline and colour. His followers thronged round him; above his head the broad blades of their spears made a spiked halo of iron points, and they hedged him from humanity by the shimmer of silks, the gleam of weapons, the excited and respectful hum of eager voices. Before sunset he would take leave with ceremony, and go off sitting under a red umbrella, and escorted by a score of boats. All the paddles flashed and struck together with a mighty splash that reverberated loudly in the monumental amphitheatre of hills. A broad stream of dazzling foam trailed behind the flotilla. The canoes appeared very black on the white hiss of water; turbaned heads swayed back and forth; a multitude of arms in crimson and yellow rose and fell with one movement; the spearmen upright in the bows of canoes had variegated sarongs and gleaming shoulders like bronze statues; the muttered strophes of the paddlers' song ended periodically in a plaintive shout. They diminished in the distance; the song ceased; they swarmed on the beach in the long shadows of the western hills. The sunlight lingered on the purple crests, and we could see him leading the

way to his stockade, a burly bareheaded figure walking
far in advance of a straggling *cortège*, and swinging
regularly an ebony staff taller than himself. The
darkness deepened fast; torches gleamed fitfully,
passing behind bushes; a long hail or two trailed in
the silence of the evening; and at last the night stretched
its smooth veil over the shore, the lights, and the
voices.

Then, just as we were thinking of repose, the watchmen of the schooner would hail a splash of paddles
away in the starlit gloom of the bay; a voice would
respond in cautious tones, and our serang, putting his
head down the open skylight, would inform us without
surprise, "That Rajah, he coming. He here now."
Karain appeared noiselessly in the doorway of the little
cabin. He was simplicity itself then; all in white;
muffled about his head; for arms only a kriss with a
plain buffalo-horn handle, which he would politely
conceal within a fold of his sarong before stepping over
the threshold. The old sword-bearer's face, the worn-
out and mournful face so covered with wrinkles that it
seemed to look out through the meshes of a fine dark
net, could be seen close above his shoulders. Karain
never moved without that attendant, who stood or
squatted close at his back. He had a dislike of an
open space behind him. It was more than a dislike
—it resembled fear, a nervous preoccupation of what
went on where he could not see. This, in view of
the evident and fierce loyalty that surrounded him,
was inexplicable. He was there alone in the midst of
devoted men; he was safe from neighbourly am-
bushes, from fraternal ambitions; and yet more than
one of our visitors had assured us that their ruler
could not bear to be alone. They said, "Even when
he eats and sleeps there is always one on the watch near

him who has strength and weapons." There was indeed always one near him, though our informants had
no conception of that watcher's strength and weapons,
which were both shadowy and terrible. We knew,
but only later on, when we had heard the story. Meantime we noticed that, even during the most important
interviews, Karain would often give a start, and interrupting his discourse, would sweep his arm back with
a sudden movement, to feel whether the old fellow
was there. The old fellow, impenetrable and weary,
was always there. He shared his food, his repose,
and his thoughts; he knew his plans, guarded his
secrets; and, impassive behind his master's agitation,
without stirring the least bit, murmured above his head
in a soothing tone some words difficult to catch.

It was only on board the schooner, when surrounded by white faces, by unfamiliar sights and sounds,
that Karain seemed to forget the strange obsession
that wound like a black thread through the gorgeous
pomp of his public life. At night we treated him in
a free and easy manner, which just stopped short of
slapping him on the back, for there are liberties one
must not take with a Malay. He said himself that on
such occasions he was only a private gentleman coming
to see other gentlemen whom he supposed as well born
as himself. I fancy that to the last he believed us to be
emissaries of Government, darkly official persons fur-
thering by our illegal traffic some dark scheme of high
statecraft. Our denials and protestations were unavail-
ing. He only smiled with discreet politeness and inquired about the Queen. Every visit began with that
inquiry; he was insatiable of details; he was fascinated
by the holder of a sceptre the shadow of which, stretching from the westward over the earth and over the
seas, passed far beyond his own hand's-breadth of

conquered land. He multiplied questions; he could never know enough of the Monarch of whom he spoke with wonder and chivalrous respect—with a kind of affectionate awe! Afterwards, when we had learned that he was the son of a woman who had many years ago ruled a small Bugis state, we came to suspect that the memory of his mother (of whom he spoke with enthusiasm) mingled somehow in his mind with the image he tried to form for himself of the far-off Queen whom he called Great, Invincible, Pious, and Fortunate. We had to invent details at last to satisfy his craving curiosity; and our loyalty must be pardoned, for we tried to make them fit for his august and resplendent ideal. We talked. The night slipped over us, over the still schooner, over the sleeping land, and over the sleepless sea that thundered amongst the reefs outside the bay. His paddlers, two trustworthy men, slept in the canoe at the foot of our side-ladder. The old confidant, relieved from duty, dozed on his heels, with his back against the companion-doorway; and Karain sat squarely in the ship's wooden armchair, under the slight sway of the cabin lamp, a cheroot between his dark fingers, and a glass of lemonade before him. He was amused by the fizz of the thing, but after a sip or two would let it get flat, and with a courteous wave of his hand ask for a fresh bottle. He decimated our slender stock; but we did not begrudge it to him, for, when he began, he talked well. He must have been a great Bugis dandy in his time, for even then (and when we knew him he was no longer young) his splendour was spotlessly neat, and he dyed his hair a light shade of brown. The quiet dignity of his bearing transformed the dim-lit cuddy of the schooner into an audience-hall. He talked of inter-island politics with an ironic and melancholy shrewdness. He had travelled

much, suffered not a little, intrigued, fought. He knew
native Courts, European Settlements, the forests, the
sea, and, as he said himself, had spoken in his time to
many great men. He liked to talk with me because
I had known some of these men: he seemed to think
that I could understand him, and, with a fine confidence, assumed that I, at least, could appreciate how
much greater he was himself. But he preferred to
talk of his native country—a small Bugis state on the
island of Celebes. I had visited it some time before,
and he asked eagerly for news. As men's names
came up in conversation he would say, "We swam
against one another when we were boys;" or, "We
had hunted the deer together—he could use the noose
and the spear as well as I." Now and then his big
dreamy eyes would roll restlessly; he frowned or
smiled, or he would become pensive, and, staring in
silence, would nod slightly for a time at some regretted
vision of the past.

His mother had been the ruler of a small semi-
independent state on the sea-coast at the head of the
Gulf of Boni. He spoke of her with pride. She had
been a woman resolute in affairs of state and of her
own heart. After the death of her first husband, un-
dismayed by the turbulent opposition of the chiefs,
she married a rich trader, a Korinchi man of no family.
Karain was her son by that second marriage, but his
unfortunate descent had apparently nothing to do
with his exile. He said nothing as to its cause, though
once he let slip with a sigh, "Ha! my land will not
feel any more the weight of my body." But he related
willingly the story of his wanderings, and told us
all about the conquest of the bay. Alluding to the
people beyond the hills, he would murmur gently, with
a careless wave of the hand, "They came over the

hills once to fight us, but those who got away never came again." He thought for a while, smiling to himself. "Very few got away," he added, with proud serenity. He cherished the recollections of his successes; he had an exulting eagerness for endeavour; when he talked, his aspect was warlike, chivalrous, and uplifting. No wonder his people admired him. We saw him once walking in daylight amongst the houses of the settlement. At the doors of huts groups of women turned to look after him, warbling softly, and with gleaming eyes; armed men stood out of the way, submissive and erect; others approached from the side, bending their backs to address him humbly; an old woman stretched out a draped lean arm— "Blessings on thy head!" she cried from a dark doorway; a fiery-eyed man showed above the low fence of a plantain-patch a streaming face, a bare breast scarred in two places, and bellowed out pantingly after him, "God give victory to our master!" Karain walked fast, and with firm long strides; he answered greetings right and left by quick piercing glances. Children ran forward between the houses, peeped fearfully round corners; young boys kept up with him, gliding between bushes: their eyes gleamed through the dark leaves. The old sword-bearer, shouldering the silver scabbard, shuffled hastily at his heels with bowed head, and his eyes on the ground. And in the midst of a great stir they passed swift and absorbed, like two men hurrying through a great solitude.

In his council hall he was surrounded by the gravity of armed chiefs, while two long rows of old headmen dressed in cotton stuffs squatted on their heels, with idle arms hanging over their knees. Under the thatch roof supported by smooth columns, of which each one had cost the life of a straight-stemmed young palm, the scent of flowering hedges drifted in warm waves. The sun was sinking. In the open courtyard suppliants walked through the gate, raising, when yet far off, their joined hands above bowed heads, and bending low in the bright stream of sunlight. Young girls, with flowers in their laps, sat under the wide-spreading boughs of a big tree. The blue smoke of wood fires spread in a thin mist above the high-pitched roofs of houses that had glistening walls of woven reeds, and all round them rough wooden pillars under the sloping eaves. He dispensed justice in the shade; from a high seat he gave orders, advice, reproof. Now and then the hum of approbation rose louder, and idle spearmen that lounged listlessly against the posts, looking at the girls, would turn their heads slowly. To no man had been given the shelter of so much respect, confidence, and awe. Yet at times he would lean forward and appear to listen as for a far-off note of discord, as if expecting to hear some faint voice, the sound of light footsteps; or he would start half up in his seat, as though he had been familiarly touched on the shoulder. He glanced back with apprehension; his aged follower whispered inaudibly at his ear; the chiefs turned their eyes away in silence, for the old wizard, the man who could command ghosts and send evil spirits against enemies, was speaking low to their ruler. Around the short stillness of the open place the trees rustled faintly, the soft laughter of girls playing with the flowers rose in clear bursts of joyous sound. At the end of upright spear-shafts the long tufts of dyed horse-hair waved crimson and filmy in the gust of wind; and beyond the blaze of hedges the brook of limpid quick water ran invisible and loud under the drooping grass of the bank, with a great murmur, passionate and gentle.

After sunset, far across the fields and over the bay, clusters of torches could be seen burning under the high roofs of the council shed. Smoky red flames swayed on high poles, and the fiery blaze flickered over faces, clung to the smooth trunks of palm-trees, kindled bright sparks on the rims of metal dishes standing on fine floor-mats. That obscure adventurer feasted like a king. Small groups of men crouched in tight circles round the wooden platters; brown hands hovered over snowy heaps of rice. Sitting upon a rough couch apart from the others, he leaned on his elbow with inclined head; and near him a youth improvised in a high tone a song that celebrated his valour and wisdom. The singer rocked himself to and fro, rolling frenzied eyes; old women hobbled about with dishes, and men, squatting low, lifted their heads to listen gravely without ceasing to eat. The song of triumph vibrated in the night, and the stanzas rolled out mournful and fiery like the thoughts of a hermit. He silenced it with a sign, "Enough!" An owl hooted far away, exulting in the delight of deep gloom in dense foliage; overhead lizards ran in the attap thatch, calling softly; the dry leaves of the roof rustled; the rumour of mingled voices grew louder suddenly. After a circular and startled glance, as of a man waking up abruptly to the sense of danger, he would throw himself back, and under the downward gaze of the old sorcerer take up, wide-eyed, the slender thread of his dream. They watched his moods; the swelling rumour of animated talk subsided like a wave on a sloping beach. The chief is pensive. And above the spreading whisper of lowered voices only a light rattle of weapons would be heard, a single louder word distinct and alone, or the grave ring of a big brass tray.

III

For two years at short intervals we visited him.
We came to like him, to trust him, almost to admire
him. He was plotting and preparing a war with patience, with foresight—with a fidelity to his purpose
and with a steadfastness of which I would have thought
him racially incapable. He seemed fearless of the
future, and in his plans displayed a sagacity that was
only limited by his profound ignorance of the rest of
the world. We tried to enlighten him, but our attempts
to make clear the irresistible nature of the forces which
he desired to arrest failed to discourage his eagerness
to strike a blow for his own primitive ideas. He did
not understand us, and replied by arguments that
almost drove one to desperation by their childish
shrewdness. He was absurd and unanswerable. Sometimes we caught glimpses of a sombre, glowing fury within him—a brooding and vague sense of wrong, and a
concentrated lust of violence which is dangerous in a
native. He raved like one inspired. On one occasion,
after we had been talking to him late in his campong,
he jumped up. A great, clear fire blazed in the grove;
lights and shadows danced together between the trees;
in the still night bats flitted in and out of the boughs
like fluttering flakes of denser darkness. He snatched
the sword from the old man, whizzed it out of the
scabbard, and thrust the point into the earth. Upon
the thin, upright blade the silver hilt, released, swayed
before him like something alive. He stepped back a

pace, and in a deadened tone spoke fiercely to the
vibrating steel: "If there is virtue in the fire, in the
iron, in the hand that forged thee, in the words spoken
over thee, in the desire of my heart, and in the wisdom
of thy makers,—then we shall be victorious together!"
He drew it out, looked along the edge. "Take," he
said over his shoulder to the old sword-bearer. The
other, unmoved on his hams, wiped the point with a
corner of his sarong, and returning the weapon to its
scabbard, sat nursing it on his knees without a
single look upwards. Karain, suddenly very calm, re-
seated himself with dignity. We gave up remonstrating after this, and let him go his way to an honourable disaster. All we could do for him was to see
to it that the powder was good for the money and the
rifles serviceable, if old.

But the game was becoming at last too dangerous;
and if we, who had faced it pretty often, thought little
of the danger, it was decided for us by some very
respectable people sitting safely in counting-houses
that the risks were too great, and that only one more
trip could be made. After giving in the usual way many
misleading hints as to our destination, we slipped away
quietly, and after a very quick passage entered the
bay. It was early morning, and even before the anchor went to the bottom the schooner was surrounded
by boats.

The first thing we heard was that Karain's mysterious sword-bearer had died a few days ago. We
did not attach much importance to the news. It was
certainly difficult to imagine Karain without his in-
separable follower; but the fellow was old, he had never
spoken to one of us, we hardly ever had heard the
sound of his voice; and we had come to look upon him
as upon something inanimate, as a part of our friend's

trappings of state—like that sword he had carried,
or the fringed red umbrella displayed during an official progress. Karain did not visit us in the afternoon as usual. A message of greeting and a present
of fruit and vegetables came off for us before sunset.
Our friend paid us like a banker, but treated us like a
prince. We sat up for him till midnight. Under the
stern awning bearded Jackson jingled an old guitar
and sang, with an execrable accent, Spanish love-songs;
while young Hollis and I, sprawling on the deck, had a
game of chess by the light of a cargo lantern. Karain
did not appear. Next day we were busy unloading, and
heard that the Rajah was unwell. The expected invitation to visit him ashore did not come. We sent friendly
messages, but, fearing to intrude upon some secret
council, remained on board. Early on the third day
we had landed all the powder and rifles, and also a six-
pounder brass gun with its carriage which we had sub-
scribed together for a present for our friend. The
afternoon was sultry. Ragged edges of black clouds
peeped over the hills, and invisible thunderstorms
circled outside, growling like wild beasts. We got
the schooner ready for sea, intending to leave next
morning at daylight. All day a merciless sun blazed
down into the bay, fierce and pale, as if at white heat.
Nothing moved on the land. The beach was empty,
the villages seemed deserted; the trees far off stood in
unstirring clumps, as if painted; the white smoke of
some invisible bush-fire spread itself low over the
shores of the bay like a settling fog. Late in the day
three of Karain's chief men, dressed in their best and
armed to the teeth, came off in a canoe, bringing a
case of dollars. They were gloomy and languid, and
told us they had not seen their Rajah for five days.
No one had seen him! We settled all accounts, and after

shaking hands in turn and in profound silence, they descended one after another into their boat, and were paddled to the shore, sitting close together, clad in vivid colours, with hanging heads: the gold embroideries of their jackets flashed dazzlingly as they went away gliding on the smooth water, and not one of them looked back once. Before sunset the growling clouds carried with a rush the ridge of hills, and came tumbling down the inner slopes. Everything disappeared; black whirling vapours filled the bay, and in the midst of them the schooner swung here and there in the shifting gusts of wind. A single clap of thunder detonated in the hollow with a violence that seemed capable of bursting into small pieces the ring of high land, and a warm deluge descended. The wind died out. We panted in the close cabin; our faces streamed; the bay outside hissed as if boiling; the water fell in perpendicular shafts as heavy as lead; it swished about the deck, poured off the spars, gurgled, sobbed, splashed, murmured in the blind night. Our lamp burned low. Hollis, stripped to the waist, lay stretched out on the lockers, with closed eyes and motionless like a despoiled corpse; at his head Jackson twanged the guitar, and gasped out in sighs a mournful dirge about hopeless love and eyes like stars. Then we heard startled voices on deck crying in the rain, hurried footsteps overhead, and suddenly Karain appeared in the doorway of the cabin. His bare breast and his face glistened in the light; his sarong, soaked, clung about his legs; he had his sheathed kriss in his left hand; and wisps of wet hair, escaping from under his red kerchief, stuck over his eyes and down his cheeks. He stepped in with a headlong stride and looking over his shoulder like a man pursued. Hollis turned on his side quickly and opened his eyes. Jackson clapped his big hand over the strings and the jingling vibration died suddenly. I stood up.

"We did not hear your boat's hail!" I exclaimed.

"Boat! The man's swum off," drawled out Hollis from the locker. "Look at him!"

He breathed heavily, wild-eyed, while we looked at him in silence. Water dripped from him, made a dark pool, and ran crookedly across the cabin floor. We could hear Jackson, who had gone out to drive away our Malay seamen from the doorway of the companion; he swore menacingly in the patter of a heavy shower, and there was a great commotion on deck. The watchmen, scared out of their wits by the glimpse of a shadowy figure leaping over the rail, straight out of the night as it were, had alarmed all hands.

Then Jackson, with glittering drops of water on his hair and beard, came back looking angry, and Hollis, who, being the youngest of us, assumed an indolent superiority, said without stirring, "Give him a dry sarong—give him mine; it's hanging up in the bathroom." Karain laid the kriss on the table, hilt inwards, and murmured a few words in a strangled voice.

"What's that?" asked Hollis, who had not heard.

"He apologizes for coming in with a weapon in his hand," I said, dazedly.

"Ceremonious beggar. Tell him we forgive a friend . . . on such a night," drawled out Hollis. "What's wrong?"

Karain slipped the dry sarong over his head, dropped the wet one at his feet, and stepped out of it. I pointed to the wooden armchair—his armchair. He sat down very straight, said "Ha!" in a strong voice; a short shiver shook his broad frame. He looked over his shoulder uneasily, turned as if to speak to us, but only stared in a curious blind manner, and again looked back. Jackson bellowed out, "Watch well on deck there!" heard a faint answer from above, and reaching out with his foot slammed-to the cabin door.

"All right now," he said.

Karain's lips moved slightly. A vivid flash of lightning made the two round sternports facing him glimmer like a pair of cruel and phosphorescent eyes. The flame of the lamp seemed to wither into brown dust for an instant, and the looking-glass over the little sideboard leaped out behind his back in a smooth sheet of livid light. The roll of thunder came near, crashed over us; the schooner trembled, and the great voice went on, threatening terribly, into the distance. For less than a minute a furious shower rattled on the decks. Karain looked slowly from face to face, and then the silence became so profound that we all could hear distinctly the two chronometers in my cabin ticking along with unflagging speed against one another.

And we three, strangely moved, could not take our eyes from him. He had become enigmatical and touching, in virtue of that mysterious cause that had driven him through the night and through the thunderstorm to the shelter of the schooner's cuddy. Not one of us doubted that we were looking at a fugitive, incredible as it appeared to us. He was haggard, as though he had not slept for weeks; he had become lean, as though he had not eaten for days. His cheeks were hollow, his eyes sunk, the muscles of his chest and arms twitched slightly as if after an exhausting contest. Of course it had been a long swim off to the schooner; but his face showed another kind of fatigue, the tormented weariness, the anger and the fear of a struggle against a thought, an idea—against something that cannot be grappled, that never rests—a shadow, a nothing, unconquerable and immortal, that preys upon life.

We knew it as though he had shouted it at us. His chest expanded time after time, as if it could not contain the beating of his heart. For a moment he had the power of the possessed—the power to awaken in the beholders wonder, pain, pity, and a fearful near sense of things invisible, of things dark and mute, that surround the loneliness of mankind. His eyes roamed about aimlessly for a moment, then became still. He said with effort—

"I came here . . . I leaped out of my stockade as after a defeat. I ran in the night. The water was black. I left him calling on the edge of black water. . . . I left him standing alone on the beach. I swam . . . he called out after me . . . I swam . . ."

He trembled from head to foot, sitting very upright and gazing straight before him. Left whom? Who called? We did not know. We could not understand. I said at all hazards—

"Be firm."

The sound of my voice seemed to steady him into a sudden rigidity, but otherwise he took no notice. He seemed to listen, to expect something for a moment, then went on—

"He cannot come here—therefore I sought you. You men with white faces who despise the invisible voices. He cannot abide your unbelief and your strength."

He was silent for a while, then exclaimed softly—

"Oh! the strength of unbelievers!"

"There's no one here but you—and we three," said Hollis, quietly. He reclined with his head supported on elbow and did not budge.

"I know," said Karain. "He has never followed me here. Was not the wise man ever by my side?

But since the old wise man, who knew of my trouble, has died, I have heard the voice every night. I shut myself up—for many days—in the dark. I can hear the sorrowful murmurs of women, the whisper of the wind, of the running waters; the clash of weapons in the hands of faithful men, their footsteps—and his voice! . . . Near . . . So! In my ear! I felt him near . . . His breath passed over my neck. I leaped out without a cry. All about me men slept quietly. I ran to the sea. He ran by my side without footsteps, whispering, whispering old words—whispering into my ear in his old voice. I ran into the sea; I swam off to you, with my kriss between my teeth. I, armed, I fled before a breath—to you. Take me away to your land. The wise old man has died, and with him is gone the power of his words and charms. And I can tell no one. No one. There is no one here faithful enough and wise enough to know. It is only near you, unbelievers, that my trouble fades like a mist under the eye of day."

He turned to me.

"With you I go!" he cried in a contained voice. "With you, who know so many of us. I want to leave this land—my people . . . and him—there!"

He pointed a shaking finger at random over his shoulder. It was hard for us to bear the intensity of that undisclosed distress. Hollis stared at him hard. I asked gently—

"Where is the danger?"

"Everywhere outside this place," he answered, mournfully. "In every place where I am. He waits for me on the paths, under the trees, in the place where I sleep—everywhere but here."

He looked round the little cabin, at the painted beams, at the tarnished varnish of bulkheads; he

looked round as if appealing to all its shabby strangeness, to the disorderly jumble of unfamiliar things that
belong to an inconceivable life of stress, of power, of
endeavour, of unbelief—to the strong life of white
men, which rolls on irresistible and hard on the edge
of outer darkness. He stretched out his arms as if to
embrace it and us. We waited. The wind and rain
had ceased, and the stillness of the night round the
schooner was as dumb and complete as if a dead world
had been laid to rest in a grave of clouds. We expected him to speak. The necessity within him tore
at his lips. There are those who say that a native will not speak to a white man. Error. No man
will speak to his master; but to a wanderer and a friend,
to him who does not come to teach or to rule, to him
who asks for nothing and accepts all things, words
are spoken by the camp-fires, in the shared solitude
of the sea, in riverside villages, in resting-places surrounded by forests—words are spoken that take no
account of race or colour. One heart speaks—another
one listens; and the earth, the sea, the sky, the passing
wind and the stirring leaf, hear also the futile tale of
the burden of life.

He spoke at last. It is impossible to convey the
effect of his story. It is undying, it is but a memory,
and its vividness cannot be made clear to another mind,
any more than the vivid emotions of a dream.
One must have seen his innate splendour, one must
have known him before—looked at him then. The
wavering gloom of the little cabin; the breathless
stillness outside, through which only the lapping of
water against the schooner's sides could be heard;
Hollis's pale face, with steady dark eyes; the energetic
head of Jackson held up between two big palms, and
with the long yellow hair of his beard flowing over the

strings of the guitar lying on the table; Karain's upright and motionless pose, his tone—all this made an impression that cannot be forgotten. He faced us across the table. His dark head and bronze torso appeared above the tarnished slab of wood, gleaming and still as if cast in metal. Only his lips moved, and his eyes glowed, went out, blazed again, or stared mournfully. His expressions came straight from his tormented heart. His words sounded low, in a sad murmur as of running water; at times they rang loud like the clash of a war-gong—or trailed slowly like weary travellers—or rushed forward with the speed of fear.

IV

THIS is, imperfectly, what he said—

"It was after the great trouble that broke the alliance of the four states of Wajo. We fought amongst ourselves, and the Dutch watched from afar till we were weary. Then the smoke of their fire-ships was seen at the mouth of our rivers, and their great men came in boats full of soldiers to talk to us of protection and peace. We answered with caution and wisdom, for our villages were burnt, our stockades weak, the people weary, and the weapons blunt. They came and went; there had been much talk, but after they went away everything seemed to be as before, only their ships remained in sight from our coast, and very soon their traders came amongst us under a promise of safety. My brother was a Ruler, and one of those who had given the promise. I was young then, and had fought in the war, and Pata Matara had fought by my side. We had shared hunger, danger, fatigue, and victory. His eyes saw my danger quickly, and twice my arm had preserved his life. It was his destiny. He was my friend. And he was great amongst us—one of those who were near my brother, the Ruler. He spoke in council, his courage was great, he was the chief of many villages round the great lake that is in the middle of our country as the heart is in the middle of a man's body. When his sword was carried into a campong in advance of his coming, the maidens whispered wonderingly under the fruit-trees,

the rich men consulted together in the shade, and a
feast was made ready with rejoicing and songs. He
had the favour of the Ruler and the affection of the poor.
He loved war, deer hunts, and the charms of women.
He was the possessor of jewels, of lucky weapons, and
of men's devotion. He was a fierce man; and I had
no other friend.

"I was the chief of a stockade at the mouth of the
river, and collected tolls for my brother from the
passing boats. One day I saw a Dutch trader go up
the river. He went up with three boats, and no toll
was demanded from him, because the smoke of Dutch
war-ships stood out from the open sea, and we were too
weak to forget treaties. He went up under the promise of safety, and my brother gave him protection.
He said he came to trade. He listened to our voices,
for we are men who speak openly and without fear;
he counted the number of our spears, he examined the
trees, the running waters, the grasses of the bank, the
slopes of our hills. He went up to Matara's country
and obtained permission to build a house. He traded
and planted. He despised our joys, our thoughts, and
our sorrows. His face was red, his hair like flame,
and his eyes pale, like a river mist; he moved heavily,
and spoke with a deep voice; he laughed aloud like
a fool, and knew no courtesy in his speech. He was a
big, scornful man, who looked into women's faces and
put his hand on the shoulders of free men as though
he had been a noble-born chief. We bore with him.
Time passed.

"Then Pata Matara's sister fled from the campong
and went to live in the Dutchman's house. She was
a great and wilful lady: I had seen her once carried
high on slaves' shoulders amongst the people, with uncovered face, and I had heard all men say that her beauty

I

was extreme, silencing the reason and ravishing the heart of the beholders. The people were dismayed; Matara's face was blackened with that disgrace, for she knew she had been promised to another man. Matara went to the Dutchman's house, and said, 'Give her up to die—she is the daughter of chiefs.' The white man refused and shut himself up, while his servants kept guard night and day with loaded guns. Matara raged. My brother called a council. But the Dutch ships were near, and watched our coast greedily. My brother said, 'If he dies now our land will pay for his blood. Leave him alone till we grow stronger and the ships are gone.' Matara was wise; he waited and watched. But the white man feared for her life and went away.

"He left his house, his plantations, and his goods! He departed, armed and menacing, and left all—for her! She had ravished his heart! From my stockade I saw him put out to sea in a big boat. Matara and I watched him from the fighting platform behind the pointed stakes. He sat cross-legged, with his gun in his hands, on the roof at the stern of his prau. The barrel of his rifle glinted aslant before his big red face. The broad river was stretched under him—level, smooth, shining, like a plain of silver; and his prau, looking very short and black from the shore, glided along the silver plain and over into the blue of the sea.

"Thrice Matara, standing by my side, called aloud her name with grief and imprecations. He stirred my heart. It leaped three times; and three times with the eye of my mind I saw in the gloom within the enclosed space of the prau a woman with streaming hair going away from her land and her people. I was angry—and sorry. Why? And then I also cried out insults and threats. Matara said, 'Now they have left

our land their lives are mine. I shall follow and strike
—and, alone, pay the price of blood.' A great wind was
sweeping towards the setting sun over the empty river.
I cried, 'By your side I will go!' He lowered his head
in sign of assent. It was his destiny. The sun had
set, and the trees swayed their boughs with a great
noise above our heads.

"On the third night we two left our land together
in a trading prau.

"The sea met us—the sea, wide, pathless, and without voice. A sailing prau leaves no track. We went
south. The moon was full; and, looking up, we said
to one another, 'When the next moon shines as this one,
we shall return and they will be dead.' It was fifteen
years ago. Many moons have grown full and withered
and I have not seen my land since. We sailed south;
we overtook many praus; we examined the creeks and
the bays; we saw the end of our coast, of our island—
a steep cape over a disturbed strait, where drift the
shadows of shipwrecked praus and drowned men
clamour in the night. The wide sea was all round us
now. We saw a great mountain burning in the midst
of water; we saw thousands of islets scattered like bits
of iron fired from a big gun; we saw a long coast of
mountain and lowlands stretching away in sunshine
from west to east. It was Java. We said, 'They are
there; their time is near, and we shall return or die
cleansed from dishonour.'

"We landed. Is there anything good in that country? The paths run straight and hard and dusty.
Stone campongs, full of white faces, are surrounded by
fertile fields, but every man you meet is a slave. The
rulers live under the edge of a foreign sword. We ascended mountains, we traversed valleys; at sunset
we entered villages. We asked everyone, 'Have you

seen such a white man?' Some stared; others laughed; women gave us food, sometimes, with fear and respect, as though we had been distracted by the visitation of God; but some did not understand our language, and some cursed us, or, yawning, asked with contempt the reason of our quest. Once, as we were going away, an old man called after us, 'Desist!'

"We went on. Concealing our weapons, we stood humbly aside before the horsemen on the road; we bowed low in the courtyards of chiefs who were no better than slaves. We lost ourselves in the fields, in the jungle; and one night, in a tangled forest, we came upon a place where crumbling old walls had fallen amongst the trees, and where strange stone idols—carved images of devils with many arms and legs, with snakes twined round their bodies, with twenty heads and holding a hundred swords—seemed to live and threaten in the light of our camp fire. Nothing dismayed us. And on the road, by every fire, in resting-places, we always talked of her and of him. Their time was near. We spoke of nothing else. No! not of hunger, thirst, weariness, and faltering hearts. No! we spoke of him and her? Of her! And we thought of them—of her! Matara brooded by the fire. I sat and thought and thought, till suddenly I could see again the image of a woman, beautiful, and young, and great and proud, and tender, going away from her land and her people. Matara said, 'When we find them we shall kill her first to cleanse the dishonour—then the man must die.' I would say, 'It shall be so; it is your vengeance.' He stared long at me with his big sunken eyes.

"We came back to the coast. Our feet were bleeding, our bodies thin. We slept in rags under the shadow of stone enclosures; we prowled, soiled and lean, about

the gateways of white men's courtyards. Their hairy
dogs barked at us, and their servants shouted from
afar, 'Begone!' Low-born wretches, that keep watch
over the streets of stone campongs, asked us who we
were. We lied, we cringed, we smiled with hate in
our hearts, and we kept looking here, looking there
for them—for the white man with hair like flame, and
for her, for the woman who had broken faith, and
therefore must die. We looked. At last in every
woman's face I thought I could see hers. We ran
swiftly., No! Sometimes Matara would whisper, 'Here
is the man,' and we waited, crouching. He came near.
It was not the man—those Dutchmen are all alike.
We suffered the anguish of deception. In my sleep
I saw her face, and was both joyful and sorry. . . .
Why? . . . I seemed to hear a whisper near me. I
turned swiftly. She was not there! And as we
trudged wearily from stone city to stone city I seemed
to hear a light footstep near me. A time came when
I heard it always, and I was glad. I thought, walking
dizzy and weary in sunshine on the hard paths of
white men—I thought, She is there—with us! . . .
Matara was sombre. We were often hungry.

"We sold the carved sheaths of our krisses—the
ivory sheaths with golden ferules. We sold the
jewelled hilts. But we kept the blades—for them.
The blades that never touch but kill—we kept the
blades for her. . . . Why? She was always by our
side. . . . We starved. We begged. We left
Java at last.

"We went West, we went East. We saw many
lands, crowds of strange faces, men that live in trees
and men who eat their old people. We cut rattans
in the forest for a handful of rice, and for a living
swept the decks of big ships and heard curses heaped

upon our heads. We toiled in villages; we wandered upon the seas with the Bajow people, who have no country. We fought for pay; we hired ourselves to work for Goram men, and were cheated; and under the orders of rough white faces we dived for pearls in barren bays, dotted with black rocks, upon a coast of sand and desolation. And everywhere we watched, we listened, we asked. We asked traders, robbers, white men. We heard jeers, mockery, threats— words of wonder and words of contempt. We never knew rest; we never thought of home, for our work was not done. A year passed, then another. I ceased to count the number of nights, of moons, of years. I watched over Matara. He had my last handful of rice; if there was water enough for one he drank it; I covered him up when he shivered with cold; and when the hot sickness came upon him I sat sleepless through many nights and fanned his face. He was a fierce man, and my friend. He spoke of her with fury in the daytime, with sorrow in the dark; he remembered her in health, in sickness. I said nothing; but I saw her every day—always! At first I saw only her head, as of a woman walking in the low mist on a river bank. Then she sat by our fire. I saw her! I looked at her! She had tender eyes and a ravishing face. I murmured to her in the night. Matara said sleepily sometimes, 'To whom are you talking? Who is there?' I answered quickly, 'No one' . . . It was a lie! She never left me. She shared the warmth of our fire, she sat on my couch of leaves, she swam on the sea to follow me. . . . I saw her! . . . I tell you I saw her long black hair spread behind her upon the moonlit water as she struck out with bare arms by the side of a swift prau. She was beautiful, she was faithful, and in the silence

of foreign countries she spoke to me very low in the
language of my people. No one saw her; no one heard
her; she was mine only! In daylight she moved with
a swaying walk before me upon the weary paths; her
figure was straight and flexible like the stem of a slender
tree; the heels of her feet were round and polished like
shells of eggs; with her round arm she made signs.
At night she looked into my face. And she was sad!
Her eyes were tender and frightened; her voice soft
and pleading. Once I murmured to her, 'You shall not
die,' and she smiled . . . ever after she smiled! . . .
She gave me courage to bear weariness and hardships.
Those were times of pain, and she soothed me. We
wandered patient in our search. We knew deception,
false hopes; we knew captivity, sickness, thirst, misery,
despair . . . . Enough! We found them! . . ."

He cried out the last words and paused. His face
was impassive, and he kept still like a man in a trance.
Hollis sat up quickly, and spread his elbows on the
table. Jackson made a brusque movement, and accidentally touched the guitar. A plaintive resonance
filled the cabin with confused vibrations and died out
slowly. Then Karain began to speak again. The restrained fierceness of his tone seemed to rise like a
voice from outside, like a thing unspoken but heard;
it filled the cabin and enveloped in its intense and
deadened murmur the motionless figure in the chair.

"We were on our way to Atjeh, where there was
war; but the vessel ran on a sandbank, and we had to
land in Delli. We had earned a little money, and
had bought a gun from some Selangore traders; only
one gun, which was fired by the spark of a stone:
Matara carried it. We landed. Many white men
lived there, planting tobacco on conquered plains,
and Matara . . . But no matter. He saw him!

. . . The Dutchman! . . . At last! . . . We crept and watched. Two nights and a day we watched. He had a house—a big house in a clearing in the midst of his fields; flowers and bushes grew around; there were narrow paths of yellow earth between the cut grass, and thick hedges to keep people out. The third night we came armed, and lay behind a hedge.

"A heavy dew seemed to soak through our flesh and made our very entrails cold. The grass, the twigs, the leaves, covered with drops of water, were gray in the moonlight. Matara, curled up in the grass, shivered in his sleep. My teeth rattled in my head so loud that I was afraid the noise would wake up all the land. Afar, the watchmen of white men's houses struck wooden clappers and hooted in the darkness. And, as every night, I saw her by my side. She smiled no more! . . . The fire of anguish burned in my breast, and she whispered to me with compassion, with pity, softly—as women will; she soothed the pain of my mind; she bent her face over me—the face of a woman who ravishes the hearts and silences the reason of men. She was all mine, and no one could see her— no one of living mankind! Stars shone through her bosom, through her floating hair. I was overcome with regret, with tenderness, with sorrow. Matara slept . . . Had I slept? Matara was shaking me by the shoulder, and the fire of the sun was drying the grass, the bushes, the leaves. It was day. Shreds of white mist hung between the branches of trees.

"Was it night or day? I saw nothing again till I heard Matara breathe quickly where he lay, and then outside the house I saw her. I saw them both. They had come out. She sat on a bench under the wall, and twigs laden with flowers crept high above her head, hung

over her hair. She had a box on her lap, and gazed into
it, counting the increase of her pearls. The Dutchman
stood by looking on; he smiled down at her; his white
teeth flashed; the hair on his lip was like two twisted
flames. He was big and fat, and joyous, and without fear. Matara tipped fresh priming from the
hollow of his palm, scraped the flint with his thumb-nail,
and gave the gun to me. To me! I took it . . .
O fate!

"He whispered into my ear, lying on his stomach,
'I shall creep close and then amok . . . let her die by
my hand. You take aim at the fat swine there. Let
him see me strike my shame off the face of the earth—
and then . . . you are my friend—kill with a sure shot.'
I said nothing; there was no air in my chest—there
was no air in the world. Matara had gone suddenly
from my side. The grass nodded. Then a bush rustled.
She lifted her head.

"I saw her! The consoler of sleepless nights, of
weary days; the companion of troubled years! I saw
her! She looked straight at the place where I crouched.
She was there as I had seen her for years—a faithful
wanderer by my side. She looked with sad eyes and
had smiling lips; she looked at me . . . Smiling
lips! Had I not promised that she should not die!

"She was far off and I felt her near. Her touch ca-
ressed me, and her voice murmured, whispered above
me, around me, 'Who shall be thy companion, who shall
console thee if I die?' I saw a flowering thicket to the
left of her stir a little . . . Matara was ready . . .
I cried aloud—'Return!'

"She leaped up; the box fell; the pearls streamed
at her feet. The big Dutchman by her side rolled
menacing eyes through the still sunshine. The gun
went up to my shoulder. I was kneeling and I was firm—

*I

firmer than the trees, the rocks, the mountains. But in front of the steady long barrel the fields, the house, the earth, the sky swayed to and fro like shadows in a forest on a windy day. Matara burst out of the thicket; before him the petals of torn flowers whirled high as if driven by a tempest. I heard her cry; I saw her spring with open arms in front of the white man. She was a woman of my country and of noble blood. They are so! I heard her shriek of anguish and fear— and all stood still! The fields, the house, the earth, the sky stood still—while Matara leaped at her with uplifted arm. I pulled the trigger, saw a spark, heard nothing; the smoke drove back into my face, and then I could see Matara roll over head first and lie with stretched arms at her feet. Ha! A sure shot! The sunshine fell on my back colder than the running water. A sure shot! I flung the gun after the shot. Those two stood over the dead man as though they had been bewitched by a charm. I shouted at her, 'Live and remember!' Then for a time I stumbled about in a cold darkness.

"Behind me there were great shouts, the running of many feet; strange men surrounded me, cried meaningless words into my face, pushed me, dragged me, supported me . . . I stood before the big Dutchman: he stared as if bereft of his reason. He wanted to know, he talked fast, he spoke of gratitude, he offered me food, shelter, gold—he asked many questions. I laughed in his face. I said, 'I am a Korinchi traveller from Perak over there, and know nothing of that dead man. I was passing along the path when I heard a shot, and your senseless people rushed out and dragged me here.' He lifted his arms, he wondered, he could not believe, he could not understand, he clamoured in his own tongue! She had her arms clasped round

his neck, and over her shoulder stared back at me
with wide eyes. I smiled and looked at her; I smiled
and waited to hear the sound of her voice. The white
man asked her suddenly, 'Do you know him?' I
listened—my life was in my ears! She looked at me
long, she looked at me with unflinching eyes, and
said aloud, 'No! I never saw him before.' . . .
What! Never before? Had she forgotten already?
Was it possible? Forgotten already—after so many
years—so many years of wandering, of companionship,
of trouble, of tender words! Forgotten already! . . .
I tore myself out from the hands that held me and went
away without a word . . . They let me go.

"I was weary. Did I sleep? I do not know. I
remember walking upon a broad path under a clear
starlight; and that strange country seemed so big, the
rice-fields so vast, that, as I looked around, my head
swam with the fear of space. Then I saw a forest.
The joyous starlight was heavy upon me. I turned
off the path and entered the forest, which was very
sombre and very sad."

V

KARAIN's tone had been getting lower and lower, as though he had been going away from us, till the last words sounded faint but clear, as if shouted on a calm day from a very great distance. He moved not. He stared fixedly past the motionless head of Hollis, who faced him, as still as himself. Jackson had turned sideways, and with elbow on the table shaded his eyes with the palm of his hand. And I looked on, surprised and moved; I looked at that man, loyal to a vision, betrayed by his dream, spurned by his illusion, and coming to us unbelievers for help—against a thought. The silence was profound; but it seemed full of noiseless phantoms, of things sorrowful, shadowy, and mute, in whose invisible presence the firm, pulsating beat of the two ship's chronometers ticking off steadily the seconds of Greenwich Time seemed to me a protection and a relief. Karain stared stonily; and looking at his rigid figure, I thought of his wanderings, of that obscure Odyssey of revenge, of all the men that wander amongst illusions; of the illusions as restless as men; of the illusions faithful, faithless; of the illusions that give joy, that give sorrow, that give pain, that give peace; of the invincible illusions that can make life and death appear serene, inspiring, tormented, or ignoble.

A murmur was heard; that voice from outside seemed to flow out of a dreaming world into the lamplight of the cabin. Karain was speaking.

"I lived in the forest.

"She came no more. Never! Never once! I lived alone. She had forgotten. It was well. I did not want her; I wanted no one. I found an abandoned house in an old clearing. Nobody came near. Sometimes I heard in the distance the voices of people going along a path. I slept; I rested; there was wild rice, water from a running stream—and peace! Every night I sat alone by my small fire before the hut. Many nights passed over my head.

"Then, one evening, as I sat by my fire after having eaten, I looked down on the ground and began to remember my wanderings. I lifted my head. I had heard no sound, no rustle, no footsteps—but I lifted my head. A man was coming towards me across the small clearing. I waited. He came up without a greeting and squatted down into the firelight. Then he turned his face to me. It was Matara. He stared at me fiercely with his big sunken eyes. The night was cold; the heat died suddenly out of the fire, and he stared at me. I rose and went away from there, leaving him by the fire that had no heat.

"I walked all that night, all next day, and in the evening made up a big blaze and sat down—to wait for him. He had not come into the light. I heard him in the bushes here and there, whispering, whispering. I understood at last—I had heard the words before, 'You are my friend—kill with a sure shot.'

"I bore it as long as I could—then leaped away, as on this very night I leaped from my stockade and swam to you. I ran—I ran crying like a child left alone and far from the houses. He ran by my side, without footsteps, whispering, whispering—invisible and heard. I sought people—I wanted men around me! Men who had not died! And again we two wandered. I sought danger, violence, and death. I

fought in the Atjeh war, and a brave people wondered
at the valiance of a stranger. But we were two; he
warded off the blows . . . Why? I wanted peace,
not life. And no one could see him; no one knew—
I dared tell no one. At times he would leave me, but
not for long; then he would return and whisper or stare.
My heart was torn with a strange fear, but could not
die. Then I met an old man.

"You all knew him. People here called him my
sorcerer, my servant and sword-bearer; but to me he
was father, mother, protection, refuge and peace.
When I met him he was returning from a pilgrimage,
and I heard him intoning the prayer of sunset. He
had gone to the holy place with his son, his son's wife,
and a little child; and on their return, by the favour
of the Most High, they all died: the strong man, the
young mother, the little child—they died; and the
old man reached his country alone. He was a pilgrim
serene and pious, very wise and very lonely. I told
him all. For a time we lived together. He said over
me words of compassion, of wisdom, of prayer. He
warded from me the shade of the dead. I begged him
for a charm that would make me safe. For a long
time he refused; but at last, with a sigh and a smile,
he gave me one. Doubtless he could command a
spirit stronger than the unrest of my dead friend, and
again I had peace; but I had become restless, and a
lover of turmoil and danger. The old man never
left me. We travelled together. We were welcomed
by the great; his wisdom and my courage are remembered where your strength, O white men, is forgotten!
We served the Sultan of Sula. We fought the Span-
iards. There were victories, hopes, defeats, sorrow,
blood, women's tears . . . What for? . . . We fled.
We collected wanderers of a warlike race and came

here to fight again. The rest you know. I am the
ruler of a conquered land, a lover of war and danger,
a fighter and a plotter. But the old man has died,
and I am again the slave of the dead. He is not here
now to drive away the reproachful shade—to silence
the lifeless voice! The power of his charm has died
with him. And I know fear; and I hear the whisper,
'Kill! kill! kill!' . . . Have I not killed enough? . . ."

For the first time that night a sudden convulsion
of madness and rage passed over his face. His wavering glances darted here and there like scared birds in a
thunderstorm. He jumped up, shouting—

"By the spirits that drink blood: by the spirits that
cry in the night: by all the spirits of fury, misfortune,
and death, I swear—some day I will strike into every
heart I meet—I . . ."

He looked so dangerous that we all three leaped to
our feet, and Hollis, with the back of his hand, sent
the kriss flying off the table. I believe we shouted
together. It was a short scare, and the next moment
he was again composed in his chair, with three white
men standing over him in rather foolish attitudes. We
felt a little ashamed of ourselves. Jackson picked
up the kriss, and, after an inquiring glance at me, gave
it to him. He received it with a stately inclination
of the head and stuck it in the twist of his sarong, with
punctilious care to give his weapon a pacific position.
Then he looked up at us with an austere smile. We
were abashed and reproved. Hollis sat sideways on
the table and, holding his chin in his hand, scrutinized
him in pensive silence. I said—

"You must abide with your people. They need
you. And there is forgetfulness in life. Even the
dead cease to speak in time."

"Am I a woman, to forget long years before an

eyelid has had the time to beat twice?" he exclaimed, with bitter resentment. He startled me. It was amazing. To him his life—that cruel mirage of love and peace—seemed as real, as undeniable, as theirs would be to any saint, philosopher, or fool of us all. Hollis muttered—

"You won't soothe him with your platitudes."

Karain spoke to me.

"You know us. You have lived with us. Why?— we cannot know; but you understand our sorrows and our thoughts. You have lived with my people, and you understand our desires and our fears. With you I will go. To your land—to your people. To your people, who live in unbelief; to whom day is day, and night is night—nothing more, because you understand all things seen, and despise all else! To your land of unbelief, where the dead do not speak, where every man is wise, and alone—and at peace!"

"Capital description," murmured Hollis, with the flicker of a smile.

Karain hung his head.

"I can toil, and fight—and be faithful," he whispered, in a weary tone, "but I cannot go back to him who waits for me on the shore. No! Take me with you . . . Or else give me some of your strength—of your unbelief . . . A charm! . . ."

He seemed utterly exhausted.

"Yes, take him home," said Hollis, very low, as if debating with himself. "That would be one way. The ghosts there are in society, and talk affably to ladies and gentlemen, but would scorn a naked human being— like our princely friend. . . . Naked . . . Flayed! I should say. I am sorry for him. Impossible—of course. The end of all this shall be," he went on, looking up at us—"the end of this shall be, that some day he will run amuck amongst his faithful subjects and send *ad patres* ever so many of them before they make up their minds to the disloyalty of knocking him on the head."

I nodded. I thought it more than probable that such would be the end of Karain. It was evident that he had been hunted by his thought along the very limit of human endurance, and very little more pressing was needed to make him swerve over into the form of madness peculiar to his race. The respite he had during the old man's life made the return of the torment unbearable. That much was clear.

He lifted his head suddenly; we had imagined for a moment that he had been dozing.

"Give me your protection—or your strength!" he cried. "A charm . . . a weapon!"

Again his chin fell on his breast. We looked at him, then looked at one another with suspicious awe in our eyes, like men who come unexpectedly upon the scene of some mysterious disaster. He had given himself up to us; he had thrust into our hands his errors and his torment, his life and his peace; and we did not know what to do with that problem from the outer darkness. We three white men, looking at the Malay, could not find one word to the purpose amongst us—if indeed there existed a word that could solve that problem. We pondered, and our hearts sank. We felt as though we three had been called to the very gate of Infernal Regions to judge, to decide the fate of a wanderer coming suddenly from a world of sunshine and illusions.

"By Jove, he seems to have a great idea of our power," whispered Hollis, hopelessly. And then again there was a silence, the feeble plash of water, the steady tick of chronometers. Jackson, with bare arms crossed, leaned his shoulders against the bulkhead of the cabin.

He was bending his head under the deck beam; his fair beard spread out magnificently over his chest; he looked colossal, ineffectual, and mild. There was something lugubrious in the aspect of the cabin; the air in it seemed to become slowly charged with the cruel chill of helplessness, with the pitiless anger of egoism against the incomprehensible form of an intruding pain. We had no idea what to do; we began to resent bitterly the hard necessity to get rid of him.

Hollis mused, muttered suddenly with a short laugh, "Strength . . . Protection . . . Charm." He slipped off the table and left the cuddy without a look at us. It seemed a base desertion. Jackson and I exchanged indignant glances. We could hear him rummaging in his pigeon-hole of a cabin. Was the fellow actually going to bed? Karain sighed. It was intolerable!

Then Hollis reappeared, holding in both hands a small leather box. He put it down gently on the table and looked at us with a queer gasp, we thought, as though he had from some cause become speechless for a moment, or were ethically uncertain about producing that box. But in an instant the insolent and unerring wisdom of his youth gave him the needed courage. He said, as he unlocked the box with a very small key, "Look as solemn as you can, you fellows."

Probably we looked only surprised and stupid, for he glanced over his shoulder, and said angrily—

"This is no play; I am going to do something for him. Look serious. Confound it! . . . Can't you lie a little . . . for a friend!"

Karain seemed to take no notice of us, but when Hollis threw open the lid of the box his eyes flew to it—and so did ours. The quilted crimson satin of the inside put a violent patch of colour into the sombre atmosphere; it was something positive to look at—it was fascinating,

VI

HOLLIS looked smiling into the box. He had lately made a dash home through the Canal. He had been away six months, and only joined us again just in time for this last trip. We had never seen the box before. His hands hovered above it; and he talked to us ironically, but his face became as grave as though he were pronouncing a powerful incantation over the things inside.

"Every one of us," he said, with pauses that somehow were more offensive than his words—"every one of us, you'll admit, has been haunted by some woman . . . And . . . as to friends . . . dropped by the way . . . Well! . . . ask yourselves . . ."

He paused. Karain stared. A deep rumble was heard high up under the deck. Jackson spoke seriously—

"Don't be so beastly cynical."

"Ah! You are without guile," said Hollis, sadly. "You will learn . . . Meantime this Malay has been our friend . . ."

He repeated several times thoughtfully, "Friend . . . Malay. Friend, Malay," as though weighing the words against one another, then went on more briskly—

"A good fellow—a gentleman in his way. We can't, so to speak, turn our backs on his confidence and belief in us. Those Malays are easily impressed—all nerves, you know—therefore . . ."

He turned to me sharply.

"You know him best," he said, in a practical tone. "Do you think he is fanatical—I mean very strict in his faith?"

I stammered in profound amazement that "I did not think so."

"It's on account of its being a likeness—an engraved image," muttered Hollis, enigmatically, turning to the box. He plunged his fingers into it. Karain's lips were parted and his eyes shone. We looked into the box.

There were there a couple of reels of cotton, a packet of needles, a bit of silk ribbon, dark blue; a cabinet photograph, at which Hollis stole a glance before laying it on the table face downwards. A girl's portrait, I could see. There were, amongst a lot of various small objects, a bunch of flowers, a narrow white glove with many buttons, a slim packet of letters carefully tied up. Amulets of white men! Charms and talismans! Charms that keep them straight, that drive them crooked, that have the power to make a young man sigh, an old man smile. Potent things that procure dreams of joy, thoughts of regret; that soften hard hearts, and can temper a soft one to the hardness of steel. Gifts of heaven—things of earth . . . .

Hollis rummaged in the box.

And it seemed to me, during that moment of waiting, that the cabin of the schooner was becoming filled with a stir invisible and living as of subtle breaths. All the ghosts driven out of the unbelieving West by men who pretend to be wise and alone and at peace—all the homeless ghosts of an unbelieving world—appeared suddenly round the figure of Hollis bending over the box; all the exiled and charming shades of loved women; all the beautiful and tender ghosts of ideals, remembered, forgotten, cherished, execrated;

all the cast-out and reproachful ghosts of friends admired, trusted, traduced, betrayed, left dead by the way—they all seemed to come from the inhospitable regions of the earth to crowd into the gloomy cabin, as though it had been a refuge and, in all the unbelieving world, the only place of avenging belief. . . . It lasted a second—all disappeared. Hollis was facing us alone with something small that glittered between his fingers. It looked like a coin.

"Ah! here it is," he said.

He held it up. It was a sixpence—a Jubilee sixpence. It was gilt; it had a hole punched near the rim. Hollis looked towards Karain.

"A charm for our friend," he said to us. "The thing itself is of great power—money, you know—and his imagination is struck. A loyal vagabond; if only his puritanism doesn't shy at a likeness . . . ."

We said nothing. We did not know whether to be scandalized, amused, or relieved. Hollis advanced towards Karain, who stood up as if startled, and then, holding the coin up, spoke in Malay.

"This is the image of the Great Queen, and the most powerful thing the white men know," he said, solemnly.

Karain covered the handle of his kriss in sign of respect, and stared at the crowned head.

"The Invincible, the Pious," he muttered.

"She is more powerful than Suleiman the Wise, who commanded the genii, as you know," said Hollis, gravely. "I shall give this to you."

He held the sixpence in the palm of his hand, and looking at it thoughtfully, spoke to us in English.

"She commands a spirit, too—the spirit of her nation; a masterful, conscientious, unscrupulous, unconquerable devil . . . that does a lot of good—incidentally . . . a lot of good . . . at times—and wouldn't stand any fuss from the best ghost out for such a little thing as our friend's shot. Don't look thunderstruck, you fellows. Help me to make him believe—everything's in that."

"His people will be shocked," I murmured.

Hollis looked fixedly at Karain, who was the incarnation of the very essence of still excitement. He stood rigid, with head thrown back; his eyes rolled wildly, flashing; the dilated nostrils quivered.

"Hang it all!" said Hollis at last, "he is a good fellow. I'll give him something that I shall really miss."

He took the ribbon out of the box, smiled at it scornfully, then with a pair of scissors cut out a piece from the palm of the glove.

"I shall make him a thing like those Italian peasants wear, you know."

He sewed the coin in the delicate leather, sewed the leather to the ribbon, tied the ends together. He worked with haste. Karain watched his fingers all the time.

"Now then," he said—then stepped up to Karain. They looked close into one another's eyes. Those of Karain stared in a lost glance, but Hollis's seemed to grow darker and looked out masterful and compelling. They were in violent contrast together—one motionless and the colour of bronze, the other dazzling white and lifting his arms, where the powerful muscles rolled slightly under a skin that gleamed like satin. Jackson moved near with the air of a man closing up to a chum in a tight place. I said impressively, pointing to Hollis——

"He is young, but he is wise. Believe him!"

Karain bent his head: Hollis threw lightly over it the dark-blue ribbon and stepped back.

"Forget, and be at peace!" I cried.

Karain seemed to wake up from a dream. He said, "Ha!" shook himself as if throwing off a burden. He looked round with assurance. Someone on deck dragged off the skylight cover, and a flood of light fell into the cabin. It was morning already.

"Time to go on deck," said Jackson.

Hollis put on a coat, and we went up, Karain leading. The sun had risen beyond the hills, and their long shadows stretched far over the bay in the pearly light. The air was clear, stainless, and cool. I pointed at the curved line of yellow sands.

"He is not there," I said, emphatically, to Karain. "He waits no more. He has departed forever."

A shaft of bright hot rays darted into the bay between the summits of two hills, and the water all round broke out as if by magic into a dazzling sparkle.

"No! He is not there waiting," said Karain, after a long look over the beach. "I do not hear him," he went on, slowly. "No!"

He turned to us.

"He has departed again—forever!" he cried.

We assented vigorously, repeatedly, and without compunction. The great thing was to impress him powerfully; to suggest absolute safety—the end of all trouble. We did our best; and I hope we affirmed our faith in the power of Hollis's charm efficiently enough to put the matter beyond the shadow of a doubt. Our voices rang around him joyously in the still air, and above his head the sky, pellucid, pure, stainless, arched its tender blue from shore to shore and over the bay, as if to envelop the water, the earth, and the man in the caress of its light.

The anchor was up, the sails hung still, and half-a-dozen big boats were seen sweeping over the bay to give us a tow out. The paddlers in the first one that came alongside lifted their heads and saw their ruler standing amongst us. A low murmur of surprise arose —then a shout of greeting.

He left us, and seemed straightway to step into the glorious splendour of his stage, to wrap himself in the illusion of unavoidable success. For a moment he stood erect, one foot over the gangway, one hand on the hilt of his kriss, in a martial pose; and, relieved from the fear of outer darkness, he held his head high, he swept a serene look over his conquered foothold on the earth. The boats far off took up the cry of greeting; a great clamour rolled on the water; the hills echoed it, and seemed to toss back at him the words invoking long life and victories.

He descended into a canoe, and as soon as he was clear of the side we gave him three cheers. They sounded faint and orderly after the wild tumult of his loyal subjects, but it was the best we could do. He stood up in the boat, lifted up both his arms, then pointed to the infallible charm. We cheered again; and the Malays in the boats stared—very much puzzled and impressed. I wondered what they thought; what he thought; . . . what the reader thinks?

We towed out slowly. We saw him land and watch us from the beach. A figure approached him humbly but openly—not at all like a ghost with a grievance. We could see other men running towards him. Perhaps he had been missed? At any rate there was a great stir. A group formed itself rapidly near him, and he walked along the sands, followed by a growing *cortége* and kept nearly abreast of the schooner. With our glasses we could see the blue ribbon on his neck and a patch of white on his brown chest. The bay was waking up. The smokes of morning fires stood in faint spirals higher than the heads of palms; people

moved between the houses; a herd of buffaloes galloped
clumsily across a green slope; the slender figures of boys
brandishing sticks appeared black and leaping in the
long grass; a coloured line of women, with water bamboos on their heads, moved swaying through a thin
grove of fruit-trees. Karain stopped in the midst of
his men and waved his hand; then, detaching himself
from the splendid group, walked alone to the water's
edge and waved his hand again. The schooner passed
out to sea between the steep headlands that shut in the
bay, and at the same instant Karain passed out of our
life forever.

But the memory remains. Some years afterwards
I met Jackson, in the Strand. He was magnificent as
ever. His head was high above the crowd. His
beard was gold, his face red, his eyes blue; he had a
wide-brimmed gray hat and no collar or waistcoat;
he was inspiring; he had just come home—had landed
that very day! Our meeting caused an eddy in the
current of humanity. Hurried people would run
against us, then walk round us, and turn back to look
at that giant. We tried to compress seven years of
life into seven exclamations; then, suddenly appeased,
walked sedately along, giving one another the news of
yesterday. Jackson gazed about him, like a man who
looks for landmarks, then stopped before Bland's
window. He always had a passion for firearms; so he
stopped short and contemplated the row of weapons,
perfect and severe, drawn up in a line behind the black-
framed panes. I stood by his side. Suddenly he said—

"Do you remember Karain?"

I nodded.

"The sight of all this made me think of him," he went
on, with his face near the glass . . . and I could
see another man, powerful and bearded, peering at him

intently from amongst the dark and polished tubes that can cure so many illusions. "Yes; it made me think of him," he continued, slowly. "I saw a paper this morning; they are fighting over there again. He's sure to be in it. He will make it hot for the caballeros. Well, good luck to him, poor devil! He was perfectly stunning."

We walked on.

"I wonder whether the charm worked—you remember Hollis's charm, of course. If it did . . . . never was a sixpence wasted to better advantage! Poor devil! I wonder whether he got rid of that friend of his. Hope so. . . . Do you know, I sometimes think that——"

I stood still and looked at him.

"Yes . . . I mean, whether the thing was so, you know . . . whether it really happened to him. . . . What do you think?"

"My dear chap," I cried, "you have been too long away from home. What a question to ask! Only look at all this."

A watery gleam of sunshine flashed from the west and went out between two long lines of walls; and then the broken confusion of roofs, the chimney-stacks, the gold letters sprawling over the fronts of houses, the sombre polish of windows, stood resigned and sullen under the falling gloom. The whole length of the street, deep as a well and narrow like a corridor, was full of a sombre and ceaseless stir. Our ears were filled by a headlong shuffle and beat of rapid footsteps and an underlying rumour—a rumour vast, faint, pulsating, as of panting breaths, of beating hearts, of gasping voices. Innumerable eyes stared straight in front, feet moved hurriedly, blank faces flowed, arms swung. Over all, a narrow ragged strip of smoky sky wound about between the high roofs, extended and motionless, like a soiled streamer flying above the rout of a mob.

"Ye-e-e-s," said Jackson, meditatively.

The big wheels of hansoms turned slowly along the edge of side-walks; a pale-faced youth strolled, overcome by weariness, by the side of his stick and with the tails of his overcoat flapping gently near his heels; horses stepped gingerly on the greasy pavement, tossing their heads; two young girls passed by, talking vivaciously and with shining eyes; a fine old fellow strutted, red-faced, stroking a white moustache; and a line of yellow boards with blue letters on them approached us slowly, tossing on high behind one another like some queer wreckage adrift upon a river of hats.

"Ye-e-es," repeated Jackson. His clear blue eyes looked about, contemptuous, amused and hard, like the eyes of a boy. A clumsy string of red, yellow, and green omnibuses rolled swaying, monstrous and gaudy; two shabby children ran across the road; a knot of dirty men with red neckerchiefs round their bare throats lurched along, discussing filthily; a ragged old man with a face of despair yelled horribly in the mud the name of a paper; while far off, amongst the tossing heads of horses, the dull flash of harnesses, the jumble of lustrous panels and roofs of carriages, we could see a policeman, helmeted and dark, stretching out a rigid arm at the crossing of the streets.

"Yes; I see it," said Jackson, slowly. "It is there; it pants, it runs, it rolls; it is strong and alive; it would smash you if you didn't look out; but I'll be hanged if it is yet as real to me as . . . as the other thing . . . say, Karain's story."

I think that, decidedly, he had been too long away from home.

THE IDIOTS

WE WERE driving along the road from Treguier to Kervanda. We passed at a smart trot between the hedges topping an earth wall on each side of the road; then at the foot of the steep ascent before Ploumar the horse dropped into a walk, and the driver jumped down heavily from the box. He flicked his whip and climbed the incline, stepping clumsily uphill by the side of the carriage, one hand on the footboard, his eyes on the ground. After a while he lifted his head, pointed up the road with the end of the whip, and said—

"The idiot!"

The sun was shining violently upon the undulating surface of the land. The rises were topped by clumps of meagre trees, with their branches showing high on the sky as if they had been perched upon stilts. The small fields, cut up by hedges and stone walls that zigzagged over the slopes, lay in rectangular patches of vivid greens and yellows, resembling the unskilful daubs of a naïve picture. And the landscape was divided in two by the white streak of a road stretching in long loops far away, like a river of dust crawling out of the hills on its way to the sea.

"Here he is," said the driver, again.

In the long grass bordering the road a face glided past the carriage at the level of the wheels as we drove slowly by. The imbecile face was red, and the bullet head with close-cropped hair seemed to lie alone, its chin in the dust. The body was lost in the bushes growing thick along the bottom of the deep ditch.

It was a boy's face. He might have been sixteen, judging from the size—perhaps less, perhaps more. Such creatures are forgotten by time, and live untouched by years till death gathers them up into its compassionate bosom; the faithful death that never forgets in the press of work the most insignificant of its children.

"Ah! there's another," said the man, with a certain satisfaction in his tone, as if he had caught sight of something expected.

There was another. That one stood nearly in the middle of the road in the blaze of sunshine at the end of his own short shadow. And he stood with hands pushed into the opposite sleeves of his long coat, his head sunk between the shoulders, all hunched up in the flood of heat. From a distance he had the aspect of one suffering from intense cold.

"Those are twins," explained the driver.

The idiot shuffled two paces out of the way and looked at us over his shoulder when we brushed past him. The glance was unseeing and staring, a fascinated glance; but he did not turn to look after us. Probably the image passed before the eyes without leaving any trace on the misshapen brain of the creature. When we had topped the ascent I looked over the hood. He stood in the road just where we had left him.

The driver clambered into his seat, clicked his tongue, and we went downhill. The brake squeaked horribly from time to time. At the foot he eased off the noisy mechanism and said, turning half round on his box—

"We shall see some more of them by-and-by."

"More idiots? How many of them are there, then?" I asked.

"There's four of them—children of a farmer near

Ploumar here. . . . The parents are dead now," he
added, after a while. "The grandmother lives on the
farm. In the daytime they knock about on this road,
and they come home at dusk along with the cattle.
. . . It's a good farm."

We saw the other two: a boy and a girl, as the driver
said. They were dressed exactly alike, in shapeless
garments with petticoat-like skirts. The imperfect
thing that lived within them moved those beings to
howl at us from the top of the bank, where they sprawled
amongst the tough stalks of furze. Their cropped
black heads stuck out from the bright yellow wall of
countless small blossoms. The faces were purple with
the strain of yelling; the voices sounded blank and
cracked like a mechanical imitation of old people's
voices; and suddenly ceased when we turned into a
lane.

I saw them many times in my wandering about the
country. They lived on that road, drifting along its
length here and there, according to the inexplicable
impulses of their monstrous darkness. They were an
offence to the sunshine, a reproach to empty heaven,
a blight on the concentrated and purposeful vigour of
the wild landscape. In time the story of their parents
shaped itself before me out of the listless answers to my
questions, out of the indifferent words heard in wayside
inns or on the very road those idiots haunted. Some
of it was told by an emaciated and sceptical old fellow
with a tremendous whip, while we trudged together
over the sands by the side of a two-wheeled cart loaded
with dripping seaweed. Then at other times other
people confirmed and completed the story: till it stood
at last before me, a tale formidable and simple, as they
always are, those disclosures of obscure trials endured
by ignorant hearts.

When he returned from his military service Jean-Pierre Bacadou found the old people very much aged. He remarked with pain that the work of the farm was not satisfactorily done. The father had not the energy of old days. The hands did not feel over them the eye of the master. Jean-Pierre noted with sorrow that the heap of manure in the courtyard before the only entrance to the house was not so large as it should have been. The fences were out of repair, and the cattle suffered from neglect. At home the mother was practically bedridden, and the girls chattered loudly in the big kitchen, unrebuked, from morning to night. He said to himself: "We must change all this." He talked the matter over with his father one evening when the rays of the setting sun entering the yard between the outhouses ruled the heavy shadows with luminous streaks. Over the manure heap floated a mist, opal-tinted and odorous, and the marauding hens would stop in their scratching to examine with a sudden glance of their round eye the two men, both lean and tall, talking in hoarse tones. The old man, all twisted with rheumatism and bowed with years of work, the younger bony and straight, spoke without gestures in the indifferent manner of peasants, grave and slow. But before the sun had set the father had submitted to the sensible arguments of the son. "It is not for me that I am speaking," insisted Jean-Pierre. "It is for the land. It's a pity to see it badly used. I am not impatient for myself." The old fellow nodded over his stick. "I dare say; I dare say," he muttered. "You may be right. Do what you like. It's the mother that will be pleased."

The mother was pleased with her daughter-in-law. Jean-Pierre brought the two-wheeled spring-cart with a rush into the yard. The gray horse galloped clumsily,

and the bride and bridegroom, sitting side by side, were
jerked backwards and forwards by the up and down
motion of the shafts, in a manner regular and brusque.
On the road the distanced wedding guests straggled in
pairs and groups. The men advanced with heavy
steps, swinging their idle arms. They were clad in
town clothes; jackets cut with clumsy smartness, hard
black hats, immense boots, polished highly. Their
women all in simple black, with white caps and shawls
of faded tints folded triangularly on the back, strolled
lightly by their side. In front the violin sang a strident
tune, and the biniou snored and hummed, while the
player capered solemnly, lifting high his heavy clogs.
The sombre procession drifted in and out of the narrow
lanes, through sunshine and through shade, between
fields and hedgerows, scaring the little birds that darted
away in troops right and left. In the yard of Bacadou's
farm the dark ribbon wound itself up into a mass of men
and women pushing at the door with cries and greetings.
The wedding dinner was remembered for months. It
was a splendid feast in the orchard. Farmers of con-
siderable means and excellent repute were to be found
sleeping in ditches, all along the road to Treguier, even
as late as the afternoon of the next day. All the coun-
tryside participated in the happiness of Jean-Pierre.
He remained sober, and, together with his quiet wife,
kept out of the way, letting father and mother reap their
due of honour and thanks. But the next day he took
hold strongly, and the old folks felt a shadow—precursor
of the grave—fall upon them finally. The world is to
the young.

When the twins were born there was plenty of room
in the house, for the mother of Jean-Pierre had gone
away to dwell under a heavy stone in the cemetery of
Ploumar. On that day, for the first time since his son's

marriage, the elder Bacadou, neglected by the cackling lot of strange women who thronged the kitchen, left in the morning his seat under the mantel of the fireplace, and went into the empty cow-house, shaking his white locks dismally. Grandsons were all very well, but he wanted his soup at midday. When shown the babies, he stared at them with a fixed gaze, and muttered something like: "It's too much." Whether he meant too much happiness, or simply commented upon the number of his descendants, it is impossible to say. He looked offended—as far as his old wooden face could express anything; and for days afterwards could be seen, almost any time of the day, sitting at the gate, with his nose over his knees, a pipe between his gums, and gathered up into a kind of raging concentrated sulkiness. Once he spoke to his son, alluding to the newcomers with a groan: "They will quarrel over the land." "Don't bother about that, father," answered Jean-Pierre, stolidly, and passed, bent double, towing a recalcitrant cow over his shoulder.

He was happy, and so was Susan, his wife. It was not an ethereal joy welcoming new souls to struggle, perchance to victory. In fourteen years both boys would be a help; and, later on, Jean-Pierre pictured two big sons striding over the land from patch to patch, wringing tribute from the earth beloved and fruitful. Susan was happy too, for she did not want to be spoken of as the unfortunate woman, and now she had children no one could call her that. Both herself and her husband had seen something of the larger world—he during the time of his service; while she had spent a year or so in Paris with a Breton family; but had been too home-sick to remain longer away from the hilly and green country, set in a barren circle of rocks and sands, where she had been born. She thought that one of the boys ought

K

perhaps to be a priest, but said nothing to her husband,
who was a republican, and hated the "crows," as he
called the ministers of religion. The christening was a
splendid affair. All the commune came to it, for the
Bacadous were rich and influential, and, now and then,
did not mind the expense. The grandfather had a new
coat.

Some months afterwards, one evening when the
kitchen had been swept, and the door locked, Jean-
Pierre, looking at the cot, asked his wife: "What's
the matter with those children?" And, as if these
words, spoken calmly, had been the portent of misfortune, she answered with a loud wail that must have
been heard across the yard in the pig-sty; for the pigs
(the Bacadous had the finest pigs in the country)
stirred and grunted complainingly in the night. The
husband went on grinding his bread and butter slowly,
gazing at the wall, the soup-plate smoking under his
chin. He had returned late from the market, where he
had overheard (not for the first time) whispers behind
his back. He revolved the words in his mind as he
drove back. "Simple! Both of them. . . . Never
any use! . . . Well! May be, may be. One must
see. Would ask his wife." This was her answer. He
felt like a blow on his chest, but said only: "Go, draw
me some cider. I am thirsty!"

She went out moaning, an empty jug in her hand.
Then he arose, took up the light, and moved slowly
towards the cradle. They slept. He looked at them
sideways, finished his mouthful there, went back
heavily, and sat down before his plate. When his wife
returned he never looked up, but swallowed a couple of
spoonfuls noisily, and remarked, in a dull manner—

"When they sleep they are like other people's children."

She sat down suddenly on a stool near by, and shook with a silent tempest of sobs, unable to speak. He finished his meal, and remained idly thrown back in his chair, his eyes lost amongst the black rafters of the ceiling. Before him the tallow candle flared red and straight, sending up a slender thread of smoke. The light lay on the rough, sunburnt skin of his throat; the sunk cheeks were like patches of darkness, and his aspect was mournfully stolid, as if he had ruminated with difficulty endless ideas. Then he said, deliberately—

"We must see . . . . consult people. Don't cry. . . . They won't all be like that . . . surely! We must sleep now."

After the third child, also a boy, was born, Jean-Pierre went about his work with tense hopefulness. His lips seemed more narrow, more tightly compressed than before; as if for fear of letting the earth he tilled hear the voice of hope that murmured within his breast. He watched the child, stepping up to the cot with a heavy clang of sabots on the stone floor, and glanced in, along his shoulder, with that indifference which is like a deformity of peasant humanity. Like the earth they master and serve, those men, slow of eye and speech, do not show the inner fire; so that, at last, it becomes a question with them as with the earth, what there is in the core: heat, violence, a force mysterious and terrible —or nothing but a clod, a mass fertile and inert, cold and unfeeling, ready to bear a crop of plants that sustain life or give death.

The mother watched with other eyes; listened with otherwise expectant ears. Under the high hanging shelves supporting great sides of bacon overhead, her body was busy by the great fireplace, attentive to the pot swinging on iron gallows, scrubbing the long table

where the field hands would sit down directly to their
evening meal.   Her mind remained by the cradle, night
and day on the watch, to hope and suffer.   That child,
like the other two, never smiled, never stretched its
hands to her, never spoke; never had a glance of recog-
nition for her in its big black eyes, which could only
stare fixedly at any glitter, but failed hopelessly to
follow the brilliance of a sun-ray slipping slowly along
the floor.   When the men were at work she spent long
days between her three idiot children and the childish
grandfather, who sat grim, angular, and immovable,
with his feet near the warm ashes of the fire.   The
feeble old fellow seemed to suspect that there was
something wrong with his grandsons.   Only once,
moved either by affection or by the sense of proprieties,
he attempted to nurse the youngest.   He took the boy
up from the floor, clicked his tongue at him, and essayed
a shaky gallop of his bony knees.   Then he looked
closely with his misty eyes at the child's face and
deposited him down gently on the floor again.   And he
sat, his lean shanks crossed, nodding at the steam
escaping from the cooking-pot with a gaze senile and
worried.

Then mute affliction dwelt in Bacadou's farmhouse,
sharing the breath and the bread of its inhabitants;
and the priest of the Ploumar parish had great cause for
congratulation.   He called upon the rich landowner,
the Marquis de Chavanes, on purpose to deliver himself
with joyful unction of solemn platitudes about the inscrutable ways of Providence.   In the vast dimness of
the curtained drawing-room, the little man, resembling a
black bolster, leaned towards a couch, his hat on his
knees, and gesticulated with a fat hand at the elon-
gated, gracefully-flowing lines of the clear Parisian
toilette from within which the half-amused, half-bored

marquise listened with gracious languor. He was exulting and humble, proud and awed. The impossible had come to pass. Jean-Pierre Bacadou, the enraged republican farmer, had been to mass last Sunday —had proposed to entertain the visiting priests at the next festival of Ploumar! It was a triumph for the Church and for the good cause. "I thought I would come at once to tell Monsieur le Marquis. I know how anxious he is for the welfare of our country," declared the priest, wiping his face. He was asked to stay to dinner.

The Chavanes returning that evening, after seeing their guest to the main gate of the park, discussed the matter while they strolled in the moonlight, trailing their long shadows up the straight avenue of chestnuts. The marquis, a royalist of course, had been mayor of the commune which includes Ploumar, the scattered hamlets of the coast, and the stony islands that fringe the yellow flatness of the sands. He had left his position insecure, for there was a strong republican element in that part of the country; but now the conversion of Jean-Pierre made him safe. He was very pleased. "You have no idea how influential those people are," he explained to his wife. "Now, I am sure, the next communal election will go all right. I shall be re-elected." "Your ambition is perfectly insatiable, Charles," exclaimed the marquise, gaily. "But, ma chère amie," argued the husband, seriously, "it's most important that the right man should be mayor this year, because of the elections to the Chamber. If you think it amuses me . . ."

Jean-Pierre had surrendered to his wife's mother. Madame Levaille was a woman of business, known and respected within a radius of at least fifteen miles. Thick-set and stout, she was seen about the country,

on foot or in an acquaintance's cart, perpetually moving, in spite of her fifty-eight years, in steady pursuit
of business. She had houses in all the hamlets, she
worked quarries of granite, she freighted coasters with
stone—even traded with the Channel Islands. She
was broad-cheeked, wide-eyed, persuasive in speech:
carrying her point with the placid and invincible
obstinacy of an old woman who knows her own mind.
She very seldom slept for two nights together in the
same house; and the wayside inns were the best places
to inquire in as to her whereabouts. She had either
passed, or was expected to pass there at six; or somebody, coming in, had seen her in the morning, or expected to meet her that evening. After the inns that
command the roads, the churches were the buildings
she frequented most. Men of liberal opinions would
induce small children to run into sacred edifices to see
whether Madame Levaille was there, and to tell her
that so-and-so was in the road waiting to speak to her—
about potatoes, or flour, or stones, or houses; and she
would curtail her devotions, come out blinking and
crossing herself into the sunshine; ready to discuss
business matters in a calm, sensible way across a table
in the kitchen of the inn opposite. Latterly she had
stayed for a few days several times with her son-in-law,
arguing against sorrow and misfortune with composed
face and gentle tones. Jean-Pierre felt the convictions
imbibed in the regiment torn out of his breast—not by
arguments, but by facts. Striding over his fields he
thought it over. There were three of them. Three!
All alike! Why? Such things did not happen to
everybody—to nobody he ever heard of. One yet—
it might pass. But three! All three. Forever useless, to be fed while he lived and . . . What
would become of the land when he died? This must be

seen to. He would sacrifice his convictions. One day he told his wife—

"See what your God will do for us. Pray for some masses."

Susan embraced her man. He stood unbending, then turned on his heels and went out. But afterwards, when a black *soutane* darkened his doorway, he did not object; even offered some cider himself to the priest. He listened to the talk meekly; went to mass between the two women; accomplished what the priest called "his religious duties" at Easter. That morning he felt like a man who had sold his soul. In the afternoon he fought ferociously with an old friend and neighbour who had remarked that the priests had the best of it and were now going to eat the priest-eater. He came home dishevelled and bleeding, and happening to catch sight of his children (they were kept generally out of the way), cursed and swore incoherently, banging the table. Susan wept. Madame Levaille sat serenely unmoved. She assured her daughter that "It will pass;" and taking up her thick umbrella, departed in haste to see after a schooner she was going to load with granite from her quarry.

A year or so afterwards the girl was born. A girl. Jean-Pierre heard of it in the fields, and was so upset by the news that he sat down on the boundary wall and remained there till the evening, instead of going home as he was urged to do. A girl! He felt half cheated. However, when he got home he was partly reconciled to his fate. One could marry her to a good fellow—not to a good for nothing, but to a fellow with some understanding and a good pair of arms. Besides, the next may be a boy, he thought. Of course they would be all right. His new credulity knew of no doubt. The ill luck was broken. He spoke cheerily to his wife. She was also hopeful. Three priests came to that christening, and Madame Levaille was godmother. The child turned out an idiot too.

Then on market days Jean-Pierre was seen bargaining bitterly, quarrelsome and greedy; then getting drunk with taciturn earnestness; then driving home in the dusk at a rate fit for a wedding, but with a face gloomy enough for a funeral. Sometimes he would insist for his wife to come with him; and they would drive in the early morning, shaking side by side on the narrow seat above the helpless pig, that, with tied legs, grunted a melancholy sigh at every rut. The morning drives were silent; but in the evening, coming home, Jean-Pierre, tipsy, was viciously muttering, and growled at the confounded woman who could not rear children that were like anybody else's. Susan, holding on against the erratic swayings of the cart, pretended not to hear. Once, as they were driving through Ploumar, some obscure and drunken impulse caused him to pull up sharply opposite the church. The moon swam amongst light white clouds. The tombstones gleamed pale under the fretted shadows of the trees in the churchyard. Even the village dogs slept. Only the nightingales, awake, spun out the thrill of their song above the silence of graves. Jean-Pierre said thickly to his wife—

"What do you think is there?"

He pointed his whip at the tower—in which the big dial of the clock appeared high in the moonlight like a pallid face without eyes—and getting out carefully, fell down at once by the wheel. He picked himself up and climbed one by one the few steps to the iron gate of the churchyard. He put his face to the bars and called out indistinctly—

"Hey there! Come out!"

"Jean! Return! Return!" entreated his wife in low tones.

He took no notice, and seemed to wait there. The song of nightingales beat on all sides against the high walls of the church, and flowed back between stone crosses and flat gray slabs, engraved with words of hope and sorrow.

"Hey! Come out!" shouted Jean-Pierre, loudly.

The nightingales ceased to sing.

"Nobody?" went on Jean-Pierre. "Nobody there. A swindle of the crows. That's what this is. Nobody anywhere. I despise it. Allez! Houp!"

He shook the gate with all his strength, and the iron bars rattled with a frightful clanging, like a chain dragged over stone steps. A dog near by barked hurriedly. Jean-Pierre staggered back, and after three successive dashes got into his cart. Susan sat very quiet and still. He said to her with drunken severity—

"See? Nobody. I've been made a fool! Malheur! Somebody will pay for it. The next one I see near the house I will lay my whip on . . . on the black spine . . . I will. I don't want him in there . . . he only helps the carrion crows to rob poor folk. I am a man. . . . We will see if I can't have children like anybody else . . . now you mind. . . . They won't be all . . . all . . . we see. . . ."

She burst out through the fingers that hid her face—

"Don't say that, Jean; don't say that, my man!"

He struck her a swinging blow on the head with the back of his hand and knocked her into the bottom of the cart, where she crouched, thrown about lamentably by every jolt. He drove furiously, standing up, brandishing his whip, shaking the reins over the gray horse

*к

that galloped ponderously, making the heavy harness leap upon his broad quarters. The country rang clamorous in the night with the irritated barking of farm dogs, that followed the rattle of wheels all along the road. A couple of belated wayfarers had only just time to step into the ditch. At his own gate he caught the post and was shot out of the cart head first. The horse went on slowly to the door. At Susan's piercing cries the farm hands rushed out. She thought him dead, but he was only sleeping where he fell, and cursed his men, who hastened to him, for disturbing his slumbers.

Autumn came. The clouded sky descended low upon the black contours of the hills; and the dead leaves danced in spiral whirls under naked trees, till the wind, sighing profoundly, laid them to rest in the hollows of bare valleys. And from morning till night one could see all over the land black denuded boughs, the boughs gnarled and twisted, as if contorted with pain, swaying sadly between the wet clouds and the soaked earth. The clear and gentle streams of summer days rushed discoloured and raging at the stones that barred the way to the sea, with the fury of madness bent upon suicide. From horizon to horizon the great road to the sands lay between the hills in a dull glitter of empty curves, resembling an unnavigable river of mud.

Jean-Pierre went from field to field, moving blurred and tall in the drizzle, or striding on the crests of rises, lonely and high upon the gray curtain of drifting clouds, as if he had been pacing along the very edge of the universe. He looked at the black earth, at the earth mute and promising, at the mysterious earth doing its work of life in death-like stillness under the veiled sorrow of the sky. And it seemed to him that to a man worse than childless there was no promise in the fertility of

fields, that from him the earth escaped, defied him,
frowned at him like the clouds, sombre and hurried
above his head. Having to face alone his own fields,
he felt the inferiority of man who passes away before
the clod that remains. Must he give up the hope of
having by his side a son who would look at the turned-
up sods with a master's eye? A man that would think
as he thought, that would feel as he felt; a man who
would be part of himself, and yet remain to trample
masterfully on that earth when he was gone! He
thought of some distant relation, and felt savage
enough to curse them aloud. They! Never! He
turned homewards, going straight at the roof of his
dwelling, visible between the enlaced skeletons of trees.
As he swung his legs over the stile a cawing flock of
birds settled slowly on the field; dropped down behind
his back, noiseless and fluttering, like flakes of soot.

That day Madame Levaille had gone early in the
afternoon to the house she had near Kervanion. She
had to pay some of the men who worked in her granite
quarry there, and she went in good time because her
little house contained a shop where the workmen could
spend their wages without the trouble of going to town.
The house stood alone amongst rocks. A lane of mud
and stones ended at the door. The sea-winds coming
ashore on Stonecutter's point, fresh from the fierce
turmoil of the waves, howled violently at the unmoved
heaps of black boulders holding up steadily short-
armed, high crosses against the tremendous rush of the
invisible. In the sweep of gales the sheltered dwelling
stood in a calm resonant and disquieting, like the calm
in the centre of a hurricane. On stormy nights, when
the tide was out, the bay of Fougère, fifty feet below
the house, resembled an immense black pit, from which
ascended mutterings and sighs as if the sands down

there had been alive and complaining. At high tide
the returning water assaulted the ledges of rock in short
rushes, ending in bursts of livid light and columns of
spray, that flew inland, stinging to death the grass of
pastures.

The darkness came from the hills, flowed over the
coast, put out the red fires of sunset, and went on to
seaward pursuing the retiring tide. The wind dropped
with the sun, leaving a maddened sea and a devastated
sky. The heavens above the house seemed to be draped
in black rags, held up here and there by pins of fire.
Madame Levaille, for this evening the servant of her
own workmen, tried to induce them to depart. "An
old woman like me ought to be in bed at this late hour,"
she good-humouredly repeated. The quarrymen drank,
asked for more. They shouted over the table as if
they had been talking across a field. At one end four
of them played cards, banging the wood with their hard
knuckles, and swearing at every lead. One sat with a
lost gaze, humming a bar of some song, which he repeated endlessly. Two others, in a corner, were quarrelling confidentially and fiercely over some woman,
looking close into one another's eyes as if they had
wanted to tear them out, but speaking in whispers that
promised violence and murder discreetly, in a venomous
sibillation of subdued words. The atmosphere in there
was thick enough to slice with a knife. Three candles
burning about the long room glowed red and dull like
sparks expiring in ashes.

The slight click of the iron latch was at that late
hour as unexpected and startling as a thunder-clap.
Madame Levaille put down a bottle she held above a
liqueur glass; the players turned their heads; the whispered quarrel ceased; only the singer, after darting
a glance at the door, went on humming with a stolid

face. Susan appeared in the doorway, stepped in, flung the door to, and put her back against it, saying, half aloud—

"Mother!"

Madame Levaille, taking up the bottle again, said calmly: "Here you are, my girl. What a state you are in!" The neck of the bottle rang on the rim of the glass, for the old woman was startled, and the idea that the farm had caught fire had entered her head. She could think of no other cause for her daughter's appearance.

Susan, soaked and muddy, stared the whole length of the room towards the men at the far end. Her mother asked—

"What has happened? God guard us from misfortune!"

Susan moved her lips. No sound came. Madame Levaille stepped up to her daughter, took her by the arm, looked into her face.

"In God's name," she said, shakily, "what's the matter? You have been rolling in mud. . . . Why did you come? . . . Where's Jean?"

The men had all got up and approached slowly, staring with dull surprise. Madame Levaille jerked her daughter away from the door, swung her round upon a seat close to the wall. Then she turned fiercely to the men—

"Enough of this! Out you go—you others! I close."

One of them observed, looking down at Susan collapsed on the seat: "She is—one may say—half dead."

Madame Levaille flung the door open.

"Get out! March!" she cried, shaking nervously.

They dropped out into the night, laughing stupidly.

Outside, the two Lotharios broke out into loud shouts. The others tried to soothe them, all talking at once. The noise went away up the lane with the men, who staggered together in a tight knot, remonstrating with one another foolishly.

"Speak, Susan. What is it? Speak!" entreated Madame Levaille, as soon as the door was shut.

Susan pronounced some incomprehensible words, glaring at the table. The old woman clapped her hands above her head, let them drop, and stood looking at her daughter with disconsolate eyes. Her husband had been "deranged in his head" for a few years before he died, and now she began to suspect her daughter was going mad. She asked, pressingly—

"Does Jean know where you are? Where is Jean?"

Susan pronounced with difficulty—

"He knows . . . he is dead."

"What!" cried the old woman. She came up near, and peering at her daughter, repeated three times: "What do you say? What do you say? What do you say?"

Susan sat dry-eyed and stony before Madame Levaille, who contemplated her, feeling a strange sense of inexplicable horror creep into the silence of the house. She had hardly realised the news, further than to understand that she had been brought in one short moment face to face with something unexpected and final. It did not even occur to her to ask for any explanation. She thought: accident—terrible accident—blood to the head—fell down a trap door in the loft. . . . She remained there, distracted and mute, blinking her old eyes.

Suddenly, Susan said—

"I have killed him."

For a moment the mother stood still, almost unbreathing, but with composed face. The next second she burst out into a shout—

"You miserable madwoman . . . they will cut your neck. . . ."

She fancied the gendarmes entering the house, saying to her: "We want your daughter; give her up:" the gendarmes with the severe, hard faces of men on duty. She knew the brigadier well—an old friend, familiar and respectful, saying heartily, "To your good health, Madame!" before lifting to his lips the small glass of cognac—out of the special bottle she kept for friends. And now! . . . She was losing her head. She rushed here and there, as if looking for something urgently needed—gave that up, stood stock still in the middle of the room, and screamed at her daughter—

"Why? Say! Say! Why?"

The other seemed to leap out of her strange apathy.

"Do you think I am made of stone?" she shouted back, striding towards her mother.

"No! It's impossible. . . . ." said Madame Levaille, in a convinced tone.

"You go and see, mother," retorted Susan, looking at her with blazing eyes. "There's no mercy in heaven —no justice. No! . . . I did not know. . . . Do you think I have no heart? Do you think I have never heard people jeering at me, pitying me, wondering at me? Do you know how some of them were calling me? The mother of idiots—that was my nickname! And my children never would know me, never speak to me. They would know nothing; neither men—nor God. Haven't I prayed! But the Mother of God herself would not hear me. A mother! . . . Who is accursed—I, or the man who is dead? Eh? Tell me. I took care of myself. Do you think I would defy the anger of God and have my house full of those things—that are worse than animals who know the hand that feeds them? Who blasphemed in the night at the very church door? Was it I? . . . I only wept and prayed for mercy . . . and I feel the curse at every moment of the day—I see it round me from morning to night . . . I've got to keep them alive—to take care of my misfortune and shame. And he would come. I begged him and Heaven for mercy. . . . No! . . . Then we shall see. . . . He came this evening. I thought to myself: 'Ah! again!' . . . I had my long scissors. I heard him shouting . . . I saw him near. . . . I must—must I? . . . Then take! . . . And I struck him in the throat above the breastbone. . . . I never heard him even sigh. . . . I left him standing. . . . It was a minute ago. How did I come here?"

Madame Levaille shivered. A wave of cold ran down her back, down her fat arms under her tight sleeves, made her stamp gently where she stood. Quivers ran over the broad cheeks, across the thin lips, ran amongst the wrinkles at the corners of her steady old eyes. She stammered—

"You wicked woman—you disgrace me. But there! You always resembled your father. What do you think will become of you . . . in the other world? In this . . . Oh misery!"

She was very hot now. She felt burning inside. She wrung her perspiring hands—and suddenly, starting in great haste, began to look for her big shawl and umbrella, feverishly, never once glancing at her daughter, who stood in the middle of the room following her with a gaze distracted and cold.

"Nothing worse than in this," said Susan.

Her mother, umbrella in hand and trailing the shawl over the floor, groaned profoundly.

"I must go to the priest," she burst out, passionately. "I do not know whether you even speak the truth! You are a horrible woman. They will find you anywhere. You may stay here—or go. There is no room for you in this world."

Ready now to depart, she yet wandered aimlessly about the room, putting the bottles on the shelf, trying to fit with trembling hands the covers on cardboard boxes. Whenever the real sense of what she had heard emerged for a second from the haze of her thoughts she would fancy that something had exploded in her brain without, unfortunately, bursting her head to pieces—which would have been a relief. She blew the candles out one by one without knowing it, and was horribly startled by the darkness. She fell on a bench and began to whimper. After a while she ceased, and sat listening to the breathing of her daughter, whom she could hardly see, still and upright, giving no other sign of life. She was becoming old rapidly at last, during those minutes. She spoke in tones unsteady, cut about by the rattle of teeth, like one shaken by a deadly cold fit of ague.

"I wish you had died little. I will never dare to show my old head in the sunshine again. There are worse misfortunes than idiot children. I wish you had been born to me simple—like your own. . . ."

She saw the figure of her daughter pass before the faint and livid clearness of a window. Then it appeared in the doorway for a second, and the door swung to with a clang. Madame Levaille, as if awakened by the noise from a long nightmare, rushed out.

"Susan!" she shouted from the doorstep.

She heard a stone roll a long time down the declivity of the rocky beach above the sands. She stepped forward cautiously, one hand on the wall of the house, and

peered down into the smooth darkness of the empty bay.
Once again she cried—

"Susan! You will kill yourself there."

The stone had taken its last leap in the dark, and she
heard nothing now. A sudden thought seemed to
strangle her, and she called no more. She turned her
back upon the black silence of the pit and went up the
lane towards Ploumar, stumbling along with sombre
determination, as if she had started on a desperate
journey that would last, perhaps, to the end of her life.
A sullen and periodic clamour of waves rolling over
reefs followed her far inland between the high hedges
sheltering the gloomy solitude of the fields.

Susan had run out, swerving sharp to the left at the
door, and on the edge of the slope crouched down behind a boulder. A dislodged stone went on downwards,
rattling as it leaped. When Madame Levaille called
out, Susan could have, by stretching her hand, touched
her mother's skirt, had she had the courage to move a
limb. She saw the old woman go away, and she remained still, closing her eyes and pressing her side to the
hard and rugged surface of the rock. After a while a
familiar face with fixed eyes and an open mouth became
visible in the intense obscurity amongst the boulders.
She uttered a low cry and stood up. The face vanished,
leaving her to gasp and shiver alone in the wilderness of
stone heaps. But as soon as she had crouched down
again to rest, with her head against the rock, the face
returned, came very near, appeared eager to finish the
speech that had been cut short by death, only a moment
ago. She scrambled quickly to her feet and said:
"Go away, or I will do it again." The thing wavered,
swung to the right, to the left. She moved this way and
that, stepped back, fancied herself screaming at it, and
was appalled by the unbroken stillness of the night.

She tottered on the brink, felt the steep declivity under
her feet, and rushed down blindly to save herself
from a headlong fall. The shingle seemed to wake up;
the pebbles began to roll before her, pursued her from
above, raced down with her on both sides, rolling past
with an increasing clatter. In the peace of the night
the noise grew, deepening to a rumour, continuous and
violent, as if the whole semicircle of the stony beach
had started to tumble down into the bay. Susan's
feet hardly touched the slope that seemed to run down
with her. At the bottom she stumbled, shot forward,
throwing her arms out, and fell heavily. She jumped
up at once and turned swiftly to look back, her clenched
hands full of sand she had clutched in her fall. The
face was there, keeping its distance, visible in its own
sheen that made a pale stain in the night. She shouted,
"Go away"—she shouted at it with pain, with fear,
with all the rage of that useless stab that could not keep
him quiet, keep him out of her sight. What did he
want now? He was dead. Dead men have no children. Would he never leave her alone? She shrieked
at it—waved her outstretched hands. She seemed to
feel the breath of parted lips, and, with a long cry of
discouragement, fled across the level bottom of the
bay.

She ran lightly, unaware of any effort of her body.
High sharp rocks that, when the bay is full, show above
the glittering plain of blue water like pointed towers of
submerged churches, glided past her, rushing to the
land at a tremendous pace. To the left, in the distance,
she could see something shining: a broad disc of light
in which narrow shadows pivoted round the centre like
the spokes of a wheel. She heard a voice calling,
"Hey! There!" and answered with a wild scream.
So, he could call yet! He was calling after her to stop.

Never! . . . She tore through the night, past the
startled group of seaweed-gatherers who stood round
their lantern paralysed with fear at the unearthly
screech coming from that fleeing shadow. The men
leaned on their pitchforks staring fearfully. A woman
fell on her knees, and, crossing herself, began to pray
aloud. A little girl with her ragged skirt full of slimy
seaweed began to sob despairingly, lugging her soaked
burden close to the man who carried the light. Somebody said: "The thing ran out towards the sea."
Another voice exclaimed: "And the sea is coming back!
Look at the spreading puddles. Do you hear—you
woman—there! Get up!" Several voices cried together. "Yes, let us be off! Let the accursed thing
go to the sea!" They moved on, keeping close round
the light. Suddenly a man swore loudly. He would go
and see what was the matter. It had been a woman's
voice. He would go. There were shrill protests from
women—but his high form detached itself from the
group and went off running. They sent an unanimous
call of scared voices after him. A word, insulting
and mocking, came back, thrown at them through
darkness. A woman moaned. An old man said
gravely: "Such things ought to be left alone." They
went on slower, shuffling in the yielding sand and
whispering to one another that Millot feared nothing,
having no religion, but that it would end badly some
day.

Susan met the incoming tide by the Raven islet and
stopped, panting, with her feet in the water. She
heard the murmur and felt the cold caress of the sea,
and, calmer now, could see the sombre and confused
mass of the Raven on one side and on the other the long
white streak of Molène sands that are left high above
the dry bottom of Fougère Bay at every ebb. She

turned round and saw far away, along the starred background of the sky, the ragged outline of the coast. Above it, nearly facing her, appeared the tower of Ploumar Church; a slender and tall pyramid shooting up dark and pointed into the clustered glitter of the stars. She felt strangely calm. She knew where she was, and began to remember how she came there—and why. She peered into the smooth obscurity near her. She was alone. There was nothing there; nothing near her, either living or dead.

The tide was creeping in quietly, putting out long impatient arms of strange rivulets that ran towards the land between ridges of sand. Under the night the pools grew bigger with mysterious rapidity, while the great sea, yet far off, thundered in a regular rhythm along the indistinct line of the horizon. Susan splashed her way back for a few yards without being able to get clear of the water that murmured tenderly all around and, suddenly, with a spiteful gurgle, nearly took her off her feet. Her heart thumped with fear. This place was too big and too empty to die in. To-morrow they would do with her what they liked. But before she died she must tell them—tell the gentlemen in black clothes that there are things no woman can bear. She must explain how it happened. . . . She splashed through a pool, getting wet to the waist, too preoccupied to care. . . . She must explain. "He came in the same way as ever and said, just so: 'Do you think I am going to leave the land to those people from Morbihan that I do not know? Do you? We shall see! Come along, you creature of mischance!' And he put his arms out. Then, Messieurs, I said: 'Before God—never!' And he said, striding at me with open palms: 'There is no God to hold me! Do you understand, you useless carcase. I will do what I

like.' And he took me by the shoulders. Then I,
Messieurs, called to God for help, and next minute,
while he was shaking me, I felt my long scissors in my
hand. His shirt was unbuttoned, and, by the candle-
light, I saw the hollow of his throat. I cried: 'Let go!'
He was crushing my shoulders. He was strong, my
man was! Then I thought: No! . . . . Must I?
. . . Then take!—and I struck in the hollow place.
I never saw him fall. Never! Never! . . . Never
saw him fall. . . . The old father never turned
his head. He is deaf and childish, gentlemen. . . .
Nobody saw him fall. I ran out . . . Nobody
saw."

She had been scrambling amongst the boulders of the
Raven and now found herself, all out of breath, standing amongst the heavy shadows of the rocky islet.
The Raven is connected with the main land by a
natural pier of immense and slippery stones. She intended to return home that way. Was he still standing there? At home. Home! Four idiots and a
corpse. She must go back and explain. Anybody
would understand. . . .

Below her the night or the sea seemed to pronounce
distinctly—

"Aha! I see you at last!"

She started, slipped, fell; and without attempting to
rise, listened, terrified. She heard heavy breathing, a
clatter of wooden clogs. It stopped.

"Where the devil did you pass?" said an invisible
man, hoarsely.

She held her breath. She recognized the voice.
She had not seen him fall. Was he pursuing her there
dead, or perhaps . . . alive?

She lost her head. She cried from the crevice where
she lay huddled, "Never, never!"

"Ah! You are still there. You led me a fine dance. Wait, my beauty, I must see how you look after all this. You wait. . . ."

Millot was stumbling, laughing, swearing meaninglessly out of pure satisfaction, pleased with himself for having run down that fly-by-night. "As if there were such things as ghosts! Bah! It took an old African soldier to show those clodhoppers. . . . But it was curious. Who the devil was she?"

Susan listened, crouching. He was coming for her, this dead man. There was no escape. What a noise he made amongst the stones. . . . She saw his head rise up, then the shoulders. He was tall—her own man! His long arms waved about, and it was his own voice sounding a little strange . . . because of the scissors. She scrambled out quickly, rushed to the edge of the causeway, and turned round. The man stood still on a high stone, detaching himself in dead black on the glitter of the sky.

"Where are you going to?" he called, roughly.

She answered, "Home!" and watched him intensely. He made a striding, clumsy leap on to another boulder, and stopped again, balancing himself, then said—

"Ha! ha! Well, I am going with you. It's the least I can do. Ha! ha! ha!"

She stared at him till her eyes seemed to become glowing coals that burned deep into her brain, and yet she was in mortal fear of making out the well-known features. Below her the sea lapped softly against the rock with a splash continuous and gentle.

The man said, advancing another step—

"I am coming for you. What do you think?"

She trembled. Coming for her! There was no escape, no peace, no hope. She looked round despairingly. Suddenly the whole shadowy coast, the blurred

islets, the heaven itself, swayed about twice, then came
to a rest. She closed her eyes and shouted—

"Can't you wait till I am dead!"

She was shaken by a furious hate for that shade that
pursued her in this world, unappeased even by death
in its longing for an heir that would be like other
people's children.

"Hey! What?" said Millot, keeping his distance
prudently. He was saying to himself: "Look out!
Some lunatic. An accident happens soon."

She went on, wildly—

"I want to live. To live alone—for a week—for a
day. I must explain to them. . . . I would tear
you to pieces, I would kill you twenty times over rather
than let you touch me while I live. How many times
must I kill you—you blasphemer! Satan sends you
here. I am damned too!"

"Come," said Millot, alarmed and conciliating. "I
am perfectly alive! . . . Oh, my God!"

She had screamed, "Alive!" and at once vanished
before his eyes, as if the islet itself had swerved aside
from under her feet. Millot rushed forward, and fell
flat with his chin over the edge. Far below he saw the
water whitened by her struggles, and heard one shrill
cry for help that seemed to dart upwards along the
perpendicular face of the rock, and soar past, straight
into the high and impassive heaven.

Madame Levaille sat, dry-eyed, on the short grass
of the hill side, with her thick legs stretched out, and
her old feet turned up in their black cloth shoes. Her
clogs stood near by, and further off the umbrella lay
on the withered sward like a weapon dropped from
the grasp of a vanquished warrior. The Marquis of
Chavanes, on horseback, one gloved hand on thigh,

looked down at her as she got up laboriously, with groans. On the narrow track of the seaweed-carts four men were carrying inland Susan's body on a hand-barrow, while several others straggled listlessly behind. Madame Levaille looked after the procession. "Yes, Monsieur le Marquis," she said dispassionately, in her usual calm tone of a reasonable old woman. "There are unfortunate people on this earth. I had only one child. Only one! And they won't bury her in con-secrated ground!"

Her eyes filled suddenly, and a short shower of tears rolled down the broad cheeks. She pulled the shawl close about her. The Marquis leaned slightly over in his saddle, and said—

"It is very sad. You have all my sympathy. I shall speak to the Curé. She was unquestionably insane, and the fall was accidental. Millot says so distinctly. Good-day, Madame."

And he trotted off, thinking to himself: I must get this old woman appointed guardian of those idiots, and administrator of the farm. It would be much better than having here one of those other Bacadous, probably a red republican, corrupting my commune.

AN OUTPOST OF PROGRESS

I

THERE were two white men in charge of the trading station. Kayerts, the chief, was short and fat; Carlier, the assistant, was tall, with a large head and a very broad trunk perched upon a long pair of thin legs. The third man on the staff was a Sierra Leone nigger, who maintained that his name was Henry Price. However, for some reason or other, the natives down the river had given him the name of Makola, and it stuck to him through all his wanderings about the country. He spoke English and French with a warbling accent, wrote a beautiful hand, understood bookkeeping, and cherished in his innermost heart the worship of evil spirits. His wife was a negress from Loanda, very large and very noisy. Three children rolled about in sunshine before the door of his low, shed-like dwelling. Makola, taciturn and impenetrable, despised the two white men. He had charge of a small clay storehouse with a dried-grass roof, and pretended to keep a correct account of beads, cotton cloth, red kerchiefs, brass wire, and other trade goods it contained. Besides the storehouse and Makola's hut, there was only one large building in the cleared ground of the station. It was built neatly of reeds, with a verandah on all the four sides. There were three rooms in it. The one in the middle was the living-room, and had two rough tables and a few stools in it. The other two were the bedrooms for the white men. Each had a bedstead and a mosquito net for all furniture. The plank floor was littered with the belongings of the white men; open half-empty boxes, town wearing apparel, old boots; all the things dirty, and all the things broken, that accumulate mysteriously round untidy men. There was also another dwelling-place some distance away from the buildings. In it, under a tall cross much out of the perpendicular, slept the man who had seen the beginning of all this; who had planned and had watched the construction of this outpost of progress. He had been, at home, an unsuccessful painter who, weary of pursuing fame on an empty stomach, had gone out there through high protections. He had been the first chief of that station. Makola had watched the energetic artist die of fever in the just finished house with his usual kind of "I told you so" indifference. Then, for a time, he dwelt alone with his family, his account books, and the Evil Spirit that rules the lands under the equator. He got on very well with his god. Perhaps he had propitiated him by a promise of more white men to play with, by and by. At any rate the director of the Great Trading Company, coming up in a steamer that resembled an enormous sardine box with a flat-roofed shed erected on it, found the station in good order, and Makola as usual quietly diligent. The director had the cross put up over the first agent's grave, and appointed Kayerts to the post. Carlier was told off as second in charge. The director was a man ruthless and efficient, who at times, but very imperceptibly, indulged in grim humour. He made a speech to Kayerts and Carlier, pointing out to them the promising aspect of their station. The nearest trading-post was about three hundred miles away. It was an exceptional opportunity for them to distinguish themselves and to earn percentages on the trade. This appointment was a favour done to beginners. Kayerts was moved almost to tears by his director's kindness. He would, he said, by doing his best, try to justify the flattering confidence, &c., &c. Kayerts had been in the Administration of the Telegraphs, and knew how to express himself correctly. Carlier, an ex-non-commissioned officer of cavalry in an army guaranteed from harm by several European Powers, was less impressed. If there were commissions to get, so much the better; and, trailing a sulky glance over the river, the forests, the impenetrable bush that seemed to cut off the station from the rest of the world, he muttered between his teeth, "We shall see, very soon."

Next day, some bales of cotton goods and a few cases of provisions having been thrown on shore, the sardine-box steamer went off, not to return for another six months. On the deck the director touched his cap to the two agents, who stood on the bank waving their hats, and turning to an old servant of the Company on his passage to headquarters, said, "Look at those two imbeciles. They must be mad at home to send me such specimens. I told those fellows to plant a vegetable garden, build new storehouses and fences, and construct a landing-stage. I bet nothing will be done! They won't know how to begin. I always thought the station on this river useless, and they just fit the station!"

"They will form themselves there," said the old stager with a quiet smile.

"At any rate, I am rid of them for six months," retorted the director.

The two men watched the steamer round the bend, then, ascending arm in arm the slope of the bank, returned to the station. They had been in this vast and dark country only a very short time, and as yet always in the midst of other white men, under the eye and guidance of their superiors. And now, dull as they were to the subtle influences of surroundings, they felt themselves very much alone, when suddenly left unassisted to face the wilderness; a wilderness rendered more strange, more incomprehensible by the mysterious glimpses of the vigorous life it contained. They were two perfectly insignificant and incapable individuals, whose existence is only rendered possible through the high organization of civilized crowds. Few men realize that their life, the very essence of their character, their capabilities and their audacities, are only the expression of their belief in the safety of their surroundings. The courage, the composure, the confidence; the emotions and principles; every great and every insignificant thought belongs not to the individual but to the crowd: to the crowd that believes blindly in the irresistible force of its institutions and of its morals, in the power of its police and of its opinion. But the contact with pure unmitigated savagery, with primitive nature and primitive man, brings sudden and profound trouble into the heart. To the sentiment of being alone of one's kind, to the clear perception of the loneliness of one's thoughts, of one's sensations—to the negation of the habitual, which is safe, there is added the affirmation of the unusual, which is dangerous; a suggestion of things vague, uncontrollable, and repulsive, whose discomposing intrusion excites the imagination and tries the civilized nerves of the foolish and the wise alike.

Kayerts and Carlier walked arm in arm, drawing close to one another as children do in the dark; and they had the same, not altogether unpleasant, sense of danger which one half suspects to be imaginary. They chatted persistently in familiar tones. "Our station is prettily situated," said one. The other assented with enthusiasm, enlarging volubly on the beauties of the situation. Then they passed near the grave. "Poor devil!" said Kayerts. "He died of fever, didn't he?" muttered Carlier, stopping short. "Why," retorted Kayerts, with indignation, "I've been told that the fellow exposed himself recklessly to the sun. The climate here, everybody says, is not at all worse than at home, as long as you keep out of the sun. Do you hear that, Carlier? I am chief here, and my orders are that you should not expose yourself to the sun!" He assumed his superiority jocularly, but his meaning was serious. The idea that he would, perhaps, have to bury Carlier and remain alone, gave him an inward shiver. He felt suddenly that this Carlier was more precious to him here, in the centre of Africa, than a brother could be anywhere else. Carlier, entering into the spirit of the thing, made a military salute and answered in a brisk tone, "Your orders shall be attended to, chief!" Then he burst out laughing, slapped Kayerts on the back and shouted, "We shall let life run easily here! Just sit still and gather in the ivory those savages will bring. This country has its good points, after all!" They both laughed loudly while Carlier thought: That poor Kayerts; he is so fat and unhealthy. It would be awful if I had to bury him here. He is a man I respect. . . . Before they reached the verandah of their house they called one another "my dear fellow."

The first day they were very active, pottering about with hammers and nails and red calico, to put up curtains, make their house habitable and pretty; resolved to settle down comfortably to their new life. For them an impossible task. To grapple effectually with even purely material problems requires more serenity

of mind and more lofty courage than people generally
imagine. No two beings could have been more unfitted
for such a struggle. Society, not from any tenderness,
but because of its strange needs, had taken care of
those two men, forbidding them all independent
thought, all initiative, all departure from routine; and
forbidding it under pain of death. They could only
live on condition of being machines. And now, released
from the fostering care of men with pens behind the
ears, or of men with gold lace on the sleeves, they were
like those lifelong prisoners who, liberated after many
years, do not know what use to make of their freedom.
They did not know what use to make of their faculties,
being both, through want of practice, incapable of independent thought.

At the end of two months Kayerts often would say,
"If it was not for my Melie, you wouldn't catch me
here." Melie was his daughter. He had thrown up
his post in the Administration of the Telegraphs, though
he had been for seventeen years perfectly happy
there, to earn a dowry for his girl. His wife was dead,
and the child was being brought up by his sisters. He
regretted the streets, the pavements, the cafés, his
friends of many years; all the things he used to see,
day after day; all the thoughts suggested by familiar
things—the thoughts effortless, monotonous, and soothing of a Government clerk; he regretted all the gossip,
the small enmities, the mild venom, and the little jokes
of Government offices. "If I had had a decent brother-
in-law," Carlier would remark, "a fellow with a heart,
I would not be here." He had left the army and had
made himself so obnoxious to his family by his laziness
ard impudence, that an exasperated brother-in-law had
made superhuman efforts to procure him an appointment in the Company as a second-class agent. Having

not a penny in the world he was compelled to accept
this means of livelihood as soon as it became quite clear
to him that there was nothing more to squeeze out of
his relations. He, like Kayerts, regretted his old life.
He regretted the clink of sabre and spurs on a fine afternoon, the barrack-room witticisms, the girls of garrison
towns; but, besides, he had also a sense of grievance.
He was evidently a much ill-used man. This made
him moody, at times. But the two men got on well together in the fellowship of their stupidity and laziness.
Together they did nothing, absolutely nothing, and enjoyed the sense of idleness for which they were paid.
And in time they came to feel something resembling
affection for one another.

They lived like blind men in a large room, aware only
of what came in contact with them (and of that only
imperfectly), but unable to see the general aspect
of things. The river, the forest, all the great land
throbbing with life, were like a great emptiness. Even
the brilliant sunshine disclosed nothing intelligible.
Things appeared and disappeared before their eyes in
an unconnected and aimless kind of way. The river
seemed to come from nowhere and flow nowhither. It
flowed through a void. Out of that void, at times,
came canoes, and men with spears in their hands would
suddenly crowd the yard of the station. They were
naked, glossy black, ornamented with snowy shells and
glistening brass wire, perfect of limb. They made an
uncouth babbling noise when they spoke, moved in a
stately manner, and sent quick, wild glances out of
their startled, never-resting eyes. Those warriors
would squat in long rows, four or more deep, before the
verandah, while their chiefs bargained for hours with
Makola over an elephant tusk. Kayerts sat on his
chair and looked down on the proceedings, under-

standing nothing. He stared at them with his round blue eyes, called out to Carlier, "Here, look! look at that fellow there—and that other one, to the left. Did you ever see such a face? Oh, the funny brute!"

Carlier, smoking native tobacco in a short wooden pipe, would swagger up twirling his moustaches, and surveying the warriors with haughty indulgence, would say—

"Fine animals. Brought any bone? Yes? It's not any too soon. Look at the muscles of that fellow— third from the end. I wouldn't care to get a punch on the nose from him. Fine arms, but legs no good below the knee. Couldn't make cavalry men of them." And after glancing down complacently at his own shanks, he always concluded: "Pah! Don't they stink! You, Makola! Take that herd over to the fetish" (the storehouse was in every station called the fetish, perhaps because of the spirit of civilization it contained) "and give them up some of the rubbish you keep there. I'd rather see it full of bone than full of rags."

Kayerts approved.

"Yes, yes! Go and finish that palaver over there, Mr. Makola. I will come round when you are ready, to weigh the tusk. We must be careful." Then turn- ing to his companion: "This is the tribe that lives down the river; they are rather aromatic. I remember, they had been once before here. D'ye hear that row? What a fellow has got to put up with in this dog of a country! My head is split."

Such profitable visits were rare. For days the two pioneers of trade and progress would look on their empty courtyard in the vibrating brilliance of vertical sunshine. Below the high bank, the silent river flowed on glittering and steady. On the sands in the middle

L

of the stream, hippos and alligators sunned themselves side by side. And stretching away in all directions, surrounding the insignificant cleared spot of the trading post, immense forests, hiding fateful complications of fantastic life, lay in the eloquent silence of mute greatness. The two men understood nothing, cared for nothing but for the passage of days that separated them from the steamer's return. Their predecessor had left some torn books. They took up these wrecks of novels, and, as they had never read anything of the kind before, they were surprised and amused. Then during long days there were interminable and silly discussions about plots and personages. In the centre of Africa they made acquaintance of Richelieu and of d'Artagnan, of Hawk's Eye and of Father Goriot, and of many other people. All these imaginary personages became subjects for gossip as if they had been living friends. They discounted their virtues, suspected their motives, decried their successes; were scandalized at their duplicity or were doubtful about their courage. The accounts of crimes filled them with indignation, while tender or pathetic passages moved them deeply. Carlier cleared his throat and said in a soldierly voice, "What nonsense!" Kayerts, his round eyes suffused with tears, his fat cheeks quivering, rubbed his bald head, and declared, "This is a splendid book. I had no idea there were such clever fellows in the world." They also found some old copies of a home paper. That print discussed what it was pleased to call "Our Colonial Expansion" in highflown language. It spoke much of the rights and duties of civilization, of the sacredness of the civilizing work, and extolled the merits of those who went about bringing light, and faith and commerce to the dark places of the earth. Carlier and Kayerts read, wondered, and began to think better of themselves. Carlier said one evening, waving his hand about, "In a hundred years, there will be perhaps a town here. Quays, and warehouses, and barracks, and—and—billiard-rooms. Civilization, my boy, and virtue—and all. And then, chaps will read that two good fellows, Kayerts and Carlier, were the first civilized men to live in this very spot!" Kayerts nodded, "Yes, it is a consolation to think of that." They seemed to forget their dead predecessor; but, early one day, Carlier went out and replanted the cross firmly. "It used to make me squint whenever I walked that way," he explained to Kayerts over the morning coffee. "It made me squint, leaning over so much. So I just planted it upright. And solid, I promise you! I suspended myself with both hands to the cross-piece. Not a move. Oh, I did that properly."

At times Gobila came to see them. Gobila was the chief of the neighbouring villages. He was a gray-headed savage, thin and black, with a white cloth round his loins and a mangy panther skin hanging over his back. He came up with long strides of his skeleton legs, swinging a staff as tall as himself, and, entering the common room of the station, would squat on his heels to the left of the door. There he sat, watching Kayerts, and now and then making a speech which the other did not understand. Kayerts, without interrupting his occupation, would from time to time say in a friendly manner: "How goes it, you old image?" and they would smile at one another. The two whites had a liking for that old and incomprehensible creature, and called him Father Gobila. Gobila's manner was paternal, and he seemed really to love all white men. They all appeared to him very young, indistinguishably alike (except for stature), and he knew that they were all brothers, and also immortal. The death of the artist, who was the first white man whom he knew intimately, did not disturb this belief, because he was firmly convinced that the white stranger had pretended to die and got himself buried for some mysterious purpose of his own, into which it was useless to inquire. Perhaps it was his way of going home to his own country? At any rate, these were his brothers, and he transferred his absurd affection to them. They returned it in a way. Carlier slapped him on the back, and recklessly struck off matches for his amusement. Kayerts was always ready to let him have a sniff at the ammonia bottle. In short, they behaved just like that other white creature that had hidden itself in a hole in the ground. Gobila considered them attentively. Perhaps they were the same being with the other—or one of them was. He couldn't decide—clear up that mystery; but he remained always very friendly. In consequence of that friendship the women of Gobila's village walked in single file through the reedy grass, bringing every morning to the station, fowls, and sweet potatoes, and palm wine, and sometimes a goat. The Company never provisions the stations fully, and the agents required those local supplies to live. They had them through the good-will of Gobila, and lived well. Now and then one of them had a bout of fever, and the other nursed him with gentle devotion. They did not think much of it. It left them weaker, and their appearance changed for the worse. Carlier was hollow-eyed and irritable. Kayerts showed a drawn, flabby face above the rotundity of his stomach, which gave him a weird aspect. But being constantly together, they did not notice the change that took place gradually in their appearance, and also in their dispositions.

Five months passed in that way.

Then, one morning, as Kayerts and Carlier, lounging in their chairs under the verandah, talked about the approaching visit of the steamer, a knot of armed men came out of the forest and advanced towards the station. They were strangers to that part of the country. They were tall, slight, draped classically from neck to heel in blue fringed cloths, and carried percussion muskets over their bare right shoulders. Makola showed signs of excitement, and ran out of the storehouse (where he spent all his days) to meet these visitors. They came into the courtyard and looked about them with steady, scornful glances. Their leader, a powerful and determined-looking negro with bloodshot eyes, stood in front of the verandah and made a long speech. He gesticulated much, and ceased very suddenly.

There was something in his intonation, in the sounds of the long sentences he used, that startled the two whites. It was like a reminiscence of something not exactly familiar, and yet resembling the speech of civilized men. It sounded like one of those impossible languages which sometimes we hear in our dreams.

"What lingo is that?" said the amazed Carlier. "In the first moment I fancied the fellow was going to speak French. Anyway, it is a different kind of gibberish to what we ever heard."

"Yes," replied Kayerts. "Hey, Makola, what does he say? Where do they come from? Who are they?"

But Makola, who seemed to be standing on hot bricks, answered hurriedly, "I don't know. They come from very far. Perhaps Mrs. Price will understand. They are perhaps bad men."

The leader, after waiting for a while, said something sharply to Makola, who shook his head. Then the man, after looking round, noticed Makola's hut and walked over there. The next moment Mrs. Makola was heard speaking with great volubility. The other strangers—they were six in all—strolled about with an air of ease, put their heads through the door of the store-room, congregated round the grave, pointed under-standingly at the cross, and generally made themselves at home.

"I don't like those chaps—and, I say, Kayerts, they must be from the coast; they've got firearms," observed the sagacious Carlier.

Kayerts also did not like those chaps. They both, for the first time, became aware that they lived in con-ditions where the unusual may be dangerous, and that there was no power on earth outside of themselves to stand between them and the unusual. They became uneasy, went in and loaded their revolvers. Kayerts said, "We must order Makola to tell them to go away before dark."

The strangers left in the afternoon, after eating a meal prepared for them by Mrs. Makola. The im-mense woman was excited, and talked much with the visitors. She rattled away shrilly, pointing here and there at the forests and at the river. Makola sat apart and watched. At times he got up and whispered to his wife. He accompanied the strangers across the ravine at the back of the station-ground, and returned slowly looking very thoughtful. When questioned by the white men he was very strange, seemed not to under-stand, seemed to have forgotten French—seemed to have forgotten how to speak altogether. Kayerts and Carlier agreed that the nigger had had too much palm wine.

There was some talk about keeping a watch in turn, but in the evening everything seemed so quiet and peaceful that they retired as usual. All night they were disturbed by a lot of drumming in the villages.

A deep, rapid roll near by would be followed by another far off—then all ceased. Soon short appeals would rattle out here and there, then all mingle together, increase, become vigorous and sustained, would spread out over the forest, roll through the night, unbroken and ceaseless, near and far, as if the whole land had been one immense drum booming out steadily an appeal to heaven. And through the deep and tremendous noise sudden yells that resembled snatches of songs from a madhouse darted shrill and high in discordant jets of sound which seemed to rush far above the earth and drive all peace from under the stars.

Carlier and Kayerts slept badly. They both thought they had heard shots fired during the night—but they could not agree as to the direction. In the morning Makola was gone somewhere. He returned about noon with one of yesterday's strangers, and eluded all Kayerts' attempts to close with him: had become deaf apparently. Kayerts wondered. Carlier, who had been fishing off the bank, came back and remarked while he showed his catch, "The niggers seem to be in a deuce of a stir; I wonder what's up. I saw about fifteen canoes cross the river during the two hours I was there fishing." Kayerts, worried, said, "Isn't this Makola very queer to-day?" Carlier advised, "Keep all our men together in case of some trouble."

II

THERE were ten station men who had been left by the Director. Those fellows, having engaged themselves to the Company for six months (without having any idea of a month in particular and only a very faint notion of time in general), had been serving the cause of progress for upwards of two years. Belonging to a tribe from a very distant part of the land of darkness and sorrow, they did not run away, naturally supposing that as wandering strangers they would be killed by the inhabitants of the country; in which they were right. They lived in straw huts on the slope of a ravine overgrown with reedy grass, just behind the station buildings. They were not happy, regretting the festive incantations, the sorceries, the human sacrifices of their own land; where they also had parents, brothers, sisters, admired chiefs, respected magicians, loved friends, and other ties supposed generally to be human. Besides, the rice rations served out by the Company did not agree with them, being a food unknown to their land, and to which they could not get used Consequently they were unhealthy and miserable. Had they been of any other tribe they would have made up their minds to die—for nothing is easier to certain savages than suicide—and so have escaped from the puzzling difficulties of existence. But belonging, as they did, to a warlike tribe with filed teeth, they had more grit, and went on stupidly living through disease and sorrow. They did very little work, and had lost their splendid physique. Carlier and Kayerts doctored them assiduously without being able to bring them back into condition again. They were mustered every morning and told off to different tasks—grass-cutting, fence-building, tree-felling, &c., &c., which no power on earth could induce them to execute efficiently. The two whites had practically very little control over them.

In the afternoon Makola came over to the big house and found Kayerts watching three heavy columns of smoke rising above the forests. "What is that?" asked Kayerts. "Some villages burn," answered Makola, who seemed to have regained his wits. Then he said abruptly: "We have got very little ivory; bad six months' trading. Do you like get a little more ivory?"

"Yes," said Kayerts, eagerly. He thought of percentages which were low.

"Those men who came yesterday are traders from Loanda who have got more ivory than they can carry home. Shall I buy? I know their camp."

"Certainly," said Kayerts. "What are those traders?"

"Bad fellows," said Makola, indifferently. "They fight with people, and catch women and children. They are bad men, and got guns. There is a great disturbance in the country. Do you want ivory?"

"Yes," said Kayerts. Makola said nothing for a while. Then: "Those workmen of ours are no good at all," he muttered, looking round. "Station in very bad order, sir. Director will growl. Better get a fine lot of ivory, then he say nothing."

"I can't help it; the men won't work," said Kayerts. "When will you get that ivory?"

"Very soon," said Makola. "Perhaps to-night. You leave it to me, and keep indoors, sir. I think you had better give some palm wine to our men to make a dance this evening. Enjoy themselves. Work better to-

*L

morrow. There's plenty palm wine—gone a little sour."

Kayerts said yes, and Makola, with his own hands, carried big calabashes to the door of his hut. They stood there till the evening, and Mrs. Makola looked into every one. The men got them at sunset. When Kayerts and Carlier retired, a big bonfire was flaring before the men's huts. They could hear their shouts and drumming. Some men from Gobila's village had joined the station hands, and the entertainment was a great success.

In the middle of the night, Carlier waking suddenly, heard a man shout loudly; then a shot was fired. Only one. Carlier ran out and met Kayerts on the verandah. They were both startled. As they went across the yard to call Makola, they saw shadows moving in the night. One of them cried, "Don't shoot! It's me, Price." Then Makola appeared close to them. "Go back, go back, please," he urged, "you spoil all." "There are strange men about," said Carlier. "Never mind; I know," said Makola. Then he whispered, "All right. Bring ivory. Say nothing! I know my business." The two white men reluctantly went back to the house, but did not sleep. They heard footsteps, whispers, some groans. It seemed as if a lot of men came in, dumped heavy things on the ground, squabbled a long time, then went away. They lay on their hard beds and thought: "This Makola is invaluable." In the morning Carlier came out, very sleepy, and pulled at the cord of the big bell. The station hands mustered every morning to the sound of the bell. That morning nobody came. Kayerts turned out also, yawning. Across the yard they saw Makola come out of his hut, a tin basin of soapy water in his hand. Makola, a civilized nigger, was very neat in his person. He threw the soapsuds skilfully over a wretched little yellow cur he had, then turning his face to the agent's house, he shouted from the distance, "All the men gone last night!"

They heard him plainly, but in their surprise they both yelled out together: "What!" Then they stared at one another. "We are in a proper fix now," growled Carlier. "It's incredible!" muttered Kayerts. "I will go to the huts and see," said Carlier, striding off. Makola coming up found Kayerts standing alone.

"I can hardly believe it," said Kayerts, tearfully. "We took care of them as if they had been our children."

"They went with the coast people," said Makola after a moment of hesitation.

"What do I care with whom they went—the ungrateful brutes!" exclaimed the other. Then with sudden suspicion, and looking hard at Makola, he added: "What do you know about it?"

Makola moved his shoulders, looking down on the ground. "What do I know? I think only. Will you come and look at the ivory I've got there? It is a fine lot. You never saw such."

He moved towards the store. Kayerts followed him mechanically, thinking about the incredible desertion of the men. On the ground before the door of the fetish lay six splendid tusks.

"What did you give for it?" asked Kayerts, after surveying the lot with satisfaction.

"No regular trade," said Makola. "They brought the ivory and gave it to me. I told them to take what they most wanted in the station. It is a beautiful lot. No station can show such tusks. Those traders wanted carriers badly, and our men were no good here. No trade, no entry in books; all correct."

Kayerts nearly burst with indignation. "Why!" he shouted, "I believe you have sold our men for these tusks!" Makola stood impassive and silent. "I—I—will—I," stuttered Kayerts. "You fiend!" he yelled out.

"I did the best for you and the Company," said Makola, imperturbably. "Why you shout so much? Look at this tusk."

"I dismiss you! I will report you—I won't look at the tusk. I forbid you to touch them. I order you to throw them into the river. You—you!"

"You very red, Mr. Kayerts. If you are so irritable in the sun, you will get fever and die—like the first chief!" pronounced Makola impressively.

They stood still, contemplating one another with intense eyes, as if they had been looking with effort across immense distances. Kayerts shivered. Makola had meant no more than he said, but his words seemed to Kayerts full of ominous menace! He turned sharply and went away to the house. Makola retired into the bosom of his family; and the tusks, left lying before the store, looked very large and valuable in the sunshine.

Carlier came back on the verandah. "They're all gone, hey?" asked Kayerts from the far end of the common room in a muffled voice. "You did not find anybody?"

"Oh, yes," said Carlier, "I found one of Gobila's people lying dead before the huts—shot through the body. We heard that shot last night."

Kayerts came out quickly. He found his companion staring grimly over the yard at the tusks, away by the store. They both sat in silence for a while. Then Kayerts related his conversation with Makola. Carlier said nothing. At the midday meal they ate

very little. They hardly exchanged a word that day.
A great silence seemed to lie heavily over the station
and press on their lips. Makola did not open the
store; he spent the day playing with his children. He
lay full-length on a mat outside his door, and the
youngsters sat on his chest and clambered all over him.
It was a touching picture. Mrs. Makola was busy
cooking all day as usual. The white men made a
somewhat better meal in the evening. Afterwards,
Carlier smoking his pipe strolled over to the store; he
stood for a long time over the tusks, touched one or two
with his foot, even tried to lift the largest one by its
small end. He came back to his chief, who had not
stirred from the verandah, threw himself in the chair
and said—

"I can see it! They were pounced upon while they
slept heavily after drinking all that palm wine you've
allowed Makola to give them. A put-up job! See?
The worst is, some of Gobila's people were there, and
got carried off too, no doubt. The least drunk woke
up, and got shot for his sobriety. This is a funny
country. What will you do now?"

"We can't touch it, of course," said Kayerts.

"Of course not," assented Carlier.

"Slavery is an awful thing," stammered out Kayerts
in an unsteady voice.

"Frightful—the sufferings," grunted Carlier with
conviction.

They believed their words. Everybody shows a
respectful deference to certain sounds that he and his
fellows can make. But about feelings people really
know nothing. We talk with indignation or enthusiasm;
we talk about oppression, cruelty, crime, devotion, self-
sacrifice, virtue, and we know nothing real beyond the
words. Nobody knows what suffering or sacrifice

mean—except, perhaps the victims of the mysterious purpose of these illusions.

Next morning they saw Makola very busy setting up in the yard the big scales used for weighing ivory. By and by Carlier said: "What's that filthy scoundrel up to?" and lounged out into the yard. Kayerts followed. They stood watching. Makola took no notice. When the balance was swung true, he tried to lift a tusk into the scale. It was too heavy. He looked up helplessly without a word, and for a minute they stood round that balance as mute and still as three statues. Suddenly Carlier said: "Catch hold of the other end, Makola—you beast!" and together they swung the tusk up. Kayerts trembled in every limb. He muttered, "I say! O! I say!" and putting his hand in his pocket found there a dirty bit of paper and the stump of a pencil. He turned his back on the others, as if about to do something tricky, and noted stealthily the weights which Carlier shouted out to him with unnecessary loudness. When all was over Makola whispered to himself: "The sun's very strong here for the tusks." Carlier said to Kayerts in a careless tone: "I say, chief, I might just as well give him a lift with this lot into the store."

As they were going back to the house Kayerts observed with a sigh: "It had to be done." And Carlier said: "It's deplorable, but, the men being Company's men the ivory is Company's ivory. We must look after it." "I will report to the Director, of course," said Kayerts. "Of course; let him decide," approved Carlier.

At midday they made a hearty meal. Kayerts sighed from time to time. Whenever they mentioned Makola's name they always added to it an opprobrious epithet. It eased their conscience. Makola gave

himself a half-holiday, and bathed his children in the
river. No one from Gobila's villages came near the
station that day. No one came the next day, and the
next, nor for a whole week. Gobila's people might
have been dead and buried for any sign of life they gave.
But they were only mourning for those they had lost
by the witchcraft of white men, who had brought
wicked people into their country. The wicked people
were gone, but fear remained. Fear always remains.
A man may destroy everything within himself, love
and hate and belief, and even doubt; but as long as
he clings to life he cannot destroy fear: the fear, subtle,
indestructible, and terrible, that pervades his being;
that tinges his thoughts; that lurks in his heart; that
watches on his lips the struggle of his last breath. In
his fear, the mild old Gobila offered extra human
sacrifices to all the Evil Spirits that had taken possession of his white friends. His heart was heavy.
Some warriors spoke about burning and killing, but
the cautious old savage dissuaded them. Who could
foresee the woe those mysterious creatures, if irritated,
might bring? They should be left alone. Perhaps in
time they would disappear into the earth as the first
one had disappeared. His people must keep away from
them, and hope for the best.

Kayerts and Carlier did not disappear, but remained
above on this earth, that, somehow, they fancied had
become bigger and very empty. It was not the absolute and dumb solitude of the post that impressed them
so much as an inarticulate feeling that something from
within them was gone, something that worked for their
safety, and had kept the wilderness from interfering
with their hearts. The images of home; the memory of
people like them, of men that thought and felt as they
used to think and feel, receded into distances made

indistinct by the glare of unclouded sunshine. And out of the great silence of the surrounding wilderness, its very hopelessness and savagery seemed to approach them nearer, to draw them gently, to look upon them, to envelop them with a solicitude irresistible, familiar, and disgusting.

Days lengthened into weeks, then into months. Gobila's people drummed and yelled to every new moon, as of yore, but kept away from the station. Makola and Carlier tried once in a canoe to open communications, but were received with a shower of arrows, and had to fly back to the station for dear life. That attempt set the country up and down the river into an uproar that could be very distinctly heard for days. The steamer was late. At first they spoke of delay jauntily, then anxiously, then gloomily. The matter was becoming serious. Stores were running short. Carlier cast his lines off the bank, but the river was low, and the fish kept out in the stream. They dared not stroll far away from the station to shoot. Moreover, there was no game in the impenetrable forest. Once Carlier shot a hippo in the river. They had no boat to secure it, and it sank. When it floated up it drifted away, and Gobila's people secured the carcase. It was the occasion for a national holiday, but Carlier had a fit of rage over it and talked about the necessity of exterminating all the niggers before the country could be made habitable. Kayerts mooned about silently; spent hours looking at the portrait of his Melie. It represented a little girl with long bleached tresses and a rather sour face. His legs were much swollen, and he could hardly walk. Carlier, undermined by fever, could not swagger any more, but kept tottering about, still with a devil-may-care air, as became a man who remembered his crack regiment. He had become hoarse, sarcastic, and inclined to say unpleasant things. He called it "being frank with you." They had long ago reckoned their percentages on trade, including in them that last deal of "this infamous Makola." They had also concluded not to say anything about it. Kayerts hesitated at first—was afraid of the Director.

"He has seen worse things done on the quiet," maintained Carlier, with a hoarse laugh. "Trust him! He won't thank you if you blab. He is no better than you or me. Who will talk if we hold our tongues? There is nobody here."

That was the root of the trouble! There was nobody there; and being left there alone with their weakness, they became daily more like a pair of accomplices than like a couple of devoted friends. They had heard nothing from home for eight months. Every evening they said, "To-morrow we shall see the steamer." But one of the Company's steamers had been wrecked, and the Director was busy with the other, relieving very distant and important stations on the main river. He thought that the useless station, and the useless men, could wait. Meantime Kayerts and Carlier lived on rice boiled without salt, and cursed the Company, all Africa, and the day they were born. One must have lived on such diet to discover what ghastly trouble the necessity of swallowing one's food may become. There was literally nothing else in the station but rice and coffee; they drank the coffee without sugar. The last fifteen lumps Kayerts had solemnly locked away in his box, together with a half-bottle of Cognâc, "in case of sickness," he explained. Carlier approved. "When one is sick," he said, "any little extra like that is cheering."

They waited. Rank grass began to sprout over the

courtyard. The bell never rang now. Days passed, silent, exasperating, and slow. When the two men spoke, they snarled; and their silences were bitter, as if tinged by the bitterness of their thoughts.

One day after a lunch of boiled rice, Carlier put down his cup untasted, and said: "Hang it all! Let's have a decent cup of coffee for once. Bring out that sugar, Kayerts!"

"For the sick," muttered Kayerts, without looking up.

"For the sick," mocked Carlier. "Bosh! . . . Well! I am sick."

"You are no more sick than I am, and I go without," said Kayerts in a peaceful tone.

"Come! out with that sugar, you stingy old slave-dealer."

Kayerts looked up quickly. Carlier was smiling with marked insolence. And suddenly it seemed to Kayerts that he had never seen that man before. Who was he? He knew nothing about him. What was he capable of? There was a surprising flash of violent emotion within him, as if in the presence of something undreamt-of, dangerous, and final. But he managed to pronounce with composure—

"That joke is in very bad taste. Don't repeat it."

"Joke!" said Carlier, hitching himself forward on his seat. "I am hungry—I am sick—I don't joke! I hate hypocrites. You are a hypocrite. You are a slave-dealer. I am a slave-dealer. There's nothing but slave-dealers in this cursed country. I mean to have sugar in my coffee to-day, anyhow!"

"I forbid you to speak to me in that way," said Kayerts with a fair show of resolution.

"You!—What?" shouted Carlier, jumping up.

Kayerts stood up also. "I am your chief," he began, trying to master the shakiness of his voice.

"What?" yelled the other. "Who's chief? There's no chief here. There's nothing here: there's nothing but you and I. Fetch the sugar—you pot-bellied ass."

"Hold your tongue. Go out of this room," screamed Kayerts. "I dismiss you—you scoundrel!"

Carlier swung a stool. All at once he looked dangerously in earnest. "You flabby, good-for-nothing civilian—take that!" he howled.

Kayerts dropped under the table, and the stool struck the grass inner wall of the room. Then, as Carlier was trying to upset the table, Kayerts in desperation made a blind rush, head low, like a cornered pig would do, and over-turning his friend, bolted along the verandah, and into his room. He locked the door, snatched his revolver, and stood panting. In less than a minute Carlier was kicking at the door furiously, howling, "If you don't bring out that sugar, I will shoot you at sight, like a dog. Now then—one —two—three. You won't? I will show you who's the master."

Kayerts thought the door would fall in, and scrambled through the square hole that served for a window in his room. There was then the whole breadth of the house between them. But the other was apparently not strong enough to break in the door, and Kayerts heard him running round. Then he also began to run laboriously on his swollen legs. He ran as quickly as he could, grasping the revolver, and unable yet to understand what was happening to him. He saw in succession Makola's house, the store, the river, the ravine, and the low bushes; and he saw all those things again as he ran for the second time round the house. Then again they flashed past him. That morning he could not have walked a yard without a groan.

And now he ran. He ran fast enough to keep out of sight of the other man.

Then as, weak and desperate, he thought, "Before I finish the next round I shall die," he heard the other man stumble heavily, then stop. He stopped also. He had the back and Carlier the front of the house, as before. He heard him drop into a chair cursing, and suddenly his own legs gave way, and he slid down into a sitting posture with his back to the wall. His mouth was as dry as a cinder, and his face was wet with perspiration—and tears. What was it all about? He thought it must be a horrible illusion; he thought he was dreaming; he thought he was going mad! After a while he collected his senses. What did they quarrel about? That sugar! How absurd! He would give it to him—didn't want it himself. And he began scrambling to his feet with a sudden feeling of security. But before he had fairly stood upright, a common-sense reflection occurred to him and drove him back into despair. He thought: If I give way now to that brute of a soldier, he will begin this horror again to-morrow—and the day after—every day—raise other pretensions, trample on me, torture me, make me his slave—and I will be lost! Lost! The steamer may not come for days—may never come. He shook so that he had to sit down on the floor again. He shivered forlornly. He felt he could not, would not move any more. He was completely distracted by the sudden perception that the position was without issue—that death and life had in a moment become equally difficult and terrible.

All at once he heard the other push his chair back; and he leaped to his feet with extreme facility. He listened and got confused. Must run again! Right or left? He heard footsteps. He darted to the left, grasping his revolver, and at the very same instant, as it seemed to him, they came into violent collision. Both shouted with surprise. A loud explosion took place between them; a roar of red fire, thick smoke; and Kayerts, deafened and blinded, rushed back thinking: I am hit—it's all over. He expected the other to come round—to gloat over his agony. He caught hold of an upright of the roof—"All over!" Then he heard a crashing fall on the other side of the house, as if somebody had tumbled headlong over a chair—then silence. Nothing more happened. He did not die. Only his shoulder felt as if it had been badly wrenched, and he had lost his revolver. He was disarmed and helpless! He waited for his fate. The other man made no sound. It was a stratagem. He was stalking him now! Along what side? Perhaps he was taking aim this very minute!

After a few moments of an agony frightful and absurd, he decided to go and meet his doom. He was prepared for every surrender. He turned the corner, steadying himself with one hand on the wall; made a few paces, and nearly swooned. He had seen on the floor, protruding past the other corner, a pair of turned-up feet. A pair of white naked feet in red slippers. He felt deadly sick, and stood for a time in profound darkness. Then Makola appeared before him, saying quietly: "Come along, Mr. Kayerts. He is dead." He burst into tears of gratitude; a loud, sobbing fit of crying. After a time he found himself sitting in a chair and looking at Carlier, who lay stretched on his back. Makola was kneeling over the body.

"Is this your revolver?" asked Makola, getting up.

"Yes," said Kayerts; then he added very quickly, "He ran after me to shoot me—you saw!"

"Yes, I saw," said Makola. "There is only one revolver; where's his?"

"Don't know," whispered Kayerts in a voice that had become suddenly very faint.

"I will go and look for it," said the other, gently. He made the round along the verandah, while Kayerts sat still and looked at the corpse. Makola came back empty-handed, stood in deep thought, then stepped quietly into the dead man's room, and came out directly with a revolver, which he held up before Kayerts. Kayerts shut his eyes. Everything was going round. He found life more terrible and difficult than death. He had shot an unarmed man.

After meditating for a while, Makola said softly, pointing at the dead man who lay there with his right eye blown out—

"He died of fever." Kayerts looked at him with a stony stare. "Yes," repeated Makola, thoughtfully, stepping over the corpse, "I think he died of fever. Bury him to-morrow."

And he went away slowly to his expectant wife, leaving the two white men alone on the verandah.

Night came, and Kayerts sat unmoving on his chair. He sat quiet as if he had taken a dose of opium. The violence of the emotions he had passed through produced a feeling of exhausted serenity. He had plumbed in one short afternoon the depths of horror and despair, and now found repose in the conviction that life had no more secrets for him: neither had death! He sat by the corpse thinking; thinking very actively, thinking very new thoughts. He seemed to have broken loose from himself altogether. His old thoughts, convictions, likes and dislikes, things he respected and things he abhorred, appeared in their true light at last! Appeared contemptible and childish, false and ridiculous. He revelled in his new wisdom while he sat by the man he had killed. He argued with himself about all things under heaven with that kind of wrong-headed lucidity which may be observed in some lunatics. Incidentally he reflected that the fellow dead there had been a noxious beast anyway; that men died every day in thousands; perhaps in hundreds of thousands—who could tell?—and that in the number, that one death could not possibly make any difference; couldn't have any importance, at least to a thinking creature. He, Kayerts, was a thinking creature. He had been all his life, till that moment, a believer in a lot of nonsense like the rest of mankind—who are fools; but now he thought! He knew! He was at peace; he was familiar with the highest wisdom! Then he tried to imagine himself dead, and Carlier sitting in his chair watching him; and his attempt met with such unexpected success, that in a very few moments he became not at all sure who was dead and who was alive. This extraordinary achievement of his fancy startled him, however, and by a clever and timely effort of mind he saved himself just in time from becoming Carlier. His heart thumped, and he felt hot all over at the thought of that danger. Carlier! What a beastly thing! To compose his now disturbed nerves—and no wonder!—he tried to whistle a little. Then, suddenly, he fell asleep, or thought he had slept; but at any rate there was a fog, and somebody had whistled in the fog.

He stood up. The day had come, and a heavy mist had descended upon the land: the mist penetrating, enveloping, and silent; the morning mist of tropical lands; the mist that clings and kills; the mist white and deadly, immaculate and poisonous. He stood up, saw the body, and threw his arms above his head with a cry like that of a man who, waking from a trance, finds himself immured forever in a tomb. *"Help!*
. . . . My God!"

A shriek inhuman, vibrating and sudden, pierced like a sharp dart the white shroud of that land of sorrow. Three short, impatient screeches followed, and then, for a time, the fog-wreaths rolled on, undisturbed, through a formidable silence. Then many more shrieks, rapid and piercing, like the yells of some exasperated and ruthless creature, rent the air. Progress was calling to Kayerts from the river. Progress and civilization and all the virtues. Society was calling to its accomplished child to come, to be taken care of, to be instructed, to be judged, to be condemned; it called him to return to that rubbish heap from which he had wandered away, so that justice could be done.

Kayerts heard and understood. He stumbled out of the verandah, leaving the other man quite alone for the first time since they had been thrown there together. He groped his way through the fog, calling in his ignorance upon the invisible heaven to undo its work. Makola flitted by in the mist, shouting as he ran—

"Steamer! Steamer! They can't see. They whistle for the station. I go ring the bell. Go down to the landing, sir. I ring."

He disappeared. Kayerts stood still. He looked upwards; the fog rolled low over his head. He looked round like a man who has lost his way; and he saw a dark smudge, a cross-shaped stain, upon the shifting purity of the mist. As he began to stumble towards it, the station bell rang in a tumultuous peal its answer to the impatient clamour of the steamer.

The Managing Director of the Great Civilizing Company (since we know that civilization follows trade) landed first, and incontinently lost sight of the steamer. The fog down by the river was exceedingly dense; above, at the station, the bell rang unceasing and brazen.

The Director shouted loudly to the steamer:

"There is nobody down to meet us; there may be something wrong, though they are ringing. You had better come, too!"

And he began to toil up the steep bank. The captain and the engine-driver of the boat followed behind. As they scrambled up the fog thinned, and they could see their Director a good way ahead. Suddenly they saw him start forward, calling to them over his shoulder: —"Run! Run to the house! I've found one of them. Run, look for the other!"

He had found one of them! And even he, the man of varied and startling experience, was somewhat discomposed by the manner of this finding. He stood and fumbled in his pockets (for a knife) while he faced Kayerts, who was hanging by a leather strap from the cross. He had evidently climbed the grave, which was high and narrow, and after tying the end of the strap to the arm, had swung himself off. His toes were only a couple of inches above the ground; his arms hung stiffly down; he seemed to be standing rigidly at attention, but with one purple cheek playfully posed on the shoulder. And, irreverently, he was putting out a swollen tongue at his Managing Director.

THE RETURN

THE inner circle train from the City rushed impetuously out of a black hole and pulled up with a discordant, grinding racket in the smirched twilight of a West-End station. A line of doors flew open and a lot of men stepped out headlong. They had high hats, healthy pale faces, dark overcoats and shiny boots; they held in their gloved hands thin umbrellas and hastily folded evening papers that resembled stiff, dirty rags of greenish, pinkish, or whitish colour. Alvan Hervey stepped out with the rest, a smouldering cigar between his teeth. A disregarded little woman in rusty black, with both arms full of parcels, ran along in distress, bolted suddenly into a third-class compartment and the train went on. The slamming of carriage doors burst out sharp and spiteful like a fusillade; an icy draught mingled with acrid fumes swept the whole length of the platform and made a tottering old man, wrapped up to his ears in a woollen comforter, stop short in the moving throng to cough violently over his stick. No one spared him a glance.

Alvan Hervey passed through the ticket gate. Between the bare walls of a sordid staircase men clambered rapidly; their backs appeared alike—almost as if they had been wearing a uniform; their indifferent faces were varied but somehow suggested kinship, like the faces of a band of brothers who through prudence, dignity, disgust, or foresight would resolutely ignore each other; and their eyes, quick or slow; their eyes gazing up the dusty steps; their eyes brown, black, gray, blue, had

118

all the same stare, concentrated and empty, satisfied and unthinking.

Outside the big doorway of the street they scattered in all directions, walking away fast from one another with the hurried air of men fleeing from something compromising; from familiarity or confidences; from something suspected and concealed—like truth or pestilence. Alvan Hervey hesitated, standing alone in the doorway for a moment; then decided to walk home.

He strode firmly. A misty rain settled like silvery dust on clothes, on moustaches; wetted the faces, varnished the flagstones, darkened the walls, dripped from umbrellas. And he moved on in the rain with careless serenity, with the tranquil ease of someone successful and disdainful, very sure of himself—a man with lots of money and friends. He was tall, well set-up, good-looking and healthy; and his clear pale face had under its commonplace refinement that slight tinge of overbearing brutality which is given by the possession of only partly difficult accomplishments; by excelling in games, or in the art of making money; by the easy mastery over animals and over needy men.

He was going home much earlier than usual, straight from the City and without calling at his club. He considered himself well connected, well educated and intelligent. Who doesn't? But his connections, education and intelligence were strictly on a par with those of the men with whom he did business or amused himself. He had married five years ago. At the time all his acquaintances had said he was very much in love; and he had said so himself, frankly, because it is very well understood that every man falls in love once in his life—unless his wife dies, when it may be quite praiseworthy to fall in love again. The girl was healthy, tall, fair, and in his opinion was well connected, well educated and intelligent. She was also intensely bored with her home where, as if packed in a tight box, her individuality—of which she was very conscious—had no play. She strode like a grenadier, was strong and upright like an obelisk, had a beautiful face, a candid brow, pure eyes, and not a thought of her own in her head. He surrendered quickly to all those charms, and she appeared to him so unquestionably of the right sort that he did not hesitate for a moment to declare himself in love. Under the cover of that sacred and poetical fiction he desired her masterfully, for various reasons; but principally for the satisfaction of having his own way. He was very dull and solemn about it—for no earthly reason, unless to conceal his feelings—which is an eminently proper thing to do. Nobody, however, would have been shocked had he neglected that duty, for the feeling he experienced really was a longing—a longing stronger and a little more complex no doubt, but no more reprehensible in its nature than a hungry man's appetite for his dinner.

After their marriage they busied themselves, with marked success, in enlarging the circle of their acquaintance. Thirty people knew them by sight; twenty more with smiling demonstrations tolerated their occasional presence within hospitable thresholds; at least fifty others became aware of their existence. They moved in their enlarged world amongst perfectly delightful men and women who feared emotion, enthusiasm, or failure, more than fire, war, or mortal disease; who tolerated only the commonest formulas of commonest thoughts, and recognized only profitable facts. It was an extremely charming sphere, the abode of all the virtues, where nothing is realized and where all joys and sorrows are cautiously toned down into pleasures and annoyances. In that serene region, then, where noble sentiments are cultivated in sufficient profusion to conceal the pitiless materialism of thoughts and aspirations Alvan Hervey and his wife spent five years of prudent bliss unclouded by any doubt as to the moral propriety of their existence. She, to give her individuality fair play, took up all manner of philanthropic work and became a member of various rescuing and reforming societies patronized or presided over by ladies of title. He took an active interest in politics; and having met quite by chance a literary man—who nevertheless was related to an earl—he was induced to finance a moribund society paper. It was a semi-political, and wholly scandalous publication, redeemed by excessive dulness; and as it was utterly faithless, as it contained no new thought, as it never by any chance had a flash of wit, satire, or indignation in its pages, he judged it respectable enough, at first sight. Afterwards, when it paid, he promptly perceived that upon the whole it was a virtuous undertaking. It paved the way of his ambition; and he enjoyed also the special kind of importance he derived from this connection with what he imagined to be literature.

This connection still further enlarged their world. Men who wrote or drew prettily for the public came at times to their house, and his editor came very often. He thought him rather an ass because he had such big front teeth (the proper thing is to have small, even teeth) and wore his hair a trifle longer than most men do. However, some dukes wear their hair long, and the fellow indubitably knew his business. The worst was that his gravity, though perfectly portentous, could not be trusted. He sat, elegant and bulky, in the drawing-room, the head of his stick hovering in front of his big teeth, and talked for hours with a thick-lipped smile (he said nothing that could be considered objectionable and not quite the thing) talked in an unusual manner—not obviously—irritatingly. His forehead was too lofty—unusually so—and under it there was a straight nose, lost between the hairless cheeks, that in a smooth curve ran into a chin shaped like the end of a snow-shoe. And in this face that resembled the face of a fat and fiendishly knowing baby there glittered a pair of clever, peering, unbelieving black eyes. He wrote verses too. Rather an ass. But the band of men who trailed at the skirts of his monumental frock-coat seemed to perceive wonderful things in what he said. Alvan Hervey put it down to affectation. Those artist chaps, upon the whole, were so affected. Still, all this was highly proper—very useful to him—and his wife seemed to like it—as if she also had derived some distinct and secret advantage from this intellectual connection. She received her mixed and decorous guests with a kind of tall, ponderous grace, peculiarly her own and which awakened in the mind of intimidated strangers incongruous and improper reminiscences of an elephant, a giraffe, a gazelle; of a gothic tower—of an overgrown angel. Her Thursdays were becoming famous in their world; and their world grew steadily, annexing street after street. It included also Somebody's Gardens, a Crescent—a couple of Squares.

Thus Alvan Hervey and his wife for five prosperous years lived by the side of one another. In time they came to know each other sufficiently well for all the practical purposes of such an existence, but they were no more capable of real intimacy than two animals feeding at the same manger, under the same roof, in a luxurious stable. His longing was appeased and became a habit; and she had her desire—the desire to

get away from under the paternal roof, to assert her
individuality, to move in her own set (so much smarter
than the parental one); to have a home of her own,
and her own share of the world's respect, envy, and
applause. They understood each other warily, tacitly,
like a pair of cautious conspirators in a profitable plot;
because they were both unable to look at a fact, a sentiment, a principle, or a belief otherwise than in the
light of their own dignity, of their own glorification,
of their own advantage. They skimmed over the
surface of life hand in hand, in a pure and frosty atmosphere—like two skilful skaters cutting figures on
thick ice for the admiration of the beholders, and dis-
dainfully ignoring the hidden stream, the stream restless and dark; the stream of life, profound and unfrozen.

Alvan Hervey turned twice to the left, once to the
right, walked along two sides of a square, in the middle
of which groups of tame-looking trees stood in respectable captivity behind iron railings, and rang at his
door. A parlourmaid opened. A fad of his wife's,
this, to have only women servants. That girl, while
she took his hat and overcoat, said something which
made him look at his watch. It was five o'clock, and
his wife not at home. There was nothing unusual in
that. He said, "No; no tea," and went upstairs.

He ascended without footfalls. Brass rods glimmered all up the red carpet. On the first-floor landing
a marble woman, decently covered from neck to instep
with stone draperies, advanced a row of lifeless toes
to the edge of the pedestal, and thrust out blindly a
rigid white arm holding a cluster of lights. He had
artistic tastes—at home. Heavy curtains caught
back, half concealed dark corners. On the rich,
stamped paper of the walls hung sketches, water-
colours, engravings. His tastes were distinctly artistic.

Old church towers peeped above green masses of foliage; the hills were purple, the sands yellow, the seas sunny, the skies blue. A young lady sprawled with dreamy eyes in a moored boat, in company of a lunch basket, a champagne bottle, and an enamoured man in a blazer. Bare-legged boys flirted sweetly with ragged maidens, slept on stone steps, gambolled with dogs. A pathetically lean girl flattened against a blank wall, turned up expiring eyes and tendered a flower for sale; while, near by, the large photographs of some famous and mutilated bas-reliefs seemed to represent a massacre turned into stone.

He looked, of course, at nothing, ascended another flight of stairs and went straight into the dressing room. A bronze dragon nailed by the tail to a bracket writhed away from the wall in calm convolutions, and held, between the conventional fury of its jaws, a crude gas flame that resembled a butterfly. The room was empty, of course; but, as he stepped in, it became filled all at once with a stir of many people; because the strips of glass on the doors of wardrobes and his wife's large pier-glass reflected him from head to foot, and multiplied his image into a crowd of gentlemanly and slavish imitators, who were dressed exactly like himself; had the same restrained and rare gestures; who moved when he moved, stood still with him in an obsequious immobility, and had just such appearances of life and feeling as he thought it dignified and safe for any man to manifest. And like real people who are slaves of common thoughts, that are not even their own, they affected a shadowy independence by the superficial variety of their movements. They moved together with him; but they either advanced to meet him, or walked away from him; they appeared, disappeared; they seemed to dodge behind walnut furniture, to be seen again, far within the polished panes, stepping about distinct and unreal in the convincing illusion of a room. And like the men he respected they could be trusted to do nothing individual, original, or startling—nothing unforeseen and nothing improper.

He moved for a time aimlessly in that good company, humming a popular but refined tune, and thinking vaguely of a business letter from abroad, which had to be answered on the morrow with cautious prevarication. Then, as he walked towards a wardrobe, he saw appearing at his back, in the high mirror, the corner of his wife's dressing-table, and amongst the glitter of silver-mounted objects on it, the square white patch of an envelope. It was such an unusual thing to be seen there that he spun round almost before he realized his surprise; and all the sham men about him pivoted on their heels; all appeared surprised; and all moved rapidly towards envelopes on dressing-tables.

He recognized his wife's handwriting and saw that the envelope was addressed to himself. He muttered, "How very odd," and felt annoyed. Apart from any odd action being essentially an indecent thing in itself, the fact of his wife indulging in it made it doubly offensive. That she should write to him at all, when she knew he would be home for dinner, was perfectly ridiculous; but that she should leave it like this—in evidence for chance discovery—struck him as so outrageous that, thinking of it, he experienced suddenly a staggering sense of insecurity, an absurd and bizarre flash of a notion that the house had moved a little under his feet. He tore the envelope open, glanced at the letter, and sat down in a chair near by.

He held the paper before his eyes and looked at half a dozen lines scrawled on the page, while he was stunned by a noise meaningless and violent, like the clash of

M

gongs or the beating of drums; a great aimless uproar that, in a manner, prevented him from hearing himself think and made his mind an absolute blank. This absurd and distracting tumult seemed to ooze out of the written words, to issue from between his very fingers that trembled, holding the paper. And suddenly he dropped the letter as though it had been something hot, or venomous, or filthy; and rushing to the window with the unreflecting precipitation of a man anxious to raise an alarm of fire or murder, he threw it up and put his head out.

A chill gust of wind, wandering through the damp and sooty obscurity over the waste of roofs and chimney-pots, touched his face with a clammy flick. He saw an illimitable darkness, in which stood a black jumble of walls, and, between them, the many rows of gaslights stretched far away in long lines, like strung-up beads of fire. A sinister loom as of a hidden conflagration lit up faintly from below the mist, falling upon a billowy and motionless sea of tiles and bricks. At the rattle of the opened window the world seemed to leap out of the night and confront him, while floating up to his ears there came a sound vast and faint; the deep mutter of something immense and alive. It penetrated him with a feeling of dismay and he gasped silently. From the cab-stand in the square came distinct hoarse voices and a jeering laugh which sounded ominously harsh and cruel. It sounded threatening. He drew his head in, as if before an aimed blow, and flung the window down quickly. He made a few steps, stumbled against a chair, and with a great effort, pulled himself together to lay hold of a certain thought that was whizzing about loose in his head.

He got it at last, after more exertion than he expected; he was flushed and puffed a little as though he had been catching it with his hands, but his mental hold on it was weak, so weak that he judged it necessary to repeat it aloud—to hear it spoken firmly—in order to insure a perfect measure of possession. But he was unwilling to hear his own voice—to hear any sound whatever—owing to a vague belief, shaping itself slowly within him, that solitude and silence are the greatest felicities of mankind. The next moment it dawned upon him that they are perfectly unattainable—that faces must be seen, words spoken, thoughts heard. All the words—all the thoughts!

He said very distinctly, and looking at the carpet, "She's gone."

It was terrible—not the fact but the words; the words charged with the shadowy might of a meaning, that seemed to possess the tremendous power to call Fate down upon the earth, like those strange and appalling words that sometimes are heard in sleep. They vibrated round him in a metallic atmosphere, in a space that had the hardness of iron and the resonance of a bell of bronze. Looking down between the toes of his boots he seemed to listen thoughtfully to the receding wave of sound; to the wave spreading out in a widening circle, embracing streets, roofs, church-steeples, fields—and travelling away, widening endlessly, far, very far, where he could not hear—where he could not imagine anything—where . . . .

"And—with that . . . . ass," he said again without stirring in the least. And there was nothing but humiliation. Nothing else. He could derive no moral solace from any aspect of the situation, which radiated pain only on every side. Pain. What kind of pain? It occurred to him that he ought to be heart-broken; but in an exceedingly short moment he perceived that his suffering was nothing of so trifling and dignified a

kind. It was altogether a more serious matter, and
partook rather of the nature of those subtle and cruel
feelings which are awakened by a kick or a horse-
whipping.

He felt very sick—physically sick—as though he had
bitten through something nauseous. Life, that to a
well-ordered mind should be a matter of congratulation, appeared to him, for a second or so, perfectly
intolerable. He picked up the paper at his feet, and
sat down with the wish to think it out, to understand
why his wife—his wife!—should leave him, should
throw away respect, comfort, peace, decency, position—
throw away everything for nothing! He set himself to
think out the hidden logic of her action—a mental
undertaking fit for the leisure hours of a madhouse,
though he couldn't see it. And he thought of his wife
in every relation except the only fundamental one. He
thought of her as a well-bred girl, as a wife, as a cul-
tured person, as the mistress of a house, as a lady; but
he never for a moment thought of her simply as a
woman.

Then a fresh wave, a raging wave of humiliation,
swept through his mind, and left nothing there but a
personal sense of undeserved abasement. Why should
he be mixed up with such a horrid exposure! It anni-
hilated all the advantages of his well-ordered past, by
a truth effective and unjust like a calumny—and the
past was wasted. Its failure was disclosed—a distinct
failure, on his part, to see, to guard, to understand. It
could not be denied; it could not be explained away,
hustled out of sight. He could not sit on it and look
solemn. Now—if she had only died!

If she had only died! He was driven to envy such
a respectable bereavement, and one so perfectly free
from any taint of misfortune that even his best friend

or his best enemy would not have felt the slightest thrill of exultation. No one would have cared. He sought comfort in clinging to the contemplation of the only fact of life that the resolute efforts of mankind had never failed to disguise in the clatter and glamour of phrases. And nothing lends itself more to lies than death. If she had only died! Certain words would have been said to him in a sad tone, and he, with proper fortitude, would have made appropriate answers. There were precedents for such an occasion. And no one would have cared. If she had only died! The promises, the terrors, the hopes of eternity, are the concern of the corrupt dead; but the obvious sweetness of life belongs to living, healthy men. And life was his concern: that sane and gratifying existence untroubled by too much love or by too much regret. She had interfered with it; she had defaced it. And suddenly it occurred to him he must have been mad to marry. It was too much in the nature of giving yourself away, of wearing—if for a moment—your heart on your sleeve. But every one married. Was all mankind mad!

In the shock of that startling thought he looked up, and saw to the left, to the right, in front, men sitting far off in chairs and looking at him with wild eyes— emissaries of a distracted mankind intruding to spy upon his pain and his humiliation. It was not to be borne. He rose quickly, and the others jumped up, too, on all sides. He stood still in the middle of the room as if discouraged by their vigilance. No escape! He felt something akin to despair. Everybody must know. The servants must know to-night. He ground his teeth . . . And he had never noticed, never guessed anything. Everyone will know. He thought: The woman's a monster, but everybody will think me a fool; and standing still in the midst of severe walnut-wood furniture, he felt such a tempest of anguish within him that he seemed to see himself rolling on the carpet, beating his head against the wall. He was disgusted with himself, with the loathsome rush of emotion breaking through all the reserves that guarded his manhood. Something unknown, withering and poison-ous, had entered his life, passed near him, touched him, and he was deteriorating. He was appalled. What was it? She was gone. Why? His head was ready to burst with the endeavour to understand her act and his subtle horror of it. Everything was changed. Why? Only a woman gone, after all; and yet he had a vision, a vision quick and distinct as a dream: the vision of everything he had thought indestructible and safe in the world crashing down about him, like solid walls do before the fierce breath of a hurricane. He stared, shaking in every limb, while he felt the de-structive breath, the mysterious breath, the breath of passion, stir the profound peace of the house. He looked round in fear. Yes. Crime may be forgiven; uncalculating sacrifice, blind trust, burning faith, other follies, may be turned to account; suffering, death itself, may with a grin or a frown be explained away; but passion is the unpardonable and secret infamy of our hearts, a thing to curse, to hide and to deny; a shame-less and forlorn thing that tramples upon the smiling promises, that tears off the placid mask, that strips the body of life. And it had come to him! It had laid its unclean hand upon the spotless draperies of his existence, and he had to face it alone with all the world looking on. All the world! And he thought that even the bare suspicion of such an adversary within his house carried with it a taint and a condemnation. He put both his hands out as if to ward off the approach of a defiling truth; and, instantly, the appalled conclave of unreal men, standing about mutely beyond the clear lustre of mirrors, made at him the same gesture of rejection and horror.

He glanced vainly here and there, like a man looking in desperation for a weapon or for a hiding place, and understood at last that he was disarmed and cornered by the enemy that, without any squeamishness, would strike so as to lay open his heart. He could get help nowhere, or even take counsel with himself, because in the sudden shock of her desertion the sentiments which he knew that in fidelity to his bringing up, to his prejudices and his surroundings, he ought to experience, were so mixed up with the novelty of real feelings, of fundamental feelings that know nothing of creed, class, or education, that he was unable to distinguish clearly between what is and what ought to be; between the inexcusable truth and the valid pretences. And he knew instinctively that truth would be of no use to him. Some kind of concealment seemed a necessity because one cannot explain. Of course not! Who would listen? One had simply to be without stain and without reproach to keep one's place in the forefront of life.

He said to himself, "I must get over it the best I can," and began to walk up and down the room. What next? What ought to be done? He thought: I will travel—no I won't. I shall face it out. And after that resolve he was greatly cheered by the reflection that it would be a mute and an easy part to play, for no one would be likely to converse with him about the abominable conduct of—that woman. He argued to himself that decent people—and he knew no others—did not care to talk about such indelicate affairs. She had gone off—with that unhealthy, fat ass of a journalist. Why? He had been all a husband ought to be. He

had given her a good position—she shared his prospects
—he had treated her invariably with great consideration. He reviewed his conduct with a kind of dismal
pride. It had been irreproachable. Then, why? For
love? Profanation! There could be no love there.
A shameful impulse of passion. Yes, passion. His
own wife! Good God! . . . And the indelicate
aspect of his domestic misfortune struck him with
such shame that, next moment, he caught himself in
the act of pondering absurdly over the notion whether
it would not be more dignified for him to induce a general belief that he had been in the habit of beating his
wife. Some fellows do . . . and anything would
be better than the filthy fact; for it was clear he had
lived with the root of it for five years—and it was too
shameful. Anything! Anything! Brutality . . .
But he gave it up directly, and began to think of the
Divorce Court. It did not present itself to him, notwithstanding his respect for law and usage, as a proper
refuge for dignified grief. It appeared rather as an
unclean and sinister cavern where men and women
are haled by adverse fate to writhe ridiculously in the
presence of uncompromising truth. It should not be
allowed. That woman! Five . . . years . . .
married five years . . . and never to see anything.
Not to the very last day . . . not till she coolly
went off. And he pictured to himself all the people he
knew engaged in speculating as to whether all that
time he had been blind, foolish, or infatuated. What
a woman! Blind! . . . Not at all. Could a
clean-minded man imagine such depravity? Evidently not. He drew a free breath. That was the
attitude to take; it was dignified enough; it gave him
the advantage, and he could not help perceiving that
it was moral. He yearned unaffectedly to see morality

(in his person) triumphant before the world. As to her—she would be forgotten. Let her be forgotten—buried in oblivion—lost! No one would allude . . . Refined people—and every man and woman he knew could be so described—had, of course, a horror of such topics. Had they? Oh, yes. No one would allude to her . . . in his hearing. He stamped his foot, tore the letter across, then again and again. The thought of sympathizing friends excited in him a fury of mistrust. He flung down the small bits of paper. They settled, fluttering at his feet, and looked very white on the dark carpet, like a scattered handful of snow-flakes.

This fit of hot anger was succeeded by a sudden sadness, by the darkening passage of a thought that ran over the scorched surface of his heart, like upon a barren plain, and after a fiercer assault of sunrays, the melancholy and cooling shadow of a cloud. He realized that he had had a shock—not a violent or rending blow, that can be seen, resisted, returned, forgotten, but a thrust, insidious and penetrating, that had stirred all those feelings, concealed and cruel, which the arts of the devil, the fears of mankind—God's infinite compassion, perhaps—keep chained deep down in the inscrutable twilight of our breasts. A dark curtain seemed to rise before him, and for less than a second he looked upon the mysterious universe of moral suffering. As a landscape is seen complete, and vast, and vivid, under a flash of lightning, so he could see disclosed in a moment all the immensity of pain that can be contained in one short moment of human thought. Then the curtain fell again, but his rapid vision left in Alvan Hervey's mind a trail of invincible sadness, a sense of loss and bitter solitude, as though he had been robbed and exiled. For a moment he ceased to be a member

*M

of society with a position, a career, and a name attached to all this, like a descriptive label of some complicated compound. He was a simple human being
removed from the delightful world of crescents and
squares. He stood alone, naked and afraid, like
the first man on the first day of evil. There are in life
events, contacts, glimpses, that seem brutally to bring
all the past to a close. There is a shock and a crash,
as of a gate flung to behind one by the perfidious hand
of fate. Go and seek another paradise, fool or sage.
There is a moment of dumb dismay, and the wanderings must begin again; the painful explaining away of
facts, the feverish raking up of illusions, the cultivation
of a fresh crop of lies in the sweat of one's brow, to
sustain life, to make it supportable, to make it fair,
so as to hand intact to another generation of blind
wanderers the charming legend of a heartless country,
of a promised land, all flowers and blessings . . .

He came to himself with a slight start, and became
aware of an oppressive, crushing desolation. It was
only a feeling, it is true, but it produced on him a
physical effect, as though his chest had been squeezed
in a vice. He perceived himself so extremely forlorn
and lamentable, and was moved so deeply by the oppressive sorrow, that another turn of the screw, he felt,
would bring tears out of his eyes. He was deteriorating. Five years of life in common had appeased his
longing. Yes, long-time ago. The first five months
did that—but . . . There was the habit—the
habit of her person, of her smile, of her gestures, of her
voice, of her silence. She had a pure brow and good
hair. How utterly wretched all this was. Good hair
and fine eyes—remarkably fine. He was surprised by
the number of details that intruded upon his unwilling
memory. He could not help remembering her foot-

steps, the rustle of her dress, her way of holding her head, her decisive manner of saying "Alvan," the quiver of her nostrils when she was annoyed. All that had been so much his property, so intimately and specially his! He raged in a mournful, silent way, as he took stock of his losses. He was like a man counting the cost of an unlucky speculation—irritated, depressed —exasperated with himself and with others, with the fortunate, with the indifferent, with the callous; yet the wrong done him appeared so cruel that he would perhaps have dropped a tear over that spoliation if it had not been for his conviction that men do not weep. Foreigners do; they also kill sometimes in such circumstances. And to his horror he felt himself driven to regret almost that the usages of a society ready to forgive the shooting of a burglar forbade him, under the circumstances, even as much as a thought of murder. Nevertheless, he clenched his fists and set his teeth hard. And he was afraid at the same time. He was afraid with that penetrating faltering fear that seems, in the very middle of a beat, to turn one's heart into a handful of dust. The contamination of her crime spread out, tainted the universe, tainted himself; woke up all the dormant infamies of the world; caused a ghastly kind of clairvoyance in which he could see the towns and fields of the earth, its sacred places, its temples and its houses, peopled by monsters—by monsters of duplicity, lust, and murder. She was a monster—he himself was thinking monstrous thoughts . . . and yet he was like other people. How many men and women at this very moment were plunged in abominations—mediated crimes. It was frightful to think of. He remembered all the streets—the well-to-do streets he had passed on his way home; all the innumerable houses with closed doors and curtained windows. Each seemed now an abode of anguish and folly. And his thought, as if appalled, stood still, recalling with dismay the decorous and frightful silence that was like a conspiracy; the grim, impenetrable silence of miles of walls concealing passions, misery, thoughts of crime. Surely he was not the only man; his was not the only house . . . and yet no one knew—no one guessed. But he knew. He knew with unerring certitude that could not be deceived by the correct silence of walls, of closed doors, of curtained windows. He was beside himself with a despairing agitation, like a man informed of a deadly secret—the secret of a calamity threatening the safety of mankind—the sacredness, the peace of life.

He caught sight of himself in one of the looking-glasses. It was a relief. The anguish of his feeling had been so powerful that he more than half expected to see some distorted wild face there, and he was pleasantly surprised to see nothing of the kind. His aspect, at any rate, would let no one into the secret of his pain. He examined himself with attention. His trousers were turned up, and his boots a little muddy, but he looked very much as usual. Only his hair was slightly ruffled, and that disorder, somehow, was so suggestive of trouble that he went quickly to the table, and began to use the brushes, in an anxious desire to obliterate the compromising trace, that only vestige of his emotion. He brushed with care, watching the effect of his smoothing; and another face, slightly pale and more tense than was perhaps desirable, peered back at him from the toilet glass. He laid the brushes down, and was not satisfied. He took them up again and brushed, brushed mechanically—forgot himself in that occupation. The tumult of his thoughts ended in a sluggish flow of reflection, such as, after the outburst of a volcano, the almost imperceptible progress of a stream of lava, creeping languidly over a convulsed land and pitilessly obliterating any landmark left by the shock of the earthquake. It is a destructive but, by comparison, it is a peaceful phenomenon. Alvan Hervey was almost soothed by the deliberate pace of his thoughts. His moral landmarks were going one by one, consumed in the fire of his experience, buried in hot mud, in ashes. He was cooling—on the surface; but there was enough heat left somewhere to make him slap the brushes on the table, and turning away, say in a fierce whisper: "I wish him joy . . . Damn the woman."

He felt himself utterly corrupted by her wickedness, and the most significant symptom of his moral downfall was the bitter, acrid satisfaction with which he recognized it. He, deliberately, swore in his thoughts; he meditated sneers; he shaped in profound silence words of cynical unbelief, and his most cherished convictions stood revealed finally as the narrow prejudices of fools. A crowd of shapeless, unclean thoughts crossed his mind in a stealthy rush, like a band of veiled malefactors hastening to a crime. He put his hands deep into his pockets. He heard a faint ringing somewhere, and muttered to himself: "I am not the only one . . . not the only one." There was another ring. Front door!

His heart leaped up into his throat, and forthwith descended as low as his boots. A call! Who? Why? He wanted to rush out on the landing and shout to the servant: "Not at home! Gone away abroad!" . . . Any excuse. He could not face a visitor. Not this evening. No. To-morrow. . . . Before he could break out of the numbness that enveloped him like a sheet of lead, he heard far below, as if in the

entrails of the earth, a door close heavily. The house
vibrated to it more than to a clap of thunder. He
stood still, wishing himself invisible. The room was
very chilly. He did not think he would ever feel like
that. But people must be met—they must be faced—
talked to—smiled at. He heard another door, much
nearer—the door of the drawing-room—being opened
and flung to again. He imagined for a moment he
would faint. How absurd! That kind of thing had
to be gone through. A voice spoke. He could not
catch the words. Then the voice spoke again, and
footsteps were heard on the first floor landing. Hang
it all! Was he to hear that voice and those footsteps
whenever any one spoke or moved. He thought:
"This is like being haunted—I suppose it will last for
a week or so, at least. Till I forget. Forget! Forget!"
Someone was coming up the second flight of stairs. Servant? He listened, then, suddenly, as though an incredible, frightful revelation had been shouted to him
from a distance, he bellowed out in the empty room:
"What! What!" in such a fiendish tone as to
astonish himself. The footsteps stopped outside the
door. He stood openmouthed, maddened and still, as
if in the midst of a catastrophe. The door-handle
rattled lightly. It seemed to him that the walls were
coming apart, that the furniture swayed at him; the
ceiling slanted queerly for a moment, a tall wardrobe
tried to topple over. He caught hold of something
and it was the back of a chair. So he had reeled
against a chair! Oh! Confound it! He gripped hard.

The flaming butterfly poised between the jaws of the
bronze dragon radiated a glare, a glare that seemed to
leap up all at once into a crude, blinding fierceness, and
made it difficult for him to distinguish plainly the

figure of his wife standing upright with her back to the closed door. He looked at her and could not detect her breathing. The harsh and violent light was beating on her, and he was amazed to see her preserve so well the composure of her upright attitude in that scorching brilliance which, to his eyes, enveloped her like a hot and consuming mist. He would not have been surprised if she had vanished in it as suddenly as she had appeared. He stared and listened; listened for some sound, but the silence round him was absolute —as though he had in a moment grown completely deaf as well as dim-eyed. Then his hearing returned, preternaturally sharp. He heard the patter of a rain-shower on the window panes behind the lowered blinds, and below, far below, in the artificial abyss of the square, the deadened roll of wheels and the splashy trotting of a horse. He heard a groan also—very distinct—in the room—close to his ear.

He thought with alarm: "I must have made that noise myself;" and at the same instant the woman left the door, stepped firmly across the floor before him, and sat down in a chair. He knew that step. There was no doubt about it. She had come back! And he very nearly said aloud "Of course!"—such was his sudden and masterful perception of the indestructible character of her being. Nothing could destroy her— and nothing but his own destruction could keep her away. She was the incarnation of all the short moments which every man spares out of his life for dreams, for precious dreams that concrete the most cherished, the most profitable of his illusions. He peered at her with inward trepidation. She was mysterious, significant, full of obscure meaning—like a symbol. He peered, bending forward, as though he had been discovering about her things he had never seen before. Unconsciously he made a step towards her—then another. He saw her arm make an ample, decided movement— and he stopped. She had lifted her veil. It was like the lifting of a vizor.

The spell was broken. He experienced a shock as though he had been called out of a trance by the sudden noise of an explosion. It was even more startling and more distinct; it was an infinitely more intimate change, for he had the sensation of having come into this room only that very moment; of having returned from very far; he was made aware that some essential part of himself had in a flash returned into his body, returned finally from a fierce and lamentable region, from the dwelling-place of unveiled hearts. He woke up to an amazing infinity of contempt, to a droll bitterness of wonder, to a disenchanted conviction of safety. He had a glimpse of the irresistible force, and he saw also the barrenness of his convictions—of her convictions. It seemed to him that he could never make a mistake as long as he lived. It was morally impossible to go wrong. He was not elated by that certitude; he was dimly uneasy about its price; there was a chill as of death in this triumph of sound principles, in this victory snatched under the very shadow of disaster.

The last trace of his previous state of mind vanished, as the instantaneous and elusive trail of a bursting meteor vanishes on the profound blackness of the sky; it was the faint flicker of a painful thought, gone as soon as perceived, that nothing but her presence—after all— had the power to recall him to himself. He stared at her. She sat with her hands on her lap, looking down; and he noticed that her boots were dirty, her skirts wet and splashed, as though she had been driven back there by a blind fear through a waste of mud. He was indignant, amazed and shocked, but in a natural, healthy way now; so that he could control those unprofitable sentiments by the dictates of cautious self-restraint. The light in the room had no unusual brilliance now; it was a good light in which he could easily observe the expression of her face. It was that of dull fatigue. And the silence that surrounded them was the normal silence of any quiet house, hardly disturbed by the faint noises of a respectable quarter of the town. He was very cool—and it was quite coolly that he thought how much better it would be if neither of them ever spoke again. She sat with closed lips, with an air of lassitude in the stony forgetfulness of her pose, but after a moment she lifted her drooping eyelids and met his tense and inquisitive stare by a look that had all the formless eloquence of a cry. It penetrated, it stirred without informing; it was the very essence of anguish stripped of words that can be smiled at, argued away, shouted down, disdained. It was anguish naked and unashamed, the bare pain of existence let loose upon the world in the fleeting unreserve of a look that had in it an immensity of fatigue, the scornful sincerity, the black impudence of an extorted confession. Alvan Hervey was seized with wonder, as though he had seen something inconceivable; and some obscure part of his being was ready to exclaim with him: "I would never have believed it!" but an instantaneous revulsion of wounded susceptibilities checked the unfinished thought.

He felt full of rancorous indignation against the woman who could look like this at one. This look probed him; it tampered with him. It was dangerous to one as would be a hint of unbelief whispered by a priest in the august decorum of a temple; and at the same time it was impure, it was disturbing, like a cynical consolation muttered in the dark, tainting the sorrow, corroding the thought, poisoning the heart. He

wanted to ask her furiously: "Who do you take me
for? How dare you look at me like this?" He felt
himself helpless before the hidden meaning of that look;
he resented it with pained and futile violence as an
injury so secret that it could never, never be redressed.
His wish was to crush her by a single sentence. He
was stainless. Opinion was on his side; morality, men
and gods were on his side; law, conscience—all the
world! She had nothing but that look. And he could
only say:

"How long do you intend to stay here?"

Her eyes did not waver, her lips remained closed;
and for any effect of his words he might have spoken
to a dead woman, only that this one breathed quickly.
He was profoundly disappointed by what he had said.
It was a great deception, something in the nature of
treason. He had deceived himself. It should have
been altogether different—other words—another sensation. And before his eyes, so fixed that at times
they saw nothing, she sat apparently as unconscious
as though she had been alone, sending that look of
brazen confession straight at him—with an air of
staring into empty space. He said significantly:

"Must I go then?" And he knew he meant nothing
of what he implied.

One of her hands on her lap moved slightly as though
his words had fallen there and she had thrown them
off on the floor. But her silence encouraged him. Possibly it meant remorse—perhaps fear. Was she thunderstruck by his attitude?　.　.　.　Her eyelids dropped.
He seemed to understand ever so much—everything!
Very well—but she must be made to suffer. It was
due to him. He understood everything, yet he judged
it indispensable to say with an obvious affection of
civility:

"I don't understand—be so good as to . . ."

She stood up. For a second he believed she intended to go away, and it was as though someone had jerked a string attached to his heart. It hurt. He remained open-mouthed and silent. But she made an irresolute step towards him, and instinctively he moved aside. They stood before one another, and the fragments of the torn letter lay between them—at their feet—like an insurmountable obstacle, like a sign of eternal separation! Around them three other couples stood still and face to face, as if waiting for a signal to begin some action—a struggle, a dispute, or a dance

She said: "Don't—Alvan!" and there was something that resembled a warning in the pain of her tone. He narrowed his eyes as if trying to pierce her with his gaze. Her voice touched him. He had aspirations after magnanimity, generosity, superiority—interrupted, however, by flashes of indignation and anxiety—frightful anxiety to know how far she had gone. She looked down at the torn paper. Then she looked up, and their eyes met again, remained fastened together, like an unbreakable bond, like a clasp of eternal complicity; and the decorous silence, the pervading quietude of the house which enveloped this meeting of their glances became for a moment inexpressibly vile, for he was afraid she would say too much and make magnanimity impossible, while behind the profound mournfulness of her face there was a regret—a regret of things done—the regret of delay—the thought that if she had only turned back a week sooner—a day sooner—only an hour sooner. . . . They were afraid to hear again the sound of their voices; they did not know what they might say—perhaps something that could not be recalled; and words are more terrible than facts. But the tricky fatality that lurks in

obscure impulses spoke through Alvan Hervey's lips
suddenly; and he heard his own voice with the excited
and sceptical curiosity with which one listens to actors'
voices speaking on the stage in the strain of a poignant
situation.

"If you have forgotten anything . . . of course
. . . I . . ."

Her eyes blazed at him for an instant; her lips
trembled—and then she also became the mouth-piece
of the mysterious force forever hovering near us; of
that perverse inspiration, wandering capricious and uncontrollable, like a gust of wind.

"What is the good of this, Alvan? . . . You
know why I came back. . . . You know that I
could not . . . "

He interrupted her with irritation.

"Then! what's this?" he asked, pointing downwards
at the torn letter.

"That's a mistake," she said hurriedly, in a muffled
voice.

This answer amazed him. He remained speechless,
staring at her. He had half a mind to burst into a
laugh. It ended in a smile as involuntary as a grimace
of pain.

"A mistake . . ." he began, slowly, and then
found himself unable to say another word.

"Yes . . . it was honest," she said very low, as
if speaking to the memory of a feeling in a remote past.

He exploded.

"Curse your honesty! . . . Is there any honesty
in all this! . . . When did you begin to be honest?
Why are you here? What are you now? . . . Still
honest? . . . "

He walked at her, raging, as if blind; during these
three quick strides he lost touch of the material world

and was whirled interminably through a kind of empty universe made up of nothing but fury and anguish, till he came suddenly upon her face—very close to his. He stopped short, and all at once seemed to remember something heard ages ago.

"You don't know the meaning of the word," he shouted.

She did not flinch. He perceived with fear that everything around him was still. She did not move a hair's breadth; his own body did not stir. An imperturbable calm enveloped their two motionless figures, the house, the town, all the world—and the trifling tempest of his feelings. The violence of the short tumult within him had been such as could well have shattered all creation; and yet nothing was changed. He faced his wife in the familiar room in his own house. It had not fallen. And right and left all the innumerable dwellings, standing shoulder to shoulder, had resisted the shock of his passion, had presented, unmoved, to the loneliness of his trouble, the grim silence of walls, the impenetrable and polished discretion of closed doors and curtained windows. Immobility and silence pressed on him, assailed him, like two accomplices of the immovable and mute woman before his eyes. He was suddenly vanquished. He was shown his impotence. He was soothed by the breath of a corrupt resignation coming to him through the subtle irony of the surrounding peace.

He said with villainous composure:

"At any rate it isn't enough for me. I want to know more—if you're going to stay."

"There is nothing more to tell," she answered, sadly.

It struck him as so very true that he did not say anything. She went on:

"You wouldn't understand. . . ."

"No?" he said, quietly. He held himself tight not to burst into howls and imprecations.

"I tried to be faithful . . ." she began again.

"And this?" he exclaimed, pointing at the fragments of her letter.

"This—this is a failure," she said.

"I should think so," he muttered, bitterly.

"I tried to be faithful to myself—Alvan—and . . . and honest to you. . . ."

"If you had tried to be faithful to me it would have been more to the purpose," he interrupted, angrily. "I've been faithful to you—and you have spoiled my life—both our lives . . ." Then after a pause the unconquerable preoccupation of self came out, and he raised his voice to ask resentfully, "And, pray, for how long have you been making a fool of me?"

She seemed horribly shocked by that question. He did not wait for an answer, but went on moving about all the time; now and then coming up to her, then wandering off restlessly to the other end of the room.

"I want to know. Everybody knows, I suppose, but myself—and that's your honesty!"

"I have told you there is nothing to know," she said, speaking unsteadily as if in pain. "Nothing of what you suppose. You don't understand me. This letter is the beginning—and the end."

"The end—this thing has no end," he clamoured, unexpectedly. "Can't you understand that? I can . . . The beginning . . ."

He stopped and looked into her eyes with concentrated intensity, with a desire to see, to penetrate, to understand, that made him positively hold his breath till he gasped.

"By Heavens!" he said, standing perfectly still in a peering attitude and within less than a foot from her.

"By Heavens!" he repeated, slowly, and in a tone whose involuntary strangeness was a complete mystery to himself. "By Heavens—I could believe you—I could believe anything—now!"

He turned short on his heel and began to walk up and down the room with an air of having disburdened himself of the final pronouncement of his life—of having said something on which he would not go back, even if he could. She remained as if rooted to the carpet. Her eyes followed the restless movements of the man, who avoided looking at her. Her wild stare clung to him, inquiring, wondering and doubtful.

"But the fellow was forever sticking in here," he burst out, distractedly. "He made love to you, I suppose—and, and . . ." He lowered his voice. "And —you let him."

"And I let him," she murmured, catching his intonation, so that her voice sounded unconscious, sounded far off and slavish, like an echo.

He said twice, "You! You!" violently, then calmed down. "What could you see in the fellow?" he asked, with unaffected wonder. "An effeminate, fat ass. What could you . . . Weren't you happy? Didn't you have all you wanted? Now—frankly; did I deceive your expectations in any way? Were you disappointed with our position—or with our prospects— perhaps? You know you couldn't be—they are much better than you could hope for when you married me. . . ."

He forgot himself so far as to gesticulate a little while he went on with animation:

"What could you expect from such a fellow? He's an outsider—a rank outsider. . . . If it hadn't been for my money . . . do you hear? . . . for my money, he wouldn't know where to turn. His

people won't have anything to do with him. The
fellow's no class—no class at all. He's useful, certainly,
that's why I . . . I thought you had enough
intelligence to see it. . . . And you . . . No!
It's incredible! What did he tell you? Do you care
for no one's opinion—is there no restraining influence
in the world for you—women? Did you ever give me a
thought? I tried to be a good husband. Did I fail?
Tell me—what have I done?"

Carried away by his feelings he took his head in both
his hands and repeated wildly:

"What have I done? . . . Tell me!
What? . . ."

"Nothing," she said.

"Ah! You see . . . you can't . . ." he
began, triumphantly, walking away; then suddenly, as
though he had been flung back at her by something
invisible he had met, he spun round and shouted with
exasperation:

"What on earth did you expect me to do?"

Without a word she moved slowly towards the table,
and, sitting down, leaned on her elbow, shading her
eyes with her hand. All that time he glared at her
watchfully as if expecting every moment to find in
her deliberate movements an answer to his question.
But he could not read anything, he could gather no
hint of her thought. He tried to suppress his desire
to shout, and after waiting awhile, said with incisive
scorn:

"Did you want me to write absurd verses; to sit and
look at you for hours—to talk to you about your soul?
You ought to have known I wasn't that sort. . . .
I had something better to do. But if you think I was
totally blind . . ."

He perceived in a flash that he could remember an

infinity of enlightening occurrences. He could recall ever so many distinct occasions when he came upon them; he remembered the absurdly interrupted gesture of his fat, white hand, the rapt expression of her face, the glitter of unbelieving eyes; snatches of incomprehensible conversations not worth listening to, silences that had meant nothing at the time and seemed now illuminating like a burst of sunshine. He remembered all that. He had not been blind. Oh! No! And to know this was an exquisite relief: it brought back all his composure.

"I thought it beneath me to suspect you," he said, loftily.

The sound of that sentence evidently possessed some magical power, because, as soon as he had spoken, he felt wonderfully at ease; and directly afterwards he experienced a flash of joyful amazement at the discovery that he could be inspired to such noble and truthful utterance. He watched the effect of his words. They caused her to glance at him quickly over her shoulder. He caught a glimpse of wet eyelashes, of a red cheek with a tear running down swiftly; and then she turned away again and sat as before, covering her face with her hands.

"You ought to be perfectly frank with me," he said, slowly.

"You know everything," she answered, indistinctly, through her fingers.

"This letter. . . . Yes . . . but . . ."

"And I came back," she exclaimed in a stifled voice; "you know everything."

"I am glad of it—for your sake," he said with impressive gravity. He listened to himself with solemn emotion. It seemed to him that something inexpressibly momentous was in progress within the room, that every word and every gesture had the importance of events preordained from the beginning of all things, and summing up in their finality the whole purpose of creation.

"For your sake," he repeated.

Her shoulders shook as though she had been sobbing, and he forgot himself in the contemplation of her hair. Suddenly he gave a start, as if waking up, and asked very gently and not much above a whisper—

"Have you been meeting him often?"

"Never!" she cried into the palms of her hands.

This answer seemed for a moment to take from him the power of speech. His lips moved for some time before any sound came.

"You preferred to make love here—under my very nose," he said, furiously. He calmed down instantly, and felt regretfully uneasy, as though he had let himself down in her estimation by that outburst. She rose, and with her hand on the back of the chair confronted him with eyes that were perfectly dry now. There was a red spot on each of her cheeks.

"When I made up my mind to go to him—I wrote," she said.

"But you didn't go to him," he took up in the same tone. "How far did you go? What made you come back?"

"I didn't know myself," she murmured. Nothing of her moved but her lips. He fixed her sternly.

"Did he expect this? Was he waiting for you?" he asked.

She answered him by an almost imperceptible nod, and he continued to look at her for a good while without making a sound. Then, at last—

"And I suppose he is waiting yet?" he asked, quickly.

Again she seemed to nod at him. For some reason

he felt he must know the time. He consulted his
watch gloomily. Half-past seven.

"Is he?" he muttered, putting the watch in his
pocket. He looked up at her, and, as if suddenly
overcome by a sense of sinister fun, gave a short, harsh
laugh, directly repressed.

"No! It's the most unheard! . . ." he mumbled
while she stood before him biting her lower lip, as if
plunged in deep thought. He laughed again in one low
burst that was as spiteful as an imprecation. He did
not know why he felt such an overpowering and sudden
distaste for the facts of existence—for facts in general
—such an immense disgust at the thought of all the
many days already lived through. He was wearied.
Thinking seemed a labour beyond his strength. He
said—

"You deceived me—now you make a fool of him
. . . It's awful! Why?"

"I deceived myself!" she exclaimed.

"Oh! Nonsense!" he said, impatiently.

"I am ready to go if you wish it," she went on,
quickly. "It was due to you—to be told—to know.
No! I could not!" she cried, and stood still wringing
her hands stealthily.

"I am glad you repented before it was too late," he
said in a dull tone and looking at his boots. "I am
glad . . . some spark of better feeling," he muttered, as if to himself. He lifted up his head after a
moment of brooding silence. "I am glad to see that
there is some sense of decency left in you," he added a
little louder. Looking at her he appeared to hesitate,
as if estimating the possible consequences of what he
wished to say, and at last blurted out—

"After all, I loved you. . . ."

"I did not know," she whispered.

"Good God!" he cried. "Why do you imagine I married you?"

The indelicacy of his obtuseness angered her.

"Ah—why?" she said through her teeth.

He appeared overcome with horror, and watched her lips intently as though in fear.

"I imagined many things," she said, slowly, and paused. He watched, holding his breath. At last she went on musingly, as if thinking aloud, "I tried to understand. I tried honestly. . . . Why? . . . To do the usual thing—I suppose. . . . To please yourself."

He walked away smartly, and when he came back, close to her, he had a flushed face.

"You seemed pretty well pleased, too—at the time," he hissed, with scathing fury. "I needn't ask whether you loved me."

"I know now I was perfectly incapable of such a thing," she said, calmly, "If I had, perhaps you would not have married me."

"It's very clear I would not have done it if I had known you—as I know you now."

He seemed to see himself proposing to her—ages ago. They were strolling up the slope of a lawn. Groups of people were scattered in sunshine. The shadows of leafy boughs lay still on the short grass. The coloured sunshades far off, passing between trees, resembled deliberate and brilliant butterflies moving without a flutter. Men smiling amiably, or else very grave, within the impeccable shelter of their black coats, stood by the side of women who, clustered in clear summer toilettes, recalled all the fabulous tales of enchanted gardens where animated flowers smile at bewitched knights. There was a sumptuous serenity in it all, a thin, vibrating excitement, the perfect security, as of an invincible ignorance, that evoked within him a transcendent belief in felicity as the lot of all mankind, a recklessly picturesque desire to get promptly something for himself only, out of that splendour unmarred by any shadow of a thought. The girl walked by his side across an open space; no one was near, and suddenly he stood still, as if inspired, and spoke. He remembered looking at her pure eyes, at her candid brow; he remembered glancing about quickly to see if they were being observed, and thinking that nothing could go wrong in a world of so much charm, purity, and distinction. He was proud of it. He was one of its makers, of its possessors, of its guardians, of its extollers. He wanted to grasp it solidly, to get as much gratification as he could out of it; and in view of its incomparable quality, of its unstained atmosphere, of its nearness to the heaven of its choice, this gust of brutal desire seemed the most noble of aspirations. In a second he lived again through all these moments, and then all the pathos of his failure presented itself to him with such vividness that there was a suspicion of tears in his tone when he said almost unthinkingly, "My God! I did love you!"

She seemed touched by the emotion of his voice. Her lips quivered a little, and she made one faltering step towards him, putting out her hands in a beseeching gesture, when she perceived, just in time, that being absorbed by the tragedy of his life he had absolutely forgotten her very existence. She stopped, and her outstretched arms fell slowly. He, with his features distorted by the bitterness of his thought, saw neither her movement nor her gesture. He stamped his foot in vexation, rubbed his head—then exploded.

"What the devil am I to do now?"

He was still again. She seemed to understand, and moved to the door firmly.

"It's very simple—I'm going," she said aloud.

At the sound of her voice he gave a start of surprise, looked at her wildly, and asked in a piercing tone—

"You. . . . Where? To him?"

"No—alone—good-bye."

The door-handle rattled under her groping hand as though she had been trying to get out of some dark place.

"No—stay!" he cried.

She heard him faintly. He saw her shoulder touch the lintel of the door. She swayed as if dazed. There was less than a second of suspense while they both felt as if poised on the very edge of moral annihilation, ready to fall into some devouring nowhere. Then, almost simultaneously, he shouted, "Come back!" and she let go the handle of the door. She turned round in peaceful desperation like one who deliberately has thrown away the last chance of life; and, for a moment, the room she faced appeared terrible, and dark, and safe—like a grave.

He said, very hoarse and abrupt: "It can't end like this. . . . Sit down;" and while she crossed the room again to the low-backed chair before the dressing-table, he opened the door and put his head out to look and listen. The house was quiet. He came back pacified, and asked—

"Do you speak the truth?"

She nodded.

"You have lived a lie, though," he said, suspiciously.

"Ah! You made it so easy," she answered.

"You reproach me—me!"

"How could I?" she said; "I would have you no other—now."

"What do you mean by . . ." he began, then checked himself, and without waiting for an answer went on, "I won't ask any questions. Is this letter the worst of it?"

She had a nervous movement of her hands.

"I must have a plain answer," he said, hotly.

"Then, no! The worst is my coming back."

There followed a period of dead silence, during which they exchanged searching glances.

He said authoritatively—

"You don't know what you are saying. Your mind is unhinged. You are beside yourself, or you would not say such things. You can't control yourself. Even in your remorse . . ." He paused a moment, then said with a doctoral air: "Self-restraint is everything in life, you know. It's happiness, it's dignity . . . it's everything."

She was pulling nervously at her handkerchief while he went on watching anxiously to see the effect of his words. Nothing satisfactory happened. Only, as he began to speak again, she covered her face with both her hands.

"You see where the want of self-restraint leads to. Pain—humiliation—loss of respect—of friends, of everything that ennobles life, that . . . All kinds of horrors," he concluded, abruptly.

She made no stir. He looked at her pensively for some time as though he had been concentrating the melancholy thoughts evoked by the sight of that abased woman. His eyes became fixed and dull. He was profoundly penetrated by the solemnity of the moment; he felt deeply the greatness of the occasion. And more than ever the walls of his house seemed to enclose the sacredness of ideals to which he was about to offer a magnificent sacrifice. He was the high priest of that temple, the severe guardian of formulas, of rites, of the pure ceremonial concealing the black doubts of life. And he was not alone. Other men, too —the best of them—kept watch and ward by the hearthstones that were the altars of that profitable persuasion. He understood confusedly that he was part of an immense and beneficent power, which had a reward ready for every discretion. He dwelt within the invincible wisdom of silence; he was protected by an indestructible faith that would last forever, that would withstand unshaken all the assaults—the loud execrations of apostates, and the secret weariness of its confessors! He was in league with a universe of untold advantages. He represented the moral strength of a beautiful reticence that could vanquish all the deplorable crudities of life—fear, disaster, sin—even death itself. It seemed to him he was on the point of sweeping triumphantly away all the illusory mysteries of existence. It was simplicity itself.

"I hope you see now the folly—the utter folly of wickedness," he began in a dull, solemn manner. "You must respect the conditions of your life or lose all it can give you. All! Everything!"

He waved his arm once, and three exact replicas of his face, of his clothes, of his dull severity, of his solemn grief, repeated the wide gesture that in its comprehensive sweep indicated an infinity of moral sweetness, embraced the walls, the hangings, the whole house, all the crowd of houses outside, all the flimsy and inscrutable graves of the living, with their doors numbered like the doors of prison-cells, and as impenetrable as the granite of tombstones.

"Yes! Restraint, duty, fidelity—unswerving fidelity to what is expected of you. This—only this—secures the reward, the peace. Everything else we should labour to subdue—to destroy. It's misfortune; it's disease. It is terrible—terrible. We must not know anything about it—we needn't. It is our duty to ourselves—to others. You do not live all alone in the world—and if you have no respect for the dignity of life, others have. Life is a serious matter. If you don't conform to the highest standards you are no one—it's a kind of death. Didn't this occur to you? You've only to look round you to see the truth of what I am saying. Did you live without noticing anything, without understanding anything? From a child you had examples before your eyes—you could see daily the beauty, the blessings of morality, of principles. . . ."

His voice rose and fell pompously in a strange chant. His eyes were still, his stare exalted and sullen; his face was set, was hard, was woodenly exulting over the grim inspiration that secretly possessed him, seethed within him, lifted him up into a stealthy frenzy of belief. Now and then he would stretch out his right arm over her head, as it were, and he spoke down at that sinner from a height, and with a sense of avenging virtue, with a profound and pure joy as though he could from his steep pinnacle see every weighty word strike and hurt like a punishing stone.

"Rigid principles—adherence to what is right," he finished after a pause.

"What is right?" she said, distinctly, without uncovering her face.

"Your mind is diseased!" he cried, upright and austere. "Such a question is rot—utter rot. Look round you—there's your answer, if you only care to see. Nothing that outrages the received beliefs can be right. Your conscience tells you that. They are the received beliefs because they are the best, the noblest, the only possible. They survive. . . ."

N

He could not help noticing with pleasure the philosophic breadth of his view, but he could not pause to enjoy it, for his inspiration, the call of august truth, carried him on.

"You must respect the moral foundations of a society that has made you what you are. Be true to it. That's duty—that's honour—that's honesty."

He felt a great glow within him, as though he had swallowed something hot. He made a step nearer. She sat up and looked at him with an ardour of expectation that stimulated his sense of the supreme importance of that moment. And as if forgetting himself he raised his voice very much.

"'What's right?' you ask me. Think only. What would you have been if you had gone off with that infernal vagabond? . . . What would you have been? . . . You! My wife! . . ."

He caught sight of himself in the pier glass, drawn up to his full height, and with a face so white that his eyes, at the distance, resembled the black cavities in a skull. He saw himself as if about to launch imprecations, with arms uplifted above her bowed head. He was ashamed of that unseemly posture, and put his hands in his pockets hurriedly. She murmured faintly, as if to herself—

"Ah! What am I now?"

"As it happens you are still Mrs. Alvan Hervey—uncommonly lucky for you, let me tell you," he said in a conversational tone. He walked up to the furthest corner of the room, and, turning back, saw her sitting very upright, her hands clasped on her lap, and with a lost, unswerving gaze of her eyes which stared unwinking like the eyes of the blind, at the crude gas flame, and blazing still, between the jaws of the bronze dragon.

He came up quite close to her, and straddling his legs
a little, stood looking down at her face for some time
without taking his hands out of his pockets. He
seemed to be turning over in his mind a heap of words,
piecing his next speech out of an overpowering abun-
dance of thoughts.

"You've tried me to the utmost," he said at last; and
as soon as he said these words he lost his moral footing,
and felt himself swept away from his pinnacle by a
flood of passionate resentment against the bungling
creature that had come so near to spoiling his life.
"Yes; I've been tried more than any man ought to be,"
he went on with righteous bitterness. "It was unfair.
What possessed you to? . . . What possessed you?
. . . Write such a . . . After five years of
perfect happiness! 'Pon my word, no one would
believe. . . . Didn't you feel you couldn't? Because you couldn't . . . it was impossible—you
know. Wasn't it? Think. Wasn't it?"

"It was impossible," she whispered, obediently.

This submissive assent given with such readiness did
not soothe him, did not elate him; it gave him, inexplic-
ably, that sense of terror we experience when in the midst
of conditions we had learned to think absolutely safe we
discover all at once the presence of a near and un-
suspected danger. It was impossible, of course! He
knew it. She knew it. She confessed it. It was
impossible! That man knew it, too—as well as any one;
couldn't help knowing it. And yet those two had been
engaged in a conspiracy against his peace—in a criminal
enterprise for which there could be no sanction of belief
within themselves. There could not be! There could
not be! And yet how near to . . . With a short
thrill he saw himself an exiled forlorn figure in a realm of
ungovernable, of unrestrained folly. Nothing could be

foreseen, foretold—guarded against. And the sensation was intolerable, had something of the withering horror that may be conceived as following upon the utter extinction of all hope. In the flash of thought the dishonouring episode seemed to disengage itself from everything actual, from earthly conditions, and even from earthly suffering; it became purely a terrifying knowledge, an annihilating knowledge of a blind and infernal force. Something desperate and vague, a flicker of an insane desire to abase himself before the mysterious impulses of evil, to ask for mercy in some way, passed through his mind; and then came the idea, the persuasion, the certitude, that the evil must be forgotten—must be resolutely ignored to make life possible; that the knowledge must be kept out of mind, out of sight, like the knowledge of certain death is kept out of the daily existence of men. He stiffened himself inwardly for the effort, and next moment it appeared very easy, amazingly feasible, if one only kept strictly to facts, gave one's mind to their perplexities and not to their meaning. Becoming conscious of a long silence, he cleared his throat warningly, and said in a steady voice—

"I am glad you feel this . . . uncommonly glad . . . you felt this in time. For, don't you see . . ." Unexpectedly he hesitated.

"Yes . . . I see," she murmured.

"Of course you would," he said, looking at the carpet and speaking like one who thinks of something else. He lifted his head. "I cannot believe—even after this— even after this—that you are altogether—altogether . . . other than what I thought you. It seems impossible—to me."

"And to me," she breathed out.

"Now—yes," he said, "but this morning? And to-morrow? . . . This is what . . ."

He started at the drift of his words and broke off
abruptly. Every train of thought seemed to lead into
the hopeless realm of ungovernable folly, to recall the
knowledge and the terror of forces that must be ignored.
He said rapidly—

"My position is very painful—difficult . . . I
feel . . ."

He looked at her fixedly with a pained air, as though
frightfully oppressed by a sudden inability to express his
pent-up ideas.

"I am ready to go," she said very low. "I have
forfeited everything . . . to learn . . . to
learn . . ."

Her chin fell on her breast; her voice died out in a
sigh. He made a slight gesture of impatient assent.

"Yes! Yes! It's all very well . . . of course.
Forfeited—ah! Morally forfeited—only morally forfeited . . . if I am to believe you . . ."

She startled him by jumping up.

"Oh! I believe, I believe," he said, hastily, and she
sat down as suddenly as she had got up. He went on
gloomily—

"I've suffered—I suffer now. You can't understand
how much. So much that when you propose a parting I
almost think. . . . But no. There is duty.
You've forgotten it; I never did. Before heaven, I
never did. But in a horrid exposure like this the
judgment of mankind goes astray—at least for a time.
You see, you and I—at least I feel that—you and I are
one before the world. It is as it should be. The world
is right—in the main—or else it couldn't be—couldn't
be—what it is. And we are part of it. We have our
duty to—to our fellow beings who don't want
to . . . to. . . . er."

He stammered. She looked up at him with wide

eyes, and her lips were slightly parted. He went on mumbling—

". . . Pain. . . . Indignation. . . . Sure to misunderstand. I've suffered enough. And if there has been nothing irreparable—as you assure me . . . then . . ."

"Alvan!" she cried.

"What?" he said, morosely. He gazed down at her for a moment with a sombre stare, as one looks at ruins, at the devastation of some natural disaster.

"Then," he continued after a short pause, "the best thing is . . . the best for us . . . for every one. . . . Yes . . . least pain—most unselfish. . . ." His voice faltered, and she heard only detached words. ". . . Duty. . . . Burden. . . . Ourselves. . . . Silence."

A moment of perfect stillness ensued.

"This is an appeal I am making to your conscience," he said, suddenly, in an explanatory tone, "not to add to the wretchedness of all this: to try loyally and help me to live it down somehow. Without any reservations—you know. Loyally! You can't deny I've been cruelly wronged and—after all—my affection deserves . . ." He paused with evident anxiety to hear her speak.

"I make no reservations," she said, mournfully. "How could I? I found myself out and came back to . . ." her eyes flashed scornfully for an instant ". . . to what—to what you propose. You see . . . I . . . I can be trusted . . . now."

He listened to every word with profound attention, and when she ceased seemed to wait for more.

"Is that all you've got to say?" he asked.

She was startled by his tone, and said faintly—

"I spoke the truth. What more can I say?"

"Confound it! You might say something human," he burst out. "It isn't being truthful; it's being brazen—if you want to know. Not a word to show you feel your position, and—and mine. Not a single word of acknowledgment, or regret—or remorse . . . . or . . . something."

"Words!" she whispered in a tone that irritated him. He stamped his foot.

"This is awful!" he exclaimed. "Words? Yes, words. Words mean something—yes—they do—for all this ' . ernal affectation. They mean something to me—to everybody—to you. What the devil did you use to express those sentiments—sentiments—pah!—which made you forget me, duty, shame!" . . . . He foamed at the mouth while she stared at him, appalled by this sudden fury. "Did you two talk only with your eyes?" he spluttered savagely. She rose.

"I can't bear this," she said, trembling from head to foot. "I am going."

They stood facing one another for a moment.

"Not you," he said, with conscious roughness, and began to walk up and down the room. She remained very still with an air of listening anxiously to her own heart-beats, then sank down on the chair slowly, and sighed, as if giving up a task beyond her strength.

"You misunderstand everything I say," he began quietly, "but I prefer to think that—just now—you are not accountable for your actions." He stopped again before her. "Your mind is unhinged," he said, with unction. "To go now would be adding crime—yes, crime—to folly. I'll have no scandal in my life, no matter what's the cost. And why? You are sure to misunderstand me—but I'll tell you. As a matter of duty. Yes. But you're sure to misunderstand me—

recklessly. Women always do—they are too—too narrow-minded."

He waited for a while, but she made no sound, didn't even look at him; he felt uneasy, painfully uneasy, like a man who suspects he is unreasonably mistrusted. To combat that exasperating sensation he recommenced talking very fast. The sound of his words excited his thoughts, and in the play of darting thoughts he had glimpses now and then of the inexpugnable rock of his convictions, towering in solitary grandeur above the unprofitable waste of errors and passions.

"For it is self-evident," he went on with anxious vivacity, "it is self-evident that, on the highest ground we haven't the right—no, we haven't the right to intrude our miseries upon those who—who naturally expect better things from us. Every one wishes his own life and the life around him to be beautiful and pure. Now, a scandal amongst people of our position is disastrous for the morality—a fatal influence—don't you see—upon the general tone of the class—very important—the most important, I verily believe, in—in the community. I feel this—profoundly. This is the broad view. In time you'll give me . . . when you become again the woman I loved—and trusted. . . ."

He stopped short, as though unexpectedly suffocated, then in a completely changed voice said, "For I did love and trust you"—and again was silent for a moment. She put her handkerchief to her eyes.

"You'll give me credit for—for—my motives. It's mainly loyalty to—to the larger conditions of our life—where you—you! of all women—failed. One doesn't usually talk like this—of course—but in this case you'll admit . . . And consider—the innocent suffer with

the guilty. The world is pitiless in its judgments.
Unfortunately there are always those in it who are only
too eager to misunderstand. Before you and before
my conscience I am guiltless, but any—any disclosure
would impair my usefulness in the sphere—in the
larger sphere in which I hope soon to . . . I
believe you fully shared my views in that matter—I
don't want to say any more . . . on—on that
point—but, believe me, true unselfishness is to bear
one's burdens in—in silence. The ideal must—must
be preserved—for others, at least. It's clear as daylight.
If I've a—a loathsome sore, to gratuitously display it
would be abominable—abominable! And often in
life—in the highest conception of life—outspokenness in
certain circumstances is nothing less than criminal.
Temptation, you know, excuses no one. There is no
such thing really if one looks steadily to one's welfare—
which is grounded in duty. But there are the weak."
. . . His tone became ferocious for an instant . . .
"And there are the fools and the envious—especially for
people in our position. I am guiltless of this terrible—
terrible . . . estrangement; but if there has been
nothing irreparable." . . . Something gloomy, like
a deep shadow passed over his face. . . . "Nothing irreparable—you see even now I am ready to trust
you implicitly—then our duty is clear."

He looked down. A change came over his expression
and straightway from the outward impetus of his
loquacity he passed into the dull contemplation of all
the appeasing truths that, not without some wonder,
he had so recently been able to discover within himself.
During this profound and soothing communion with his
innermost beliefs he remained staring at the carpet,
with a portentously solemn face and with a dull vacuity
of eyes that seemed to gaze into the blankness of an

*N

empty hole. Then, without stirring in the least, he continued:

"Yes. Perfectly clear. I've been tried to the utmost, and I can't pretend that, for a time, the old feelings—the old feelings are not. . . ." He sighed. . . . "But I forgive you. . . ."

She made a slight movement without uncovering her eyes. In his profound scrutiny of the carpet he noticed nothing. And there was silence, silence within and silence without, as though his words had stilled the beat and tremor of all the surrounding life, and the house had stood alone—the only dwelling upon a deserted earth.

He lifted his head and repeated solemnly:

"I forgive you . . . from a sense of duty—and in the hope . . ."

He heard a laugh, and it not only interrupted his words but also destroyed the peace of his self-absorption with the vile pain of a reality intruding upon the beauty of a dream. He couldn't understand whence the sound came. He could see, foreshortened, the tear-stained, dolorous face of the woman stretched out, and with her head thrown over the back of the seat. He thought the piercing noise was a delusion. But another shrill peal followed by a deep sob and succeeded by another shriek of mirth positively seemed to tear him out from where he stood. He bounded to the door. It was closed. He turned the key and thought: that's no good. . . . "Stop this!" he cried, and perceived with alarm that he could hardly hear his own voice in the midst of her screaming. He darted back with the idea of stifling that unbearable noise with his hands, but stood still distracted, finding himself as unable to touch her as though she had been on fire. He shouted, "Enough of this!" like men shout in the tumult of a riot, with a red face and starting eyes; then, as if swept away before another burst of laughter, he disappeared in a flash out of three looking-glasses, vanished suddenly from before her. For a time the woman gasped and laughed at no one in the luminous stillness of the empty room.

He reappeared, striding at her, and with a tumbler of water in his hand. He stammered: "Hysterics— Stop—They will hear—Drink this." She laughed at the ceiling. "Stop this!" he cried. "Ah!"

He flung the water in her face, putting into the action all the secret brutality of his spite, yet still felt that it would have been perfectly excusable—in any one—to send the tumbler after the water. He restrained himself, but at the same time was so convinced nothing could stop the horror of those mad shrieks that, when the first sensation of relief came, it did not even occur to him to doubt the impression of having become suddenly deaf. When, next moment, he became sure that she was sitting up, and really very quiet, it was as though everything—men, things, sensations, had come to a rest. He was prepared to be grateful. He could not take his eyes off her, fearing, yet unwilling to admit, the possibility of her beginning again; for, the experience, however contemptuously he tried to think of it, had left the bewilderment of a mysterious terror. Her face was streaming with water and tears; there was a wisp of hair on her forehead, another stuck to her cheek; her hat was on one side, undecorously tilted; her soaked veil resembled a sordid rag festooning her forehead. There was an utter unreserve in her aspect, an abandonment of safeguards, that ugliness of truth which can only be kept out of daily life by unremitting care for appearances. He did not know why, looking at her, he thought suddenly of to-morrow, and why the thought called out a deep feeling of unutterable, discouraged

weariness—a fear of facing the succession of days.
To-morrow! It was as far as yesterday. Ages elapsed
between sunrises—sometimes. He scanned her features like one looks at a forgotten country. They were
not distorted—he recognized landmarks, so to speak;
but it was only a resemblance that he could see, not the
woman of yesterday—or was it, perhaps, more than the
woman of yesterday? Who could tell? Was it something new? A new expression—or a new shade of
expression? or something deep—an old truth unveiled,
a fundamental and hidden truth—some unnecessary,
accursed certitude? He became aware that he was
trembling very much, that he had an empty tumbler in
his hand—that time was passing. Still looking at her
with lingering mistrust he reached towards the table to
put the glass down and was startled to feel it apparently
go through the wood. He had missed the edge. The
surprise, the slight jingling noise of the accident annoyed him beyond expression. He turned to her
irritated.

"What's the meaning of this?" he asked, grimly.
She passed her hand over her face and made an
attempt to get up.

"You're not going to be absurd again," he said.
"'Pon my soul, I did not know you could forget yourself to that extent." He didn't try to conceal his
physical disgust, because he believed it to be a purely
moral reprobation of every unreserve, of anything in
the nature of a scene. "I assure you—it was revolt-
ing," he went on. He stared for a moment at her.
"Positively degrading," he added with insistence.

She stood up quickly as if moved by a spring
and tottered. He started forward instinctively. She
caught hold of the back of the chair and steadied herself. This arrested him, and they faced each other

wide-eyed, uncertain, and yet coming back slowly to the reality of things with relief and wonder, as though just awakened after tossing through a long night of fevered dreams.

"Pray, don't begin again," he said, hurriedly, seeing her open her lips. "I deserve some little consideration —and such unaccountable behaviour is painful to me. I expect better things. . . . I have the right. . . ."

She pressed both her hands to her temples.

"Oh, nonsense!" he said, sharply. "You are perfectly capable of coming down to dinner. No one should even suspect; not even the servants. No one! No one! . . . I am sure you can."

She dropped her arms; her face twitched. She looked straight into his eyes and seemed incapable of pronouncing a word. He frowned at her.

"I—wish—it," he said, tyrannically. "For your own sake also. . . ." He meant to carry that point without any pity. Why didn't she speak? He feared passive resistance. She must. . . . Make her come. His frown deepened, and he began to think of some effectual violence, when most unexpectedly she said in a firm voice, "Yes, I can," and clutched the chair-back again. He was relieved, and all at once her attitude ceased to interest him. The important thing was that their life would begin again with an every-day act—with something that could not be misunderstood, that, thank God, had no moral meaning, no perplexity— and yet was symbolic of their uninterrupted communion in the past—in all the future. That morning, at that table, they had breakfast together; and now they would dine. It was all over! What had happened between could be forgotten—must be forgotten, like things that can only happen once—death for instance.

"I will wait for you," he said, going to the door. He had some difficulty with it, for he did not remember he had turned the key. He hated that delay, and his checked impatience to be gone out of the room made him feel quite ill as, with the consciousness of her presence behind his back, he fumbled at the lock. He managed it at last; then in the doorway he glanced over his shoulder to say, "It's rather late—you know—" and saw her standing where he had left her, with a face white as alabaster and perfectly still, like a woman in a trance.

He was afraid she would keep him waiting, but without any breathing time, he hardly knew how, he found himself sitting at table with her. He had made up his mind to eat, to talk, to be natural. It seemed to him necessary that deception should begin at home. The servants must not know—must not suspect. This intense desire of secrecy; of secrecy dark, destroying, profound, discreet like a grave, possessed him with the strength of a hallucination—seemed to spread itself to inanimate objects that had been the daily companions of his life, affected with a taint of enmity every single thing within the faithful walls that would stand forever between the shamelessness of facts and the indignation of mankind. Even when—as it happened once or twice—both the servants left the room together he remained carefully natural, industriously hungry, laboriously at his ease, as though he had wanted to cheat the black oak sideboard, the heavy curtains, the stiff-backed chairs into the belief of an unstained happiness. He was mistrustful of his wife's self-control, unwilling to look at her and reluctant to speak, for it seemed to him inconceivable that she should not betray herself by the slightest movement, by the very first word spoken. Then he thought the silence in the room was becoming dangerous, and so excessive as to produce the effect of an intolerable uproar. He wanted to end it, as one is anxious to interrupt an indiscreet confession; but with the memory of that laugh upstairs he dared not give her an occasion to open her lips. Presently he heard her voice pronouncing in a calm tone some unimportant remark. He detached his eyes from the centre of his plate and felt excited as if on the point of looking at a wonder. And nothing could be more wonderful than her composure. He was looking at the candid eyes, at the pure brow, at what he had seen every evening for years in that place; he listened to the voice that for five years he had heard every day. Perhaps she was a little pale—but a healthy pallor had always been for him one of her chief attractions. Perhaps her face was rigidly set—but that marmoreal impassiveness, that magnificent stolidity, as of a wonderful statue by some great sculptor working under the curse of the gods; that imposing, unthinking still-ness of her features, had till then mirrored for him the tranquil dignity of a soul of which he had thought himself—as a matter of course—the inexpugnable possessor. Those were the outward signs of her difference from the ignoble herd that feels, suffers, fails, errs—but has no distinct value in the world except as a moral contrast to the prosperity of the elect. He had been proud of her appearance. It had the perfectly proper frankness of perfection—and now he was shocked to see it unchanged. She looked like this, spoke like this, exactly like this, a year ago, a month ago —only yesterday when she. . . . What went on within made no difference. What did she think? What meant the pallor, the placid face, the candid brow, the pure eyes? What did she think during all these years? What did she think yesterday—to-day; what would she think to-morrow? He must find out. . . . And yet how could he get to know? She had been false to him, to that man, to herself; she was ready to be false—for him. Always false. She looked lies, breathed lies, lived lies—would tell lies—always— to the end of life! And he would never know what she meant. Never! Never! No one could. Impossible to know.

He dropped his knife and fork, brusquely, as though by the virtue of a sudden illumination he had been made aware of poison in his plate, and became positive in his mind that he could never swallow another morsel of food as long as he lived. The dinner went on in a room that had been steadily growing, from some cause, hotter than a furnace. He had to drink. He drank time after time, and, at last, recollecting himself, was frightened at the quantity, till he perceived that what he had been drinking was water—out of two different wine glasses; and the discovered unconsciousness of his actions affected him painfully. He was disturbed to find himself in such an unhealthy state of mind. Excess of feeling—excess of feeling; and it was part of his creed that any excess of feeling was unhealthy—morally unprofitable; a taint on practical manhood. Her fault. Entirely her fault. Her sinful self-forgetfulness was contagious. It made him think thoughts he had never had before; thoughts disintegrating, tormenting, sapping to the very core of life—like mortal disease; thoughts that bred the fear of air, of sunshine, of men— like the whispered news of a pestilence.

The maids served without noise; and to avoid looking at his wife and looking within himself, he followed with his eyes first one and then the other without being able to distinguish between them. They moved silently

about, without one being able to see by what means, for
their skirts touched the carpet all round; they glided
here and there, receded, approached, rigid in black and
white, with precise gestures, and no life in their faces,
like a pair of marionettes in mourning; and their air of
wooden unconcern struck him as unnatural, suspicious,
irremediably hostile. That such people's feelings or
judgment could affect one in any way, had never
occurred to him before. He understood they had no
prospects, no principles—no refinement and no power.
But now he had become so debased that he could not
even attempt to disguise from himself his yearning to
know the secret thoughts of his servants. Several
times he looked up covertly at the faces of those girls.
Impossible to know. They changed his plates and
utterly ignored his existence. What impenetrable
duplicity. Women—nothing but women round him.
Impossible to know. He experienced that heart-
probing, fiery sense of dangerous loneliness, which
sometimes assails the courage of a solitary adventurer in
an unexplored country. The sight of a man's face—he
felt—of any man's face, would have been a profound
relief. One would know then—something—could understand. . . . He decided he must have men
servants. He would engage a butler as soon as possible.
And then the end of that dinner—which had seemed to
have been going on for hours—the end •came, taking
him violently by surprise, as though he had expected in
the natural course of events to sit at that table for ever
and ever.

But upstairs in the drawing-room he became the
victim of a restless fate, that would, on no account,
permit him to sit down. She had sunk on a low easy-
chair, and taking up from a small table at her elbow a
fan with ivory leaves, shaded her face from the fire.

The coals glowed without a flame; and upon the red glow
the vertical bars of the grate stood out at her feet,
black and curved, like the charred ribs of a consumed
sacrifice.   Far off, a lamp perched on a slim brass rod,
burned under a wide shade of crimson silk: the centre,
within the shadows of the large room, of a fiery twilight
that had in the warm quality of its tint something
delicate, refined and infernal.   His soft footfalls and the
subdued beat of the clock on the high mantel-piece
answered each other regularly—as if time and himself,
engaged in a measured contest, had been pacing together through the infernal delicacy of twilight towards
a mysterious goal.

He walked from one end of the room to the other
without a pause, like a traveller who, at night, hastens
doggedly upon an interminable journey.   Now and
then he glanced at her.   Impossible to know.   The
gross precision of that thought expressed to his practical
mind something illimitable and infinitely profound, the
all-embracing subtlety of a feeling, the eternal origin of
his pain.   This woman had accepted him, had abandoned him—had returned to him.   And of all this he
would never know the truth.   Never.   Not till death—
not after—not on judgment day when all shall be
disclosed, thoughts and deeds, rewards and punish-
ments, but the secret of hearts alone shall return, forever unknown, to the Inscrutable Creator of good and
evil, to the Master of doubts and impulses.

He stood still to look at her.   Thrown back and with
her face turned away from him, she did not stir—as if
asleep.   What did she think?   What did she feel?   And
in the presence of her perfect stillness, in the breathless
silence, he felt himself insignificant and powerless before her, like a prisoner in chains.   The fury of his
impotence called out sinister images, that faculty of

tormenting vision, which in a moment of anguishing sense of wrong induces a man to mutter threats or make a menacing gesture in the solitude of an empty room. But the gust of passion passed at once, left him trembling a little, with the wondering, reflective fear of a man who has paused on the very verge of suicide. The serenity of truth and the peace of death can be only secured through a largeness of contempt embracing all the profitable servitudes of life. He found he did not want to know. Better not. It was all over. It was as if it hadn't been. And it was very necessary for both of them, it was morally right, that nobody should know.

He spoke suddenly, as if concluding a discussion.

"The best thing for us is to forget all this."

She started a little and shut the fan with a click.

"Yes, forgive—and forget," he repeated, as if to himself.

"I'll never forget," she said in a vibrating voice. "And I'll never forgive myself. . . ."

"But I, who have nothing to reproach myself . . ." he began, making a step towards her. She jumped up.

"I did not come back for your forgiveness," she exclaimed, passionately, as if clamouring against an unjust aspersion.

He only said "oh!" and became silent. He could not understand this unprovoked aggressiveness of her attitude, and certainly was very far from thinking that an unpremeditated hint of something resembling emotion in the tone of his last words had caused that uncontrollable burst of sincerity. It completed his bewilderment, but he was not at all angry now. He was as if benumbed by the fascination of the incomprehensible. She stood before him, tall and indistinct,

like a black phantom in the red twilight. At last
poignantly uncertain as to what would happen if he
opened his lips, he muttered:

"But if my love is strong enough . . ." and
hesitated.

He heard something snap loudly in the fiery stillness.
She had broken her fan. Two thin pieces of ivory fell,
one after another, without a sound, on the thick carpet,
and instinctively he stooped to pick them up. While
he groped at her feet it occurred to him that the woman
there had in her hands an indispensable gift which nothing else on earth could give; and when he stood up he
was penetrated by an irresistible belief in an enigma, by
the conviction that within his reach and passing away
from him was the very secret of existence—its certitude,
immaterial and precious! She moved to the door, and
he followed at her elbow, casting about for a magic word
that would make the enigma clear, that would compel
the surrender of the gift. And there is no such word!
The enigma is only made clear by sacrifice, and the
gift of heaven is in the hands of every man. But they
had lived in a world that abhors enigmas, and cares for
no gifts but such as can be obtained in the street. She
was nearing the door. He said hurriedly:

" 'Pon my word, I loved you—I love you now."

She stopped for an almost imperceptible moment to
give him an indignant glance, and then moved on.
That feminine penetration—so clever and so tainted by
the eternal instinct of self-defence, so ready to see an
obvious evil in everything it cannot understand—filled
her with bitter resentment against both the men who
could offer to the spiritual and tragic strife of her feelings nothing but the coarseness of their abominable
materialism. In her anger against her own ineffectual
self-deception she found hate enough for them both.

What did they want? What more did this one want? And as her husband faced her again, with his hand on the door-handle, she asked herself whether he was unpardonably stupid, or simply ignoble.

She said nervously, and very fast:

"You are deceiving yourself. You never loved me. You wanted a wife—some woman—any woman that would think, speak, and behave in a certain way—in a way you approved. You loved yourself."

"You won't believe me?" he asked, slowly.

"If I had believed you loved me," she began, passionately, then drew in a long breath; and during that pause he heard the steady beat of blood in his ears. "If I had believed it . . . . I would never have come back," she finished, recklessly.

He stood looking down as though he had not heard. She waited. After a moment he opened the door, and, on the landing, the sightless woman of marble appeared, draped to the chin, thrusting blindly at them a cluster of lights.

He seemed to have forgotten himself in a meditation so deep that on the point of going out she stopped to look at him in surprise. While she had been speaking he had wandered on the track of the enigma, out of the world of senses into the region of feeling. What did it matter what she had done, what she had said, if through the pain of her acts and words he had obtained the word of the enigma! There can be no life without faith and love—faith in a human heart, love of a human being! That touch of grace, whose help once in life is the privilege of the most undeserving, flung open for him the portals of beyond, and in contemplating there the certitude immaterial and precious he forgot all the meaningless accidents of existence: the bliss of getting, the delight of enjoying; all the protean and enticing

forms of the cupidity that rules a material world of
foolish joys, of contemptible sorrows.   Faith!—Love!—
the undoubting, clear faith in the truth of a soul—the
great tenderness, deep as the ocean, serene and eternal,
like the infinite peace of space above the short tempests
of the earth.   It was what he had wanted all his life—
but he understood it only then for the first time.   It
was through the pain of losing her that the knowledge
had come.   She had the gift!   She had the gift!   And
in all the world she was the only human being that
could surrender it to his immense desire.   He made a
step forward, putting his arms out, as if to take her to
his breast, and, lifting his head, was met by such a look
of blank consternation that his arms fell as though they
had been struck down by a blow.   She started away from
him, stumbled over the threshold, and once on the landing turned, swift and crouching.   The train of her
gown swished as it flew round her feet.   It was an un-
disguised panic.   She panted, showing her teeth, and
the hate of strength, the disdain of weakness, the eternal
preoccupation of sex came out like a toy demon out of
a box.

"This is odious," she screamed.

He did not stir; but her look, her agitated movements,
the sound of her voice were like a mist of facts thickening between him and the vision of love and faith.   It
vanished; and looking at that face triumphant and
scornful, at that white face, stealthy and unexpected,
as if discovered staring from an ambush, he was coming
back slowly to the world of senses.   His first clear
thought was: I am married to that woman; and the
next: she will give nothing but what I see.   He felt
the need not to see.   But the memory of the vision,
the memory that abides forever within the seer made
him say to her with the naïve austerity of a convert

awed by the touch of a new creed, "You haven't the gift." He turned his back on her, leaving her completely mystified. And she went upstairs slowly, struggling with a distasteful suspicion of having been confronted by something more subtle than herself— more profound than the misunderstood and tragic contest of her feelings.

He shut the door of the drawing-room and moved at hazard, alone amongst the heavy shadows and in the fiery twilight as of an elegant place of perdition. She hadn't the gift—no one had. . . . He stepped on a book that had fallen off one of the crowded little tables. He picked up the slender volume, and holding it, approached the crimson-shaded lamp. The fiery tint deepened of the cover, and contorted gold letters sprawling all over it in an intricate maze, came out, gleaming redly. "Thorns and Arabesques." He read it twice, "Thorns and Ar . . . ." The other's book of verses. He dropped it at his feet, but did not feel the slightest pang of jealousy or indignation. What did he know? . . . What? . . . The mass of hot coals tumbled down in the grate, and he turned to look at them . . . Ah! That one was ready to give up everything he had for that woman —who did not come—who had not the faith, the love, the courage to come. What did that man expect, what did he hope, what did he want? The woman—or the certitude immaterial and precious! The first unselfish thought he had ever given to any human being was for that man who had tried to do him a terrible wrong. He was not angry. He was saddened by an impersonal sorrow, by a vast melancholy as of all mankind longing for what cannot be attained. He felt his fellowship with every man—even with that man—especially with that man. What did he think now? Had he ceased to wait—and hope? Would he ever cease to wait and hope? Would he understand that the woman, who had no courage, had not the gift—had not the gift!

The clock began to strike, and the deep-toned vibration filled the room as though with the sound of an enormous bell tolling far away. He counted the strokes. Twelve. Another day had begun. To-morrow had come; the mysterious and lying to-morrow that lures men, disdainful of love and faith, on and on through the poignant futilities of life to the fitting reward of a grave. He counted the strokes, and gazing at the grate seemed to wait for more. Then, as if called out, left the room, walking firmly.

When outside he heard footsteps in the hall and stood still. A bolt was shot—then another. They were locking up—shutting out his desire and his deception from the indignant criticism of a world full of noble gifts for those who proclaim themselves without stain and without reproach. He was safe; and on all sides of his dwelling servile fears and servile hopes slept, dreaming of success, behind the severe discretion of doors as impenetrable to the truth within as the granite of tombstones. A lock snapped—a short chain rattled. Nobody shall know!

Why was this assurance of safety heavier than a burden of fear, and why the day that began presented itself obstinately like the last day of all—like a to-day without a to-morrow? Yet nothing was changed, for nobody would know; and all would go on as before—the getting, the enjoying, the blessing of hunger that is appeased every day; the noble incentives of unappeasable ambitions. All—all the blessings of life. All—but the certitude immaterial and precious—the certitude of love and faith. He believed the shadow of it had been with him as long as he could remember; that invisible presence had ruled his life. And now the shadow had appeared and faded he could not extinguish his longing for the truth of its substance. His desire of it was naïve; it was masterful like the material aspirations that are the groundwork of existence, but, unlike these, it was unconquerable. It was the subtle despotism of an idea that suffers no rivals, that is lonely, inconsolable, and dangerous. He went slowly up the stairs. Nobody shall know. The days would go on and he would go far—very far. If the idea could not be mastered, fortune could be, man could be—the whole world. He was dazzled by the greatness of the prospect; the brutality of a practical instinct shouted to him that only that which could be had was worth having. He lingered on the steps. The lights were out in the hall, and a small yellow flame flitted about down there. He felt a sudden contempt for himself which braced him up. He went on, but at the door of their room and with his arm advanced to open it, he faltered. On the flight of stairs below the head of the girl who had been locking up appeared. His arm fell. He thought, "I'll wait till she is gone"—and stepped back within the perpendicular folds of a *portière*.

He saw her come up gradually, as if ascending from a well. At every step the feeble flame of the candle swayed before her tired, young face, and the darkness of the hall seemed to cling to her black skirt, followed her, rising like a silent flood, as though the great night of the world had broken through the discreet reserve of walls, of closed doors, of curtained windows. It rose over the steps, it leaped up the walls like an angry wave, it flowed over the blue skies, over the yellow sands, over the sunshine of landscapes, and over the pretty pathos of ragged innocence and of meek starva-

tion. It swallowed up the delicious idyll in a boat and
the mutilated immortality of famous bas-reliefs. It
flowed from outside—it rose higher, in a destructive silence. And, above it, the woman of marble, composed
and blind on the high pedestal, seemed to ward off
the devouring night with a cluster of lights.

He watched the rising tide of impenetrable gloom
with impatience, as if anxious for the coming of a
darkness black enough to conceal a shameful surrender.
It came nearer. The cluster of lights went out. The
girl ascended facing him. Behind her the shadow of a
colossal woman danced lightly on the wall. He held
his breath while she passed by, noiseless and with heavy
eyelids. And on her track the flowing tide of a tene-
brous sea filled the house, seemed to swirl about his feet,
and rising unchecked, closed silently above his head.

The time had come but he did not open the door.
All was still; and instead of surrendering to the reasonable exigencies of life he stepped out, with a rebelling
heart, into the darkness of the house. It was the abode
of an impenetrable night; as though indeed the last
day had come and gone, leaving him alone in a darkness
that has no to-morrow. And looming vaguely below
the woman of marble, livid and still like a patient
phantom, held out in the night a cluster of extinguished
lights.

His obedient thought traced for him the image of an
uninterrupted life, the dignity and the advantages of
an uninterrupted success; while his rebellious heart
beat violently within his breast, as if maddened by the
desire of a certitude immaterial and precious—the
certitude of love and faith. What of the night within
his dwelling if outside he could find the sunshine in
which men sow, in which men reap! Nobody would
know. The days, the years would pass, and . . . .

He remembered that he had loved her. The years
would pass . . . And then he thought of her as
we think of the dead—in a tender immensity of regret,
in a passionate longing for the return of idealized per-
fections. He had loved her—he had loved her—and
he never knew the truth . . . The years would
pass in the anguish of doubt . . . He remembered
her smile, her eyes, her voice, her silence, as though he
had lost her forever. The years would pass and he
would always mistrust her smile, suspect her eyes; he
would always misbelieve her voice, he would never
have faith in her silence. She had no gift—she had no
gift! What was she? Who was she? . . . The
years would pass; the memory of this hour would grow
faint—and she would share the material serenity of an
unblemished life. She had no love and no faith for any
one. To give her your thought, your belief, was like
whispering your confession over the edge of the world.
Nothing came back—not even an echo.

In the pain of that thought was born his conscience;
not that fear of remorse which grows slowly, and slowly
decays amongst the complicated facts of life, but a
Divine wisdom springing full-grown, armed and severe
out of a tried heart, to combat the secret baseness of
motives. It came to him in a flash that morality is
not a method of happiness. The revelation was terrible. He saw at once that nothing of what he knew
mattered in the least. The acts of men and women,
success, humiliation, dignity, failure—nothing mattered. It was not a question of more or less pain, of
this joy, of that sorrow. It was a question of truth or
falsehood—it was a question of life or death.

He stood in the revealing night—in the darkness that
tries the hearts, in the night useless for the work of
men, but in which their gaze, undazzled by the sun-

shine of covetous days, wanders sometimes as far as the stars. The perfect stillness around him had something solemn in it, but he felt it was the lying solemnity of a temple devoted to the rites of a debasing persuasion. The silence within the discreet walls was eloquent of safety but it appeared to him exciting and sinister, like the discretion of a profitable infamy; it was the prudent peace of a den of coiners—of a house of ill-fame! The years would pass—and nobody would know. Never! Not till death—not after . . .

"Never!" he said aloud to the revealing night.

And he hesitated. The secret of hearts, too terrible for the timid eyes of men, shall return, veiled forever, to the Inscrutable Creator of good and evil, to the Master of doubts and impulses. His conscience was born—he heard its voice, and he hesitated, ignoring the strength within, the fateful power, the secret of his heart! It was an awful sacrifice to cast all one's life into the flame of a new belief. He wanted help against himself, against the cruel decree of salvation. The need of tacit complicity, where it had never failed him, the habit of years affirmed itself. Perhaps she would help . . . He flung the door open and rushed in like a fugitive.

He was in the middle of the room before he could see anything but the dazzling brilliance of the light; and then, as if detached and floating in it on the level of his eyes, appeared the head of a woman. She had jumped up when he burst into the room.

For a moment they contemplated each other as if struck dumb with amazement. Her hair streaming on her shoulders glinted like burnished gold. He looked into the unfathomable candour of her eyes. Nothing within—nothing—nothing.

He stammered distractedly.

"I want . . . I want . . . to . . . to . . . know . . . ."

On the candid light of the eyes flitted shadows; shadows of doubt, of suspicion, the ready suspicion of an unquenchable antagonism, the pitiless mistrust of an eternal instinct of defence; the hate, the profound, frightened hate of an incomprehensible—of an abominable emotion intruding its coarse materialism upon the spiritual and tragic contest of her feelings.

"Alvan . . . I won't bear this . . . ." She began to pant suddenly, "I've a right—a right to—to—myself . . . ."

He lifted one arm, and appeared so menacing that she stopped in a fright and shrank back a little.

He stood with uplifted hand . . . The years would pass—and he would have to live with that unfathomable candour where flit shadows of suspicions and hate . . . The years would pass—and he would never know—never trust . . . The years would pass without faith and love. . . .

"Can you stand it?" he shouted, as though she could have heard all his thoughts.

He looked menacing. She thought of violence, of danger—and, just for an instant, she doubted whether there were splendours enough on earth to pay the price of such a brutal experience. He cried again:

"Can you stand it?" and glared as if insane. Her eyes blazed, too. She could not hear the appalling clamour of his thoughts. She suspected in him a sudden regret, a fresh fit of jealousy, a dishonest desire of evasion. She shouted back angrily—

"Yes!"

He was shaken where he stood as if by a struggle to break out of invisible bonds. She trembled from head to foot.

"Well, I can't!" He flung both his arms out, as if to push her away, and strode from the room. The door swung to with a click. She made three quick steps towards it and stood still, looking at the white and gold panels. No sound came from beyond, not a whisper, not a sigh; not even a footstep was heard outside on the thick carpet. It was as though no sooner gone he had suddenly expired—as though he had died there and his body had vanished on the instant together with his soul. She listened, with parted lips and irresolute eyes. Then below, far below her, as if in the entrails of the earth, a door slammed heavily; and the quiet house vibrated to it from roof to foundations, more than to a clap of thunder.

He never returned.

THE LAGOON

THE white man, leaning with both arms over the roof of the little house in the stern of the boat, said to the steersman—

"We will pass the night in Arsat's clearing. It is late."

The Malay only grunted, and went on looking fixedly at the river. The white man rested his chin on his crossed arms and gazed at the wake of the boat. At the end of the straight avenue of forests cut by the intense glitter of the river, the sun appeared unclouded and dazzling, poised low over the water that shone smoothly like a band of metal. The forests, sombre and dull, stood motionless and silent on each side of the broad stream. At the foot of big, towering trees, trunkless nipa palms rose from the mud of the bank, in bunches of leaves enormous and heavy, that hung unstirring over the brown swirl of eddies. In the stillness of the air every tree, every leaf, every bough, every tendril of creeper and every petal of minute blossoms seemed to have been bewitched into an immobility perfect and final. Nothing moved on the river but the eight paddles that rose flashing regularly, dipped together with a single splash; while the steersman swept right and left with a periodic and sudden flourish of his blade describing a glinting semicircle above his head. The churned-up water frothed alongside with a confused murmur. And the white man's canoe, advancing upstream in the short-lived disturbance of its own making, seemed to enter the portals of a land from which the very memory of motion had forever departed.

The white man, turning his back upon the setting sun, looked along the empty and broad expanse of the sea-reach. For the last three miles of its course the wandering, hesitating river, as if enticed irresistibly by the freedom of an open horizon, flows straight into the sea, flows straight to the east—to the east that harbours both light and darkness. Astern of the boat the repeated call of some bird, a cry discordant and feeble, skipped along over the smooth water and lost itself, before it could reach the other shore, in the breathless silence of the world.

The steersman dug his paddle into the stream, and held hard with stiffened arms, his body thrown forward. The water gurgled aloud; and suddenly the long straight reach seemed to pivot on its centre, the forests swung in a semicircle, and the slanting beams of sunset touched the broadside of the canoe with a fiery glow, throwing the slender and distorted shadows of its crew upon the streaked glitter of the river. The white man turned to look ahead. The course of the boat had been altered at right-angles to the stream, and the carved dragon-head of its prow was pointing now at a gap in the fringing bushes of the bank. It glided through, brushing the overhanging twigs, and disappeared from the river like some slim and amphibious creature leaving the water for its lair in the forests.

The narrow creek was like a ditch: tortuous, fabulously deep; filled with gloom under the thin strip of pure and shining blue of the heaven. Immense trees soared up, invisible behind the festooned draperies of creepers. Here and there, near the glistening blackness of the water, a twisted root of some tall tree showed amongst the tracery of small ferns, black and dull, writhing and motionless, like an arrested snake. The short words of the paddlers reverberated loudly between the thick and sombre walls of vegetation. Darkness oozed out from between the trees, through the tangled maze of the creepers, from behind the great fantastic and unstirring leaves; the darkness, mysterious and invincible; the darkness scented and poisonous of impenetrable forests.

The men poled in the shoaling water. The creek broadened, opening out into a wide sweep of a stagnant lagoon. The forests receded from the marshy bank, leaving a level strip of bright green, reedy grass to frame the reflected blueness of the sky. A fleecy pink cloud drifted high above, trailing the delicate colouring of its image under the floating leaves and the silvery blossoms of the lotus. A little house, perched on high piles, appeared black in the distance. Near it, two tall nibong palms, that seemed to have come out of the forests in the background, leaned slightly over the ragged roof, with a suggestion of sad tenderness and care in the droop of their leafy and soaring heads.

The steersman, pointing with his paddle, said, "Arsat is there. I see his canoe fast between the piles."

The polers ran along the sides of the boat glancing over their shoulders at the end of the day's journey. They would have preferred to spend the night somewhere else than on this lagoon of weird aspect and ghostly reputation. Moreover, they disliked Arsat, first as a stranger, and also because he who repairs a ruined house, and dwells in it, proclaims that he is not afraid to live amongst the spirits that haunt the places abandoned by mankind. Such a man can disturb the course of fate by glances or words; while his familiar ghosts are not easy to propitiate by casual wayfarers

o

upon whom they long to wreak the malice of their human master. White men care not for such things, being unbelievers and in league with the Father of Evil, who leads them unharmed through the invisible dangers of this world. To the warnings of the righteous they oppose an offensive pretence of disbelief. What is there to be done?

So they thought, throwing their weight on the end of their long poles. The big canoe glided on swiftly, noiselessly, and smoothly, towards Arsat's clearing, till, in a great rattling of poles thrown down, and the loud murmurs of "Allah be praised!" it came with a gentle knock against the crooked piles below the house.

The boatmen with uplifted faces shouted discordantly, "Arsat! O Arsat!" Nobody came. The white man began to climb the rude ladder giving access to the bamboo platform before the house. The juragan of the boat said sulkily, "We will cook in the sampan, and sleep on the water."

"Pass my blankets and the basket," said the white man, curtly.

He knelt on the edge of the platform to receive the bundle. Then the boat shoved off, and the white man, standing up, confronted Arsat, who had come out through the low door of his hut. He was a man young, powerful, with broad chest and muscular arms. He had nothing on but his sarong. His head was bare. His big, soft eyes stared eagerly at the white man, but his voice and demeanour were composed as he asked, without any words of greeting—

"Have you medicine, Tuan?"

"No," said the visitor in a startled tone. "No. Why? Is there sickness in the house?"

"Enter and see," replied Arsat, in the same calm manner, and turning short round, passed again through the small doorway. The white man, dropping his bundles, followed.

In the dim light of the dwelling he made out on a couch of bamboos a woman stretched on her back under a broad sheet of red cotton cloth. She lay still, as if dead; but her big eyes, wide open, glittered in the gloom, staring upwards at the slender rafters, motionless and unseeing. She was in a high fever, and evidently unconscious. Her cheeks were sunk slightly, her lips were partly open, and on the young face there was the ominous and fixed expression—the absorbed, contemplating expression of the unconscious who are going to die. The two men stood looking down at her in silence.

"Has she been long ill?" asked the traveller.

"I have not slept for five nights," answered the Malay, in a deliberate tone. "At first she heard voices calling her from the water and struggled against me who held her. But since the sun of to-day rose she hears nothing—she hears not me. She sees nothing. She sees not me—me!"

He remained silent for a minute, then asked softly—"Tuan, will she die?"

"I fear so," said the white man, sorrowfully. He had known Arsat years ago, in a far country in times of trouble and danger, when no friendship is to be despised. And since his Malay friend had come unexpectedly to dwell in the hut on the lagoon with a strange woman, he had slept many times there, in his journeys up and down the river. He liked the man who knew how to keep faith in council and how to fight without fear by the side of his white friend. He liked him—not so much perhaps as a man likes his favourite dog—but still he liked him well enough to help and ask no questions, to think sometimes vaguely and hazily in the midst of his own pursuits, about the lonely man and the long-haired woman with audacious face and triumphant eyes, who lived together hidden by the forests—alone and feared.

The white man came out of the hut in time to see the enormous conflagration of sunset put out by the swift and stealthy shadows that, rising like a black and impalpable vapour above the tree-tops, spread over the heaven, extinguishing the crimson glow of floating clouds and the red brilliance of departing daylight. In a few moments all the stars came out above the intense blackness of the earth and the great lagoon gleaming suddenly with reflected lights resembled an oval patch of night sky flung down into the hopeless and abysmal night of the wilderness. The white man had some supper out of the basket, then collecting a few sticks that lay about the platform, made up a small fire, not for warmth, but for the sake of the smoke, which would keep off the mosquitos. He wrapped himself in the blankets and sat with his back against the reed wall of the house, smoking thoughtfully.

Arsat came through the doorway with noiseless steps and squatted down by the fire. The white man moved his outstretched legs a little.

"She breathes," said Arsat in a low voice, anticipating the expected question. "She breathes and burns as if with a great fire. She speaks not; she hears not—and burns!"

He paused for a moment, then asked in a quiet, incurious tone—

"Tuan . . . will she die?"

The white man moved his shoulders uneasily and muttered in a hesitating manner—

"If such is her fate."

"No, Tuan," said Arsat, calmly. "If such is my fate.

I hear, I see, I wait. I remember . . . Tuan, do you remember the old days? Do you remember my brother?"

"Yes," said the white man. The Malay rose suddenly and went in. The other, sitting still outside, could hear the voice in the hut. Arsat said: "Hear me! Speak!" His words were succeeded by a complete silence. "O Diamelen!" he cried, suddenly. After that cry there was a deep sigh. Arsat came out and sank down again in his old place.

They sat in silence before the fire. There was no sound within the house, there was no sound near them; but far away on the lagoon they could hear the voices of the boatmen ringing fitful and distinct on the calm water. The fire in the bows of the sampan shone faintly in the distance with a hazy red glow. Then it died out. The voices ceased. The land and the water slept invisible, unstirring and mute. It was as though there had been nothing left in the world but the glitter of stars streaming, ceaseless and vain, through the black stillness of the night.

The white man gazed straight before him into the darkness with wide-open eyes. The fear and fascination, the inspiration and the wonder of death—of death near, unavoidable, and unseen, soothed the unrest of his race and stirred the most indistinct, the most intimate of his thoughts. The ever-ready suspicion of evil, the gnawing suspicion that lurks in our hearts, flowed out into the stillness round him—into the stillness profound and dumb, and made it appear untrustworthy and infamous, like the placid and impenetrable mask of an unjustifiable violence. In that fleeting and powerful disturbance of his being the earth enfolded in the starlight peace became a shadowy country of inhuman strife, a battle-field of phantoms terrible and charming, august or ignoble, struggling ardently for the possession of our helpless hearts. An unquiet and mysterious country of inextinguishable desires and fears.

A plaintive murmur rose in the night; a murmur saddening and startling, as if the great solitudes of surrounding woods had tried to whisper into his ear the wisdom of their immense and lofty indifference. Sounds hesitating and vague floated in the air round him, shaped themselves slowly into words; and at last flowed on gently in a murmuring stream of soft and monotonous sentences. He stirred like a man waking up and changed his position slightly. Arsat, motionless and shadowy, sitting with bowed head under the stars, was speaking in a low and dreamy tone—

". . . for where can we lay down the heaviness of our trouble but in a friend's heart? A man must speak of war and of love. You, Tuan, know what war is, and you have seen me in time of danger seek death as other men seek life? A writing may be lost; a lie may be written; but what the eye has seen is truth and remains in the mind!"

"I remember," said the white man, quietly. Arsat went on with mournful composure—

"Therefore I shall speak to you of love. Speak in the night. Speak before both night and love are gone—and the eye of day looks upon my sorrow and my shame; upon my blackened face; upon my burnt-up heart."

A sigh, short and faint, marked an almost imperceptible pause, and then his words flowed on, without a stir, without a gesture.

"After the time of trouble and war was over and you went away from my country in the pursuit of your desires, which we, men of the islands, cannot understand, I and my brother became again, as we had been before, the sword-bearers of the Ruler. You know we

were men of family, belonging to a ruling race, and more
fit than any to carry on our right shoulder the emblem
of power. And in the time of prosperity Si Dendring
showed us favour, as we, in time of sorrow, had showed
to him the faithfulness of our courage. It was a time
of peace. A time of deer-hunts and cock-fights; of idle
talks and foolish squabbles between men whose bellies
are full and weapons are rusty. But the sower watched
the young rice-shoots grow up without fear, and the
traders came and went, departed lean and returned fat
into the river of peace. They brought news, too.
Brought lies and truth mixed together, so that no man
knew when to rejoice and when to be sorry. We heard
from them about you also. They had seen you here
and had seen you there. And I was glad to hear, for I
remembered the stirring times, and I always remembered you, Tuan, till the time came when my eyes
could see nothing in the past, because they had looked
upon the one who is dying there—in the house."

He stopped to exclaim in an intense whisper, "O
Mara bahia! O Calamity!" then went on speaking a
little louder:

"There's no worse enemy and no better friend than a
brother, Tuan, for one brother knows another, and in
perfect knowledge is strength for good or evil. I loved
my brother. I went to him and told him that I could
see nothing but one face, hear nothing but one voice.
He told me: 'Open your heart so that she can see
what is in it—and wait. Patience is wisdom. Inchi
Midah may die or our Ruler may throw off his fear of a
woman!' . . . I waited! . . . You remember
the lady with the veiled face, Tuan, and the fear of our
Ruler before her cunning and temper. And if she
wanted her servant, what could I do? But I fed the
hunger of my heart on short glances and stealthy

words. I loitered on the path to the bath-houses in the
daytime, and when the sun had fallen behind the forest
I crept along the jasmine hedges of the women's courtyard. Unseeing, we spoke to one another through the
scent of flowers, through the veil of leaves, through the
blades of long grass that stood still before our lips; so
great was our prudence, so faint was the murmur of our
great longing. The time passed swiftly . . . and
there were whispers amongst women—and our enemies
watched—my brother was gloomy, and I began to
think of killing and of a fierce death. . . . We are
of a people who take what they want—like you whites.
There is a time when a man should forget loyalty and
respect. Might and authority are given to rulers, but
to all men is given love and strength and courage. My
brother said,'You shall take her from their midst. We
are two who are like one.' And I answered, 'Let it be
soon, for I find no warmth in sunlight that does not
shine upon her.' Our time came when the Ruler and all
the great people went to the mouth of the river to fish
by torchlight. There were hundreds of boats, and on
the white sand, between the water and the forests,
dwellings of leaves were built for the households of the
Rajahs. The smoke of cooking-fires was like a blue
mist of the evening, and many voices rang in it joyfully.
While they were making the boats ready to beat up the
fish, my brother came to me and said, 'To-night!' I
looked to my weapons, and when the time came our
canoe took its place in the circle of boats carrying the
torches. The lights blazed on the water, but behind the
boats there was darkness. When the shouting began
and the excitement made them like mad we dropped
out. The water swallowed our fire, and we floated back
to the shore that was dark with only here and there the
glimmer of embers. We could hear the talk of slave-

girls amongst the sheds. Then we found a place
deserted and silent. We waited there. She came.
She came running along the shore, rapid and leaving no
trace, like a leaf driven by the wind into the sea. My
brother said gloomily, 'Go and take her; carry her into
our boat.' I lifted her in my arms. She panted.
Her heart was beating against my breast. I said, 'I
take you from those people. You came to the cry of
my heart, but my arms take you into my boat against
the will of the great!' 'It is right,' said my brother.
'We are men who take what we want and can hold it
against many. We should have taken her in daylight.'
I said, 'Let us be off'; for since she was in my boat I
began to think of our Ruler's many men. 'Yes. Let
us be off,' said my brother. 'We are cast out and this
boat is our country now—and the sea is our refuge.'
He lingered with his foot on the shore, and I entreated
him to hasten, for I remembered the strokes of her
heart against my breast and thought that two men
cannot withstand a hundred. We left, paddling down-
stream close to the bank; and as we passed by the creek
where they were fishing, the great shouting had ceased,
but the murmur of voices was loud like the humming of
insects flying at noonday. The boats floated, clustered
together, in the red light of torches, under a black roof
of smoke; and men talked of their sport. Men that
boasted, and praised, and jeered—men that would
have been our friends in the morning, but on that night
were already our enemies. We paddled swiftly past.
We had no more friends in the country of our birth.
She sat in the middle of the canoe with covered face;
silent as she is now; unseeing as she is now—and I
had no regret at what I was leaving because I could
hear her breathing close to me—as I can hear her
now."

He paused, listened with his ear turned to the doorway, then shook his head and went on:

"My brother wanted to shout the cry of challenge—one cry only—to let the people know we were freeborn robbers who trusted our arms and the great sea. And again I begged him in the name of our love to be silent. Could I not hear her breathing close to me? I knew the pursuit would come quick enough. My brother loved me. He dipped his paddle without a splash. He only said, 'There is half a man in you now—the other half is in that woman. I can wait. When you are a whole man again, you will come back with me here to shout defiance. We are sons of the same mother.' I made no answer. All my strength and all my spirit were in my hands that held the paddle—for I longed to be with her in a safe place beyond the reach of men's anger and of women's spite. My love was so great, that I thought it could guide me to a country where death was unknown, if I could only escape from Inchi Midah's fury and from our Ruler's sword. We paddled with haste, breathing through our teeth. The blades bit deep into the smooth water. We passed out of the river; we flew in clear channels amongst the shallows. We skirted the black coast; we skirted the sand beaches where the sea speaks in whispers to the land; and the gleam of white sand flashed back past our boat, so swiftly she ran upon the water. We spoke not. Only once I said, 'Sleep, Diamelen, for soon you may want all your strength.' I heard the sweetness of her voice, but I never turned my head. The sun rose and still we went on. Water fell from my face like rain from a cloud. We flew in the light and heat. I never looked back, but I knew that my brother's eyes, behind me, were looking steadily ahead, for the boat went as straight as a bushman's dart, when it leaves the end of the sumpitan. There was no better paddler, no better steersman than my brother. Many times, together, we had won races in that canoe. But we never had put out our strength as we did then—then, when for the last time we paddled together! There was no braver or stronger man in our country than my brother. I could not spare the strength to turn my head and look at him, but every moment I heard the hiss of his breath getting louder behind me. Still he did not speak. The sun was high. The heat clung to my back like a flame of fire. My ribs were ready to burst, but I could no longer get enough air into my chest. And then I felt I must cry out with my last breath, 'Let us rest!' . . . 'Good!' he answered; and his voice was firm. He was strong. He was brave. He knew not fear and no fatigue . . . My brother!''

A murmur powerful and gentle, a murmur vast and faint; the murmur of trembling leaves, of stirring boughs, ran through the tangled depths of the forests, ran over the starry smoothness of the lagoon, and the water between the piles lapped the slimy timber once with a sudden splash. A breath of warm air touched the two men's faces and passed on with a mournful sound—a breath loud and short like an uneasy sigh of the dreaming earth.

Arsat went on in an even, low voice.

"We ran our canoe on the white beach of a little bay close to a long tongue of land that seemed to bar our road; a long wooded cape going far into the sea. My brother knew that place. Beyond the cape a river has its entrance, and through the jungle of that land there is a narrow path. We made a fire and cooked rice. Then we lay down to sleep on the soft sand in the shade of our canoe, while she watched. No sooner had I closed my eyes than I heard her cry of alarm. We leaped up. The sun was halfway down the sky already, and coming in sight in the opening of the bay we saw a prau manned by many paddlers. We knew it at once; it was one of our Rajah's praus. They were watching the shore, and saw us. They beat the gong, and turned the head of the prau into the bay. I felt my heart become weak within my breast. Diamelen sat on the sand and covered her face. There was no escape by sea. My brother laughed. He had the gun you had given him, Tuan, before you went away, but there was only a handful of powder. He spoke to me quickly: 'Run with her along the path. I shall keep them back, for they have no firearms, and landing in the face of a man with a gun is certain death for some. Run with her. On the other side of that wood there is a fisherman's house—and a canoe. When I have fired all the shots I will follow. I am a great runner, and before they can come up we shall be gone. I will hold out as long as I can, for she is but a woman—that can neither run nor fight, but she has your heart in her weak hands.' He dropped behind the canoe. The prau was coming. She and I ran, and as we rushed along the path I heard shots. My brother fired—once —twice—and the booming of the gong ceased. There was silence behind us. That neck of land is narrow. Before I heard my brother fire the third shot I saw the shelving shore, and I saw the water again; the mouth of a broad river. We crossed a grassy glade. We ran down to the water. I saw a low hut above the black mud, and a small canoe hauled up. I heard another shot behind me. I thought, 'That is his last charge.' We rushed down to the canoe; a man came running from the hut, but I leaped on him, and we rolled together in the mud. Then I got up, and he lay still at my feet. I don't know whether I had killed him or not. I and Diamelen pushed the canoe afloat. I heard yells behind me, and I saw my brother run across the glade. Many men were bounding after him, I took her in my arms and threw her into the boat, then leaped in myself. When I looked back I saw that my brother had fallen. He fell and was up again, but the men were closing round him. He shouted, 'I am coming!' The men were close to him. I looked. Many men. Then I looked at her. Tuan, I pushed the canoe! I pushed it into deep water. She was kneeling forward looking at me, and I said, 'Take your paddle,' while I struck the water with mine. Tuan, I heard him cry. I heard him cry my name twice; and I heard voices shouting, 'Kill! Strike!' I never turned back. I heard him calling my name again with a great shriek, as when life is going out together with the voice—and I never turned my head. My own name! . . . My brother! Three times he called—but I was not afraid of life. Was she not there in that canoe? And could I not with her find a country where death is forgotten—where death is unknown!"

The white man sat up. Arsat rose and stood, an indistinct and silent figure above the dying embers of the fire. Over the lagoon a mist drifting and low had crept, erasing slowly the glittering images of the stars. And now a great expanse of white vapour covered the land: it flowed cold and gray in the darkness, eddied in noiseless whirls round the tree-trunks and about the platform of the house, which seemed to float upon a restless and impalpable illusion of a sea. Only far away the tops of the trees stood outlined on the twinkle of heaven, like a sombre and forbidding shore—a coast deceptive, pitiless and black.

Arsat's voice vibrated loudly in the profound peace.

"I had her there! I had her! To get her I would have faced all mankind. But I had her—and——"

His words went out ringing into the empty distances. He paused, and seemed to listen to them dying away very far—beyond help and beyond recall. Then he said quietly—

"Tuan, I loved my brother."

A breath of wind made him shiver. High above his head, high above the silent sea of mist the drooping leaves of the palms rattled together with a mournful and expiring sound. The white man stretched his legs. His chin rested on his chest, and he murmured sadly without lifting his head—

"We all love our brothers."

Arsat burst out with an intense whispering violence—

"What did I care who died? I wanted peace in my own heart."

He seemed to hear a stir in the house—listened—then stepped in noiselessly. The white man stood up. A breeze was coming in fitful puffs. The stars shone paler as if they had retreated into the frozen depths of immense space. After a chill gust of wind there were a few seconds of perfect calm and absolute silence. Then from behind the black and wavy line of the forests a column of golden light shot up into the heavens and spread over the semicircle of the eastern horizon. The sun had risen. The mist lifted, broke into drifting patches, vanished into thin flying wreaths; and the unveiled lagoon lay, polished and black, in the heavy shadows at the foot of the wall of trees. A white eagle rose over it with a slanting and ponderous flight, reached the clear sunshine and appeared dazzlingly brilliant for a moment, then soaring higher, became a dark and motionless speck before it vanished into the blue as if it had left the earth forever. The white man,

standing gazing upwards before the doorway, heard in
the hut a confused and broken murmur of distracted
words ending with a loud groan. Suddenly Arsat
stumbled out with outstretched hands, shivered, and
stood still for some time with fixed eyes. Then he
said—

"She burns no more."

Before his face the sun showed its edge above the
tree-tops rising steadily. The breeze freshened; a great
brilliance burst upon the lagoon, sparkled on the
rippling water. The forests came out of the clear
shadows of the morning, became distinct, as if they had
rushed nearer—to stop short in a great stir of leaves, of
nodding boughs, of swaying branches. In the merciless
sunshine the whisper of unconscious life grew louder,
speaking in an incomprehensible voice round the dumb
darkness of that human sorrow. Arsat's eyes wandered
slowly, then stared at the rising sun.

"I can see nothing," he said half aloud to himself.

"There is nothing," said the white man, moving to
the edge of the platform and waving his hand to his
boat. A shout came faintly over the lagoon and the
sampan began to glide towards the abode of the friend
of ghosts.

"If you want to come with me, I will wait all the
morning," said the white man, looking away upon the
water.

"No, Tuan," said Arsat, softly. "I shall not eat or
sleep in this house, but I must first see my road. Now
I can see nothing—see nothing! There is no light and
no peace in the world; but there is death—death for
many. We are sons of the same mother—and I left him
in the midst of enemies; but I am going back now."

He drew a long breath and went on in a dreamy tone:
"In a little while I shall see clear enough to strike—to

strike. But she has died, and . . . now . . .
darkness. '

He flung his arms wide open, let them fall along his
body, then stood still with unmoved face and stony
eyes, staring at the sun. The white man got down into
his canoe. The polers ran smartly along the sides of
the boat, looking over their shoulders at the beginning
of a weary journey. High in the stern, his head muffled
up in white rags, the juragan sat moody, letting his
paddle trail in the water. The white man, leaning with
both arms over the grass roof of the little cabin, looked
back at the shining ripple of the boat's wake. Before
the sampan passed out of the lagoon into the creek he
lifted his eyes. Arsat had not moved. He stood lonely
in the searching sunshine; and he looked beyond the
great light of a cloudless day into the darkness of a
world of illusions.

JOSEPH CONRAD

A Biographical Note

JOSEPH CONRAD was born on 3rd December 1857, at Berdiczew in Podolia, one of the Ukrainian provinces of Poland long under Russian Tsarist rule. He was the only child of Apollo Nałęcz Korzeniowski and his wife Evelina Bobrowska, and he was christened Józef Teodor Konrad Nałęcz Korzeniowski. His parents were of the landowner class, and his father was deeply involved in the secret national Polish movement. Apollo had literary interests too, wrote poetry and criticism and translated from the French and German.

When Conrad was three his father was arrested by the Russian authorities and exiled to Northern Russia, his wife and child being allowed to go with him under the same conditions of banishment. Evelina's health broke down and she died in exile in 1865. Two years later Apollo was given conditional parole, but seven years of privation had also told on him physically, and he died in Cracow in 1869, leaving the orphaned Conrad in the care of his maternal uncle, Tadeusz Bobrowski.

Between the ages of fifteen and seventeen Conrad astonished his uncle and tutor by expressing from time to time a determination to go to sea, a strange calling to people belonging inland and traditionally devoted to agricultural pursuits. Conrad persisted and in September 1874 he travelled to Marseilles to become a seaman. He spoke French fluently and had one or two introductions to people in the port. After some experience on two sailing ships, he became one of a syndicate of four young men who bought the sixty-ton *Tremolino* and sailed her on contraband activities until she was deliberately wrecked as described in a chapter in *The Mirror of the Sea*. More of this phase of Conrad's life is told in the story *The Arrow of Gold*.

Conrad's first English ship was the *Mavis*, which he joined at Marseilles in April 1878, and it was aboard that vessel that he arrived at Lowestoft two months later and saw England for the first time. After some coastal trips in another ship, he joined as ordinary seaman a 'wool-clipper' sailing to Australia. Returning to London at the end of January 1880 he passed examination as second mate in June of that year.

From then on he served as officer on several ships, voyaging to many parts of the world, particularly across the Indian Ocean, and in and around the Malay Archipelago and the Gulf of Siam. These are the scenes of some of his best-known stories, *Youth, Almayer's Folly, An Outcast of the Islands, The Nigger of the 'Narcissus,' The Secret Sharer, Typhoon, Lord Jim, Victory, Falk, The Rescue, The Shadow-Line,* and others. He passed his mate's examination in July 1883, and on 11th November 1886 he succeeded in the final seamanship test and obtained his Master Mariner's Certificate. Conrad's accounts of these examinations are in *A Personal Record*. He became a naturalized British subject on 19th August 1886.

In 1890 he went to the Belgian Congo to command a river steamer—realization of a hope expressed as a child when he put his finger on a map of Central Africa and said he would go there one day. From his experiences in the Congo Conrad was physically weakened but psychologically awakened, and his writing career dates from this period, for he was then writing his first book, *Almayer's Folly*. Years later he gave his Congo story in one of his finest books, *Heart of Darkness*.

His last ship was the *Torrens*, a renowned sailing vessel, which he left in October 1893. It happened that John Galsworthy (not then a writer) was a passenger on part of this last voyage, joining the ship at Adelaide; years later he gave a picture of Conrad at the first meeting: 'He was superintending the stowage of cargo. Very dark he looked in the burning sunlight—tanned, with a peaked brown beard, almost black hair, and dark brown eyes, over which the lids were deeply folded. He was thin, not tall, his arms very long, his shoulders broad, his head set rather forward. He spoke to me with a strong, foreign accent. He seemed to me strange on an English ship. For fifty-six days I sailed in his company. . . . Many evening watches in fine weather we spent on the poop. Ever the great teller of a tale, he had already nearly twenty years of tales to tell. . . . At Cape Town, on my last evening, he asked me to his cabin, and I remember feeling that he outweighed for me all the other experiences of that voyage. . . .'

Conrad took about five years to write *Almayer's Folly*, which, having been read and recommended by Edward Garnett, was published in April 1895. Encouraged by Garnett and other editors to continue writing, he settled down to a shore life, marrying Miss Jessie George of London on 24th March 1896. His early books were appreciated by a discriminating public and praised by eminent writers such as H. G. Wells, John Galsworthy, Henry James, and R. B. Cunninghame Graham; but none of his books attracted a wide circle of readers until *Chance*, 1913. It is now generally agreed that his greatest stories were written round about the turn of the century: *Lord Jim* came out in 1900, and *Nostromo*, published in 1904, is regarded by many as his masterpiece. Between *Nostromo* and *Chance* came those remarkable novels, totally unconnected with the sea, *The Secret Agent* and *Under Western Eyes*.

During most of his married and writing life Conrad lived in various houses in Kent, occasionally making visits lasting some months to the Continent, usually France or Poland. He had two sons, Borys, born in January 1898, and John Alexander, born in August 1906. He and his family were on a visit to Austrian Poland when war broke out in 1914, and they went through some excitement and hardship in getting out of enemy territory via Italy and the Mediterranean.

His last two novels (*The Rover* and *Suspense*, the latter unfinished) were of the Napoleonic period and set in the Mediterranean, the first sea he had known, and some of the characters had their prototypes in friends of his youthful days there. *The Rover*, probably the best of his later books, has something of both of his adopted countries in it, France, the Rover's native land, and England, in her sailors at war with France. Poland is in it also in spirit, because the author was himself a Rover from that native land of his. Mrs Conrad has said that a sort of homing instinct was on Conrad towards the end of his life. But he remained in Kent, in his English home, Oswalds, in the village of Bishopsbourne, with his English family, writing until the end. Although he had been ailing for some years his death came suddenly, after a heart attack, on the morning of 3rd August 1924. He is buried in Canterbury, and the stone on his grave bears his Polish name.

A. J. H.

A SELECT BIBLIOGRAPHY

CONRAD'S WORKS

(1) 1895   *Almayer's Folly—A Story of an Eastern River.*

(2) 1896   *An Outcast of the Islands.*

(3) 1897   *The Nigger of the 'Narcissus'—A Tale of the Sea.* (First edition to include Preface, 1914.)

(1) 1898   *Tales of Unrest.* (Contents: 'Karain, a Memory,' 'The Idiots,' 'An Outpost of Progress,' 'The Return,' 'The Lagoon.')

(4) 1900   *Lord Jim—A Tale.*

(5) 1902   *Youth: A Narrative; and Two Other Stories.* (Contents: 'Youth,' 'Heart of Darkness,' 'The End of the Tether.')

(3) 1903   *Typhoon, and Other Stories.* (Contents: 'Typhoon,' 'Amy Foster,' 'Falk,' 'To-morrow.')

(6) 1903   *Romance—A Novel.* (In collaboration with Ford Madox Hueffer.)

(7) 1904   *Nostromo—A Tale of the Seaboard.*

(8) 1906   *The Mirror of the Sea—Memories and Impressions.*

(9) 1907   *The Secret Agent—A Simple Tale.*

(10) 1908   *A Set of Six.* (Contents: 'Gaspar Ruiz,' 'The Informer,' 'The Brute,' 'An Anarchist,' 'The Duel,' 'Il Conde.')

(11) 1911   *Under Western Eyes.*

(8) 1912   *A Personal Record.* (First published under the title *Some Reminiscences.*)

(12) 1912   *'Twixt Land and Sea—Tales.* (Contents: 'A Smile of Fortune,' 'The Secret Sharer,' 'Freya of the Seven Isles.')

(13) 1913   *Chance—A Tale in Two Parts.*

(14) 1915   *Victory—An Island Tale.*

(15) 1915   *Within the Tides—Tales.* (Contents: 'The Planter of Malata,' 'The Partner,' 'The Inn of the Two Witches,' 'Because of the Dollars.')

(15) 1917   *The Shadow Line—A Confession.*

(16) 1919   *The Arrow of Gold—A Story between Two Notes.*

(17) 1920   *The Rescue—A Romance of the Shallows.*

(18) 1921   *Notes On Life and Letters.* (Essays, mainly from periodicals; thirteen in Part I on Letters, and thirteen in Part II on Life.)

(19) 1923   *The Rover.*

(20) 1925   *Suspense—A Napoleonic Novel.*

(21) 1925   *Tales of Hearsay.* (Contents: 'The Warrior's Soul,' 'Prince Roman,' 'The Tale,' 'The Black Mate.')

(21) 1926   *Last Essays.* (Nineteen essays, uncollected in book form at the time of his death.)

       1923–8   Uniform Edition of the Works of Joseph Conrad, with an Author's Note to each volume.

           (Reissued as Collected Edition, 1946–54, 21 volumes. The numbers against the titles in the above list show where two works are contained in one volume in the Collected Edition.)

SELECT BIBLIOGRAPHY

LETTERS

The Life and Letters of Joseph Conrad (2 vols.), edited by G. Jean-Aubry, 1927. *Letters from Joseph Conrad, 1895–1924*, edited, with an Introduction, by Edward Garnett, 1928. *Letters from Joseph Conrad to Richard Curle*, 1928. *Letters of Joseph Conrad to Marguerite Poradowska*, New York, 1940. *Joseph Conrad: Letters to William Blackwood and David S. Meldrum*, edited by W. Blackburn, 1959.

BIOGRAPHICAL AND CRITICAL WRITINGS ON CONRAD

Joseph Conrad, A Study, by Richard Curle, 1914. Essay in *Notes on Novelists*, by Henry James, 1914. *Joseph Conrad*, by Hugh Walpole, 1916. Essay on Conrad in *A Book of Prefaces*, by H. L. Mencken, 1917. *Joseph Conrad, A Personal Remembrance*, by Ford Madox Ford, 1924. Essay on Conrad in *The Common Reader*, by Virginia Woolf, 1925. *Joseph Conrad as I knew Him*, by Jessie Conrad, 1926. 'Reminiscences of Conrad' and 'Preface to Conrad's Plays' in *Castles in Spain*, by John Galsworthy, 1927. *The Last Twelve Years of Joseph Conrad*, by Richard Curle, 1928. *The Polish Heritage of Joseph Conrad*, by Gustav Morf, 1930. *Joseph Conrad's Mind and Method*, by R. L. Mégroz, 1931. *Joseph Conrad and His Circle*, by Jessie Conrad, 1936. *Joseph Conrad, Some Aspects of the Art of the Novel*, by Edward Crankshaw, 1936. Introductory Essay by Edward Garnett to *Conrad's Prefaces to his Works*, 1937. *Joseph Conrad, the Making of a Novelist*, by John D. Gordan, 1940. *Joseph Conrad, England's Polish Genius*, by M. C. Bradbrook, 1941. Introduction by A. J. Hoppé to *The Conrad Companion*, 1946. *The Great Tradition* (George Eliot, Henry James, and Joseph Conrad), by F. R. Leavis, 1948. *Joseph Conrad*, by Oliver Warner, 1951. *Conrad, a Re-assessment*, by D. Hewitt, 1952. *Six Great Novelists*, by Walter Allen, 1955 (Conrad is the sixth subject). *The Mirror of Conrad*, by E. H. Visiak, 1955. *The Sea Dreamer: Life of Conrad*, by G. Jean-Aubry, 1957. *Joseph Conrad*, by Thomas Moser, 1957. *Joseph Conrad, A Study in Non-conformity*, by Osborn Andreas, 1959. *Joseph Conrad, A Critical Biography*, by Jocelyn Baines, 1960.

BIBLIOGRAPHIES

A Bibliography of the Writings of Joseph Conrad, 1895–1921, by T. J. Wise, 1921. *A Conrad Memorial Library*, collected by G. T. Keating, New York, 1929, with 'Check List of Additions,' 1938. *Joseph Conrad at Mid-Century, Editions and Studies, 1895–1955*, by K. A. Lohf and E. P. Sheehy, 1959.

EVERYMAN'S LIBRARY: A Selected List

BIOGRAPHY

CLASSICAL

ESSAYS AND BELLES-LETTRES

FICTION

3

HISTORY

ORATORY

POETRY AND DRAMA

REFERENCE

ROMANCE

SCIENCE

THEOLOGY AND PHILOSOPHY

TRAVEL AND TOPOGRAPHY